KU-523-531

REPUBLIC

REPUBLIC

Wallis Peel

CHIVERS

British Library Cataloguing in Publication Data available

This Large Print edition published by BBC Audiobooks Ltd, Bath, 2008.
Published by arrangement with the Author.

U.K. Hardcover ISBN 978 1 405 64462 4
U.K. Softcover ISBN 978 1 405 64463 1

Copyright © Wallis Peel 2006

The right of Wallis Peel to be identified as the author of the work has
been asserted herein in accordance with the Copyright, Designs and
Patents Act 1988.

With the exception of certain well-known historical figures, all the other
characters in this book are fictitious and any resemblance to actual
people, living or dead, is purely imaginery.

All rights reserved.

Printed and bound in Great Britain by
Antony Rowe Ltd., Chippenham, Wiltshire

For
Nigel J Roberts

PART ONE

1645

CHAPTER ONE

'You, Mistress, come here!'

Sarah Turner blinked, looked around hastily, then realised, with a guilty flush, the officer's finger pointed at herself.

'Me?' she asked, struggling to avoid a tremor in her voice.

'Yes, you!'

Sarah took a deep breath and willed her features into a compliance which masked the trepidation in her heart. The crowd parted uneasily for her mare as she pushed forward to where the officer and his men stood guard. At this time of day, Bristol's numerous entrances were always thronged and it was unusual for the guards to single out any individual, let alone a female.

'Well?' Sarah asked evenly, praying her thumping heart remained known only to herself. The Royalist officer looked at her coldly. He ran his eyes over the mare she rode, then turned his attention back to the rider.

'What are you doing here?' he barked.

Sarah felt her cheeks deepen and she struggled to maintain her composure, cursing at the same time to herself. The guards had been changed yet, even so, wasn't it odd for her to be called before them? She did not make the mistake of licking her lips even

3

though they had gone very dry.

'I'm visiting an old friend,' she managed to explain evenly, sharply conscious the slowly moving throng was looking at her with interest, then suddenly she went on to the attack. 'Why do you ask? Everyone knows about my visits,' she said with a hot little rush of words. 'Your colleagues do.'

The Royalist officer gave a grunt, which could have meant anything. 'I don't!'

Sarah fastened a leash on her rising temper. It would never do to antagonise this new officer, his power was too great, but it was incredibly bad luck the normal guards had been rotated.

'That's a fine mare,' the Royalist said, running his experienced eye over the mount.

Sarah knew she must get in first. 'Yes, that's why she is a lady's ride,' she said swiftly. 'She was a wedding present to me from my husband who was killed here one evening,' she said and paused for emphasis. 'He was a Royalist officer too.'

The officer hesitated fractionally. 'Was?' he asked dubiously.

Sarah held his gaze coldly. 'He was shot in the back one night,' she explained, 'the killer was never caught.'

The officer realised she had flat-footed him and he went red with annoyance. Why hadn't he been warned? He was conscious of the Bristolians shuffling past, pedestrians, riders

4

and horse-drawn vehicles—all of them eyeing him—and he grumbled under his breath. Over two-thirds of these citizens hated King Charles because Bristol was a trading city and the traders had made it very plain they favoured Parliament and Oliver Cromwell.

'Very well, pass,' he said grudgingly, making a mental note to do some back-checking.

Sarah nodded a polite thanks, which she did not feel, and hastily pulled back to join the people streaming into the city, her mind whirling with implications. Was this challenge coincidental? Her mind swirled uneasily and she guided her mare through to the back street, to turn off to Martin's house.

With relief, she saw the open gates and dismounted briskly as Robert, the young son of Bessie, Martin's housekeeper, came to take the reins. He was a shy youth, never said two words where one would do and Sarah was unsure whether she liked him or not.

Dismissing him, she hastened up the two back steps to enter the kitchen where Bessie, red-cheeked against the heat, was banging iron pans on the stove.

'Is the master in, Bessie?' Sarah asked. Bessie was another strange one, like her illegitimate son. Sarah realised she had been coming to this house for years but knew nothing at all about Bessie. She smothered a sigh of exasperation.

'He's in his study, Sarah,' Bessie told her,

5

then became riveted with stirring something vigorously, ignoring the guest.

Sarah gave a tiny shake to her head, and, knowing the way, walked along the passage, carrying the small saddlebag, which held cheese from her village home. She never failed to bring something with her. Martin appreciated her gifts and they also gave her the perfect excuse when food was difficult to get in Bristol in wartime.

She tapped on the study door, then entered without waiting, and Martin Penford looked up quickly, a little startled at her appearance. He gave her a brief nod towards a chair before turning his attention back to the column of figures.

Sarah sank down thankfully, still confused and alarmed. She eyed Martin surreptitiously while he worked. He was such a sweetie, yet, recently, he had changed in a subtle way which, at times, disconcerted her. She sat back in the chair, musing on how strangely it had all turned out. Martin Penford had been her father's executor; later, after her parents' dual death from disease, he had given her away when she married Captain Joseph Turner. Was it her present circumstances that had made Martin change? There were visits when he was distinctly standoffish with her, although, on other occasions, she sometimes fancied she had seen something else reflected in his eyes. It was all very confusing, which irked her straightforward nature.

Martin had already totalled the figures but made a pretence of going through them again, to control the ache in his heart. How he loved this lovely Sarah Turner, and how devastated he had been at her wedding. Widowhood had suggested fresh hope, which had then been stilled as political activities took over emotional ones.

He saw she was wearing green, a colour she favoured and which complemented her fair hair and skin. The only slight jarring note was the vivid blueness in her direct eyes. Her short marriage had been childless, so her figure was superb and, with her upright carriage and healthy strength from much horse riding, she epitomised everything desirable in a young female. It was this that worried him deeply. He was twenty years her senior and how could he speak now?

Finally he lay down his quill pen, sat back in his chair and regarded her thoughtfully.

'What is it?' he asked quietly.

Sarah took a deep breath. 'I was challenged at the gate,' she said quickly, then, biting her lip, frowned heavily. 'And last week Royalists rode through our village. Why should they do that when they know it's all Royalist territory now?'

Martin Penford pursed his lips thoughtfully. He considered her statement and facts at his disposal known to only one other person,

7

surely?

Sarah studied his perplexity. Martin was a good-looking man and carried his years well. He did not look forty, which was, she calculated, his age, twice her own. He was of average height but with powerful shoulders and a trim body. His brown eyes matched his hair, yet his skin was pale. It was as if he did not get enough fresh air but Bessie had told her, on her last visit, that he walked twice a day. Sometimes she fancied there was an odd little something about him, which reminded her of someone but, rack her brains as she might, she could think of no possible connection. Right now, Martin's features were gravely stern as he turned back to her.

'Who have you talked to?' he asked abruptly.

Sarah was shocked at this. 'Why no one, of course. Don't forget it's my neck on the line and anyhow, I've never been a gossip,' she added hotly.

Martin knew this latter statement was true, which was why he had approached her. At the time, it had seemed one of his better ideas but now reservations filled him. Yet what else could he do? The Royalists were not fools. They suspected just about everyone, which was, he admitted, natural, when Bristol was known to be a hotbed of Parliamentary sympathies.

He muttered a low curse. 'Your servants.

8

They must know or have guessed. Tell me about them.'

Again he shocked Sarah. 'Of course they don't know. It's impossible and I've told you about them before,' she protested. If there was a leak it was not at her end. She opened her mouth to argue but the glint in Martin's eyes changed her mind. With a tiny shake of her head, she obeyed. 'There's Mary at home, my housekeeper, Nellie Witchell who comes in as a daily, Jack in the stables, and that's all. They came with the house when Joseph bought it for our marriage.'

Martin chewed his lip. 'But you meet regularly,' he said quietly. 'How do you explain that when the weather is bad?' he persisted.

Sarah threw him an impish grin. 'They all think I'm horse mad and eccentric. Even the village considers me slightly crazy since becoming a widow. I come and go as and when I like and if my servants don't like it, they don't say anything either. I am the mistress, after all,' she reminded him. 'And what about this end?'

'Here?' Martin asked, put out at this flanking attack. 'Bessie's been with me since Robert was born. They're like family.'

Sarah turned this over, then narrowed her eyes. 'But what about your spice business customers?'

He gave a snort. 'Fat lot of them there are now,' he said coldly. 'With the blockade and all

9

the Royalists, I can hardly get any goods in to sell; just nutmegs and peppers from the West Indies. At the rate things are going, the business will collapse. Like every trader in this city, I'm living a hand-to-mouth existence. When I think of the commerce in London . . .' He shook his head with exasperation. 'The few customers who do come making enquiries, do so as pure buyers for what wares I manage to ship in. The other is kept totally secret for my own safety too,' he told her a little acidly.

'Well, it's not him,' she said firmly.

He knew that more than she did but decided it might be better to go over the facts once more.

'You met him?' he asked, tongue in cheek.

Sarah took a deep breath. Why did Martin keep hashing over old facts? 'I met him when Colonel Massey attacked Chipping Sodbury on the night he relieved Yate Court then destroyed it with the Court's own canon. I was out riding when this pompous, arrogant, obnoxious Ironside's officer apprehended me as a spy . . .' She paused, shaking her head. 'Me—a spy! Anyhow, Colonel Massey made me stay with them most of the night while they relieved their garrison at Yate Court and only then was I released. My servants were in a real state when I rode home with the dawn. The next thing I knew was a strange man accosting me out riding, leaving a message for me to meet him at a given point. I nearly didn't go

10

either, I can tell you but, when I did—it was him. Only this time—' She paused, sorting out tangled thoughts.

'Go on,' he encouraged, having a positive reason for wanting to know.

Sarah threw him a limp smile. 'He was different. Rather nice really, but when he approached me to be your courier, I was flabbergasted. I was at a loose end, as you know, so I was glad to think I was doing something to help England get rid of King Charles, though we don't seem to be doing much about it.'

He ignored that aside. He was far more up to date with information than his courier and had no intention of putting her right either.

Sarah continued, staring at the large old trunk he kept against the window.

'When I knew I was to come to you, that was my second shock. I never guessed you were involved in . . .'

'Never say the word. Don't even think it,' Martin told her quickly. 'It's an ugly word and discovery means execution,' he reminded her.

'There's only one person who can be the leak,' Sarah told him suddenly. 'His man Walter!'

He knew this was incorrect. Personnel checks had been too stringent but again it would be imprudent for her ever to know more than was necessary. He simply looked blandly at her.

11

Sarah felt her cheeks redden. 'Oh, it couldn't be him because he was checked out!' she guessed lamely, then gave an impatient shake of her shoulders. 'In that case, the business at the gate must simply be coincidental or it means the Royalists are tightening their grip on the city.'

'You hide my messages carefully?' he asked delicately.

Sarah eyed him and wondered how prudish he really was. An imp of mischief filled her.

'Of course, in that one place a female has that a man doesn't!' she replied, tongue in cheek, amused to see him turn scarlet now and give a little wriggle on his chair. She felt a flash of pity for his embarrassment. 'They're in waterproof packaging, perfectly safe, and removed before being handed over, of course,' she finished saucily.

'Sarah!' he growled, realising she was poking fun at him, which made his heart ache. How he longed to take her in his arms but knew he would not. England and Republicanism had to come first. Too many brave men had already died in battle, and it was not finished yet. While Prince Rupert held Bristol and the King was at large, the country teetered and headed towards bankruptcy, with natural Continental enemies waiting on the sidelines to pick up the pieces for themselves.

Sarah took pity on him. 'Do you have a message for me this time?' she asked quietly.

12

He grunted and eyed her thoughtfully. 'This one is most important,' he said as he removed a small, slender roll of thin paper from under his small clothes. 'It's imperative this gets through. It covers the latest troop dispositions and armaments.'

'I'll get it to my contact this week,' Sarah promised him gently. Why hadn't she seen the strain lines on his face before? She led a double life but for Martin it was far worse. He had to observe, collate and numerate the information first of all. What an incredible memory he had when he took his daily walks. Her heart swelled for him and she reached out to touch his hand.

He looked warmly at her, took a deep breath and pushed temptation away. 'Work!' he grunted. 'Go and hide this. When will you be in again?'

'Next week as usual,' Sarah told him as she stood. 'I'll bring more food in with me. How are things here in Bristol for the citizens?'

He shook his head. 'Bad, and they'll get worse before they get better. There's also some plague around, here and there. It only needs one fool Royalist to do or say the wrong thing and there'll be a revolt here which Rupert will be hard put to control. That's one of the reasons the guards at the city gates are edgy,' he told her, then turning, opened a drawer at his desk.

Sarah saw him remove something, hold it in

13

his hand, then study her carefully. How strange, there was that odd look in his eyes once more, which she only saw now and again. He was two people in one but which was the true man?

'I'd like you to have this,' he told her slowly, then opened his hand to show the brooch.

Sarah gasped. 'It's lovely,' she said, her brow puckering, as she looked at him quizzically.

Martin understood and cursed himself. Why couldn't he speak his mind and tell of his great love? Yet how could he? Each day was a bonus one because of the risks he ran. It would be grossly unfair to ask her to pledge herself to him under such dire circumstances, yet he wanted nothing more than to stamp his ownership upon her.

'It was my mother's,' he grunted. 'I'd like you to wear it as a small thank-you for what you are doing for the cause. Perhaps one day, when it's all over and we've rid the land of kings, we might . . .' and he knew his voice tailed off miserably.

In a clairvoyant flash, Sarah understood and she bit her lip. She liked Martin very much. She admired and respected him but had never anticipated his feelings towards her were anything out of the ordinary. She hesitated, uncertain what to do. She could not refuse his delightful gift yet would acceptance be interpreted wrongly?

'Thank you, Martin,' she said and taking the

14

brooch, pinned it to her blouse. 'It's so lovely, but . . .' and she floundered to an uncertain halt.

It was his turn to read the signals incorrectly. She was embarrassed, he told himself quickly. It was too expensive a gift without a more solemn declaration which circumstances stopped him from making. He waggled one hand. 'You'd better be off,' he said gruffly, to hide his feelings. 'Get that message to your contact as quickly as possible,' he added and turned back to his desk, sitting, dismissing her with his actions.

Oh Martin, Sarah thought. You are such a dear and I love you, but like a big, older brother. She said nothing, a wistful smile on her face as she left the study and went back into the kitchen.

'Off then, Sarah?' Bessie asked, pausing from her cooking.

Sarah nodded wanly. Martin's unexpected action had suddenly deflated her, as a vision of future problems arose before her eyes. She wondered if she dared question Bessie but decided against this. Who was to say what Bessie did not relate afterwards to Martin? She gave a tiny shake to her head. If anything, Bessie was in Martin's age group and the housekeeper adored him. How could Martin be so blind? And who was Robert's unknown father? She would have loved to question Bessie but dare not. Bessie was deep and

15

mysterious; the kind of person to whom it was impossible to get close and, it crossed her mind to wonder whether Robert knew who his father was. Bessie was a fine, buxom woman, overweight from tasting her own cooking but a wonderful homemaker. Robert seemed a fine, clean-cut young man and, deep down, probably regarded Martin as a surrogate father already. Oh damn all men, she told herself. They are simply too complicated.

She collected her horse and, mounting, rode thoughtfully back towards the city gate, her eyes everywhere, noting and observing. The inhabitants did not look well. Once they had been finely dressed but there was a shabby air about them. Passing a few stalls, she noted goods were sparse and she bit her lip. Despite the vast number of Royalist troops in the city, what would happen if the citizens should revolt? It was an interesting question until, turning, she gazed up at the enormous, thick, impregnable walls of the castle. How could a foe outside possibly storm and take such an impregnable city as Bristol? She wondered what dead Joseph would have thought about this. It was eerie to think that she, a Royalist's widow, was a courier for Parliament but Sarah knew she only followed her breeding. Her father had been in trade, and she too was heartily sick of a king who ruled without calling a Parliament. England had to be a better country without the likes of King

16

Charles, surely?

*   *   *

Two days later, with heart throbbing in anticipation, Sarah rode out from her village home, Martin's coded message hidden in a pocket. She picked a path towards Yate Park, basking in the early spring sunshine. There had been frost the previous evening and, with forethought, she had stolen from her kitchen when Mary's back was turned. Such antics amused her but Mary was sometimes too sharp. For her mistress to take food and drink on a morning ride would only have produced questions.

She was careful as she rode at a slow trot, scanning the surrounding area which she knew intimately but she had the countryside to herself. As she neared the ruins of what had been the once proud Yate Court, he appeared and lifted a hand to show the coast was clear. At this, she cantered forward and marvelled at herself. How could she have so disliked him that day so long ago? Now, whenever she saw him, something squeezed her heart yet, at the same time, she prudently kept a distance between them emotionally. She acknowledged she was tangled and confused because, even now, at this moment of approach to him, her heart thundered.

'Hello there!' James Hawkins called as she

17

stopped and dismounted. He took the mare's reins and anchored them next to those of his large, black stallion who snorted with interest.

'I cold-camped here last night,' he explained, as he eyed the small bag hopefully. 'Field rations get boring after a while,' he added, grinning down at her.

Sarah knew he was the most powerful, masculine person she'd ever met. Always there came from him, as if frosting off ice, an aura of carefully controlled explosion and savagery. There was a rugged handsomeness to his features which pulled her, and his grey eyes never failed to make her marvel. They were the exact shade of a cloud just before a rainstorm. He towered over her with his six feet, yet he was light and swift in movement despite a strong, well muscled frame.

James' heart soared at the sight of her. When the initial proposal to use her had reached him he had snorted with annoyance. As if the war wasn't difficult enough without dragging women into it when their erratic emotions were only too well known. Their first meeting had been a clash of personalities and he had not been amused to send his man, Walter Hamlyn, to make an initial contact with her but orders were to be obeyed, not ignored to suit his whims. On their second meeting though, he had recognised a rebellious, kindred spirit; a difference to any other female he'd met before and, during their many

18

meetings, his regard had started to soar. When this had changed to something else, he was uncertain. It was enough for him to know he looked forward to their meetings with delight as well as natural apprehension. If only there was time to conduct a proper courtship but, always at this point, he hesitated. She had been widowed once; would she wish to put herself into this dangerous position a second time? He was a serving soldier, to say nothing of his other life.

He cast a swift gaze around and saw that the stag stood aside of his herd and was not agitated, which meant they were alone at the ruins.

'I thought that might be the case,' Sarah told him and laughingly handed over the small saddlebag. 'Cheese, new bread and some thin wine,' she explained. 'There's ginger in the wine,' she added.

He unstopped the flask and took a long pull. 'That's good,' he told her, standing with long booted feet slightly apart, helmet tipped back, his leather body shield just catching the thin sun's rays.

Sarah reached into her pocket and brought out the message. She never looked at them because she knew they were coded. She handed it to him.

James took it and slipped it into a pocket inside his chest protector. 'Any problems?' he asked casually.

Sarah paused a moment. 'Not really but I was challenged,' she said and explained the event she had related to her Bristol contact.

He stilled at this, frowning heavily. 'I don't think I like the sound of that,' he said finally, after thinking a few moments. He was only too well aware that the Royalists had no scruples where espionage agents were concerned, even if they should be but humble, female couriers.

Sarah gave a little shrug. 'Martin asked me a lot of questions but I know I'm not responsible for any leak. How can I be?' she asked reasonably.

'Tell me all,' he said gruffly while his mind worked at top speed. It was possible that Prince Rupert had tightened up on all of Bristol's city gates but it was odd troops should be in her village too. He frowned. Something didn't smell right yet he could not finger anything.

'What does Penford think about it all?' he wanted to know next. Sarah gave a little sigh. 'He never says what he thinks,' she told him. 'He swears a leak from his end is out of the question. His business has just about broken down and he only has a handful of customers. Spices are not getting into the port and Bessie and her son have been with him since Robert was born. They're more like family. I think perhaps it might just be Prince Rupert flexing his muscles because there's a distinct undercurrent of tension in the city now.'

20

He grunted then his eyes narrowed as she moved. Her jacket opened and he spotted her new brooch.

'That's new,' he said and nodded.

Sarah looked down, looked up and pulled a little face. 'Martin gave it to me,' she explained. 'I think it's just a token of esteem for my work,' she added a little lamely.

'That belonged to his mother!'

Sarah was astonished. 'How on earth do you know that?'

James muttered to himself. That was a bad slip, which showed exactly how much she affected him. Was he slipping?

'I knew his family,' he hurried to cover his lapse.

'Before the troubles began?' Sarah prodded.

James nodded then swivelled his gaze. Her eyes were so direct and questioning.

'Well, you never said!'

James struggled with himself It would be only too simple to blacken Penford's name but he was too big to do that. 'We knew each other long ago. We never got on. It's unfortunate really that we have to work together,' he ended, forcing a grin on his lips which failed to reach his eyes.

Sarah eyed him shrewdly. She sensed there was a lot kept back from her now and itched to question, yet refrained. This big, strong man could never be bullied and did it really matter? She had ridden to see him with such a happy heart yet now he stood there scowling like a little boy. She cast her mind around for a neutral topic of conversation.

James raged inwardly. Of course Penford would try to impress her. Rewards for work given, my eye, he told himself sourly. He was out to catch her and who could blame him? Sarah Turner was worth netting. She was a fine girl with incredible spirit and not short on beauty either. He cursed the damned war. If only he were not a serving officer with his neck only ever inches from disaster.

'Excuse my sudden black mood,' he said swiftly, aware she had gone cool and hurt. 'Living a double life can make a man down at times.'

Sarah bit her lip with doubt. There was something horribly wrong.

'What is it?' she whispered and touched one hand.

James looked down at her then made up his mind, once and for all, before it was too late. 'I've fallen in love with you,' he said in a low voice, 'yet how can I court you in my position? Penford is available at all times.'

Sarah caught her breath. He had said it, admitted it and shown jealousy.

She smiled up at him, her heart swelling with happiness. He was so different from long-dead Joseph who had epitomised the Gay Cavaliers with his outrageously fancy clothes and feathers in his hats. James was utilitarian, always businesslike and, because of this, more evidently lethal. Life with him would be an incredible adventure; yet a finger of caution touched her heart. She had married so young, pushed into it by her parents who had, despite their trade connections, liked the dashing Captain Turner. For Sarah, it had been a simple case of leaving her father's authority to go to that of a husband's. Now though, she was free, single, comfortably off financially but, most of all, totally independent. As a widow, no chaperon was needed by her because she was no simpering virgin. She belonged to no man so did she want to anchor herself down again—even with this magnificent male?

Marriage was a wonderful invention for men, but for women it was nothing but a delicate form of bondage.

'Have I upset you?' he breathed in one ear as he gathered her into his arms. Sarah still hesitated. How could she explain so he'd understand? No man would, but did she want to go through the rest of her life lying in a half-empty bed? She extemporised swiftly.

'Martin leads a dangerous, double life too,' she said softly.

He released her and scowled. Her arrow had struck its target. Martin Penford saw her more often than himself. There were occasions when the messages had to be picked up by Walter Hamlyn and it hit him, he must act and now. To hell with the war, he added to himself.

23

'I love you,' he repeated slowly and looked deep into her eyes. 'How do you feel about me, Sarah? Please tell me.'

Sarah pulled away. 'Oh James,' she groaned. How could she face those eyes with a lie? How far did physical attraction go in making a marriage? With herself and Joseph, their few months together had been nothing but a gorgeous romp. There had not been the time for settled domesticity and, deep down, although she had liked Joseph, she admitted she had never felt any flaring love. What came from this man before her was unlike anything she'd yet experienced but still she hesitated uncomfortably.

'Sarah!' he demanded.

'I do like you, James,' she told him slowly but missed the way he flinched.

'Is that all?' he asked, then touched the brooch. 'You wear Penford's token though? Are you spoken for?'

'No, I am not,' Sarah replied hotly. 'I belong to no one but myself. It's all very well for men. Marriage is fine but what about the female? I'd only become a chattel again and I'll not have it. I'm me. I'm independent. I'm free. You men never understand.'

'For God's sake, is that all?' and he laughed. 'I thought it was something traumatic.'

'If that isn't, what is?' she shot back, feeling her temper rise. He was impossible and, damn his eyes, why did he have to bring such a

24

subject up now? It was Martin's brooch which had started all this. 'I'm not ready even to think about marrying again and that's that.'

He was amused at her flaring belligerence. 'I'm mad about you,' he told her, drawing her back again, feeling her resistance forced to crumble before his superior strength. 'Let's forget about marriage then, until the country is at peace again but you can wear my token too.' He paused, eyeing her carefully. 'And if your precious freedom is so important too you, I vow, here and now, that when we marry you can do as you like.'

'What do you mean? I've not said I'll marry you or anyone!'

He grinned wolfishly down at her. 'You will,' he predicted, 'because I'm the only man tough enough for you, my wild, spirited Sarah!'

'Let me go. Now! This instant!'

He ignored her, bent and kissed her slowly, savouring her taste, taking in the fine scent which came from her clothes.

Sarah was livid with him. He was going too far and too fast. Then his words registered.

'Do you mean it?' she managed to get out when he paused for breath. 'What about children?'

He knew he was winning and pressed home his advantage. 'Two would be nice but only if you want them. There are methods,' he hinted delicately. 'Now will you wear my pledge too? I did bring something with me,' he tempted with a smirk.

Sarah looked at him with sharp, fond exasperation. She went back over his words and knew instinctively he had not made them lightly. Deep down, she knew it was quite impractical to continue to live alone. She had a flashing vision of a lonely old age and a sharp prescience he would be very good and strong in bed, which had not been Joseph's metier.

'Sarah! Say something! Just don't stand looking at me like that!'

'All right,' she capitulated suddenly and felt a flare of excitement race through her. Life could not be boring with this man and there was still England to bring to peace. She had ample time in which to change her mind if she chose.

'Very well. I'll wear it but I don't know what Martin will think,' she said thoughtfully.

'Serve him right,' he grunted and dived into another pocket, delighted with himself for his foresight.

'What do you mean?' she asked, suddenly puzzled.

'He wants to marry you too.'

'What!' she gasped, astounded then frowned. 'How do you know?'

He eyed her. 'I had occasion to meet him not so long ago and we rowed, as we have always done. He dropped a few hints about you and himself so that's why he gave you his brooch.'

'Oh no!' Sarah groaned. 'That's going to make it very awkward when I next see him but . . . how dare you discuss me!'

He grinned at her expression: 'We didn't actually do that. It was more a case of a lot of heavy hints.'

'Really!' Sarah shot back. 'How on earth am I going to face him again?'

He had already worked that one out. 'Wear mine out of sight and don't tell him . . . but don't accept any more gifts. Make an excuse,' he advised coolly 'I still have to work with him though I doubt it'll be for much longer. The armies will soon be moving now that spring is here and once tactics for taking Bristol have been completed, your work will have finished completely, as will Penford's.'

She watched him unfasten a tiny package made from a white kerchief, edged with lace. It was a strange object for an Ironside's man to possess. It was more suitable for a flamboyant Cavalier.

James opened his hand and displayed the locket. It was round, of patterned gold, suspended from a chain, woven like a rope. He pressed the side and it opened showing, inside, a few short strands of his hair.

'My pledge,' he said gruffly as he fastened it around her throat. 'Will it do?' he asked with sudden anxiety.

Sarah was thrilled and nodded enthusiastically as her fingers caressed the lovely object. She wondered from whom he had obtained it. He read her mind and smiled a little sadly.

'It was my mother's,' he explained in a soft voice. 'With this I plight my troth!' he added seriously, eyes steady on hers but with a subtle question.

Sarah knew this was the moment of truth. What she said now, would decide the rest of her life. She had to believe his words and vow and knew, deep down, this man would never lie to her.

'I accept,' she replied simply then, standing on tiptoes, kissed him gently. 'But let's keep it a secret, please?'

He hugged her and felt his penis harden with longing, enough to make him groan at its ache. How he wanted her body—but discipline took over. He had many miles to ride with a message of incalculable value because, at this work, Penford was outstanding.

'Damn the war,' he groaned. 'I'll have to get this back for transmission to London,' he said, touching his pocket in which lay Penford's message.

'Will you be here next week?' she asked him hopefully.

He pulled a face. 'God knows, I don't,' he said in a low voice. 'I might have to send Hamlyn.'

'He is trustworthy?' Sarah asked suddenly, thinking back to Martin's interrogation.

28

'Walter?' He let out a harsh laugh. 'He'd die for me. No, Penford is right to be concerned, but there's no chance of a leak my end. I report to one person only, whose name even you don't know. Even Massey only guesses and would never dare say aloud. No, just be careful at the Bristol end.'

Sarah sensed how his mood had changed. From being a suitor he had reverted to the alert, highly trained and ever-suspicious soldier.

'You'll be riding back a different way?' he checked.

Sarah nodded soberly. Right from the start, she had realised the necessity not to set patterns. Which villages had open Parliamentary or Royalist sympathies were not easy to guess. People were inclined to sit on the fence until something happened to involve them directly.

'You leave first while I watch your back trail then I'll go. God, there's going to be another frost tonight or I'm a Dutchman,' he said with a groan, thinking of the miles yet to ride. He unfastened the two sets of reins and helped her mount, then carefully studied the deer herd. They grazed peacefully and the stag only kept a watchful eye on their presence.

'No one around,' he grunted. 'Take care, my dear, fiery Sarah. Just in case Martin's right and there is a leak somewhere, though God knows who's the culprit. If I find out—' He

29

stopped, his voice sinking to a growl, 'And Penford is no soft pushover when it comes to the crunch either.'

'James!'

'Shh!' he crooned up at her as she sat her saddle, not wanting to leave him now. Suddenly, filled with enormous apprehension without quite knowing why, he reached round and gave a hefty slap to her mare's quarters, then hastily side-stepped as the mare flung out a hoof in warning. 'Off!' he growled, masking his own worries. As she cantered away he stood and shook his head. He had a sudden, deep gut feeling that he did not like. Dear God, why the hell had Penford started all this in the first place? Espionage was no game for a female; yet, he was forced to admit to himself, many a female could succeed as courier where a man was instantly suspected. Damn King Charles, he told himself sourly. It was all his fault in the first place.

CHAPTER TWO

Martin Penford left the inn casually and, while tightening his girth, looked around. This inn was always busy but now that spring had finally come, the activity was almost frenetic. He mounted his horse clumsily, aware he was not the world's best horse-man and swung him around to head towards the selected place.

He could imagine the mood he would be in and meetings were best kept to the bare minimum but, after much deep thought, he had decided this was necessary. He felt as taut as a bowstring as he trotted onwards, now and again throwing a swift look around. He turned and headed towards the small copse of deciduous trees and spotted Hawkins' big black horse right away. Hawkins nodded at him and they placed their horses side by side, each waiting for the other to speak first.

'Let's walk up this lane a bit,' James said, knowing someone had to speak. Penford could be mulish at times. 'I want to see if anyone follows us,' he explained.

'I took care no one followed me from Bristol,' Martin told him quickly, knowing perfectly well he had gone onto the defensive. Hawkins always had this effect upon him. Of all the men in the country he had to work with, it was ridiculously wrong it should be Hawkins. Yet, he told himself honestly, there were few men who could match Hawkins for efficiency, reliability and downright courage.

They walked for a quarter of a mile. 'Anyone?' he asked when Hawkins halted to look behind.

'No, but we're still just in sight of the inn. Perhaps we should move aside?'

Martin grunted. 'No need to get so elaborate. We're not kids at this game.'

31

James threw him a look. Now what was eating him? When Penford was in a mood he became impossible. 'It has to stop!' he barked unceremoniously.

'What has?' Martin shot back, drawing himself to his full height, nearly matching James Hawkins.

'You know perfectly well I'm on about Sarah carrying on this assignment. It's too bloody dangerous for her!'

'Don't you think I know that, man? But what the hell else can I do? They are strip-searching men now at the gates if they have the slightest suspicion; and you know how the Royalists treat spies?'

James gave a heavy sigh. 'I know, I know, it's just that . . .' and he halted uncertainly.

'You've had all the latest information but what happens if we stop using her and Lord Chichester sends in more men from Ireland? Cromwell has to know what he faces in Bristol. Be your age.'

'Don't snarl at me unless you're prepared to back it up with your fists,' James grated back, his heart sinking. As always, their meeting looked like degenerating into another verbal brawl.

'Bloody hell!' Martin exploded. 'Do you think I enjoy using a female? Christ, if I could get a man out in safety I'd do so but there's not a snowball in hell's chance I'd get away with that now.'

James grunted. Penford was right, as usual, which added irritation to the fury this man could always arouse in him. 'There has to be a leak somewhere.'

'Not at my end, there isn't,' Martin snapped quickly, 'and Sarah's not stupid enough to talk. She knows the penalty. I've questioned her about her servants and she's adamant they know nothing, can't even suspect because she's built up precedents in seeing you and coming in to me. If it's neither of us, then that leaves your man Hamlyn and those who saw you the first time you met her with Massey and his dragoons.'

'Hamlyn's in the clear, that I swear. As to our first meeting?' James paused to consider, then shook his head. 'Most unlikely. Massey's men are totally loyal to him, at all times. Anyhow, nothing had been thought of then, let alone decided. She was just another civilian rider who happened to be in the wrong place at the wrong time. No more, no less.'

'I don't believe in coincidences,' Martin growled.

'Neither do I,' James agreed, 'so where does that leave us?'

'Up a bloody tree with nowhere else to go,' Martin said sourly. 'How many paid informers do you run?' James probed. Martin never liked divulging information even to someone as safe as James Hawkins but he could see the sense and validity of the question.

33

'Four,' he managed to get out in a low voice, as if the tree's branches might overhear.

'What are their instructions?'

'They are simply to watch at the guarded gates, passing to and fro as simple citizens; no more, no less. They're told nothing. They have no names. They watch no one particular person. It's just a blanket observation of enemy activities. They're men I've known for years but, even so, I trust none of 'em with details.'

James took a deep breath. 'One of them has to be a double agent. The King is paying more to one man than you.'

Martin had already worked that one out. 'You're probably right but you know the double agent is the most difficult man to flush out.'

James thought hard, biting his lip. Time was of the essence now. Both of them knew this, yet Sarah's safety now overrode all else in his opinion.

'There can't really, be much more information for Sarah to bring out. Surely we have a plant in Ireland to cover Lord Chichester? You've sent out minute details of the gun batteries. We know Prince Rupert's strength. I say Sarah should stop this work. It's too bloody dangerous by half,' James told him bluntly. Then a thought occurred to him. 'Are *you* under observation personally?'

Martin gave a tiny shrug. 'It's distinctly

possible but then, who isn't in Bristol right now?' He paused and took a deep breath. 'It's weird you should bring this up but there are days when I get a gut feeling which bothers me and I don't know why either.' He flashed a look at the younger man. 'If anything should happen to me, my Will is with Lawyer Benson, you know him. Benson and his clerk are Executors and my affairs are in order.'

James was shocked. 'Good God! You're serious!'

Martin managed a wan smile. 'I'm mortal, more like.'

James was stunned into a rare silence. He eyed his companion and took a deep breath, distinctly disturbed. Penford was acting and speaking out of character.

His features softened as he stared at his companion. Martin Penford had a whimsical twist to his lips though his eyes reflected bleak sadness.

'You'll win,' Martin murmured heavily.

'Win? Win? Of course we'll win England's freedom from a king!'

Martin shook his head. 'No, I mean Sarah Turner. I gave her my brooch but when I saw her last week, I noted she wore a fine locket under her blouse.'

James stiffened, ready for a shouting match, and then quietened, feeling sharply uncomfortable. He had never seen such a sad look in the other's eyes before.

35

'I love Sarah very much but I know I'm twenty years too old for her. If the political situation had been different, then I'd have given you a run for your money but, as it is . . .' His voice tailed off unhappily. Then his expression hardened. 'You'd better treat her right, Hawkins, by God you had.'

James had nothing to say. Penford had always been incredibly sharp with a perception matched by few, which explained his great value to Parliament's cause and his location in Bristol. Yet he could not crow. The other's unhappiness came off him in an aura almost strong enough to touch.

Martin ignored him for a moment, turning something over in his mind; then he gave a tiny nod.

'I think, just as a precaution, you'd better know a few facts apart from where my Will is. Whatever message I have for Sarah I hold in the old spice jar in the cellar. It's in the small wall cupboard and with it are the spices and peppers for Bessie's use. It stands to one side, half hidden by shadow. Got that?'

James nodded. 'Right!'

'Here's a copy of my Will but it's sealed for now. There's a key around my neck. It opens the trunk. I keep all Parliament's funds in there to pay informers. It's in gold sovereigns. Comes in by ship as cargo for the spice business, which, incidentally, is just about defunct through lack of supplies. There are

36

also half a dozen diamonds hidden under the trunk's bottom. There's a false board. It all belongs to the cause, for the Republic's use when we win. My personal money is lodged with a financier known to Benson.'

He had never known Penford so low and depressed. Much more of this and he'd be affected too. With a grunt, he decided to change the man's mood with provocation.

'Well,' he drawled, 'I must say you're a real Jeremiah today. What's up with you? Being a bad loser?' he mocked.

Martin reined to a halt, turned and sparks shot from his eyes. 'One day you'll go too far,' he growled angrily. 'I can still take you if I've a mind to it.'

James barked a harsh laugh. 'That's a matter of opinion!'

Martin glowered at him, all else forgotten. Jesus, he told himself. How I detest you. I always have and I always will. To think you'll get Sarah—and then, with a great effort of will, he controlled himself and switched to another safer topic.

'Have you seen the boss lately?' he made himself drawl, though an ugly glint still showed in his eyes.

James did not miss this but decided he need provoke no more. He gave a short nod. 'As a matter of fact I did, only last week. I arranged with Massey to be gone for a few days. I gave both a verbal and written report.'

'Including Sarah?'

James nodded soberly. 'I had to. She's now in that famous little black book, I bet, as well as us two.'

This thought suddenly tickled Martin's fancy and lightened his mood. 'I bet King Charles would give half his Kingdom to get his hands on that black book. I wonder where it's kept?' he mused. Then another thought struck him. 'Does Sarah know about . . . him?'

James shook his head firmly. 'I've not told her, for her own safety. She's never mentioned his name so obviously she's in total ignorance and that's how it should remain.'

Martin knew this made sense. His mind switched tracks. 'There has to be a leak but I know it can't be a customer. As I've said, there are few enough now and, of those, they're all dedicated Parliamentarians, I'd swear to that. Anyhow, I never discuss politics, too dangerous in these times.'

'Close it down,' James advised firmly. 'Halt anything which might jeopardise Sarah's life.'

'You understand what that will mean?'

'Of course I do! I'm not that dumb!'

James turned in the saddle and idly looked around. The sun was weak but climbing higher. Something caught his attention and he focused hard then, turning his head, looked from his eye corner. He knew a sideways vision often gave more detail than a frontal one. He heard Penford rabbiting on about something but ignored him. They had turned their horses and walked slowly back towards their meeting place.

Martin became aware he had been talking to the fresh air. 'What's the matter? You've not heard a word I've just said!'

'We're under observation,' James grunted uneasily. 'Someone in the inn has one of those new, small telescopes. I've just seen the sun flash on the lenses.'

'What!' Martin gasped, but kept his gaze fixed upon his companion. If Hawkins was correct, a direct stare would give the game away. He gritted his teeth and willed himself to study Hawkins' face.

'Hell!' James swore. 'Someone has followed you and now they've seen us together. Turn your horse around and we'll walk back up the lane again so we can vanish beneath the skyline. Once there, we bolt. You get back to the city but go in by another gate.'

Martin was shocked. 'I've been ultra careful,' he protested.

James threw him a grim look. 'This proves the leak's from your end. Not mine. No one knew I was coming here today; not even Massey.'

'Hamlyn?'

James shook his head. 'He's away on a special duty for me. Impossible!' he growled. 'That inn's big enough to have a patrol hidden around the rear.'

39

'You've a long way to go to Gloucester,' Martin said uneasily.

James grimaced and nodded. 'My horse is hard and fit and I've two pistols under this lot,' he said, indicating his leather coat, 'as well as this saddle carbine. This does it though. Stop Sarah, right away. It's far too dangerous now. I'll have nothing happen to her.'

'I agree,' Martin grated, furious with this unexpected situation that reflected gravely upon his security. He could have sworn there had been no breach but this day was no coincidence. 'I'll tell her next week when she comes in, it's the last trip.'

James did not even like this but it would be utter folly for him to approach Sarah at her home, even though he did know its locality. He was honest enough to know he was more valuable to the cause that one humble, female courier. This fact galled but there was nothing else either of them could do.

They reached the end of the lane again and halted dubiously. 'At least we are out of carbine range,' James muttered and eyed Penford.

'You'd better go.'

Martin took a deep breath. 'I doubt we'll be able to meet again like this,' he said slowly. 'The Royalist espionage network must be better than I thought. Make sure this is reported upstairs.'

James looked backwards. 'As I suspected, a

patrol has appeared. Who the hell is the informer though? One of your men has definitely been turned. Find him and . . .'

'Kill him!' Martin growled. He looked over at James, eyes narrow and hard.

James knew he would not hesitate; neither would he if in the same situation. There was simply too much at stake; too many good men's lives, the whole future of England.

'I'm off,' Martin said and threw a hard look at James. 'You can get stuffed!' he said with a mocking leer.

James gave a short bark: 'And up yours, Penford, too!'

Martin thumped with his heels, turned his horse and cantered off at a tangent. James watched him for a few paces, threw another calculating look to his rear, then released his stallion. The black leaped forward in a fly jump before unleashing himself in his powerful gallop.

By the time the patrol of six men reached the spot, there was no sign of man or horse. The leader muttered to himself. No rider would catch that black horse, and which way had the other rider gone? He bent, studied the various paths that were cluttered with hoof prints. He was too much of a townsman to be able to read fresh from old tracks. With an oath, he shook his head and turned back to his men.

'Return!' he ordered sharply. They would

go back to the city gate but it was obvious Penford would re-enter by a different one and would, no doubt, have an unshakeable alibi for this time. It was also, he told himself, likely that Penford was a brilliant liar, so what was the point? If an attempt was made to arrest an upstanding Bristol citizen on a flimsy excuse, all hell would break loose and it would be his head on Prince Rupert's block. 'Back to Lawford's Gate, at the double.'

CHAPTER THREE

Sarah approached the Lawford Gate with every nerve twanging. As the queue neared the guardhouse she noted it was the unfriendly officer again and their eyes met. It was nearly ten days since she had crossed swords with him and she prayed he would be more amenable this time.

As she neared, she held his eyes. Not in a direct challenge, which would have been foolish, but with open friendliness. She guessed this would disconcert the officer, so managed to twist her lips into a faint smile as well, though she cursed him silently under her breath. He gave her the briefest of nods, then passed her through. Sarah failed to see him turn and throw another meaningful glance at a junior officer who promptly followed on foot.

Bristol was crowded as usual and had started to stink. It was not just a case of too many people, as well as the troops, but also the normal, fetid smells of any city when the sun increased its temperature and whose sewerage system left a lot to be desired.

After the fresh country smells, Sarah found her nostrils crinkling with disgust. It was with a little personal shock that she realised she had once lived in such crowded conditions with her parents and then Joseph. She had taken these odours for granted, as something quite normal. It wasn't until Joseph had bought the country cottage that she had learned what fresh air truly was. Now she writhed. Nothing would persuade her to live in a city again.

She hastened the mare to her fastest walk, weaving between the throng, and gave a sigh of relief as she turned up the lane to Martin's house. She halted the mare, noted the gate was open but Robert had not appeared. He was obviously busy doing something for Martin and had not heard the mare's hooves. Sarah swung down and unfastened the little saddlebag. Inside was freshly made butter but how long it would stay like that in this city heat was a moot point.

'Robert!' Sarah called brightly but, when he still did not appear, she gave a shrug, led her mare forward and into a stall. She was perfectly capable of managing all stable duties, and quietly and efficiently removed the bridle, slipped on a halter and forked some hay into a corner. It was odd Robert still had not come. What on earth could he be doing? Martin would not be pleased to know she was having to do this work.

Martin! She bit her lip anxiously. What was his attitude going to be? She wondered if there was any way he could know about herself and James? Had the two men met since she last saw James? Were words exchanged? Long ago she had gathered there was no love lost between the two men and, without their political alliance, they might have become sworn and deadly enemies.

It suddenly occurred to her that Martin's horse was not present, then her face brightened. That explained Robert's absence. He had been sent on some errand, so Sarah walked briskly to the back door, opened it and stepped into the small lobby which led directly to the kitchen.

'Hello, Bessie. It's me again!'

There was silence. Sarah stood uncertainly, wondering why something weird started to slide down her spine. She studied the kitchen. The fire had burned out which meant no hot meals this day. That was strange in itself because Martin had a healthy appetite for well cooked food. Her eyes flashed around the large, stone-flagged kitchen but everything looked normal.

She walked to the fire, picked up the poker

to stir some life into the ashes, then changed her mind. That fire went out hours ago. Another ice finger slid down her spine and, holding her breath, Sarah opened the door into the hall.

'Martin!' she called anxiously but only silence echoed back at her ears. The house was utterly silent and she stood uncertainly, feeling apprehension grow. Why did the hair at the nape of her neck begin to prickle? Walking on tiptoes, Sarah padded up the passage and faced the door to Martin's study. It was shut although this, in itself, was not unusual. Taking a deep breath, she rapped three times and waited, wondering why her heart had started to thud unevenly.

There was no response so, grasping the handle firmly, she quietly turned it, opened the door and peeped warily into the room. It was a room never well lit by the sun; almost gloomy even on a summer's day and Martin invariably had a fire, except during a heat wave. Her eyes flew to the fire; it still burned but only as a tiny glow, tickling the base of one apple log.

She took a deep breath and stepped fully into the room, eyes swivelling around. Martin sat in his favourite working chair at his desk, hunched over it. She could just see his head, resting on his forearms where he had fallen asleep.

'Martin! Your fire is going out! Shall I make it up for you?'

He did not reply and, heart now thundering wildly, Sarah stepped forward on tiptoes, rounded the desk and looked carefully. She froze, her eyes refusing to believe what they saw, while one hand flew to her open mouth. Her instinct was to scream but caution silenced this action.

Martin's body weight rested evenly on his bent forearms. The large knife was buried slightly to one side of his spine, sunk deep almost to the hilt. Sarah blinked, gave a muted sob, bit her lip and froze with shock and fear. She gulped, shocked and scared out of her wits with legs that had turned lifeless. She knew she was rooted to the spot, quite unable to take it all in, her eyes fixed on the hilt sticking from Martin's back.

She closed her eyes, counted slowly to ten, opened them and forced a revolting stomach into quiescence again. She would not be sick. Her fists clenched and unclenched as she looked around for help or a clue. The old chest still stood in the corner but now the lid was up and she could see the two hasps had been broken. There were objects strewn on the floor around the trunk, some papers, two small coins, a tiny ornamental dagger and nothing else. She walked over and peered inside. The trunk was empty. Sarah's shoulders slumped wearily. Murder with robbery as the motive but Martin, dear, sweet Martin who had never harmed a fly! Brave, courageous Martin who

46

loved her, she now knew, but who never made a nuisance of himself; Martin whom she had known since a little girl when her father first took her to meet him.

Dear God, who had done this and where were Bessie and Robert? She came back, bent and studied Martin's face. His eyes were open and registered shock so the killer was known enough to come into the room and considered friendly enough for Martin to be his normal self at his desk.

Why had Robert vanished on the horse? It was not a very good animal and not really capable of carrying two people. Surely to God Robert and Bessie were not dual killers? She padded to the fire and picked up the long, iron poker, feeling a sudden, vital urge for a weapon without knowing why. She felt herself start to shiver and her eyes lifted to the laths. She knew she should go and investigate upstairs but dare she? Sarah retreated to the door and stood, dithering uncertainly. Should she get help from the Royalists but what if there were secret papers around? Then commonsense returned. If there were, Martin would have them so hidden they would take a lot of finding. If only James were here, and a little sob broke from her lips.

It was the tiniest of creaks but her overstrained nerves jumped with shock as her ears registered the unexpected sound. Her heart started its awful banging again and her face twisted with terror. The killer was coming back. He must have been here all the time, hidden in the house and now he was coming for her. The sound came again and she was galvanised into action. She sprang back into Martin's room, shot silently behind the door and lifted the poker, grasping it with both hands.

The sound approached. It was unsteady, uncoordinated, hesitant but steadily nearing. She heard a creak that was the back door swinging on its hinges though she knew perfectly well she had shut it. Sarah sank back against the wall, lips drawn back in a silent snarl. No killer would attack her without reaction. The poker rose an inch higher as the uncertain steps approached, almost like those of a drunk, heading towards Martin's room.

Sarah licked her dry lips, terrified out of her senses then the voice croaked raggedly:

'Mistress Sarah! Are you there? I heard you arrive?'

Robert staggered into the room, reeling a little, blood streaming down his face. His lips were split, one eye half-closed and blood seeped from his nostrils.

Sarah sagged with relief and she could not have moved to save her life. She could barely recognise the young man whom she had seen grow from boy to youth. His face looked as if it had been pulped and tears cascaded down both cheeks.

Robert turned, stared miserably into her eyes, hands held from his sides pitifully and burst into tears, sobbing like a small child. Sarah lowered the poker a little, was this a trap? She strained to hear, heard nothing but Robert's wild sobs and ventured another step nearer.

'Mistress, they've killed him,' Robert wailed.

Sarah was galvanised into action at last. She lowered the poker but prudently kept it in her left hand; with her right, she grabbed Robert's arm, pulled him from the room, slammed the door shut and took him into the kitchen; Bessie's room.

She thrust Robert into a chair, placed the poker against the table leg in a convenient position and worked the pump. She hastily pushed a bowl under then turned back to Robert. His face was a red mask. Gently, grabbing a cloth, she started to dab the blood away while the tears turned into frantic sobs of distress.

Sarah stopped, turned and eyed the cupboards. All cooks worth their salt kept brandy somewhere. She hunted around, found a small cask, grabbed two pewter mugs and poured out two generous tots.

'Get this down you, Robert, first of all. We can talk later after I've cleaned you up a bit,' she told him firmly.

He lifted large, puppy-like eyes to her, brimming with more tears but drank the brandy in large gulps. Sarah sank down on another stool and sipped hers more carefully; she was unused to strong spirit but God, this was one drink she did need. The brandy hit her stomach with a punch, stirred her blood into action and her shoulders sagged a moment. Her mind had, she knew, gone a complete blank.

Finally she put the mug down and recommenced cleaning Robert's face. One tooth was loose. One eye was rapidly closing and should really have raw steak on it but, apart from this, his face was simply split and bruised. He had been thrashed by large fists. As a young man, he would have no chance against whoever had done this.

'Right, now go to the water jug and wash your face thoroughly,' she told him firmly. 'Then tell me everything.'

When Robert returned to sit opposite her, he was not so ghastly looking but she realised he would be a mess in the morning from bruises. However, he was young, and youth was resilient.

'Now, talk,' she commanded gently.

'My father killed the master,' Robert began.

Sarah was astounded. 'Your father?' she stammered. 'But I thought . . .' and her voice tailed off tactfully. She sensed suddenly this ice was very thin, yet she must know everything.

'It was all planned and I never knew,' Robert started again wearily. 'I never thought

50

my mother would be a party to . . .'

'Bessie as well?' Sarah gasped, now deeply shocked. Was she hearing correctly?

Robert nodded miserably. 'I didn't know anything until a few hours ago . . .' and his voice croaked tremulously.

'Go on,' Sarah encouraged, taking another drink of the brandy, desperate for it herself. Bessie? Martin's housekeeper and cook for years? Bessie whom she suspected had always had a soft spot for her master. It was impossible! Then a thought struck her. But Bessie who? What had she ever known about Bessie?

'It all started a few weeks ago when Fletcher turned up when the master was out on one of his walks. I realise now, he had waited until then.'

'Fletcher?'

'He's my father, damn him to hell!'

Robert halted, then struggled to gather his thoughts into a coherent story. 'I've often wondered who my father was but my mother would never discuss him with me so, in the end, I gave up asking. It even crossed my mind as to whether it might be Master Martin,' Robert admitted, with a wan smile.

'Go on.'

'All Mother ever said to me was that he was well bred. Anyhow he turned up unexpectedly at the back door. Mother opened it, took one look at his face, went white, then sent me from

51

the room. What was said I don't know but, after an hour, just before Master was due back, he came out and Mother was holding his hand. I kept myself out of the way, I can tell you, because there was something about him I didn't like.'

'Your mother?'

'She was a changed woman. She seemed to blossom, even sang while she worked but she still would say nothing to me, so whenever he came I made myself scarce. I couldn't tell the master, there was nothing then to tell.'

That was a mistake, Sarah thought. With his connections, Martin could have conducted some quiet investigation but Robert was not to know.

'It all came to a head last evening, I suppose. Mother told me we were all going away with Fletcher to start a new life. I was horrified and argued with her but to no avail, as you can imagine. Mother was bewitched by that damned man. He only had to beckon his finger and she trotted to obey his slightest whim. It nauseated me, I can tell you, Mistress. I didn't want to leave Master Martin. I've lived here since I was born and what did Fletcher ever do for Mother and me? Bugger all. Yet there was Mother, flashing winsome smiles at him . . .' and Robert's voice cracked before, taking a deep breath, he was able to continue.

'I told her I wasn't going. My place was here. I liked my work. Then this morning,

52

when he came, I hid but so I could overhear. Fletcher said he'd found out that Master Martin was a spy for Parliament, of all things. Mother believed him though. He said Master was now under suspicion and could be picked up at any time and this was one house not to be connected with. I could see he threw Mother into a flummox; I was watching through the keyhole by now. Fletcher also mentioned you, Mistress, and that you were under observation as well, being so close to master and visiting him on such a regular basis. I must admit, Mother demurred at that but Fletcher overrode her. He said we would have to leave, all of us and that it was only right and proper that we should take money with us. Master obviously must have funds for paying agents and mother mentioned a trunk in the study. I was able to see Fletcher brighten at that, then he started whispering to her. I didn't like it, I can tell you but I didn't know what to do. Master was in his room. I did think of bursting in but would he have believed me . . . a youth?'

Sarah eyed him and refrained from nodding. It would only make Robert feel more guilty.

'Continue,' she encouraged.

'I was so sick with it all I went out to the stables and found a big grey horse there. His! I debated what to do, then decided there was nothing for it, I must warn Master.'

53

'You went and saw him?'

Robert groaned. 'I did but it was too late. I suppose Mother made some excuse to go into Master's study and Fletcher was on her tail. Master was quite off guard. Fletcher just slipped behind him, I think, while Mother kept him talking and that was it. I came back just then and saw the end result. I think Mother was horrified though. I don't think she realised Fletcher meant murder. I stood there frozen, unable to take it all in while Fletcher roared at Mother, forced open the trunk, dived in and put things into a small sack. Money I guess, from the sounds he made. Mother then went to him and started to argue.'

'What did he do?'

'Back-handed her,' Robert said grimly. 'I charged forward . . . after all, she is my mother, and he turned on me. He's a big man. He beat me. I think he meant to kill me too but Mother clung to his arm and screamed at me to run.'

'And you did?'

'I ran like hell to the stables. I was hurting so I couldn't think straight but I've always had a hiding place there. There is a loose board; by pulling this aside and turning sideways, I managed to wriggle behind the wall. I stayed there. I was scared, Mistress.'

'So would anyone be with a grain of sense,' Sarah placated gently.

'Anyhow, Fletcher came out dragging Mother with him. This time she was crying, in

54

a real state, but Fletcher dominated. He shoved her up on the back of Master's horse, mounted his own and rode off. I think perhaps I must have slept then. I only awoke when you stabled your mare but I was still frightened. I didn't know whether to approach you or not. By now I didn't know who could be trusted. Finally I plucked up courage to come into the house and . . .' Robert finished with a pitiful look in his eyes.

Sarah let out a long, heavy sigh and shook her head. Dear God, when she had left her home this morning it had been with a light, gay heart. Now she felt as if she would never be able to smile again.

'I didn't even know your mother could ride,' she mused.

'She can, but like an empty sack, she'll not get far on a horse,' Robert said thoughtfully. He was more in control of himself now he had told his story and Mistress Sarah was so rock solid. He looked hopefully at her and waited for her to sort out this mess.

'This is a Royalist city,' Sarah murmured, thinking hard. 'They'd only have to ride to the docks and they could sail away anywhere,' she pointed out to Robert.

His jaw dropped. 'I never thought of that . . . and they have all Master's money!'

Sarah studied Robert. From not knowing him before, and even being uncertain as to whether she liked him, she felt her heart swell for him. He looked over at her like a trusting puppy.

'Where do you stand in this war, Robert?' she asked warily.

Robert did not hesitate. 'I wasn't really interested, Mistress,' he said thoughtfully, then his jaw hardened. 'But if Royalists have done this to Master, then I'm for Parliament.'

Sarah eyed him and took a gamble. James would not approve but these were certainly unusual and tragic circumstances.

'He too,' she told him simply.

Robert gazed at her, a frown on his brow He had recovered from the shock. The brandy had worked but, most of all, he had shifted the awful disaster on to someone else's back. He was bright and intelligent. As Sarah watched him she could swear she could see the wheels turning in his head.

'Then Master did work for Parliament and you too!' he breathed with awe. 'My father was correct at that!'

Sarah gave him a sad smile. 'I admit to nothing and Robert, if you want some wise advice, you know nothing either!'

He took her warning, noting the serious look in her eyes. In half a day he had grown from boy to man. Life could never be the same for him again. His heart swelled as he regarded this fine lady and, in a flash, he became her servant for life. That he would not always agree with her would be immaterial.

56

When the chips ever fell down the wrong way, Robert knew his life belonged to Sarah Turner.

'I'll do anything to bring Fletcher to Justice,' he said with quiet intensity.

'And your mother?' Sarah asked him in a low voice.

That made Robert hesitate but only for a heartbeat of time. 'She too,' he said but there was a catch in his voice. 'Master didn't deserve what happened to him.'

No, Sarah thought, he certainly did not. Never, in a month of Sundays, would Martin have suspected Bessie. Why should he? Mother and son had lived with him for over a decade. They were part and parcel of his life. What had come over Bessie? Was Fletcher so charismatic he had turned her head with platitudes or was Bessie more obtuse than Sarah had realised? Was it incredible bad luck Fletcher had come to Bristol? She thought about this carefully then realised it must have been fate. Finally, her mind switched to more practical matters.

Something still bothered Sarah. 'I wonder,' she began, hesitating.

Robert waited, holding his breath. Sarah continued. 'You said Fletcher back-handed your mother? I wonder if he was playing both ends to the middle?' she mused.

Robert gazed at her, quite bewildered. 'Mistress?'

57

Sarah explained herself, thinking rapidly. 'I don't think Fletcher was an out and out Royalist. I think he may have acted like that but really he basically wanted money for his own ends. He is a pure criminal. There's nothing political about him at all, which means . . .'

'The Royalists will want him too,' Robert gasped, understanding her reasoning.

'How badly hurt are you, Robert?'

He pulled a face. 'Not that bad, Mistress.'

'Now listen carefully and don't ask questions which I will not be able to answer. I have my purse here. I'll give you some sovereigns and what I want you to do is this. Go and buy a horse, and get a good one too, then ride to Gloucester. I'll give you a note which must be put in the hands of one man only; no one else, no matter what. This is vitally important. At the sane time, you must *not* tell the man what has happened here. Say you are just a messenger and you know nothing. Can you do that?'

Again Robert did not hesitate. He nodded eagerly. Anything would be better than staying here now.

'Right!' Sarah said decisively 'I'll have to go back into Martin's study to get quill and writing material and then . . .' She eyed Robert carefully. 'I have to search this property before I leave.'

He understood in a flash. 'Incriminating

58

papers against Parliament?'

'Something like that,' Sarah prevaricated, delighted and rather surprised at his wits. Astounded, she was only just discovering what made this young man tick, and rather liked the reality.

'Are you game to be with me?' she asked in a low voice.

Robert gulped, then nodded. 'What are we looking for?'

'Papers, anything written down, whether we can read it or not.' She paused. 'I'll be taking them with me, hidden under my shirt.'

'Come on then, Mistress. Two heads are said to be better than one,' though his cheeks had paled again.

Without giving him chance to change his mind, Sarah led the way back into the study. She stared at Martin, her lips tightening. Dear God, someone was going to pay for this and Fletcher was top of her list. They searched. Each worked methodically going through the desk's drawers, under the floor covering, checking the trunk, poking fingers everywhere. It was Robert who discovered the loose board at the trunk's base.

'Prise it off,' Sarah told him.

When he had done so, the small packet of stones fell into Robert's hand and he passed them to her. She gently unrolled the white material and examined the contents.

'Diamonds!' she explained to Robert. 'I'll

take those with me too.'

Finally, when they had exhausted everywhere, Sarah studied the neat roll of papers, covered in Martin's neat, intricate handwriting and she rolled them up into a small cylinder then, turning her back, slipped them under her riding shirt next to her skin.

'What about the cellar?' Robert asked her as she stood, contemplating going home. She was sure nothing had been overlooked.

'Cellar?'

Robert nodded and blushed. 'I loved Master so much I used to watch him when I shouldn't,' he confessed. 'He'd often go down to the cellar where the few spices are kept and handle the old spice jar next to the peppers?"

Sarah's eyes opened wide with astonishment. 'Let's get down there then.'

Robert's spying proved accurate. He went directly to the wall cupboard and pointed to a range of small bottles and packets wrapped in waterproof cloths.

'The spices,' he explained.

Sarah eyed them thoughtfully. If that was all Martin had had, business had just about ground to a halt. She saw a tall, glass spice jar standing tucked under the far corner of the shelf. Gingerly she took it down, removed the glass stopper and peered inside.

'There's something here,' she muttered, teasing it out with her fingers.

A thin roll of paper slid into her hand and

60

she recognised the same type as that which Martin used to hand to her. Slowly she opened it, and read.

'Hawkins, I'm doubly uneasy and I don't know why. Stop Sarah from any more trips. I think my time here has ended and it might be prudent for me to bolt for my neck's safety. The business must go to pot until we have made England a Republic. Watch yours. Penford.'

'Well,' she muttered to herself, 'a message in plain language!' That was odd in itself. When had Martin placed it there? She realised she'd never know and her face became grim. She showed the brief, succinct message to Robert.

'So Master suspected something but . . .' he paused and sighed heavily '. . . never my mother. He had no chance at all.'

Sarah agreed but refrained from comment. Had Martin, through complacency, made the one fatal error? Had he been too involved in espionage for far too long? Again, she told herself, this was another puzzle which would never be solved now.

'Come on, let's go,' she said with a sore heart. 'You leave first. I'll follow you in ten minutes.'

'The Master?' Robert asked nervously.

'I'm going to report his murder to the

61

Royalists. Give them something to do,' she said maliciously.

Robert hesitated as something occurred to him. 'But if they saw you ride in through the gate, won't they wonder why it has taken you so long to tell them, Mistress?'

'Ten out of ten, Robert!' she praised. 'You're thinking better than me.' She paused to work it all out in her head. She could afford no error now. 'You get on your way with that note. Afterwards go to my home and wait for me, but make sure you slip away unnoticed. There might just be a Royalist prowling around right now.'

'I'll slip over the stable roof into the next yard,' Robert told her. 'But you?'

Sarah forced a smile on her face that went nowhere near her eyes. 'I'll have had the longest attack of the vapours, from shock, anyone can have.'

Robert had to grin. He didn't feel like it. Indeed, only an hour ago he was convinced he would never smile again but there was something so wonderfully strong and reassuring about Mistress Turner. His heart went out to her. He had lost his mother. Was it possible he had discovered a surrogate one?

CHAPTER FOUR

James was in a foul mood and knew it. He was desperately short of sleep because it had seemed a long ride back from London. He had spent too much time dodging Royalist patrols and, by the time he arrived at base camp, even his powerful stallion plodded with head hanging low. The final straw had been being awoken much too early when a sentry had insisted he spoke to him. With a thundercloud on his face, he had been lost for words when Robert faced him. Only Sarah's far too brief message had managed to drive the fatigue waves away temporarily.

Once he had grasped the essence, which appeared to be critically urgent, he had pushed tiredness away. He knew he had great reserves of strength and this blunt, almost demanding message meant he must dip into them generously.

'Right,' he had grunted to the sentry, 'feed this young man then . . .' He had paused, uncertain what to do with him.

Robert had solved the problem for him. 'I'm to go to Mistress Turner's home and wait for her,' he had volunteered.

'Right, sentry, see to his wants. Give him a fresh horse and, young man, go where you've been told.'

James always kept a spare horse, a nondescript brown animal of good quality although nowhere near that of his favourite black. A sudden thought occurred to him. 'And get my black shod,' he ordered. It was always extremely wise to have new shoes. There was no telling when or where he had to ride and a loose shoe could be catastrophic.

*   *   *

The ride down from Gloucester had almost drained him and, at the ruins, it was a struggle to keep his eyes open. He thanked God for the park's deer herd. They made superb sentinels so he allowed himself the luxury of a few brief catnaps. It was the stag that alerted him to Sarah's approach and he frowned heavily as she rode at a brisker pace than normal. Something heavy landed in his stomach with a thud. Whatever it was, it was certainly not good and he grimaced to himself.

As Sarah reined back to a halt he stepped forward to help. Her mare was skittish this morning, facing a strange horse. He hoped to god she wasn't coming into season. He'd never dare come near her riding his stallion.

'Oh, James!' Sarah gasped, falling into his arms.

'Sarah! What the hell's happened?' Surely those were not tears? His blood chilled.

'I've bad news. Very bad indeed,' Sarah told

him, biting her bottom lip.

He took a deep breath. That much was obvious. 'Spit it out then.'

'It's Martin. He's dead. He was murdered!'

'Good God!' James exclaimed. This was the last thing he had expected to hear. For a few seconds his wits left him as he stared at her horrified while seeing the tears flood down her cheeks; tears of delayed shock, and having to break such news.

'You are quite . . . sure?'

Sarah nodded dumbly. 'I'm afraid so. It was a knife,' she told him.

'Over here. Sit on this rubble and start right at the beginning. Miss nothing out,' he instructed her.

Sarah obeyed, bowing her head for a few moments. She had been all right when she'd risen, though her night had been sleepless. So why this flood of weeping? She gulped and sobbed, struggling to control herself, sensing he barely managed to restrain his impatience. Finally, with an enormous effort, she forced the tears away, collected herself together and related her story. He listened in total, appalled silence.

When she had finished he was silent, shoulders slightly bent as his mind revolved with shock. He had considered himself a hardened veteran of warfare and there was nothing left in life to shock him. Now he knew better. Penford dead and, worst of all, knifed in the back. His jaw tightened. He could feel her eyes on him, big and questioning but he had to gather himself together, as memories stormed back.

His breath came out in a heavy sigh as he lifted his gaze to look into her questioning eyes:

'We were brothers,' he told her simply.

Sarah was astounded. 'Brothers? But your names . . .' She halted, mind wobbling with confusion. This information was something she would never have guessed, even under torture.

'I don't understand,' she managed to get out at last.

James grimaced. 'My mother married very young. He was the first-born and I was the last. In between we had brothers and sisters but none survived to become adults through various diseases and illnesses. Our parents died when I was sixteen.'

'That's incredible!' she exclaimed, then something hit her. Now at last it was clear. 'How weird. Do you know, for ages I always fancied there was something about Martin which I'd seen in another person but I could never make the connection. Now I do! He always had a very subtle likeness to you when in a happy mood. Why couldn't I see this before?' Then she frowned. 'But your names?'

James explained. 'Hawkins is only a cover name. My real one is David James Penford

66

and only one other person, apart from you, now knows this. Even Massey doesn't.'

'I never guessed,' Sarah murmured with awe.

'That was the general idea,' he replied grimly, 'only Thurloe knew.'

Thurloe, who is he? Sarah wondered. Had she heard that name before? She crinkled her forehead with bewilderment. Where did this strange man fit into this picture? Quite suddenly she became aware just how little she really did know.

'We never got on,' James continued in a low voice. 'Indeed, there were times when we loathed each other. I guess it was a personality clash. Whatever, we fought. Sometimes verbally and other times physically. Honours were about even, I guess if a score had been taken. We only had one thing in common but this was of such critical, vital importance, it meant we were doomed to work together despite our emotional feelings. Our politics were the same, identical to the last dot. Sometimes both of us thought it was crazy we should have such a close working relationship and each of us, individually, complained but Thurloe had no time for such nonsense. We had a job to do and do it we would, even if it meant supping with the devil in the process.'

That name again, Sarah thought wildly. Yet she sensed this was hardly the moment to plague him with questions.

'It's strange,' James continued in a low voice. 'He'd had a presentiment only the last time we met. I was ready to poo-hoo it, but I didn't. I'm glad now. So the old sod has gone but in what a way,' he growled. 'I want vengeance because, no matter what, we came from the same parents. He must be avenged.'

Sarah kept quiet. Privately she considered this an impossibility. Someone as sharp as Fletcher would have left the region days ago. She lifted up her shirt and extracted the neat roll of papers.

'Thank God you had the sense to look for these,' James said, flipping through them rapidly. 'That's his code book. If the Royalists had got hold of it, our code would have had to be changed but it would have taken us time to learn this. Damn! I'll have to go to Thurloe with this news,' he murmured but more to himself than her. Sleep, though, he must have. A tired man could so easily put himself into an unknown hazard. He felt her eyes on him, large, questioning and worried.

'You've done very well, Sarah. I'm proud of you. Now about his body . . .'

'That's been taken care of.'

'What?'

'The Royalists did indeed have their suspicions. When I came out, after Robert had slipped away, there was a young Royalist officer lingering just a little too near the door.'

'What did you do?' he asked quickly.

68

Sarah gave him a malicious grin. 'Walked up to him, screamed blue murder then let myself faint in his arms.'

He had to smile, picturing it all. 'You'd just discovered the body, I take it?'

Sarah shook her head. 'No, I didn't know how long he'd known I was inside, so I told him I'd fainted with shock. After he had helped me recuperate enough to talk, I collected my wits together and tore into him. I lambasted him for allowing such crime to take place in Bristol and I was disgusted with what Prince Rupert expected the citizens to contend with.'

He took a deep breath. 'You didn't overdo it?' he asked anxiously.

Sarah shook her head. 'He was so young and pliable. It was like taking a comfit from a small child.'

'You made a deposition?'

'Yes, and gave them the house keys. After all, I've everything of value which you now hold.'

'This is going to put the cat among the Royalist pigeons with a vengeance,' he told her thoughtfully. 'Be very circumspect for a while now. Your work is finished but pay close attention to what you say and to whom. It's quite likely there are Royalist sympathisers in your village; men in the King's pay.'

Sarah nodded soberly Quite suddenly, she was glad her work had ended. Nothing could

69

ever be the same again though she knew she would have to ride out, to make a cover for her servants. It would never do for her to stay at home after so much wandering.

'There's something else you can do though. See Lawyer Benson. He has Martin's Will. There's also the business. Half of it's mine though, from what he said when we last met, it's just about on its last legs until peace comes.'

'I'd like to help, where I can,' she said sincerely. Her heart went out to this strong man. She guessed his set features hid a multitude of churning emotions but who would guess from his expression? Was it that which made him such a clever agent? She knew she was brimful with questions but could ask none at this time.

'When will I see you again?' she wanted to know.

He turned and gave her his complete attention. 'I don't know,' he replied honestly. 'My time and my life are not yet my own. One thing I do know though, Walter Hamlyn is getting the fastest discharge my army has ever known and he's coming down to your home, hot foot, as a guard.'

'Eh?' Sarah gasped, 'I have Jack and there will be Robert!'

'Kids!' he snorted. 'Hamlyn is a highly trained soldier even if a little lame in one shoulder from an old pike wound. No, for my peace of mind, Sarah, I insist. I still have much work to do and I can't do this properly, worrying about your safety, now can I?' he asked reasonably.

She gave a rueful nod. It seemed all rather exaggerated but, as a soldier and officer, she presumed he must know best. What her servants were going to say about it all, she did not like to think.

'My servants will question,' she began hesitantly.

'Spin them a yarn, anything, but make them realise my man stays as guard,' he told her firmly.

Sarah was dubious about this. It was all very well having servants, but it made privacy impossible and motives out of the question. She said nothing; it would be grossly unfair to add to his load. She studied him as he stood, face bleak, immersed in complicated personal thoughts. She felt suddenly totally excluded. He seemed to have forgotten she was present. Then he turned back to her.

'The best thing I've done in my life was meet you,' he said soberly. 'I'm glad you went on that ride so I could abduct you,' he told her, trying to lighten his mood and failing completely. Too many problems and upsets had descended too sharply, altogether.

'Oh, James,' she murmured, touching one of his hands.

'I swear, when I can, I want to marry you.

71

No more waiting. No more being alone. No more camp meals. I want a proper home, a wife, children in due course and some peace and comfort. I've done more than my share for England. I'm not asking too much, am I?'

Sarah shook her head sadly. 'But when will that be?'

He paused. 'I wish I knew. The trouble is with espionage, it's easy to get into, if a man has the right talents but it's bloody hard to break away again. The man at the top has tremendous power. He can wield that power to suit himself and inveigle a man to continue to work whether he wishes to or not. How to sever links without being under the threat of compulsion? I don't know. Martin was the only person whom I knew doing such work. Obviously there are others, many others, but the top man keeps distances between. No one knows more than another name, for security purposes, either up or down the line. An espionage agent, by virtue of his work, puts himself in a position whereby he can be blackmailed to continue, morally or otherwise.'

Sarah felt herself chill. It made a future sound horrendous; one in which, by this admission, he would never be wholly free so where did that leave marital stability? Then she gave herself a shake. They'd manage. Others did, because she knew her love for this brave man was something deep, rare and lasting. If only no other problems reared their ugly heads in the near future.

'Anyhow, back to business. Where will you want it paid?'

Sarah was taken aback again. 'What paid?'

'Your remuneration, of course. Parliament pays generously for services rendered.'

'Goodness me! I never once thought of money,' Sarah exclaimed truthfully. Her expression amused James. How he loved this wild-spirited girl; how he yearned to give her his name. He took her head between his hands, bent and kissed her slowly, enforcing his hold on her emotions. Sarah melted and moulded to him. One hand slid up and touched the back of his neck and she felt herself crushed against his body. She had a flashing vision of the two of them, in a great bed at night and she knew, with instinct, it would always be good.

He drew back first, pulling a face. 'I can't stay,' he groaned. 'I'll have to ride back to Gloucester, have a discreet word with Massey, get my head down for a few hours, then ride to London. It means leaving you to deal with everything this end, though Benson will be a pillar of strength.'

'That's all right, James. Our turn will come, won't it?' she asked herself.

*   *   *

73

Mary Compier was not amused. As a housekeeper, she took her duties as seriously as did her son Jack in the stables, but Mistress Turner puzzled her. Although they got on well, without undue familiarity, there were times when Mary was annoyed. Today was one. The mistress was out on horseback, yet again, and here was this strange young man insisting he await her return.

She didn't like it at all and had already sent her friend Nellie Witchell to alert Jack. In all her life, Mary had never seen such a face. It was grotesquely swollen, heavily bruised and the young man had a determination that was untoward in one so young.

Mary was not as tall as Sarah but she was enormous. She did not so much walk as waddle or roll. Her cheeks were always brightly flushed from exertion, or the heat of the kitchen fire, yet, surprisingly, she was exceedingly strong. Her arms were powerful from years of lifting heavy pans from here to there and also pummelling dough for bread-making.

When her bosom friend came in they made a strange pair. Nellie towered over Mary but was stringy, yet she too did not lack strength. Her hair, like Mary's, was just starting to show grey threads and, when they stood together, each with hands on hips, they made a formidable combination.

Sarah eyed them with a sinking heart while,

to one side, Robert stood a little miserably. He needed little to sense the fat woman's hostility and it was with considerable relief that he had heard Mistress Turner return.

'He says you told him to wait here!' Mary started ominously.

Sarah decided there was only one way to act. Her two workers, whom she privately though of as The Pair, had their hackles up. 'That's right,' she began smoothly. 'This is Robert who is coming to live with us,' she told them and paused before exploding a bomb which would irritate Mary even more, 'and another person will be living with us too. His name is Walter Hamlyn.'

'Well, Mistress,' Mary started, her breasts beginning to heave like twin mountains under an eruption, 'two more men to cook for and . . .'

'. . . wash for and their rooms,' Nellie ended for her, then flashed a look at Mary.

Oh you wretched pair, Sarah thought. Not all that long ago they had been at daggers drawn; Mary jealous of her superior position and Nellie doing her best to muscle in and become an aide. Now they had combined forces to protest as much as any servant dare. She loved both of them, respected them but there were days when she could cheerfully knock their heads together.

'Of course, if it's all going to be too much for you both I can make other extra arrangements,' she said cunningly.

They bridled together. Again they eyed each other and Sarah swore she could see some kind of message pass between them. Bearing in mind James' comments and his position, to say nothing of their hoped-for future, Sarah knew she must regularise the situation forthwith. She could only be generous. Surely The Pair would not bite the hand that fed them?

'I've decided we need more live-in help. Why don't you move in, Nellie? You could rent your cottage so you'd have other income and I'm sure you and Mary can work out duties to suit yourself. Because,' she paused heavily, 'there are certainly two more men to look after, and who knows what the future might not bring.'

The Pair stiffened, quivered, threw a questioning look at each other, then turned back to Sarah with bated breath and a silent question.

'I can't say any more at the moment,' Sarah continued blandly. This would all give them something else to think about and, hopefully, still a multitude of questions. 'So will one of you sort a room out for Robert, please?'

Mary spoke for both of them. 'Robert who, Mistress?'

Sarah saw the battered young man flinch. 'Just Robert for the time being,' she replied, then taking his arm she led Robert into her

76

private sitting room and shut the door firmly.

'Take no notice of them,' she said kindly and fancied she saw Robert's lips quiver once more. He must be exhausted and miserable about a blank future. 'Do you only ever go under your first name?'

'Yes, Mistress. Mother would never let me know what she called herself and I'll certainly not use Fletcher's name,' he replied stiffly.

Sarah nodded thoughtfully. 'Leave it for the time being. Now, what am I going to do with you? Schooling?'

'No, Mistress. I'd like to continue where Master Martin left off. I'd like to be in the spice business.'

Sarah was startled and pursed her lips. 'First of all, nothing can be done there until the Will has been read. You see, there is another partner and I can't say more than that. It's going to take time to sort everything out and, anyhow, it would mean living in the city again. At the moment, where? Then there's the war, oh, it's all such a horrible mess,' she said, more to herself now.

'Perhaps I can stay here until something can be arranged. I can work in the stables. I am experienced,' Robert said, in a little rush of words. He was desperately anxious to have a home, any home but, most of all, an anchor where he could feel safe and wanted. Despite his contempt for his mother's action, he missed her desperately. At sixteen years, he

77

felt bereft.

'That's fine,' Sarah soothed, reading his mind and near panic. 'Just muddle in here and don't take any notice of The Pair.' Then she gave a little chuckle, 'And don't let on that's what I call them, please. They'd become quite impossible!' she confided.

Robert's heart expanded and a little smile appeared. The nightmare was too recent to vanish overnight but now he dared to hope and his heart went out even more to Sarah Turner.

Sarah stood, rested a hand on his shoulder and smiled encouragingly. She realised she found it necessary to look at eye level. Robert was going to make a tall man but then, she reminded herself, Fletcher had been big and not gross with it either. She allowed herself to wonder where he and Bessie were now. James would take vengeance but how could he find them? They could have sailed anywhere. She was sufficiently worldly wise to know that money, especially gold coins, opened many doors without questions being asked. Surely to God, something could be done by someone, some time?

'There's a horse coming, Mistress,' Robert said urgently, turning and nodding at the window.

Sarah stared, working matters out. Taking into account time and distance, she had a shrewd idea who this caller was. She patted

Robert's shoulder again, took him out, flashed an appealing look at The Pair and nodded in Robert's direction.

'He's hungry,' she explained, not really knowing whether he was or not but, at the same time, perfectly well aware that The Pair loved nothing more than filling the male stomach. It would be an ideal way to break lots of thick ice into multiple shards.

She opened the back door and looked up at the stranger, rather surprised. She was uncertain exactly who she expected. Certainly not a man in his twenties, perhaps only a couple of years older than herself, who sat his horse stiffly. Why, she thought, he's a real carrot top. Ginger red hair stood up from his head in a wiry brush, only slightly above normal military length. He had a fair, handsome face marred by a batch of freckles. He wore the clothes of a travelling journeyman but there was no mistaking the stamp. His back was straight though he appeared to favour the left shoulder. He was well armed with carbine, pistol and sword; utilitarian weapons with neither gloss nor ornamentation. At her appearance, he vaulted to the ground, slammed his feet together and only just restrained himself from saluting.

'Hamlyn, ma'am, at your service and under orders,' he barked.

Sarah gave a tiny little cough, more a clearing of her throat, because she was so

79

amused. How naive men could be at times. Did James and this man think that civilian dress hid military bearing? This young man shrieked soldier at her.

'Orders?' Sarah then asked, with a tiny frown. Now what game was James playing at? For a few seconds she felt annoyance; she was not a child; then common sense returned. This was a compliment, albeit a back-handed one. He considered he was protecting his property and territory—her.

'Yes, ma'am. To protect and guard you,' Hamlyn barked.

'Mr Hamlyn, please relax. You're not on a parade ground and you are supposed to be a civilian!' she chided with amusement. 'You're acting just like a soldier.'

Walter Hamlyn eyed her, relaxed half an inch, then gave a deep sigh. 'That's what I was, Mistress, until a few hours ago,' he grumbled.

Sarah wondered if his words held a trace of resentment. 'And you don't fancy a civilian life?'

'I liked being a soldier, ma'am.'

'Oh!' was all Sarah could manage at that. It was all very well for James to be dogmatic but it was she who would have this young man on the property. If he had started to grow chips on both shoulders, then she wished he would go away.

Walter wondered about her. He was still bemused by what had happened to him. Only that morning, barely a few hours ago, the captain had bellowed for him. He had trotted to his private room and been surprised when the captain shut the flap to his quarters.

'Hamlyn, there's your discharge, effective immediately.'

Walter was almost pole-axed with shock. It had taken him a few minutes to find speech. 'Sir, what have I done?'

The Captain had grinned. 'Nothing, but I want you for something that's pretty important to me.'

Without stopping to think, Walter had blurted out words which he immediately regretted, 'For your secret work, sir?'

The captain had eyed him for two seconds then sprung forward, grabbed him at the throat and flung him, back down over a trestle table.

'Who told you?' he had snarled.

Walter had been servant to Captain Hawkins for a long time. He had reckoned he knew every mood of his officer. Certainly the look on Hawkins' face had appalled him. The big officer's eyes glowered with ferocity. His right hand squeezed Walter's throat while his left rammed him down crushingly on the table.

'Talk, damn you to hell!'

Walter writhed, squeaked and finally managed to get out some words. 'No one, sir, and that's the truth, so help me God!'

Hawkins, teeth bared in a grimace of rage,

pressed down harder on his throat and Walter felt panic. He struggled to free himself and breathe but he was no match for the more powerful man. There was something quite terrifying about the light in Hawkins' eyes. He tried to lift one hand to hit out even though that would be considered a military offence but he could feel himself going. There was a red mist before his eyes; the blood drummed in his ears and speech was impossible. His eyes held those of Hawkins and, for a few crazy seconds, he wondered if his officer had gone mad through overstrain.

He gasped, moved his lips and the stranglehold relaxed a fraction. 'It is the truth, sir, I worked it out. The horseshoes . . .'

Hawkins' hand had eased another fraction and the burning fire slowly died in his eyes as bewilderment and wariness replaced it.

'Horseshoes?' he grated, then with a grunt, stood straight again.

Walter half fell on the tent's floor, which was hard, packed earth. He dropped to his knees and frantically fought to breathe freely. Gradually the red mist vanished but, when he looked up, his officer still regarded him balefully. Walter knew he was in the most terrible peril. He was nearer to death than at any time on the battlefield.

'Explain, and it had better be good!'

Walter pulled himself erect but found he must still lean, with one hand, on the table edge with slumped shoulders. God, that had been a close call and he wasn't out of the woods yet. There was still a slightly maniacal gleam in those grey eyes.

'It's true, sir,' he panted, then made himself take a deep breath. 'Though it took me a while to work it all out and Colonel Massey helped.'

'What?'

'Your black stallion has worn out more shoes than any horse in this troop and the next. That meant long, very hard riding over great distances where there were roads; which meant cities. It obviously wasn't Bristol and what's the next most important city to us? London. Why should a captain keep going to London? Why should one lone captain keep disappearing erratically when all other officers' movements were known to the Colonel at all times? Twice Colonel Massey sent for you and I explained you were away. When the Colonel did not query this, I started to think. If any other officer had been absent so often, there would have been a full-scale enquiry. Colonel Massey simply accepted the situation. All this added up to something highly secretive, sir.' He paused. 'Something so hush-hush that even Colonel Massey had no authority over your movements which, in turn, meant you had to be reporting to someone very high up. Again, that pointed to one place only where we are in great force. London.'

'Damnation!' Hawkins had sworn, then

stamped two paces away, face serious, obviously thinking deeply. Suddenly he had whipped around and strode back.

'Who else thinks on these lines?' he had barked angrily.

Again Walter was deeply shocked and rather frightened. 'No one to my knowledge, sir. Certainly no one has ever questioned me.' He stopped, thinking deeply before continuing, 'I think probably it's because you've always acted like this and it's an accepted thing. Also, you always place your tent at the extreme edge of the living quarters and your stallion is kept apart too. You don't mix with the other officers. You eat alone. Indeed, one servant said you were a lone wolf and he even pitied me working for you. I hope you believe me sir, because, if you don't, I've no idea how to prove to you that what I'm saying is the truth.'

Very gradually, the Captain had relaxed though he kept flashing wary looks at Walter.

'Oh very well,' he grunted finally. 'I believe you because the story is too simple to be invented but you say one word, or even hint one word of what you've said and I'll shoot you out of hand *and* no one in authority will do a damned thing about it either. Got that?'

'Yes, sir!'

'Right,' Hawkins grunted; seeing sheer fright still present had softened his tone. 'For your own safety you must also keep your

84

intuition to yourself. Now I want you out of the army to guard a lady for me. No, don't flinch. You won't be a lap puppy. This lady is very dear to me and I have it in the back of my mind, that one day her life might be in peril. Look, sit down, man but, first of all, get us a tankard of ale each.'

This astounding order had been enough to convince Walter of the officer's genuine concern.

'I'm going to tell you the story of a murder in Bristol. Pin your ears back,' the Captain had said and Walter obeyed.

He was appalled at what was related and relaxed properly. No wonder the officer had reacted at his simple statement. He suddenly felt very sorry for Fletcher when the Captain met him because meet him he would. Hawkins had a very long memory and an even longer arm.

'So, you see, the lady and her home must have a guard because I'm going to marry her. That doesn't mean, of course, you're going to be nothing but a guard there. I'll have other assignments for you in due course after you've trained those two boys on that place to act as men. Can you do that?'

'Would I have a free hand, sir?'

Hawkins had grinned wolfishly. 'Down to the nth degree,' he assured him. 'I'll have a note for you to give to the lady who is Mistress Turner.'

85

'I think that'd be a worthwhile job, sir but what about pay . . . ?'

The officer had merely grunted. 'You'll never find me ungenerous,' he promised and Walter believed him. 'Just guard that lady, her servants and property with your life whenever I'm away—and I can't leave the army yet, worse luck,' Hawkins had added gloomily.

'Is my discharge honourable, sir?'

'Very, because you've been a good soldier, man.'

With that, Walter was fairly well satisfied yet, deep down, he couldn't say he relished the idea of petticoat duty. He eyed the lady who faced him warily.

'I'm ordered to give you this, ma'am,' he said, diving into a pocket to pass over a sealed note. Sarah took it, her first letter from James. She opened it, turning to be private.

'This man is to train yours in what he knows best. Cooperate so I don't get the vapours.'

Sarah's lips twitched. No address, no signature, brief, blunt, and to the point. How like James not to use two words when one sufficed. How security-conscious he was.

'Very well, Walter,' Sarah said, turning back. 'It's all in your hands, though how Jack, my stableman and a young boy called Robert, will shape up or even agree, is another matter. I'm not getting involved,' she grinned, then looked over to one side. From this angle, there was an excellent view of the long road to Bristol, open, without trees, and today, with good spring visibility, she could see a long way. 'However,' she began again, 'I think to the villagers, you are another stable worker and odd job man; especially right now.'

'Ma'am?'

'There's a Royalist patrol heading in this direction,' she grimaced. 'Don't antagonise them, Walter. It will only make life even more difficult. Go into the stables, please.'

Walter hastened to obey and took up a position by a half-open door, a pistol in his hand, to the astonishment of the gangly Jack Compier who had been talking to Robert. The young men threw a questioning look at each other, peered over at their mistress, eyed the strange man up, and down and prudently retreated to the far end of the passage.

Sarah waited with trepidation. She had been expecting this and had prepared, what she hoped was a smooth story, more truth than lies, so she would not trip herself up in any future interrogation.

'Captain!' she smiled up at the leader, as the patrol halted in a little flurry of dust. He dismounted, his men copying him as, almost casually, they ranged themselves around the property and stable yard. Sarah felt her heart start to thump uneasily. What did they know?

What had they guessed?

'Would you like to come in for refreshments?' she asked, forcing an artificial smile on her face. Without another word, she turned on her heel and led the way, throwing a quick prayer that Mary and Nellie had their wits about them. Then it dawned upon her she had no idea where The Pair stood politically, which meant another worry. 'Ale in my sitting room, please,' she asked sweetly and led the officer inside and closed the door before turning to face him.

Sarah's heart sank. This was no callow youth. This man was old enough to be her father so would know all about life. He had a grizzled face, set in stern lines, with penetrating brown eyes which would miss nothing, she knew. Mary came in with a tray and two pewter tankards of ale. Sarah nodded to him. He took one, then after she had sat, he copied, perching on the rim of the chair as if it were a gin trap.

'Can I help you?' Sarah began. She was in no mood for a fencing session with verbal traps being laid. 'I take it this visit is to do with that awful murder?'

'Why yes, ma'am. What can you add to what you told our man before?'

'Nothing,' Sarah replied bluntly and waited uneasily.

He stared back at her unflinchingly. 'Why did you visit Penford so regularly?'

Sarah forced herself to give an exasperated sigh. 'I explained all this before,' she said evenly. 'I'd known Martin Penford since a small child. He had done a lot of work for my family. After my parents and then my husband died, I kept in touch. It was, I admit, a loose arrangement initially but when food started to get scarce in the city I made a point of riding in weekly with home products from here. We are, of course, just about self-sufficient.'

The officer frowned heavily, not at all impressed. He went on to a more direct attack. 'I'm astonished and disappointed to know a Royalist's widow should associate with a proven spy.'

Sarah knew she must be quick. Her eyebrows lifted, her expression changed and she managed a little laugh of amusement. 'What! Martin, a spy? Goodness me, that's the most ridiculous idea I've heard this year,' she shot back, then decided her own attack was now in order. She drew herself up very erect and fixed him with a glower. 'And I'm put out too, I might add. If you dare to come here with such a preposterous, even downright idiotic idea, then you leave me no alternative other than to think you've been drinking. How dare you imbibe to the extent you don't know what you're saying? I'll not have it,' Sarah snapped, standing, breathing fire and fury, which was no sham by now. 'I'm going to write a strong complaint to Prince Rupert and you, Mr

Officer, can get out of my home, off my land and away from my life.'

The Royalist was staggered. He considered he had met all forms of verbal resistance, lies and tongue-twistings in his long campaign of prisoner interrogation but this direct assault was outside his experience. For a few seconds, he felt doubt flash through him, then pushed this away firmly. Penford had been a Parliamentarian spy, without a shadow of a doubt. However, perhaps such a cunning rogue had merely used this widow as a front. He eyed her. Did she mean what she said or was this her bluff?

Sarah read his mind. She had him reeling. She pressed home her advantage. 'I'm not bluffing,' she said in a cold, low voice. 'I have to see Lawyer Benson, and the facts will be presented to him with precise instructions from me.'

The officer launched himself at her from this new angle. 'Why see Benson? You're not related to the deceased, are you?'

Sarah realised her mistake but covered as quickly as possible. 'I don't know,' she told him. 'Once or twice he hinted, because of my parents' old connections, there might be a little token for me when he died,' she shot back, inventing rapidly. 'Long ago he informed me who his lawyer was,' Sarah said firmly and then launched an assault from a fresh direction. 'And what exactly are you doing to catch the murderer, this man Fletcher?'

He pounced. 'How do you know his name?'

'Because his illegitimate son now lives here,' Sarah cooed sweetly. 'I'm thinking of adopting him as a brother or something which, incidentally, is another reason I'll be seeing Lawyer Benson but, he doesn't know this yet. I don't want to make promises that might be hard to keep but he's homeless now and parentless. He's also been through a nightmare experience.'

'I'll be speaking to him too,' the Royalist grunted. Somehow this interview was not going as he had planned. Again the doubt reared its head. Perhaps this widow lady did indeed know nothing of Penford's activities? In which case, he realised he must tread very carefully indeed. After all, she was a Royalist officer's widow.

'He's a minor,' Sarah riposted, 'and there will be no questioning without myself or Lawyer Benson present. Is that clear? I'll not have you or anyone browbeating that young boy after his experience.'

The officer dried up. He knew when he was beaten. His jaw stiffened. He would go. He would not come back but he would certainly make sure, in the future, that a most discreet watch was kept upon this property. Thank God, the King had loyal citizens in this village as well as those who must favour Parliament. It crossed his mind to wonder where this lady stood but he did not quite dare bring himself to ask.

After the patrol had departed, Sarah and Walter met. 'Over the field,' she told him.

Strolling slowly, Sarah related what had taken place. Walter listened with a grave expression. 'I should really report this, ma'am but it would be most unwise to run a pigeon service from this address at present. That's something for the future. I don't like committing events to paper either, just in case,' he said shortly.

'Neither do I,' Sarah agreed, 'so we do nothing until . . .'

'. . . I can speak to the Captain personally,' Walter finished for her, though when that would be he was uncertain. He did have a slim line of communication but this meant riding away, leaving the property and the lady unguarded. One snap glance at the young men here had shown him he had much work do but first he had to get their cooperation and trust. There was also the matter of the female house servants.

Sarah was ahead of him there. 'I'll tell my women,' she said thoughtfully, 'but it'll be a watered-down version, of course. They might try to pump you as you'll be living in the house though,' she warned carefully.

Walter grinned at her. Quite suddenly, he decided he liked this lady. She did not flare up or go into emotional hysterics. She might indeed be a suitable mate for his beloved Captain, after all. Suddenly, this assignment no longer palled. Indeed, it might even get interesting enough to produce excitement.

CHAPTER FIVE

Sarah was there first. She was wildly excited to see James again and also bubbled to tell him the astonishing news. It was true, that, when she thought deeply about this totally unexpected situation, she did experience a tiny grain of doubt but when this happened she simply told herself not to be silly.

Walter rode a discreet two horse lengths to her rear except as they approached the court's ruins. Then he rode ahead, eyes swivelling in all directions, his alertness making a giggle rise to Sarah's lips. Wasn't he countryman enough to rely upon the animals? She'd have to have a discreet word with him about the habits of a stag guarding his harem of does. Or perhaps he was just being ultra-conscientious as she was his Captain's intended?

It was just over four weeks since her last awful meeting with him. Even Walter had not appeared to know where James had been but then, Sarah reminded herself, perhaps he had been instructed not to say? Really, she thought with a touch of pique, I am twenty-two and can look after myself. She had been amused to be guarded day and night initially, but now the novelty had worn off. It was irksome to have a shadow every step she took, and worse when out riding. She felt as if her precious freedom was wilfully contained and this, she told herself grimly, she would not tolerate. She was not a wedded possession yet and, even when she was, such stifling restrictions would have to be lifted or more than sparks would fly.

'All clear, ma'am,' Walter cried as he completed a thundering circle of the ruins, almost sending the stag into hysterics.

'The deer, Walter!' Sarah cried, pointing. 'There's no need to be quite like that while the animals are at this end of the park,' she told him gently.

Walter looked at her, then at the deer herd and blushed. Sarah averted her gaze to hide a grin. Now she had embarrassed him but honestly, she told herself, he did deserve it. It seemed soldiers' lives lacked certain aspects of education away from the battlefield.

'The master comes, ma'am,' Walter said suddenly, and pointed. 'Come into the ruins and I'll halter your mare to that stump.'

Sarah watched him canter up, holding the stallion under tight control. The horse was fresh which meant James had not ridden too far, so from where had he come? She decided not to ask, suspecting she'd get no clear answer even if she did.

'James,' she cried happily as Walter took his horse, walked all three mounts to one side and posted himself as guard at a discreet distance.

'Sarah! By God, I've missed you!' James cried and took her in his arms.

He kissed her with hunger then let his hands travel over her breasts, grunting a little. 'Mine,' he murmured, and Sarah's eyebrows twitched.

'Walter's around,' warned Sarah discreetly.

He was unimpressed. 'He'd better be looking elsewhere, studying the scenery then. Incidentally, I want a word with him first before we can catch up with news. How's he settled down at your place?'

Sarah gave a throaty chuckle. 'I don't go near the men. I don't interfere. I know better, but Walter's happy in the home, being ruined by The Pair, my female servants and putting on a bit of weight. As to the outside, well,' she drawled, stopping mischievously, 'I noted this morning Jack has a black eye and one of Walter's lips is swollen. I think perhaps discipline is being enforced the hard way. Not with Robert though. Jack is like his mother. A bit of a quiet law unto himself.'

'Yes, Robert,' James said thoughtfully. 'Hamlyn!' he bawled. 'Give me five,' he said to Sarah then strode over to talk seriously to his man who had, Sarah was amused to note, reverted to the soldier again, standing at rigid attention.

95

When he came back, expression a little reserved, Sarah guessed it was concerned with military matters.

'I'm thinking of adopting Robert,' she told him, 'perhaps as a brother.'

'That's a good idea, but why not wait until we're married and he can be a son?' James suggested. 'Give him stability, which he needs, and he's a decent young fellow from what Walter's said just as Jack Compier is, apparently, knuckle-headed.'

Sarah led the way to a ruined wall that was just wide enough to double as a seat.

'Talk,' he invited and she did. He listened intently to everything relating to the patrol, frowning heavily at times.

'You did well. No more problems from that angle?'

Sarah shook her head. She was not quite ready to relate her other news. She had just received a sharp spear of instinct; this might cause a problem between them.

'My brother?' he got out at last.

Sarah's expression saddened. 'He was buried in that little church near his house,' she told him gently. 'Myself and Lawyer Benson attended plus, I think, some Royalists officers in civilian dress.'

'That figures,' he rated coldly. 'So Benson's dealt with the Will. I'll have to think of making arrangements for Martin's share of the business, even if it is virtually defunct. With

96

mine, once peace comes, it means perhaps there could be a big business there. I might have to install a trusted manager until I get my discharge.'

Sarah took a deep breath. He was not going to like this. She could feel it in her bones.

'Actually, James, I have a copy of the Will in my saddle bag but the gist of Martin's wishes is that I'm his sole legatee for everything.'

He was stunned. 'What!'

She nodded and watched him carefully. Men could be so unreasonably jealous at times and, deep down, much as she adored this powerful man, there had not been time to get to know him intimately. A wartime courtship had to be a thready affair.

'Martin also tied everything up in a "Use for my own benefit" absolutely and no one can touch it, even a husband.'

'The cunning, old . . .' James swore. 'Striking back at me from the grave. That's him all over,' he exploded a little irrationally. Glowering at the park, James was stiff with barely suppressed anger and Sarah felt a chill slide down her spine.

'Well, one thing's for certain,' James started. 'I don't hold with such nonsense between husband and wife. It doesn't give a foundation of trust, does it? I'll have a word with Benson when the war allows and I'll sort something out,' he promised. It was eerie the way Martin had been able to do this, James thought, stiff

97

with anger. It was simply an extension of the bad blood that had always flowed between them since the very early days.

'I'm sorry you don't like it,' Sarah started cautiously, 'but I do.'

It was his turn to go still and look at her with astonishment. Had he heard correctly?

'Oh James, this is an extension of what we discussed ages ago; about a wife's freedom in these hidebound days. I don't hold with any of that. I should have the right to live as I like and use any income as I wish. After all, it's not unusual among the upper class for fathers to leave inheritances to daughters in a Use that no husband can ever touch. Don't you see, this gives a wife security. She doesn't feel so . . .' and Sarah hunted for the correct word to make him understand. 'She doesn't feel . . . bought!'

'I've never heard such bloody rubbish in all my life,' he snorted with genuine shock and outrage. 'Such an idea is a downright insult to a husband's masculinity. It is his job to manage everything, to take care of his wife and family. It's his duty, his responsibility. Anyhow, most females are totally incompetent at managing their effects and affairs. They're far too emotional and hysterical,' he told her firmly, eyes narrowing a little.

Sarah started to bristle. So her instinct had been correct. Well, she told herself grimly, start as you intend to go on or married life will

98

be hell.

'I'm perfectly capable of managing my affairs,' she replied coldly. 'I'm neither emotional, hysterical nor a congenital idiot, thank you, James!'

'I never implied you were,' he shot back, astounded at the set look on her face, her narrowed eyes and stiff jaw. Now what the hell was eating her? He was being perfectly reasonable and sane. All men were masters in their homes. Not wives. Start as you intend to go on, he added to himself grimly. Sarah is strong-minded. Don't let her trample over you.

They glowered at each other, both pulling back so that a few inches of air space separated them.

'If dear Martin went to the trouble of leaving me his half-share of the business, his house and effects and his working capital, then handle it I will. Not you, Benson or any other male. I wouldn't dream of insulting Martin's memory. He left it to me for a purpose so that I would always be wholly independent.'

James snorted. 'He left it to you like that to cause trouble between us because I have you. He always was a rotten loser, blast him.'

'Don't you dare speak ill of the dead who can't defend themselves!' Sarah snapped hotly.

'He was my brother, not yours!' he shouted at her.

Sarah bridled, her cheeks turning scarlet with mortification. 'Don't raise your voice and use that tone to me. I'm not one of your soldiers!' she hurled back at him. 'You're just jealous!'

'Jealous! Me?' he bellowed, standing up with a jump. 'That's just what I mean. It's impossible for a man to have a reasonable argument with a woman because, in five seconds, once she realises she is losing, she goes all hysterical and downright stupid.'

Sarah leapt to her feet. 'I'm not stupid. Right from the start you were obtuse, arrogant, bombastic and one of the most unpleasant men I've had the misfortune to meet,' she raged, between set teeth, eyes fiery with him.

'You don't know anything about spices!' he hurled back at her.

'I'm a woman and probably know a damned sight more than a thick-headed soldier like you!'

'You want your backside tanning,' he growled and meant it. Sarah's hand shot to her waist belt, under her tunic. She rode nowhere without a knife.

'You lay one hand on me and I'll slit your gizzard,' she hissed and meant it.

He was shocked at this. He studied the fury in her eyes, saw where her hand lay, made an intelligent guess and kept still.

'You don't know anything about commerce and finance,' he accused. He was desperately shocked and hurt. Not just by her attitude but because of his brother's underhand trick. Dear God, he'd give anything to have five minutes with big brother Martin right now. He'd thrash him to within an inch of his life. Then he blanched at the direction of his thoughts. With a swallow he turned and studied the deer herd for the want of somewhere to look. This obdurate attitude of Sarah was something new; it did not bode well for marital harmony. Of course, she was cockahoop with her inheritance and that confounded Use which, he knew perfectly well, he'd be unable to break even with England's cleverest lawyer. So where did that leave him with Sarah? Was physical attraction enough? Doubts arose sharply.

Sarah glowered at him. She was stung, deeply hurt at his fresh arrogance and knew she had reached an impasse with him. Thank God she had found out this side of his nature before a wedding. Life with him would be no better than before. She would lose every ounce of freedom and independence. She would have to go to him for everything. Why, she told herself grimly, your soul won't be your own. She knew it then. It was finished and done with. Dear Heavens, what a close escape she'd had. Even dear, gentle Joseph had always been very much aware he was the master in the house—and go through that again? Never, she vowed silently.

'Men would never do business with a woman anyhow,' James growled, turning back to her.

Sarah refused to rise to any fresh argumentative bait. 'There's nothing more to say then, is there, James? It's fortunate for both of us all this has come to light now and not later.'

He studied her face. Her expression was bleak, her eyes cold, little chips of sapphires. She faced him proudly, head held high, jaw far too stiff and unyielding. What a lucky escape he'd had, he told himself. She'd be a real shrew in no time at all and home life would become hell.

'Yes,' he agreed in a low tone, yet he knew he lied. But give ground first he would not.

'That's it then,' Sarah replied calmly, yet why did her heart thunder and what was the matter with her eyes? How stupid there should be a prickle behind both of them. She took a deep breath. The sooner she was away from here the better. She dived under her riding shirt, fumbled and brought forth his token, handing it back. 'I presume this was your mother's. I suggest you give it to the kind of weak-kneed, simpering, syncopated female who will lick your arrogant boots to order.'

She knew she was now being bitchy but she felt tears humiliatingly near. She would not give him the satisfaction of seeing them. He'd think he'd beaten her and he'd only throw emotional hysterics at her.

'With pleasure,' James growled, taking the

pledge back. 'At least the next time I'll see it decorates the neck of someone who has more sense in her little finger than you have in your dogmatic head!'

'Walter!' Sarah screeched. 'My mare. Now!'

'Yes, Hamlyn, get her out of my sight!' he roared.

Walter Hamlyn nearly leaped a foot in the air. He hastily unfastened the mare and trotted over. He opened his mouth to comment then changed his mind. He was sufficiently worldly wise to see that he faced two people who, at that exact moment, loathed each other's guts.

Walter helped Sarah to mount and, the second she had found her stirrups, Sarah kicked furiously and her mare leaped forward in a sharp canter. Walter flashed a hapless look at her retreating back, then at his Captain. He opened his mouth to speak, then decided otherwise. Taking a deep breath, muttering a curse under his breath, he raced back for his own horse to leave the black stallion plunging in frustrated loneliness.

'My gawd,' he told himself, 'those two have had a real upper and downer. What came into both of them? I thought they had the makings of a fine couple.'

He clapped with his own heels and his horse chased after the rapidly vanishing mare. James scowled moodily, kicked the ground, walked over to his stallion and controlled it fiercely.

'And don't you start,' he snarled at his

103

favourite horse. 'I've had enough for one day,' he roared as he vaulted into the saddle.

The stallion promptly humped his back and shot forward in a series of harsh bucks, legs drumming a ramrod tattoo and, for a number of seconds, James was hard put to stay with his mount. 'Oh, very well, if that's how you damned well feel, gallop then and get it out of your system,' he bellowed at the flattened ears and they tore across the park at a wild, savage pace.

*   *   *

The Pair were puzzled. For a while Sarah had been a happy, contented person hugging some delightful secret to herself then, out of the blue, she had altered to one of snappy moodiness.

'What is the matter with her?' Mary asked her friend.

Nellie did not reply straight away. She loved Mary dearly but her friend was not exactly overloaded with brains. Nellie, on the other hand, knew she was sometimes too quick and sharp for her own good. There was also the matter of Walter Hamlyn. It was strange how he had arrived, out of the blue. From where? Who had sent him? Why? And look how he chased Jack and Robert about. Not that it did either of them any harm because, Nellie thought, Jack can be a bit lazy at times. Walter

104

had certainly gingered him up.

Mary studied her friend. She knew Nellie was much cleverer but she was not at all jealous. Indeed it was nice to throw a problem at Nellie and watch her solve it.

'It's a man!' Nellie grunted at last. 'And there's been a lovers' tiff.'

Mary was shocked. 'Well,' she began uncertainly, 'but who? There's no one in the village who's courting Mistress I'm sure.'

Nellie shook her head. 'He's in the army,' Nellie added. 'That's where Walter's from. He has army written all over him and he's nothing but a guard here. Who would guard us? No, it's the mistress,' she said shrewdly.

Mary considered all this. Mistress Sarah had certainly been living an odd life in the past months then there was that awful business of the murder of her father's old friend. Robert arriving. Walter. The Royalist patrol. She stood still, perturbed about something but unable to see the nettle to grasp it.

'Which army though?' she asked slowly.

That was a fine point, Nellie thought. 'Does it matter?' she asked slowly. 'Soldiers are soldiers surely and both sides are Englishmen.'

'Well,' Mary began doubtfully, 'some are for the King and others against, so which side would he be on, Nellie?'

'Would you mind, Mary?' Nellie asked gently.

Mary shook her head firmly. 'Black is black

is black,' she replied.

Nellie laughed at that. There were odd times, rare ones it was true, when Mary came out with an enigmatical but truthful reply once the puzzle of her sentence had been solved.

'So you don't care,' she remarked.

Mary shrugged. 'What good does caring matter to servants like us?' she asked shrewdly. 'All I want to do is get on with my life with the minimum fuss and bother; all this fighting, Englishmen killing each other. I think it's very wrong and, for what? Just so another lot can run the country and who is to say they'll do a better job than a king?'

'Your Jack is getting on better with Walter now,' Nellie remarked calmly. Mary laughed. 'A hiding now and again hasn't done him any harm.'

Nellie considered. 'So much so that Walter, Jack and Robert are as thick as thieves. Did you know pigeons had arrived and they're being kept in the stable loft?'

Mary did not. 'What on earth for?'

Still Mary did not see what was, to Nellie, so obviously plain, that it screamed.

'That Walter is still a soldier and those pigeons are for carrying secret messages.'

'Nellie, no!' Mary gasped, at last on the same wavelength. 'Does that mean . . . ?'

Nellie nodded. 'I think that's why Mistress spent so much time riding into Bristol for so long and a situation which ended up in a murder.'

Mary was astounded. She'd never have worked that out and she gazed at her friend with admiration. 'You mean . . . ?'

Nellie nodded. 'That's why Walter's a guard here and why he's taught Jack and Robert to use those pistols so well. Some man, Mr Mystery perhaps, is worried about who might be around. I think you and I should keep a careful watch too.'

'Except they've had a row!' Mary reminded her.

'Lovers do!' Nellie replied with a sniff.

Mary lapsed into silence. All of a sudden, she felt a sharp flash of genuine unease. It was true there were now three males on the property, but against a killer? She bit her lip. 'I don't like any of it,' she added unhappily.

'Neither do I, but there's nothing we can do except watch,' Nellie replied evenly, 'and just hope Mistress will stop being pig-headed and get herself married to a strong man.'

Mary thought about that carefully. 'It might be six of one and half a dozen of the other,' she said with sharp wisdom. 'There's the mistress now. She's called Walter and they're walking. Now what?'

Sarah strolled with Walter across the stable yard to the fence which was at one side.

'When will the armies move, Walter?' she asked and saw his eyes narrow. 'I would like to know.'

107

Walter had to grin at the naiveté of the question. 'So would many people, Mistress, including Prince Rupert. Only Cromwell and Fairfax will know, the rest of us have to guess. This year I'd think,' he added thoughtfully. The longer Parliament was denied Bristol, then the more difficult their campaign would be. King Charles was around Oxford, which placed him midway between the capital and the west's most important city and seaport.

Sarah nodded to herself. She too had thought along these lines. 'I shall be making the odd trip into Bristol, now and again,' she began coolly, 'and I'll not need a bodyguard as Robert will be with me. I intend to arrange his future work,' she explained but had no intention of going into details. These would only be related back to that awful man because, she knew, Walter had some communication link with James Hawkins, pigeons or otherwise.

Walter demurred. 'That won't do, Mistress,' he replied firmly. 'My job is to guard you and guard you I will.'

Sarah shook her head. 'No you won't,' she replied equally stiffly. 'I'm nothing to do with James Hawkins and my welfare is not his concern either, I might add. I'm not a six-year-old and Robert seems to be capable with a pistol now.'

Walter pulled a face. 'That's a matter of opinion, mistress,' he started, politely but firmly. 'He's still only a boy and . . .'

'And I'm not being tailed by a bodyguard morning, noon and night!'

Walter read her mood. What the hell had those two hurled at each other? Thank God he was single yet, he mused suddenly, what a crying shame this situation was. Some people could be so bull-necked.

'If you send me away, Mistress, I shall simply get lodgings in the village and camp at your gate all the time. You can't stop me following you,' he replied politely but forcefully. 'I shall continue as originally ordered until told to do otherwise.'

'Oh!' Sarah stormed angrily. 'You're as bad as him!' she shouted. 'You men think you run life; well let me tell you, you're not running my life.'

In a fury of temper, Sarah marched away from him, and headed back to her home, a thundercloud on her face. The Pair spotted this from the window where they had been peeping. They flashed a look at each other and, as one, prudently marched into the very large larder, to start a clearing-up session there. Mistress Turner in a rage could be quite impossible.

CHAPTER SIX

Walter knew he was over-tired. Learning did not come easily to him yet the Captain had been insistent. They met surreptitiously, unknown to anyone. A time was always chosen, like evening stables, when Jack and Robert were on the property, enabling Walter to ride away with a clear conscience. He took his duties very seriously and the mood of the mistress had been related in detail.

'Continue to follow and guard her, to the best of your ability, Hamlyn,' he had been told. 'She's stubborn.'

Walter eyed his officer. And so are you, he told himself. He would not dare to venture such an opinion aloud because the Captain's features were set in his old, bleak mask.

'Those pigeons are organised?'

'Yes, sir. Jack and Robert were surprised when I said I alone would handle them. They have their suspicions, sir, as do the house servants, but no one's asked me anything direct.'

'If they do, tell 'em to mind their own bloody business,' had been the curt reply.

'What news, sir?' Walter did not hesitate to ask. 'The mistress and Robert have started to ride into Bristol once a month.'

'Have they by God! What the hell for?'

Walter had not been told but he was a good guesser. 'I've followed them to that lawyers, then to the house where the murder took place and finally just around the city,' he explained.

James was puzzled and frowned to work it out. Now what mischief was Sarah planning? Good God, didn't he have enough worries without this? But yet, his other half reminded him ruthlessly, she's nothing to you, is she? He knew she was his life, if he replied to himself truthfully, but how to bring her to heel? His heel. She was such a deep, complex character with a will of iron. She's been a widow too long, he told himself morosely; long enough to get grandiose ideas about what a wife could and could not do.

'Sir?' Walter interrupted his sour thoughts.

'Don't get yourself tangled up with the weaker sex, Hamlyn, otherwise they'll drive you mad. Weaker sex, my foot. When a female goes on the warpath, the devil himself must turn tail and bolt!' he grumbled.

Walter's tongue slipped into his cheek. He had no intention of offering any reply. Whatever he might say, even in innocence, could rebound on him when the captain was in this mood. God help any Royalists who might have the misfortune to cross his path.

'And you needn't look so bloody innocent either!' James growled, eyeing his man's bland expression. 'Here, take this,' he ordered, pulling a thin book from between his shirt and

111

jacket. 'It's a code book. Learn it and let no one else see it. When it's been digested, burn it. When you send a message by pigeon, stop and code it up, no matter what. Nothing in plain language. Is that clear?'

Walter's heart sank. He only hoped he could do this. Then something occurred to him. 'If you are going to be on the move between . . .' he halted, still unsure how far he could go when the captain was in a mood.

James realised his quandary. It was grossly unfair of him to take his temper out on a good man who could not really answer back. 'I've set up a system of messengers which is why you must always use code. There might be a slight delay, now and again, for a message to reach me but get there, eventually, it will.'

'Right, sir,' Walter said, eyeing the thin book, placing it carefully in a secure pocket. 'And the mistress?'

'Do the best you can. At least she has the boy with her,' James grumbled again. 'But why all this traipsing around Bristol? What's it like in there now?'

'Pretty bad, sir. There have been more outbreaks of the plague. The Royalist troops are getting distinctly edgy. The citizens are the same and, frankly, it won't need much to panic the civilians,' Walter told him, then plucked up courage. 'Will Bristol begin with a siege or a direct attack, sir?'

James threw him a sharp look. He smelled

the wishes of an old soldier. Hamlyn wanted to be in it. 'It might start off as a siege but it will quickly develop into an all-out attack. Fairfax and Cromwell have regular patrols around the place, though we've heard that Prince Rupert is itching for fighting to start.'

James threw him a grin then. 'Actually, Rupert has been a fool. The Clubmen will come down on our side with a vengeance. You know our leaders, Cromwell and Fairfax, have always insisted the ordinary people be paid a fair price for their goods especially when sequestrated. Rupert has allowed his men to plunder. I can tell you, in confidence of course, that 3,000 Clubmen have moved up from Somerset and another 2,000 are due to come down from Gloucestershire.'

Walter considered this. 'They're untrained though, sir.'

'True! True! But you should know better than to underestimate angry men even if they only have home-made weapons. Also, I expect they'll be given tasks like guarding the ferries at Rownham or excavating the ground for our batteries. Whatever, they'll make a fine reserve for us.'

'I should be in the fight,' Walter grumbled, so agitated at the thought of being left out, he forgot to add sir. 'Not guarding petticoats!'

James threw him a sharp look. He opened his mouth to bellow something about orders and changed his mind. Walter wore a dour

113

look, almost a sulk. His brows were set in a heavy scowl and there was an ugly glow in his eyes. James knew he must be tactful. He did not want to lose this excellent man but after a pike wound years ago, he did not make the best fighting material. He thought quickly. He knew where he would be, he'd had his orders a while now. Suddenly he took pity on his man.

'Well, I might be able to arrange something,' he drawled meaningfully.

Walter brightened and looked at him hopefully. 'I can still shoot, sir.'

James made a snap decision, risky though it might be, but he understood a man's urge to prove himself.

'Now that Jack and Robert are armed, I guess the property wouldn't miss you for a week. Everywhere is going to be in such an uproar, I doubt anything untoward will happen at the Turner property, and those women servants are not fools. I'll send you a personal pigeon message to join me for a scrap.'

Walter beamed at him now, his good humour completely restored. 'That's more like it, sir.'

'Just make sure you leave that property with all weapons fully primed and loaded.'

Walter nodded eagerly. 'I obtained a small pistol for the Mistress too.'

'Excellent!' James praised. 'What's she like?'

Walter grinned. 'Not bad, to say she's only a

learner. When she gets more practice and experience I think she might outshoot a few men.'

'Is that so?' James drawled. Trust Sarah to be able to do everything well or not at all. Dear God, what on earth had happened to the pair of them but, more to the point, how could they both disentangle themselves from their stupid quarrel without either losing face? Hamlyn obviously knew everything. He had been within distance of hearing their row but he had said not a word. His tact had been superb, yet James had a vague feeling Hamlyn sometimes itched to express an opinion. He wanted to ask about Sarah, how she was, did she ever mention him, but he was still too proud for this. He muttered a string of army curses under his breath. Women, he groaned to himself.

Walter read his mind and decided a change of subject was in order. 'Surely Rupert will try probes, sir?'

James brought his mind back to military matters. 'Whatever he tries this month might well rebound on him,' he grinned wolfishly. 'Just you stay available if you still want to see some fun and action.'

*   *   *

'This is awful, Robert,' Sarah groaned as their horses picked their way through the city's

115

hopelessly crowded streets. Perhaps she had been imprudent to visit Bristol in August after all. It was so stifling hot and Bristol's stench was abominable.

'I've never seen such crowds, Sarah,' Robert agreed, keeping his horse next to hers.

'It's all these confounded Royalist troops. At least we had no problem at Lawford's gate but I bet it will be a long wait to get out,' she murmured half to herself.

Robert had the same opinion and was uneasy. They should have stayed in the village but this recent Sarah was like a cat on hot bricks. She couldn't stay still for a moment. She seemed driven on by something, but what?

He thought it was crazy to enter Bristol. Already there was military activity in numerous skirmishes as Parliament tested the Royalist strength at the various gates. Most people with horse sense, he told himself with agitation, were hell bent on leaving the city before the real fight started. What possessed Sarah to do the opposite? Was she being contrary for some reason? He wished he could understand. He wished he had some authority to stop her. He could do nothing at all but guard her. Why had Walter taken it into his head to be away at this precise moment? What had been in that pigeon's message that Walter had grabbed so enthusiastically? Questions hammered at him from all directions as he rode miserably behind Sarah's mare.

Sarah did not understand herself either. She was so desperately unhappy that activity, frenetic action, of any kind, was the order of each and every day. Never before had country life so bored her. Never before had she thought she would miss James so much and the hurt grew daily. How could he be so mean and old-fashioned? It was so unfair. She was still amazed at his vituperation for his dead brother that, whenever she thought back to their row, her blood chilled. Surely whatever bad feeling there had been between James and Martin had all been wiped away by his horrendous death? Not so in James' eyes, it seemed.

Why she had the constant urge to come so often to Bristol, she could not say except that she could think of nowhere else to go where there was activity. Also, unknown to Robert, she had conducted a correspondence with lawyer Benson.

Whether James, as the other partner, would agree seemed unlikely but at least, with her half share from Martin, she had sufficient finance to branch out on her own if necessary. This was where Robert would come in.

The horses fought their way through the throng of citizens and neither liked it but there was neither room nor space to kick out, let alone bolt.

'We're going down to the water,' Sarah called over to Robert. He looked as thoroughly miserable as she felt. He did not like it here; more to the point, he did not like her being here. How providential it was that Walter had vanished only that morning, with a flurry of hooves. He's gone to that man, she told herself. Good riddance to the pair of them.

'Why?' Robert called back, then moved up more closely to Sarah's side.

Sarah bent over to explain. 'At long last Martin's old house has been sold,' she began, 'and I've found a property on the wharf, which will be ideal for the business when the peace comes.'

Robert was puzzled. 'But I thought there was another partner?' he asked delicately.

Sarah's lips tightened. 'So there is and if he doesn't like what I've done then he can do the other thing.'

Robert took a deep breath. Sarah was still in an argumentative mood. He'd better keep his mouth shut. He was deeply disturbed. As he rode, he had taken the trouble to listen to comments and asides from the citizens: Prince Rupert had sent out a sally only two days ago when a number of Parliamentarians were taken prisoner. Now, cockahoop, the Prince spoiled for the real fighting to start. What about the guns though? He was also appalled at the filth and stench in the overcrowded city. Sewerage, always a problem in the hot weather, was out of control. No refuse had

118

been removed. The plague was in various sections of the city. Food was desperately short. Drinking water was doubtful, yet here they were, voluntarily entering such a pesthole. He knew that Sarah had told The Pair not to worry if they stayed overnight in the city, which was madness. Where?

Sarah eyed him, reading his mind, feeling sudden guilt at his being here. Bristol could hold no happy memories for him. If only she had been able to come in alone.

'We're staying overnight at the property I'm going to buy. Mr Benson will have arranged palliasses for us and there are two stalls for the horses. We have rations in our saddle bags so we will be all right.'

'I don't like it, and how do we know we can get out when we want to?' Robert asked with worry. 'What if the Parliamentarians decide to make their attack while we are trapped here?'

Sarah had considered that and dismissed it. 'A siege takes a long time to organise,' she replied smoothly, her good sense completely gone while her heart broke for her lost love. If Walter returned, and found her missing, he would have a fit. Sarah gave a tiny sniff. Let him, she thought. He can go and tittle-tattle to "him" and they will both perhaps learn I'm a free agent to do as I like, not to move only when they say. Yet why did this defiance make her heart ache even more? She had a flashing memory of the warm strength and security of

119

James' arms. Directly afterwards though, she had another flashback—of him in a cold rage with a totally unnecessary, obdurate stance against her plans.

*   *   *

Less than half a mile away, Captain James Hawkins, took a deep breath, eyed the situation in general, then turned to Walter Hamlyn with a wide grin.

'I thought that pigeon would bring you hot foot,' he teased.

'Yes, sir,' Walter returned. He was not taken in by his officer's apparent good humour. He knew his man only too well. Were those new crease lines on his brow? Why did his smile fail to reach his eyes? Why did his stance have that edge of brittle alertness as if the man was tensed, ready to explode in any direction?

James felt Walter's eyes fixed on him steadily and knew he was far from being himself. He was so keen for action, any action, that he felt fit to jump from his skin. Something must be done to remove the awful heartache, deep hurt and bitter disappointment. When he thought back to his rosy plans, it seemed inconceivable these had collapsed to ashes. He dare not look ahead to the future now. It would only appear empty and lonely. Sometimes, in the past week, his shoulders had slumped and, as he reviewed the

120

possible years ahead, the pain in his heart had been as physically unbearable as toothache.

What was Sarah doing right now? Riding her mare around the countryside, he supposed. Gloating over her inheritance, making plans, not thinking of him any more. How could his world so collapse just because of one big brother? He gritted his teeth and clenched one fist.

Walter needed little imagination to understand his mood and he cursed to himself. How could two people, so well suited, be so utterly stupid? It was quite beyond him. He realised it might pay to distract his officer. That mood he was in was a dangerous one. When reason gave way to pure rage, troubles rose. A fighting man should not have emotional worries to cloud his judgement.

'What is the exact military position, sir?' he asked quietly.

James turned to him, his ugly train of thought broken. It did cross his mind to wonder exactly how much Walter guessed or knew then, firmly, he shut domestic problems away.

'Today Prince Rupert made a sally with a thousand horse and much foot infantry but he might have saved his energy. The weather is on our side. We've had some rain, which has made the going difficult for horses, and I bet it was hell for the men. I attended a council of war held by Fairfax and it's been decided, for the sake of Bristol's citizens, that there will be no siege after all. It's best to have a direct attack, end it once and for all.'

'I see,' Walter said thoughtfully. 'Do you know the dispositions?'

James nodded. 'Colonel Weldon's four regiments of foot and three of horse are to attack the southern ramparts. Six hundred top-rate men have been picked to storm other areas. Montague's brigade—four foot and two of horse—have been given a tough spot. They have to attack Lawford's Gate. Prior's Hill Fort will be another hard one to crack open and that's Rainsborough's job. Colonel Pride will attack the fort while Okey's dragoons make a feint advance towards Washington's Breech. Do you follow me, man?'

Walter nodded. He had taken the trouble to study the area with the officer's map when alone.

'Washington's Breach is a nasty one, sir,' he murmured thoughtfully, 'but what about Fleetwood's men?'

James nodded. 'They're on the Durdham Downs and their job is to move around, wherever a weakness shows.'

'A roving commission!'

James gave a grunt. 'The sailors will attack the Water Fort so really, when you think about it, everywhere is covered nicely.'

'Except for the unexpected,' Walter said quietly.

122

James looked at him sharply. 'True,' he agreed, 'but I'm sure nothing can arise which we can't cope with.'

'What time does the attack commence, sir?'

James threw him a wolfish grin. 'At exactly two o'clock in the morning which, if it doesn't catch the Royalists with their breeches down, should at least find them bleary-eyed,' he halted then, frowning again.

Walter stifled a groan. Surely he was not thinking about her again? This would never do just before a battle. Within a few hours, many good Englishmen would have met their Maker.

'The great problem though,' James started slowly, 'is that I have been forbidden to take part in the fighting.'

Walter was aghast. 'What, sir? Why?'

James grimaced. 'It seems I'm considered too valuable to risk losing my skin,' he growled. 'Direct orders from London. However . . .' he paused to throw a wicked look at his man. 'I'll not disobey orders, an officer cannot do that, but then, on the other hand, if I should happen to have wandered from here to there, I might accidentally find myself being made to fight, if you see what I mean?'

Walter started to chuckle. 'You're right, sir. You cannot just sit here all day like sour cheese. You must move around to observe and if the enemy should see you, and pick a fight, then that's most certainly not your fault. After all, no officer can duck an issue, can he?'

James let out the first genuine laugh for a long time. 'You're a man after my own heart, Hamlyn. So just after midnight, shall we leave our horses somewhere handy and take ourselves a little walk?' he asked maliciously.

Walter nodded enthusiastically. 'I've not had any walking exercise for a long time, sir. It'll make a change from horseback.'

Rank difference was forgotten as, working together, each checked his weapons, paying particular attention to pistols and carbines then, grinning at each other like two small boys, they sauntered off.

*   *   *

Sarah awoke with a violent start. What was that awful noise? Thunder? Impossible, she thought, then eyes opening wide, she understood. Hastily standing and kicking the palliasse aside, she ran across the room, opened the door and met Robert coming from the room where he had dossed down for the night.

'Robert,' Sarah cried. 'I think the fighting to take the city has started. It's not going to be a siege after all.'

Robert groaned. He licked his lips; he wanted to throw an accusation at Sarah but knew he could not.

124

'The horses!' Sarah cried. 'They'll be petrified. Those bangs are large ones. Quick, downstairs to them,' she cried.

With Robert at her heels, she thundered down the wooden stairs, her feet clattering as she blessed the fact neither of them had undressed. Quite suddenly, what had seemed a delightful adventure and escape from rural boredom only yesterday, had turned into what promised to be a nightmare. Lawyer Benson had certainly been put out when he understood her plan to camp in the empty house. He had argued, but Sarah had made him back down. After all, she was a client of some note and she simply would not tolerate another man presuming to give her orders.

'I'm only staying for two nights,' she had told him frostily. 'I want to study the house properly.'

'But mistress, this will be highly irregular,' Benson had started, perhaps just a little too pompously, without meaning it insultingly, and Sarah had flared. 'I'll do what I want, when I want and I don't give a damn for what people think. If they have sewer minds then that is their misfortune. This young man is hardly likely to attempt rape!'

'Mistress Turner!' Benson had cried, scandalised now. 'Your partner will . . .'

Sarah had exploded. 'My partner can go and take a running jump,' she spat back. 'If he doesn't like what I'm doing then I'll buy him

125

out and he can go and . . .' Sarah knew she had nearly let out an extremely crude expletive. She bit it back just in time to save the stuffy lawyer's shock from turning to a heart attack. She knew he had sent his own family out to the country until the city's situation was resolved, but Sarah answered to no man, damn them all.

Now though, Sarah thought quickly as they hurried into the tiny stable yard, perhaps she might have been imprudent and was endangering Robert as well.

Guilt almost overwhelmed her. They slowed and approached their two horses who were in stalls, tied with halters. Neither appeared unduly perturbed.

'Shut the top door,' Robert advised knowingly. 'They'll be all right.' I hope, he added to himself.

Sarah turned to him, one hand on his shoulder. 'Robert, I'm sorry. I shouldn't have come but . . .' She hesitated miserably. 'I've not been myself lately.'

He threw her a lop-sided grin. 'That's all right and, anyhow, if the battle has started there's nothing we can do but keep our heads down,' he said sagely.

Sarah gulped and nodded. Suddenly the night air exploded again with the sound of canon and they both jumped. The noise ratio started to increase as men's voices broke in, roars, bellows and, now and again, shrieks of pain. Sarah threw a look around in panic.

Sound seemed to come from all directions at once.

Robert understood in a flash. 'It's an attack at all points together,' he gasped. He eyed the nearby water, looked around and studied the night sky, punctured by flashes. There was a fresh smell now, which made their nostrils flare. The powder of pistol and carbine balls' explosions; the acrid stench drifting down from the cannons' assault and, Robert grabbed her hand.

'Let's get under cover,' he suggested wisely.

Sarah knew she had been almost rooted with shock. The deep bangs, the smaller ones, the general noise and hubbub of men hell-bent on killing each other, made a cacophony of sound she had never imagined possible. Intermingled with this bedlam, were the cries of the frightened citizens, the screams of panicking horses in stalls, the howling of frightened dogs, all juxtaposing into a sound wave which grew larger and noisier each minute.

She fled with Robert into the empty house she had bought and flinched constantly. It hit her that James was out there somewhere. Perhaps for all she knew, he might be injured or, worse, already dead. Great tears oozed from her eyes and she groaned to herself. How stupid and pointless had been their quarrel. She flinched as she remembered the hot words she had hurled at him. Even if he lived

127

through this attack, he would never forget. How could she hope he might forgive? Oh you stupid, little fool, she berated herself.

They huddled together in the house's small hallway, waiting, flinching, hardly daring to breath as smoke now started to plume downwards with the wind's change. The noise tempo increased. Sometimes the men's roars sounded so near then they receded and both of them knew it was the wind.

Sarah knew time had ceased to exist. This was a nightmare the likes of which she would never forget. Sometimes there were sounds very close of men running, orders being bellowed and she guessed it was the defenders, racing to another point.

'I wonder if we are winning,' Robert muttered. He itched to leave and find a place for better observation but knew he would never leave Sarah now. She was white-faced and tears trickled quietly down her cheeks. It was as if the appalling noise had released some terrible tension under which she had been living, something so big it had forced her to act out of character. Robert thought of The Pair and Jack. If they knew and realised . . . he shook his head. Why, oh why had Walter decided to leave just now? Then it hit him. He had known about this battle! He was here, in it somewhere with . . . at this stage his mind boggled. Who was the mysterious military man involved? He had overheard The Pair's

128

comments and made his own deduction as to Sarah's misery. He let out a deep sigh of unease.

'Robert,' Sarah said suddenly, going to the door, fidgeting a little. 'There's something wrong,' she added.

'What?'

'I don't know except I feel something . . . here!' Sarah told him and touched the pit of her stomach. 'I wonder what time it is? The fight's been going on for hours. It must be dawn yet there's so much smoke about . . . I'm uneasy.'

Robert frowned, stood with her and peered about hopefully. There appeared to be some kind of lull. Certainly the cannon were quieter. Did that mean their men were nearly in the city?

'There's an awful lot of smoke,' Sarah told hint 'Let's go up that street and find out what's going on.'

'But Sarah . . .' Robert started to protest, but she was gone, walking rapidly up to the part of the old city, jam-packed with narrow streets and houses almost touching.

The noise crescendo rose as Robert tore after her, panting slightly against all the smoke. At the top, Sarah halted and leaned back against a house wall. The street was heaving with people, all surging agitatedly towards her, screaming, pushing, and shoving each other. It was bedlam, noise, and confusion.

'What's happening?' Robert gasped and grabbed a man's arm. He was wild-eyed with fear, breathing hard.

The man turned to him, labouring to breathe in the thickly, descending smoke. 'It's the Royalists. Because they are losing, Prince Rupert has told them to set fire to the city. There are people, women, children and animals trapped back there, and, with this wind, the fire's coming this way. Get out while you can. Get to a gate and escape!' he bellowed and was gone, swallowed up in a surge of maddened citizens.

'Oh my God!' Sarah exclaimed. 'Surely Rupert can't have done such an awful thing?'

Robert knew he must have. 'We must get back to the water, the horses!'

Sarah gasped with horror. The wind blew strongly towards them and she grabbed Robert's hand in panic, turned and tried to break through the maddened throng. It was impossible. They were drawn along against their will, hopelessly trapped in the centre of a stream of terrified people. Around them the bedlam was penetrated by the most harrowing screams and screeches as trapped animals started to burn.

Robert struggled valiantly, but his strength was feeble against that of these berserk people. Then, with luck, he saw a door handle. He grabbed it with one hand and savagely held

Sarah with the other.

'To me!' he roared at her. Sarah fought to obey. She staggered backwards, nearly bowled over, gasping and coughing to breathe, trying not to faint in the appalling heat. Suddenly with the will to live powerful, she struck out with her free hand. She made it into a fist, then used both feet, fighting like a wild cat to remain erect. Anyone who went down now would be trampled to death.

With his muscles creaking, Robert kept his grip, lips drawn back, teeth bared in a snarl of maximum effort; then Sarah was with him. They flattened themselves against a wall, sobbing with effort, coughing, eyes running wildly 'Which way?' Robert roared. Even though he knew Bristol so well, he had lost his bearings in the uproar, confusion and smoke.

Sarah knew it did not matter, just as long as they were not trapped again in a surging horde of maddened people. 'Down there!' she sobbed and, hand in hand, they lurched to one side, down a narrow alley. Panting violently, struggling to breathe, hardly able to see, they rolled like drunks, bouncing against walls as others followed them blindly, then pushed past.

The noise was dreadful, an assault upon their ears, and, finally, Sarah had to halt, lean against a gatepost and hold her ribs with head bowed.

'Can you make it, Sarah?' Robert asked

131

anxiously. He was almost done in himself; how much worse for Sarah hampered with her long riding skirt. He looked at her filthy face; she had stopped crying but the tears had left clean runnels down cheeks liberally coated with ash. Sarah made herself look around. They should be going downhill towards the water. Her eyes opened wide with horror. On their opposite flank, a waving red and yellow curtain roared towards them; devouring, spitting, crackling and smothering with its heat.

'Oh no!' Sarah gasped and pointed: 'Look!'

Robert jerked his head around and recognised where he was at last. He shook himself, his shoulders slumped and he turned to her, his own tears now flowing. Sarah watched, frozen in time, as Martin's old home exploded into flames. They roared up and out, leapfrogged on to the next building, inexorable in their advance. For a crazy, fleeting second, Sarah thought the cremation was like that for a Viking's funeral.

'Royalists!' Robert shouted at her and pointed where weaving figures appeared through the billowing smoke. 'They're trying to put the fire out!'

'Stupid fools!' Sarah rasped. Her throat felt dreadful. 'What chance do they have now with this wind?'

'It's not quite so strong!' Robert roared back.

'Trust Prince Rupert to change his mind,

but how many have died because of his stupidity?' Sarah shrieked at him, starting to get a little hysterical.

Robert felt as scared as at any time in his young life. Nothing had prepared him for this horror. People still raced around—citizens wildly trying to find their way to the dock's water and refuge. No one had thought for anyone else. Such was the panic and pandemonium.

'Try that way!' Sarah pointed and jumped forward, staggering with near exhaustion. People barged past them. She bounced off walls, stumbled, coughing until she felt like retching. She could only hope to God Robert was at her heels because, suddenly, she knew where she was and the narrow street headed downwards. She halted at a corner and peered hopefully to her rear. People cannoned past, pushing, jolting and hitting her out of their panicky way. Robert had gone.

'Robert!' she screamed frantically, turned and started to hit and claw her way back again. It was murder. The smoke fluctuated. Sometimes it swirled low, completely blinding her, then it lifted, twirling over her head. People continued to fight past her, all intent on one direction and the water's safety. She peered with streaming eyes then, in a little doorway, spotted Robert's crumpled form.

'Oh my God, Robert!' she wailed, half fell over him, flinched as a boot kicked her side,

133

then his head was in her lap. His eyes fluttered and blood trickled from one side of his head. 'Robert, get up. You must. The fire!' she shouted at him, saw he was still bemused and, standing, fought to pull him erect. Fortunately his body was still skinny so, labouring hard, one shoulder under his armpit, Sarah fought savagely to head downwards again. She knew she could not go much farther. Her strength was fading. Her legs were wobbling yet she must move. 'Help me!' she screeched as people pushed by, but each was intent only upon personal safety. 'Robert!' she cried. 'Try and walk, help me!' she begged with wild sobs.

Somehow, with a superhuman effort, Robert made his legs move. His steps were erratic, tiny; but, gradually, spitting and swearing at those who tried to push her out of their way, Sarah guided them back down to the dock's edge. It was crowded. Little boats had appeared. People jumped into them, capsized them, screamed and shouted making a worse pandemonium.

'Aside!' Sarah grunted then, spotting a doorway, she pushed them both into it, away from the maddened crowd.

Robert blinked up at her, forced his feet to stand flat and, with an effort, was able to take his own body weight.

Royalist soldiers were everywhere now, frantically trying to douse what they had started. Robert shook his head, his wits returning. He looked up at Sarah, eyes still wide with shock.

'The crowd knocked you down?' Sarah gasped at him, guessing.

He gave a little shake to his head but decided not to do that again. 'I was hit from behind. I just caught a flashing glimpse of a piece of wood ascending, then I was down.'

'What?' Sarah cried, shocked beyond belief; then she eyed him. He was obviously mistaken. In the madness that they had experienced, anything could have happened but she wisely decided not to argue with him. 'Can you manage now?'

Robert read her mind. He frowned, struggling to remember. There had been so many wild people surging along, fighting their way through, going faster than Sarah could manage. He closed his eyes, thought back and bit his lip. Had he imagined it? He was sure he had seen a cudgel of wood falling with enough warning from his periphery vision to enable him to twist his head. One blow had landed just above his ear, otherwise, the back of his skull would have been stoved in.

'I was hit,' he protested, a little mulishly, 'I did not imagine it.'

Sarah eyed him sharply and saw resentment flare in his eyes. She pulled a face. 'With all that mad throng, obviously someone wanted you out of his way. We were both going too slow, but fancy people being like that;

135

behaving worse than animals,' she told him hotly.

Robert nodded slowly. That must have been it because, he remembered now, wild, staring eyes, a mouth open, bellowing something, then the blackness.

'The horses!' he said then, remembering. They both staggered forward, trying to estimate the fire's strength. It would take the Royalists time to put out the conflagration and, as they tottered up towards the house with its tiny yard, they could hear wild squeals inside. Sarah felt tears well.

'We must release them,' she moaned. 'At least they'll get the chance to gallop to safety. Surely to God even Royalists don't take it out on horses!' she wailed. The thought of losing her beloved mare was unbearable.

'Come on then!' Robert cried, making himself shuffle into a faster pace. His head still hurt but he was thinking clearer now. They hurried in to the stables where the two horses, wild-eyed with the noise and smoke, fought their restraints. Each reached up, slipped a halter then stood back. The horses spun on their heels and clattered from the yard. Sarah felt the tears flood again. She would never see her mare again. She was realistic enough to know that, when caught, the valuable, highly bred mare would be purloined by someone.

Robert understood. 'Down to the water's edge again, Sarah,' he shouted, grabbing her attention, snatching her hand. He felt all right now but something niggled him. He was puzzled but unable to think straight. There was still too much happening at once. Why should anyone cudgel him? He would have been easy to elbow aside. He knew he still only had a youth's strength compared to that of some of the panicky Bristolians. Then, with a tiny, and still cautious shake of his head, he pushed the matter away. They were both alive, unlike some unfortunates. Prince Rupert would have a lot to answer for. If only they could see the ochre-eyed leather jackets of some Parliamentarians. They would know then that the Royalists were truly defeated.

CHAPTER SEVEN

'By God, I feel more like a man again!' James grunted, slowly slipping his pistol back into its holster.

Walter grinned over at him. They were slightly the worse for wear. Each of them had a minor sabre wound on the forearm; only the left was protected by leather. Both of them had dishevelled dress, helmets slightly askew and they breathed hard.

'Me too, sir!'

James took a deep breath. 'I suppose we'd better stroll back to the main area,' he mused.

'Just in case I'm wanted, but you stick with me, Hamlyn. We might be lucky enough to find Royalists escaping in our direction,' he laughed wickedly.

'I doubt that, sir,' Walter told him and pointed. 'Our troops are well into the city now but there's certainly been more smoke that I anticipated. You don't suppose our fire set that off? It must be hell for the citizens.'

James strode over to a tiny group of brother officers, all of whom had been on horse but were now dismounted.

'What started the fire?' he called, after taking a quick look that Fairfax and Cromwell were not around. He knew he had cunningly disobeyed orders and was ready to argue to defend himself, but information was also of importance.

'It's all over bar the shouting,' one of the officers told him, wiping a red sword blade clean on some grass. 'Prince Rupert set fire to the place though. It wasn't us. Did it in a fit of pique when he knew he was losing.'

James swore. 'Has he been taken prisoner?'

'No, they are parlaying now. There's talk that we'll let him go, march out with colours flying!'

Walter heard this and frowned perturbed. James turned back to him. 'No, we've not gone crazy,' he explained. 'If we do this, can't you imagine the disastrous effect on King Charles and his remaining men? Gamesmanship!' he

138

chuckled.

Walter sniffed. He was more practical. 'Those men though can fight us another day, sir.'

James considered, then slowly shook his head, looking sideways as wild-eyed horses raced up towards them from the city. 'Catch those mounts!' he bellowed, waving his arm, setting men into motion. Horses were worth their weight in gold to soldiers. He turned back to Walter. 'No,' he began, 'the King is beaten. Oh, there will be some shouting and arguing, one thing and another, but, from now on, the war is over, to all extents and purposes. This will have bled the King dry. He's finished and doomed too. Parliament will rule and England will no longer be an archaic monarchy but a republic at last.'

Walter nodded. He wanted to be convinced but was still a little unsure. If it were up to him, Prince Rupert's army would all be taken prisoner. James read him. It was often like this. The foot soldiers, not the officers, were always the more bloodthirsty.

'Well, Hamlyn,' he drawled with a grin, 'you've had your fight. And now?'

Walter pulled a face. 'I suppose I'd better go and get back to the village,' he muttered. He wanted to stay where the action was. James understood.

'You'll not be missing anything and you've been away for two days,' he pointed out. 'I'd be pleased to know you were back on guard again. Who knows where runaway Royalists might not pop up; hungry, on foot, ready to cause trouble as the losers,' he pointed out cunningly. He could have made the issue an order but was too wise for that.

'That's true!' Walter replied with a nod. 'I don't know where my horse is though,' he said, looking around hopefully. 'I'll take one of those,' he said, nodding in the direction of where the terrified city horses were gradually being caught and roped together.

'Right, I'll stroll over with you and authorise it,' James agreed.

The horses milled in a large, hastily roped off stockade with troops around, eyeing them with interest, intent on making a personal selection when allowed to.

'Not bad,' James drawled, 'quite decent stock in fact.'

Walter looked around then frowned a little uncertainly. He gave a shake to his head, squinted sideways, then turned for another frontal stare. He held his breath, taking time to make sure he was correct, then touched his officer's arm.

'Sir?' he said, an odd note in his voice. 'That mare. She's an absolute double to the one Mistress Turner rides.'

James was startled. 'What? That's impossible.'

'It *is* her mare.'

140

'It can't be!'

They both studied the mare who stood, rope around her neck, head high, eyes rolling with agitation, pulling back and flicking her tail in warning.

Walter muttered in a low voice. 'The correct colour; small white blaze on her face; two tiny white coronets, the correct height and weight. It is her double,' he breathed with awe. He stepped forward. A foot soldier held the mare on a long rope.

'She's mine!' he growled.

Walter flashed an appealing look at James. 'Not now, she's not,' he barked.

The trooper scowled, hesitated, then discipline reared its ugly head and he thrust the rope into Walter's hands.

'Trust the officers to pick the best even when they don't catch 'em!' he grumbled, slightly under his breath.

Walter caught the words, as did James, but both ignored them. 'Shhh, girl,' Walter crooned and slowly extended his right hand. The mare was still frightened, but from him came a familiar, reassuring scent. Her ears came forward, her nostrils flared and slowly, warily, she advanced two steps, then, lowering her head, nuzzled Walter's hand. 'It is her, sir,' he cried with alarm.

'Good God, man. I believe you are right but, what the hell is she doing here now?' he said, with rising alarm.

An ugly little thought rose in Walter's head. He licked suddenly dry lips and turned to James, eyes big with alarm. 'Sir,' he began nervously, 'I've been away two days. I told you the mistress had been riding an awful lot into Bristol. You don't suppose . . .'

'In your absence she did it again!' James bellowed, finishing the sentence for him. That was just the wild, crazy, independent, bloody-minded act Sarah would do. At this, of all times. And Bristol had been burning, Bristol had been a war zone. He blanched with a fear he had never felt in battle.

He turned and roared at some soldiers. 'Volunteer platoon needed right now!' he roared, making every eye fix upon him. 'Give me that mare, Hamlyn. Grab another horse, mount up those who are willing,' he shouted, springing into the saddle.

Walter scurried around, seizing the first free horse saddled and waiting.

'That's mine!' a voice bellowed at him, which Walter ignored, thrusting his feet into stirrups far too short. He had neither the time nor the finesse to adjust them. There was a wild scramble as men copied, grabbing horses from anywhere, hastening to follow the officer who was, already, cantering frantically towards the smouldering city.

'Arms!' James called over his shoulders. 'Swords only!' he ordered. They would be far more effective than pistols in a confined space.

Walter rode frantically, caught up with his officer and shouted at him. 'Let me lead, sir. I know where she used to go!'

'Hurry!' James bellowed at him, which was, he suddenly realised, utterly impossible. They had to slow to push their way through a gate held by their own men. James' rank guaranteed their immediate passage, though it was a case of a slow, frustrating walk through citizens, still in a state of panic. Odd enemy troops still skirmished around but, at sight of the Ironsides, hastily and discreetly vanished up side streets, except for a few. These were fought out and glad enough to surrender with honour. 'Keep moving back to the gate!' James ordered them. He couldn't be bothered with prisoners and, anyhow, more and more of their men were now pouring in. Only the castle remained aloof and still royal, but its time was very limited now.

It was an appalling ride. The troopers closed up to ride in a tight phalanx but, even then, they made heavy going. Many of the citizens, Parliamentarians to the core, were delighted to see them. They cried greetings, patted the horses, wanted to engage in conversation or else bellowed horror stories of the fire.

James turned to check behind. 'Keep tight up behind me!' he shouted and hoped the lead man had enough wit to pass his order backwards. Walter rode ahead very slowly;

143

utterly appalled at the city's shocking state. Smoke and ashes clung everywhere. Some buildings were gutted. From others came the smell of burned meat, but whether man or animal, he neither knew nor wished to find out.

He racked his brains to remember the way, badly disorientated, then he halted uncertainly, looking around with shock. He turned to James and pointed.

'That's the house Mistress sold, or what's left of it.'

James studied the locality and knew he stared at his brother's old home. Sold, he asked himself in bewilderment, then realised Benson had always had his Power of Attorney. How dare Sarah sell his brother's house though without consulting him! Then fright returned. She might be dead. Perhaps it was her body which produced the ghastly smells which reached his nostrils. He swallowed, his throat had gone dry and he licked parched lips. It was an inferno of heat but he knew terror was affecting him, not that.

'I think it was down here, sir!' Walter cried, pointing.

'What was?'

'A house I think Mistress intended to buy,' he explained.

Again James felt wrath rise to conflict with terror. There was much he did not know, it appeared, but Sarah's safety was now

144

paramount. The people, starting to come to their senses now the fire had died down to isolated, smouldering patches, moved out of the troopers' way. At the water's edge they halted, bemused at the spectacle of boats, people in them and the water, plus the general confusion.

Walter looked around. 'There, sir! I'm sure that's the house,' he pointed.

James rode the mare forward, highly alert for enemy still with fight in them and, at that identical moment, Sarah and Robert staggered from the house. They confronted each other with amazement.

Sarah's eyes opened wide while Robert's creased into a relieved grin—an officer and, this time, from the correct side.

'James!' Sarah exclaimed, stepping forward as he vaulted from the saddle. 'And with my mare!' she cried with delight. 'I never thought I'd see her again.'

James' eyes swept her. He took in the tear runnels, the general filth, the stench of the fire and shock waves which gave little trembles to her hands as she patted her mare's neck.

His relief was enough to make him feel sick. He flung a look behind and gave a nod. The senior trooper intelligently disposed his men around them in a wide circle, far enough back to give the officer and the lady privacy. Walter also discreetly retreated, flashing a meaningful look at Robert.

'What on earth are you doing here?' Walter asked him, leading him well away, slightly around a corner.

Robert's shoulders slumped with relief. 'It's quite a story,' he started.

Yes, Walter thought, I bet it is and I have a shrewd idea what's going to happen shortly, he told himself grimly, He saw the senior trooper had the men on top alert, not looking at the couple, but watching the surrounding area with three of them checking buildings.

James felt himself sag with total relief. 'What's been going on, Sarah?' he asked in a reasonable voice.

Sarah felt her heart swell with happiness at seeing him again, then the bite in his words stayed her act of flinging herself into his arms. She pulled herself straight with as much dignity as she could muster in her filthy condition.

'I don't know what you mean,' she replied with asperity. Oh, James, her heart ached, don't start all over again, I beg you, she implored silently.

He flinched as she stuck her head up with stiff jaw and he felt the wave of misery grow once more. She was going to get awkward again. His relief at finding her safe after his awful shock produced the only possible reaction. His temper exploded.

'You stupid, little bitch,' he snarled at her. 'Only someone as dumb as you would be here

146

in wartime when everyone, even a two-year-old child, knew a battle was due to take place,' he raged down at her.

'Why you horrible, insufferable, jumped-up bully!' she spat back at him.

'And who the hell gave you permission to sell *my* brother's house? You certainly are a cocky little miss and you want taking down more than a peg or two.'

Now Sarah exploded. 'Good job I did, otherwise you'd have lost its value because did you have a protection on it? I bet not! But I sold it and I have the money safely lodged with Mr Benson.'

'He had no business conveying that property!' he hurled at her.

'You gave him Power of Attorney. He told me so and at least he had the sense to see the business foresight of my scheme, which you won't because you are nothing but a dumb soldier!' she spat at him.

'It's high time someone bent you over and thrashed some sense into you!'

'If you think you're the man to do it, why hide your troopers then?'

They glowered at each other, both in pure rage, neither willing either to back down or consider the other's point of view. Fire raged in Sarah's eyes and her fingers were tense, ready to spring at and claw him. He boiled with anger. Even Martin had never dared this temerity. He itched to backhand her.

147

It was unfortunate they both moved at the same time. Sarah took a step slightly forward, really only adjusting her balance. She felt bone weary and wanted nothing more than to go home, bathe, then cry and cry with misery and frustration.

James had been standing tensed, feet too wide apart. Now he readjusted his stance, which meant he moved two inches nearer to her. His mind swirled with horror at their position while his heart ached. Looking at her, seeing her proud, indomitable spirit, made him realise that if he could not have her, he would never marry.

Both were far too strung up to have good sense left. Each interpreted the other's move as one of hostility. Sarah sprang forward, right hand extended to hit his cheek. He instinctively brought up his forearm to push her aside. Within seconds, they were brawling; Sarah spitting fire and fury, trying to claw and kick at the same time, James struggling to parry and defend his eyes while, at the same time, attempting to turn her to thrash her backside.

At that identical moment, Walter reappeared from around the corner where he had finally brought Robert up to date with a brief résumé and left him with the alert troopers. He took in the scene, only ten paces away, with shocked, total disbelief.

'Sir! Mistress!' he cried with horror. It was a

long time since he had witnessed such a common, utterly disgusting brawl in public. He ran forward, stood one second, bemused with their disgraceful behaviour, then he acted. He grabbed Sarah's arm, tipping her off balance and she tumbled heavily to the ground. He swung round, balled his fist and slammed it against his officer's jaw.

James was taken completely unawares. He reeled, stumbled, then he too crashed to the hard cobbles. The pair of them lay there. Sarah was shocked. Not quite sure what had happened, she looked up at Walter with disbelief.

'Walter!' she protested.

'Hamlyn,' James growled, shocked beyond measure, 'that's a court martial offence!'

'I'm sick to death of you two!' Walter bellowed down at both of them. He stood with his hands on his hips, carrot-coloured hair poking from under his askew helmet, eyes glowing, cheeks red with rare anger. 'I've never seen such a disgusting exhibition,' he shouted. 'You are behaving like two alley cats. You should be ashamed of yourselves. You call yourself a lady, mistress? I think I know serving maids with better manners than you. As to you, sir, first of all it is *not* a court martial offence as I'm a civilian and that's your doing, not mine,' he grated harshly. 'And your behaviour is a total disgrace to that of any officer. I think I've had more than enough of the pair of you. I was better off in the ranks than putting up with your childish tantrums,' he shouted, making sure they understood he joined them together. 'If you two think I'm going to allow my good and respectable name to be involved with a couple who brawl in public like a pair of squabbling whores, then you both have another think coming. I don't need either of you, now or in the future. I'm man enough to make my own way in life and I'll do this mixing with civilised people, not common street urchins, which is what the pair of you are. You disgust me! Both of you!' He stopped to catch his breath, rather astounded with himself but not displeased. He meant every word he said and knew this was the end. Who would want to be around a stupid, childish pair like these two? They would drive a man insane with their jealousies, rows and common behaviour.

'Walter!' Sarah cried, deeply hurt. She liked him very much and suddenly felt waves of shame seep over her.

'Hamlyn!' James growled, but without the bite in his voice. He knew he'd never find such a fine, upstanding, loyal servant again if he looked over the whole of England.

'I'm sick to the bottom of my guts with the pair of you,' Walter continued, his own rarely seen temper in full spate. 'You can both get yourselves well and truly stuffed. I'm off, and good riddance to you.'

150

'Christ!' James blasphemed, struggling to his feet, grabbing Sarah's arm to steady her as she copied. 'He bloody well means it. I didn't know he had it in him!'

'Neither did I!' Sarah gasped, more deeply shocked than for years. 'We can't let him go. He's irreplaceable!'

'But . . .' he began with rare uncertainty.

'James!' she cried. 'Do something! Stop him! Walter!' she wailed.

'Hamlyn! Come back here, damn you, man!'

Walter strode on, hell-bent on going. It was the very first time in his life he had spoken to his betters with such words, but he felt good and sad at the same time. He heard boots thundering after him, then a hand grabbed his arm and swung him around. A smaller hand clasped his other. He was forced to halt as they turned him to face them.

Tears cascaded down Sarah's face while James' eyes were incredibly hurt. He waited, in pointed, very ominous silence.

James understood first. 'I'm sorry,' he said hastily. 'I mean it, Sarah, I apologise!'

Sarah understood. 'I'm so sorry too. I don't know what came over me. I am sincere, Walter,' she pleaded, now in a downright panic.

Walter's jaw was set in an iron band. His narrow eyes glinted as he looked first to the officer then the lady. He waited, eyebrows elevated, lips very tight, nostrils pinched with

151

his anger.

'Please, Walter,' Sarah begged unashamedly, 'don't leave me.'

James cleared his throat. 'God damn it, Hamlyn, I've never begged or pleaded in my life but I'd take it as a favour of great esteem, if you'd reconsider,' he got out, in a little rush of words.

They waited, holding their breath, rather frightened by this new, totally unexpected Walter. He looked at them in turn, taking his time, building up the tension deliberately, and driving his point well and truly home.

'Well,' he began slowly, letting a more even tone enter his voice. 'I may be willing to think about it. On conditions though!'

Sarah caught her breath and flashed a worried look at James. He licked his lips.

'Conditions?' he asked quietly.

Walter nodded at each in turn. 'I always thought you two were made for each other but something got into the pair of you and it's grown and grown. Nothing can be bad enough for two suited people to fall out over something, whether trivial or not. If you want me to stay I *might* be willing to think about it *and* put you two on trial, if you kiss and make up whatever it was which bugged both of you, then sit down and talk it out like adults, not a pair of half-brained kids.'

Walter was amazed with himself but kept his expression stiff. He did not know himself. Was this what war did to a man? Certainly never before in his life had he dared to stand up to his betters, let alone threaten them. At the same time, deep inside his heart, he was touched that the mere threat of his going could produce such an instantaneous reaction. Walter had no family. He had always been a natural loner and now he felt something queer, a funny lump lodged in his throat. These two fools wanted him. He longed to hug both of them but made himself stand cold and withdrawn.

James turned to Sarah, eyebrows lifted in a silent question. A little smile touched the corner of her lips. She waggled her shoulders before giving a small nod of assent. Without more ado, James bent, kissed her, took his time in doing it and enjoyed every second. Sarah felt herself melting into his arms with their strength and security. Bless Walter, she told herself. That man has horse sense, James added silently. He's worth his weight in golden sovereigns.

Walter cleared his throat and a twinkle showed in his eyes when they broke apart.

'Very well,' he told them quietly, 'but there's no need to make a meal of it in public,' though his rebuke was mild now. Once more he looked at them in turn. Sarah blushed and broke eye contact. James felt his cheek go red and he hastily sniffed and looked to one side. Walter's tongue touched his cheek but now he wisely stayed silent. He felt himself swell with pride, gave an eloquent sniff, jiggled two steps then chuckled his amusement and delight.

'Bloody carrot-tops!' James growled. 'Never could control 'em!'

'Oh Walter, I think you're lovely!' Sarah crooned.

'Right then, Mistress, I'm taking you and Robert home. As to you, sir, it might be prudent for you to show your face in the right quarters or you might indeed be in trouble with higher authority,' he reminded his officer.

'Oh Christ yes!' James said. 'I'll have to go, Sarah. I'll call when I can and we'll start . . .'

'. . . to make plans,' she finished for him. Her heart was bursting with joy, and she knew she would have eternal gratitude for Walter Hamlyn, as long as she lived. She also guessed that James would feel the same.

CHAPTER EIGHT

'Well,' James drawled, sitting in her best chair, booted feet sprawled before him, a tankard of Mary's ale in his right fist. The Pair had been agog at his arrival and studied him with immense interest, enough to make Sarah go scarlet. She had been glad to usher him into her room and shut the door. It was wonderful to have him here, in her home at long last.

154

'You've not kissed me,' she said pertly.

He eyed her and chuckled. 'I'll see to that matter later,' he said placidly. 'Right now I'm comfortable and I've no intention of moving for one hour.'

Sarah's face fell. 'Is that all the time you have, James?'

He pulled a face. 'I'm afraid so,' and flashed her a look. 'You know my work,' he said gently, 'and though the King's bolt is shot, there are still pockets of resistance plus the King himself. Once we take him prisoner, it should all end and life can slowly get back to normal.'

'With Cromwell as head of the country?'

James nodded with satisfaction. 'Yes, though it's tragic so many men have had to die. No,' he said with a deep, satisfied sigh, 'peace will seem strange I must admit.'

Sarah bit her lip. 'But when we are married, surely you won't still have to . . . ?'

'Work for Thurloe? I'm afraid so, because the King has an heir and I'm too experienced now. What will happen is young men will have to be brought on but that will take time.'

Sarah frowned. 'You mentioned Thurloe before but never explained. Can you tell me now, James?'

He took a deep breath. 'Thurloe? What a man he is. His name is John Thurloe and he was brought up as a lawyer. Right now, he is secretary to a commissioner of Parliament. He is a very clever man. His metier in life is information, the formation and maintenance of the Republic of England and its safekeeping for all time with the best espionage system the world has ever known. Thurloe is earmarked for very high places, you mark my words, and I also predict that one day his power in England will be considerable. I work directly for him. Myself and a few hand-picked others whose names even I don't know. Only one person knows every agent, and that is Thurloe. He keeps a detailed record in a famous little black book. When Thurloe commands, I jump.'

'Oh!'

'Yes,' James echoed, then threw her a sharp look. 'This means, even married, I expect to be at his beck and call for a long time. Which means, you independent young woman, you can run the business to your heart's delight.'

Sarah knew she was flushing, though, peeping at him, she saw the twinkle in his eyes. Something occurred to her though. 'Will that mean danger for you?' she asked nervously.

James knew better than to lie to her. 'It's possible,' he admitted, 'but I'm well used to that. There will always be a faction of Royalists. They'll never take kindly to England being run by someone without the right to the crown. In this village, you'll have them. It is quite possible, over a period of time, a guerrilla faction might be organised which means Thurloe will always want to know who

156

stands where, why and for how long. Eventually, these diehard Royalists will get their own espionage system going too. Plot and counter plot, I'm afraid.'

Sarah's face fell. He was not making their future rosy but it was his work, and, she suspected, something he enjoyed doing. She would have to learn to live with him coming and going erratically. But then, she reminded herself, how sweet his arrivals would be. With this thought, her face brightened.

'Now about Robert,' James began, nodding sagely to himself. 'How about adopting him as our son the day after we are married? He's a fine young man. I'd like my own sons cut from his cloth,' he hinted mischievously.

Sarah twinkled back at him. 'I'll have to see what I can do then,' she paused, thinking back. 'It's strange, Robert swears he was attacked that time in Bristol and I phoo-hooed it. I wonder though if he was correct?'

He stilled. 'Why?'

'When we returned from Bristol, Mary told me they'd seen a stranger in our area and she'd simply forgotten to tell me.'

'Description?' he asked sharply. 'Clubman?'

Sarah shook her head hopelessly. 'None. I'm afraid Mary's not very bright that way. Now if it had been Nellie . . .' her voice tailed off.

James considered. With all the general uproar there had been in the build-up to

Bristol's attack, there were many strangers about including the Clubmen coming down from Gloucestershire in this north side of the city. He murmured to himself.

'There will be days when I'll want Walter with me, even though he's set up such an excellent pigeon service. Robert?'

Sarah shook her head. 'He wants to live in Bristol in the house and work at the business. It wouldn't surprise me if, when he's older, he doesn't leave to sail the seas for spices.'

'That only leaves Jack on the place,' James murmured, not very happy at this thought. 'I'll have to get another man here. A discharged soldier who has been wounded enough to be no good to an army but still all right for a home guard.'

Sarah decided to change the subject. James was worried, yet she herself considered a clubman explanation logical. 'Tell me more about Cromwell,' she invited.

He was surprised at this conversation change. 'Him? He's another astute man. Rank, wealth and position mean nothing to him at all. What does count is the man himself. His ability, his courage; money is ignored. I think he will be a good man for England.' Then he paused uncertainly. 'The only reservation I have is the religious, Puritan faction. They are inclined to be every bit as dogmatic as the King was in not calling a Parliament. With the Puritans it's religion and I'm not sure that is a very good thing' He stopped, his mind flitting to another subject. 'I think it might be prudent for you to know how to handle the pigeons,' he told her. 'Just in case you wanted to get an urgent message to me when Walter accompanies me.'

Sarah nodded. This made sense. 'When can we marry?' she asked him practically, turning to the most important topic. She had a flashing vision of both of them in bed and, as she did so, she felt her thighs flood with moisture. It had been a long time, she reminded herself. Too long, and she was young, with a healthy appetite.

He read her mind and grinned. 'Within the month,' he promised.

*   *   *

'Come on, Robert. Let's ride and I'll show you where James and I used to meet in secret,' she said, bubbling happily. Walter looked at her whimsically. A pigeon had come and he had to go into Bristol on a short errand though he planned to return well before nightfall.

'Are you armed, boy?' he challenged quickly.

Robert nodded and displayed his pistol. 'And you, mistress?' Sarah showed him the tiny one, tucked into a small holster which hung from her waist belt. She felt cluttered up with it but wore it for James' peace of mind. There

159

was no need, she was sure. Any roving clubmen had disappeared since James went and the countryside was tranquil again. The sun shone and it was going to be a gorgeous day with the hint of an early autumn frost.

Sarah mounted her mare while Robert picked a large brown who had comfortable paces. 'We're just going around the old Court,' Sarah told Jack. He was inclined to worry now since being spiced up by Walter's sharp tongue. Indeed, Sarah told herself with a giggle, Walter had gingered them all up. Certainly she and James were most circumspect with Walter now. That one awesome display of temper with his harsh, biting words had shaken both of them. She noted even James was studiously correct with Walter now; anxious not to arouse such ginger passion again. Indeed, Walter had changed before their eyes. Now he was an assured man. Confident, even a little more polished as he copied herself and James, and very much his own man now he had learned he was wanted for himself. They were all fond of him and, very gradually, Sarah realised Walter was slipping into the position of a much loved, powerful brother. With the Pair and Jack, Sarah realised they had wonderful staff who had changed to become friends. Quite suddenly her whole future glowed in a way that, only a few weeks ago, had seemed utterly impossible.

'Let's ride!' she called gleefully to Robert

and pushed her mare into a springy canter. He followed then, heeling his horse, and rode by her side. It was mildly warm with a light breeze and it was fun to ride stirrup to stirrup across a land at peace. How really wonderful it was to be alive on this gorgeous day, Sarah thought, then laughed aloud. Robert grinned, chuckled and did the same. This was . . . fun!

'Goodness, these horses are fresh!' Sarah exclaimed as she tussled with her mare and, throwing a look at Robert, she noted he too was working his hands. His big horse, although a good weight carrier, lacked her mare's speed so she struggled not to go too far ahead. It would only aggravate Robert's horse the more.

They rode only a short while before pulling back to a walk, leading right out into the open countryside. There were no signs of life and Robert kept looking around keenly. He had much to learn about the region.

After a few moments he halted and turned his horse, frowning with concentration. 'That's odd, we are being followed,' he murmured.

Sarah stopped and also stared. He was correct. Way in the distance but approaching rapidly was a solitary rider. She was puzzled. She knew most of the villagers' stances in the saddle from familiarity but not this. 'A stranger.'

They watched the man approach, then a little something started to grow in Robert's mind. A hundred yards from them, the man

161

stopped and regarded them keenly. He was big with a heavy beard and rode his horse well.

'No!' Robert said in a low voice. 'It can't be, but it is.'

Sarah was bewildered. On Robert's face was horror. 'Is what?'

'I was right. I knew it!' Robert told her with rising agitation. 'It is he. He was the one who hit my head in Bristol. I remember that beard only too well and . . .' He paused, his voice sinking low. 'I know exactly who he is too.'

Sarah regarded the rider, noting he had two pistols fastened to his saddle. She felt a strong tide of alarm and looked at Robert urgently.

'Who is it?' she asked quickly.

'My father! Fletcher!' Robert replied bluntly.

'Good God!' Sarah exclaimed, totally bemused for a few seconds then her wits sprang into action and it all became clear. 'Of course,' she gasped. 'What utter fools we've been. Where's the best place to hide anything? Under one's nose. He's been in Bristol all this time and we presumed erroneously he'd sailed away. He bumped into you in the city fire, saw the panic, realised his chance and tried to kill you; because you, Robert, are the only true witness. He must eliminate you if he wishes to stay in the city with a different political colour. Why didn't we all see this before? It's you he's after now too.'

Robert quietly nodded his head. But where

was his mother? It had obviously not entered Sarah's head that she too must be removed. He drew his pistol, sharply conscious that his aim was not yet what it might be. Sarah copied, although she knew hers was little more than a toy unless used at very close range. It flashed into Sarah's mind to question Robert's pistol accuracy. If only Walter were here, and James.

Fletcher walked his horse purposefully towards them while Sarah calculated. 'Robert,' she hissed, 'divide and rule. When I give the word, turn to the right. I'll go to the left and fire as we go. Make sure he's within range though,' she warned, feeling fright consume her.

There was something wickedly inexorable about Fletcher's advance. 'Now!' she screeched.

Both horses were whipped aside and Sarah's mare, a very fast animal, was swiftly out of pistol range. She threw a snap look behind and saw that Fletcher had turned for Robert. She pulled up her mare and wheeled to give chase. Robert's slower horse was rapidly being overtaken. Why didn't he fire? Then it hit her, Robert did not know how, when riding fast. Dear God, Fletcher was catching up with him. She heeled her mare viciously and chased them.

She saw Fletcher lift his pistol and, even at a gallop, sight and fire. There was the violent bark then Robert lurched in his saddle, swayed

163

and slowly fell.

Sarah drew her toy pistol and, teeth bared, rode madly towards Fletcher who turned, hauled his horse to a halt, calmly sheathed one pistol and removed the second. Sarah felt herself bouncing erratically. She would never hit the man even while he was at a standstill. She saw the danger, lowered her pistol fractionally, and started to make her mare perform flying changes, altering her silhouette all the time. It was horsemanship of the highest calibre as the mare changed forelegs every few paces. Sarah's groin muscles ached with the strain but, she saw, Fletcher was baulked. As they neared, she lifted her pistol again. He did the same and both fired together.

Sarah's ball was far too distant. It drooped way in front of Fletcher, landing with a harmless plop on the earth. His ball, larger and heavier, hit Sarah in her left forearm as the mare changed legs again. Without this sudden sideways swerve, the ball would have entered her chest. As it was, the power and pain made her lurch precariously while Fletcher stared with disbelief.

The pain was horrendous and Sarah gasped then, looking ahead, she saw Robert sprawled on the ground, unmoving. Something snapped in her. Rage, injustice, fear and pain all combined and she went berserk. She turned her mare, rammed with her heels and charged,

164

at a flat-out gallop, at Fletcher's flank.

Before he had time to react with shock, at this totally unexpected tactic, she was on him. The mare, seeing the collision, acted as any horse would under these circumstances. At the identical moment of impact she half-reared to protect herself. Her large hooves whipped through the air, her speed and body weight lethal.

Fletcher and his horse went down with a bellow and scream from his mount. The mare plunged her front hooves down for instinctive footing. They landed on both man and horse, then she was gone, her hind hooves kicking backwards for speed.

Sarah slumped, grasping the pommel, on the verge of coming off. The pain waves made her eyes swim then slowly, almost elegantly, she rolled over the mare's left shoulder. She landed heavily, badly winded and the mare galloped off, kicking her heels in equine fashion at such a fright.

Sarah lay still a moment, confused, hurt and tearful then, making an almighty effort, she half rolled and, favouring her bleeding arm, staggered to her feet. She stumbled over to Robert, dropped on her knees and studied the ugly ball hole high up in his back. Dear God, was he dead already? Moving gently, wincing with her own pain, she touched his neck and slumped with relief, as she felt the huge neck artery throb under her fingers.

165

Turning, she saw a twitching movement from Fletcher. Taking a deep breath, she staggered to her feet and lurched awkwardly over to him. One swift assessing look told her all. Many ribs had been broken on one side and the lung was lethally punctured. Blood seeped from Fletcher's mouth, but he was still alive, though fighting for breath, wincing with pain.

With a great effort, he looked up at her. 'That boy?'

"He'll live,' Sarah threw down at him, not at all sure this was true. 'So you have failed, you butcher. Where is Bessie?'

His brown eyes mocked her even though his spirit was faltering. 'That old fool? I dumped her, of course. She'd served her purpose.'

'Where?' Sarah rasped with an effort. Her arm was red and sticky with her blood and pain waves made her eyes mist but, fighting valiantly, she forced unconsciousness away. 'Where?' she cried harshly. 'You've nothing to lose by telling me, because you're dying, Fletcher.'

He went into an agonised paroxysm of coughing, sweat dappling his forehead. He knew she was correct. He had gambled and lost. For once, the dice had turned right against him.

'White Bull in Bristol,' he managed to get out, 'stupid cow she is! I nearly pulled it off too. Got the old man. Nearly finished the kid in Bristol. My mistake was in not taking you out first, though.'

He went into another burst of laboured coughing, the blood flowing faster; pink lung blood.

'Tell me,' he struggled to speak, 'was I right?'

Sarah failed to understand. She was in abject misery. Robert lying desperately wounded, perhaps even dying; herself in pain, out here in the countryside alone. Yet she knew it was vital, even imperative, that she witnessed Fletcher die. It would remove the hoodoo for all time.

'About what?' she got up with an effort, willing herself to keep erect and not faint.

'You and Penford were both spies for Parliament?'

Sarah took a deep breath, made herself concentrate, and replied. There was no harm to be done now.

'Yes,' she told him bluntly.

'Clouds,' he gasped, 'it's going so dark,' he grunted.

Sarah threw a brief look at the blue sky with no clouds in sight. 'Glad I was right about something, at least,' he groaned, before his head slumped with a jerk.

She studied him for a minute then, making a great effort, bent and felt for his heart. There was no pumping; he was really dead. Robert! She must get help. Wearily, with her arm liberally covered now in blood, she staggered back to him and knelt again, feeling his neck. He was still alive but what to do? She forced herself to think calmly.

The mare had halted and now grazed, snatching the grass in gulps. Fletcher's horse was dead, its neck broken. Robert's horse had bolted from sight. Biting her lip, with a great effort of will, Sarah staggered slowly toward her mare. Thank God she had always built up friendship and trust with her mounts. The mare lifted her head, continued chewing, but eyed her approach. Speaking softly, Sarah slowly extended her hand and grasped the reins. The mare stilled; then, with each movement agony, Sarah straightened the nearside stirrup and eyed the saddle. Just how could she mount with only one arm? But she had to. If only the mare would stand and not fidget.

She stroked her nose, affectionately patted her neck, licked very dry lips then, moving haltingly, biting her bottom lip, she placed one foot in the stirrup, took a deep breath, willed herself to forget her left arm, grasped the cantle and, with an inelegant sprawl, landed in her saddle.

The mare dithered two steps then stilled as discipline and training took over. 'Good girl,' Sarah crooned, feeling like death warmed up. 'Now, take me home and I can't help you either,' she winced. 'We must get help for

Robert!'

It was as if the animal sensed something unusual. She walked sedately, tail switching, head ducking but made no attempt to break into a trot. Sarah swore afterwards that the journey had taken hours. It was a living nightmare but the village finally showed. She approached from an angle because her home was isolated. The mare plodded into the stable yard with Sarah slumped in the saddle.

'Help!' Sarah called weakly. She knew she was going to fall again and winced at the thought of landing heavily on the cobbles.

A startled Walter appeared. He had just returned and been engaged in talk with jack and Robert.

'Good God!' he exclaimed. 'Mistress Sarah! What the hell's happened?' he cried and ran to her, just catching her as she slid sideways.

'Jack! Robert!'

The men ran up and slowly lowered her, gently easing her bloody arm. Sarah took a deep breath, then turned to reliable Walter.

'Robert's badly wounded, perhaps even dying. Over towards the common,' she managed to get out. 'It was his father, Fletcher, Martin's killer. Get to him quickly. Mine is only a flesh wound,' she managed to tell them, then quite suddenly fainted.

Walter reacted rapidly. 'Jack, harness up the cart, then fetch The Pair,' he bellowed, holding Sarah's inert body. The Pair arrived in shocked

169

horror, and took Sarah inside. Walter hastily threw his saddle on a fresh horse then, with Jack driving the light cart, they headed away.

The Pair did not panic and Nellie took over. She was the one experienced with herbs and hers were the steady hands and head. The Pair laid Sarah on the bed, bathed the wound and Nellie examined it thoroughly. The pistol ball had passed through the flesh and the wise woman grunted. She worked swiftly, packed it with herbs she kept in the kitchen, bound it, then together they managed to get Sarah up the stairs and into her bed.

As they came back, Mary eyed her friend. 'What on earth can have happened? I wonder if this was to do with the stranger, a few weeks ago, who asked me those questions about young Robert? Oh dear! I wish I had thought to mention him the same day. Perhaps this is all my fault,' she wailed and broke into a flood of tears.

Nellie suspected it was but recriminations achieved nothing. Walter had gone for Robert who was more seriously wounded she imagined, from what had been bellowed at her. She swiftly reviewed her private apothecary collection, then hastily built up the fire for hot water. Nellie had no medicinal training; what she did have was a natural instinct, a head full of herbal knowledge and practical common sense. She was also unflappable and, when the need arose, could take over a situation with brisk orders.

When they brought Robert back, and after Nellie had examined him, she was dubious.

She looked over at Walter who had, automatically, taken charge, as the senior male. 'It's not good. That ball must come out. There is only one thing going for him, and that is his youth. You men hold him down because I'm going to have to hurt him a lot, an awful lot,' Nellie said with set jaw.

Even in his comatose state, Robert writhed and fought the pain as Nellie probed delicately for the ball in his back. It took the combined strengths of Jack, Walter and Mary to pin him down on the kitchen table.

Nellie worked carefully, feeling the ball's path then, holding her breath, using an instrument of her own invention, she managed to get under the ball. 'Now!' she grunted.

With a steady pull she eased the ball up and out, then Robert slumped into unconsciousness. Knowing this, Nellie worked with greater rapidity. She packed the wound with herbs, after allowing it to bleed freely, and then inserted a clean, hollow straw to keep it open. Finally she wrapped Robert's torso in fresh linen and stood up straight, eyeing him doubtfully.

'It's out of my hands, now,' she said slowly. 'Prayers might just be the order of the day,' she told them all. 'Get him into his bed and leave the rest to Mary and me.'

Afterwards she slumped down on a kitchen stool and Walter, hunting for the brandy cask, poured them all a generous drink. 'Here's to Nellie,' he toasted solemnly.

She blushed and shook her head. 'And to Sarah for managing to ride back. How she mounted with that arm is beyond me.'

Walter agreed, then moving silently, he slipped from the kitchen and headed for the pigeons. He took a deep breath. There was no time to code up. He was too shaken with all that had happened; he doubted he could remember coherently. He scribbled his message in sparse, blunt words:

Home at once. Hamlyn

Then he fastened it inside the tiny leg container, took the bird out, held it for a few seconds then tossed it high. The pigeon rose, circled a few times and then took off in a straight line to the next handler.

*   *   *

The black stallion's gallop had slowed to a ragged canter. Even the powerful horse was nearly at the end of his tether. His rider was in a worse state. James was not only exhausted but in a cold rage. What the hell had come over Hamlyn? How many times had he dinned it into him not to use plain language? Only coded messages were to be sent to him. Did he think, because of the events in Bristol, that he had assumed rights? If so, he would very quickly disabuse him! He was also disappointed with Hamlyn. Never before had he disobeyed a legitimate order and, James told himself, he now knew the situation in depth. James had considered it prudent to tell him that day he had taken Sarah to the court's ruins. A man without the full facts could not answer sensibly, so what the hell has got into Hamlyn? What kind of crazy message was it he'd sent; "home at once". He fumed to himself. He itched to gallop, get there, blast Hamlyn, then have a quick word with Sarah and be about his work. It was only by the grace of God the message had reached him so swiftly but, even then, twenty-four hours had elapsed.

He rode into the yard in a furious black rage, saw Hamlyn right away, vaulted from the saddle, left the exhausted horse quite unattended, and strode over, wrath bristling from every hair.

Walter weighed up the situation and decided to get in first. 'The mistress and Robert have been shot by your brother's murderer. The mistress will be all right but Robert is another matter,' he said with a rush of words.

James halted abruptly in mid stride, jaw gaped and words stuck in his throat. Had he heard correctly?

173

'That's right, sir. It's been bad here, very bad. We have been lucky not to have had both of them killed.'

James continued to stare in total silence. He swore afterwards that his mind had ceased to function. Then he took a deep breath, gave a shake to his head, turned and strode into the kitchen, opening the back door with a thud.

'Quiet!' Nellie shouted. He had made her jump. 'There are very sick people here!'

Again James froze, went scarlet and hesitated. 'Can I see them, Sarah first?' he asked with sudden respect. The thin woman was furious with him and he cursed himself. He had plunged in with two left feet, both size twenty. 'Please,' he added respectfully and politely.

'Very well but don't thump about in those boots, mister, and you're not to stay with the mistress if she's asleep. I'll come with you and check,' Nellie told him firmly.

He was led upstairs and went on exaggerated tiptoe. It was the first time he'd been to the upper storey of the house. Nellie peeped into a room with an open door, eyed up the situation, then gave him a brief nod with a severe frown.

James softly walked in. 'Sarah,' he whispered, shocked at what he saw.

She had managed to sit up with her arm bandaged and in a sling; her cheeks were white and she lay back, almost lethargically. Not his

174

bouncy Sarah at all. He drew up a chair, gently taking her free hand.

'Can you talk and tell me what happened? Don't if it's going to tire you,' he added hastily, aware of the thin woman's possible anger if he did the wrong thing.

Sarah threw him a wan smile. 'I think it's been the shock as much as anything,' she began, then related her tale. He listened intently, shaking his head at some points.

'Fletcher made fools of all of us,' Sarah ended, 'and now poor Robert is so ill.'

James had to know. 'Gangrene?'

Sarah pulled a face. 'It's early days to say but Nellie thinks he might be all right. She says there's no smell on him and she changes the dressings regularly. It's awful for Robert. Walter holds him. That man is a rock,' Sarah told him. 'We must never lose him.'

Sarah eyed him and James shook his head with a groan. 'It was me who sent him on an errand into Bristol. Thank God he came back in time to organise.'

'You are quite sure Fletcher is dead?'

Sarah nodded firmly. 'Very sure and anyhow, the Sheriff came out. Walter sent Jack for him . . . and his body has been removed.'

'Well, thank heavens that enemy has gone for good but it was a close-run thing indeed. In Bristol all this time. Bessie! What about her?'

'Fletcher said she was at the White Bull, wherever that is,' Sarah told him. She felt a yawn coming. Much as she loved her adored James, all she wanted to do now was sleep for hours and hours.

He saw this and stood at the moment Nellie popped her head in. She assessed the situation, looked at James and pointed firmly to the open door. Meekly he obeyed but paused to rest a hand on the thin shoulder. 'Thank you,' he whispered, 'now Robert.'

He studied the young man without speaking. He had seen many battlefield wounds and dying men. He examined the young man's cheeks, listened to his breathing, bent and sniffed the region of the wound, then straightened slowly.

'He'll make it. It will take time, of course, but he will live. Mistress, I am honoured you live in this house and when I marry the Mistress you will get a handsome pay rise,' he said, then, before the startled Nellie could demur, he bent and gave her a smacking kiss.

Nellie turned scarlet as Mary appeared, then what he had said registered. 'Marry the mistress?' she cried and flashed a glowing look at Mary. 'You were right on that,' she told her friend. 'I owe you three pennies.'

'What's this? Gambling, ladies?' James whispered with amusement. 'Tut tut,' he said and, diving into his breeches, pulled out his purse. He opened it, extracted two gold coins and presented one to each of them. He had a shrewd idea they might not have seen such

176

wealth before. 'To celebrate my nuptials, in advance,' he suggested slyly.

Before they could get too embarrassed, he went back down the stairs and out into the yard. He opened his mouth to make his usual bellow then remembered. 'Hamlyn,' he called in a low voice.

Walter appeared, eyebrows raised in question. 'They'll do, including the young one; thanks for all you've done,' and he gave Walker four gold coins.

He looked at the property. This would soon be his home and his heart warmed to it. Then his mind reverted to more critical matters.

'If you come with mc in the morning, what about the guard situation here?' he asked thoughtfully. He did not think there was more cause for alarm but he was a prudent and wary soldier.

Walter was ahead of him again. 'There's only Jack who will never be the world's best shot,' he replied, 'so when I'm away, I've arranged for the loan of male servants from the clothier up the road. The whole village has been shocked at what happened and they descended here in a drove, wanting to help, indeed getting in the way. I compromised by asking for guards.'

'Good man,' James praised, and then his face went stern. 'I have to go into Bristol in the morning. There's someone I need to see,' he added grimly. 'So get a pigeon off. Code up a

177

message to say I've been delayed because of a domestic crisis. We'll leave as soon as the sun is up,' he finished. He would not take a fresh horse and go into Bristol today. Deep inside, he boiled with cold rage, the more deadly variety than the hot bubbling stuff.

'Where to, sir?'

'The White Bull. Do you know it by any chance?'

Walter thought, and then nodded. 'It's not too far from Master Penford's old house. It's a pretty big tavern with many floors, and it escaped the fire if I remember correctly,' and Walter threw him a look. 'With arms, sir?'

James gave a slow nod. It was unlikely one female had a guard but he did not intend to be caught napping. It was only by the grace of God there had not been a double murder here.

Walter waited to see if there was going to be any more explanation but, when he saw this was not so, he did not mind. If it was the officer's private business and he was simply there as a guard, he would see only what his officer wanted him to see, even if he did have both eyes wide open and focused correctly.

*   *   *

James frowned uneasily. Down here, in this cellar room, the stink was disgusting and the crone who sat and warily eyed him was scrawny. Long ago Sarah had provided him with a detailed description of Bessie, and James realised, this hag bore not the slightest resemblance. Yet his enquiries had sent him down here to this old woman, who worked as a lowly cleaner.

She was thin and old, ragged clothes hung limply on her frame. Her face, filthy dirty as if it rarely saw hot water was creased and in her eyes there was an odd, hunted, drawn look. She could not meet his gaze directly but eyed him from a half-bowed head. He thought she resembled a cur who was whipped often.

'Your name is Bessie?' he said coldly.

She continued to stare at the damp cellar stones. To one side was a miserable truckle bed with a straw palliasse. It too was never wholly dry and she knew, if she lived, the joint ills would eventually cripple her. Live? Did she want to? And Bessie knew she could not care less. What was the point of it all now? All that could be said for this place was that it gave a roof over her head and the miserable work provided just enough food to keep body and soul together.

'Have you any idea who I am?' James continued remorselessly.

Bessie did not but she knew he was trouble. Everyone was trouble to her now since that dreadful day when *he* had come back into her life.

James realised this silence was not a sulk. It was the silence of the terrified and the beaten.

179

Nothing he did to this woman could make her feel more wretched than she did right now.

'My brother was your old master, Martin Penford,' he said coldly.

This time there was a reaction. She lifted her head and her eyes filled with tears. 'The master?' she mumbled. 'But he is dead.'

'I know he's bloody well dead,' James hurled at her. 'Fletcher killed him and your hands might just as well have been on the knife. My brother gave you a home, you and your bastard son. For over a decade he looked after you and how did you repay him? With treason of the highest order.'

Bessie's heavy heart could not, she knew, sink lower but there was something coldly mesmerising about this strange big man. She studied him carefully and gradually managed to catch the resemblance.

'Fletcher's not here,' she managed to get out at last.

'Because he's dead!' James barked down at her.

Bessie's eyes opened wide with shock and then, slowly, gradually, a little something else flared in them; the tiniest vestige of hope. 'Killed ... dead?' she asked with a quaver.

'But only after he tried to murder your son Robert and Mistress Sarah!'

'Robert. My son! Oh, that dreadful man. But you said tried? He lives?' Bessie asked hopefully, one dirty hand going to her wizened face as tears welled afresh.

'He'll live,' James told her and wondered why he found it necessary to explain. Walter stood back two paces but could overhear everything. Somehow, James knew, this was not going as he had planned. What vengeance could he take on this crone to give satisfaction? She was at the bottom of a pit which she'd dug for herself.

'And Mistress Sarah too?'

He gave a brusque nod then, relenting a little, explained what had happened. Bessie heard him out in silence, then her shoulders slumped as he finished and continued to stare at her with those cold grey eyes.

'Talk!' James barked.

Bessie took a deep breath. Dare she hope if she did, the day might end better than it had begun?

'We all make mistakes but I made the biggest of them all. It really started years ago when he made me pregnant, gave me lots of promises that were all lies. He did give me a little money and I fled from London with it. I found my post with Master Penford and confessed all. Yes, he did take me and my baby in. Yes, he did look after me and don't you think I'll ever feel free from guilt. Of course I won't. There's a ghost who haunts me every night; the picture of Fletcher plunging that knife in Master's back. He bumped into me accidentally then told me another of his

181

fanciful stories. I was so stupid. I believed him a second time. He made more promises and because Robert was such a fine young man, I really and truly thought he'd changed. He had not. He was hand in glove with some guards at one of the gates. He guessed what Master was doing, before I ever did. Then he worked it out that Master must have money to pay his men. He even worked it out that the Mistress was involved, which I thought was absolute rubbish. Then he made fresh promises, about us all going and starting a new life again.' She paused, reliving the horror before continuing. 'I had no idea he had murder in mind. I tried to stop him. He hit me afterwards, then beat up Robert, but luckily Robert fled and vanished somewhere. The next thing I knew was he had me on a horse and we rode all round Bristol. I could not understand why but I realise now he was checking to see if we were followed. Finally, he brought me here and that's where we've been holed up ever since.'

'My brother's money?'

Bessie gave it to him straight. 'I never saw any of it. Fletcher gambled with dice; then when it was all gone, because he was a loser, he said he'd have to find another fool and start again. I was terrified. It was very bad in the fire. He went out and I thought he'd gone but then he came back, all pleased with himself. But recently he had done a lot of riding. I don't know where. I sometimes think he must have been looking for someone and now I understand. He wanted Robert dead as witness then, with Parliament holding Bristol, he would have been quite free to start up living here again, more openly. He had changed his appearance. Robert would not have known him.'

'He did,' James growled at her and related the incident of the fire.

Bessie shuddered and the tears became a flood. With wracking sobs she took time to pull herself together again. 'Thank God Robert took after me, not him.'

Than she eyed the big man. 'What are you going to do?' she asked nervously.

'I could take you to law, James drawled slowly, which he knew was accurate, 'but I don't think you are worth it.' He looked around. 'This is like a pig pen and I guess it suits you, so here you can stay. If you can drag yourself up by your boot straps then so be it, but let me tell you, you have no son Robert. When I marry, my wife and myself will adopt him as ours. You have forfeited all right and that can be your major punishment. You make any attempt to go near him or contact him in any way, and I promise you, you'll be tried and executed for your part in my brother's murder. I mean every word I say. I hope you believe me?' he asked in a slow, rasping tone.

Bessie did. She nodded feebly. It was all over and done with. If she had the means, she would commit suicide but even this was denied her. She had nothing except her wasted, dirty and half-starved body. It did not seem it would ever be possible for her to redeem herself. She sagged, her misery even greater yet, somehow, a load was lifted from her back. Slowly she raised her head and held the big man's gaze, nodding slowly.

'I do!' she confirmed.

James gave a grunt. Suddenly, all this had turned so distasteful, he fidgeted to get away and back out into fresh, country air. He flashed Walter a look and stomped from the cellar, back up the stone steps. Outside, he breathed in Bristol's ever-fetid air.

'Hell,' he muttered to himself, then turned to Walter. 'I came here for vengeance. Blood for blood, but I've done nothing. What can a man do against someone as pitiful as that?'

Walter considered in his thoughtful way. 'You've inflicted the greatest vengeance possible on a mother,' he replied slowly. 'Will you ever tell Robert?'

James considered. 'Should I?'

Walter shook his head. 'It's all in the past. It's history, let it lie. What good will knowing ever do? It's true, Robert will always wonder, but let him. In a few years time, he'll have girls on his mind,' he advised sagely.

'By God, you're right!' James exclaimed. 'Come on, Hamlyn, I feel in desperate need of a drink. You'll drink with me, no rank, remember?' he grinned, feeling great relief at a rotten job done well.

They strode for their horses, led them up the road and went into the first suitable tavern.

Later James explained to Sarah. She was well on the way to recovery with her natural health and resilience.

'Walter was right,' Sarah told him after thinking about everything. 'Robert will never know from any of us. Then she flashed a look of mischief at him. 'Thank God we managed to keep Walter. We must never lose him. This place would grind to a halt.'

He grunted his agreement. 'I'll think about each word before I say it if I'm in a mood,' he promised. 'Now, when do we get married?'

PART TWO

1650

CHAPTER NINE

Sarah knew she had the fidgets again and wondered what on earth was the matter with her. She had everything surely to make total earthly happiness. Was she going queer or something? She had two splendid children, a boy and a girl, a very loving husband, incredible servants, no money worries and an adopted son who worked in Bristol as manager to the family spice firm, and horses to ride.

She was bored; incredibly, totally, screamingly bored. There was nothing whatsoever for her to do. The Pair looked after the children and were well on their way to spoiling them, she sometimes thought, then discipline would be restored and there would be peace again, albeit temporarily.

The property manager was Walter who had grown into a strong, fine man. He had married a clothier's daughter and, in his own home in the village, was their respected and highly trusted right hand. Jack had blossomed too, which was surprising because he had a dour nature. He had watched Walter, then promptly copied him.

James. Dear lovable James; yet he never seemed to be at home. That's not strictly true, she chided herself. He was at home as often as he could but he was also away, sometimes for a month at a time. What he did, she never asked. She did not have to. He was still working for that man Thurloe on Cromwell's behalf and here was another irritation.

Sarah did not like their life. James had said long ago that the Puritans were hidebound and it appeared they would, one day, stamp their beliefs on the whole of the country. Perhaps, she thought, her own personal rot had set in when King Charles was tried, in his own court, and then executed. That was terribly wrong. A lot seemed to go amiss then with Colonel Pride and his army in Parliament and that dreadful list of his. All those men considered hostile to the army were denied admittance to Parliament. Which was worse? A king who refused to call one or an army man who selected whom should enter?

Then the King's sentence was, in Sarah's opinion, quite barbaric. The trial had been a total mockery of justice, which did not say a lot for Parliament, and James was a true Parliamentarian. She had considered it wiser over the years, to steer clear of politics particularly when her own beliefs began to crumble. The vote to execute the king had been one only, and this she had nearly thrown at James, only just managing to restrain herself. Their times together were so erratically few, she had vowed she would never cause dissention so she kept her mouth shut.

The Pair did not like the situation either.

She had overheard them one day. She had stood behind the closed kitchen door, on the point of opening it and eavesdropped shamelessly.

'It's wrong,' Mary had said forcefully.

'That's true. Fancy Parliament's soldiers having the right to enter homes on Sundays and that's going to apply to Feast Days too. Ale licences are going to be withdrawn and swearing has to stop with fines on a sliding scale,' Nellie had added, then laughed. 'Though how they intend to stop men swearing makes an interesting question.'

'I don't hold with those Puritans,' Mary grumbled. 'Our lives and our homes are not going to be our own any more. It wasn't like this when we had a king,' she complained.

No, it wasn't, Sarah thought. Now there was all this latest uproar with Prince Charles marching to battle; more fighting, more Englishmen killing each other. Had the country gone stark raving mad or was it her, out of step?

If only she and James had common ground on matters political, but she knew they were now poles apart. She wondered if he was at the Battle of Worcester where, rumour had it, Prince Charles was fighting gamely to gain back his executed father's crown. Deep down, Sarah did not give him any chance at all. Parliament and Cromwell were simply far too strong.

191

Had the Battle of Worcester ended? Sometimes news took time to reach them out here in the country. Robert only visited once a month because he had found the love of his life, lawyer Benson's daughter Jane, which had astounded Sarah. She had wondered about the girl, then been enchanted when she finally met her. How on earth had stuffy Benson managed to produce such a charming, sweet creature? She and Robert were made for each other.

Suddenly, she felt a violent urge to get out and ride and ride and ride. The morning was young. She had her mare who was still a good ride even if not, perhaps, quite as fast. She could take a leather flask of wine and some food. At the thought, her face brightened. She would do it and blow her depression away into the fresh air.

Walter prepared her mount for her and eyed her as she mounted. 'Armed, mistress?' he asked from force of habit. Sarah patted the holster attached to the saddle. Ever since the Fletcher episode she never rode unarmed and, over the years, had turned herself into a competent shot, so much so that Walter had given her a larger, more deadly pistol. Even he did not deem it necessary for his mistress to have a guard. The recent fighting was nowhere in their area and he had gained considerable respect for Mistress Penford since Fletcher's death. Indeed, that one event had produced mutual admiration all round. 'Where do you intend to ride?' he still asked though, from force of habit.

Sarah considered. 'Up to the high land, then off in the direction of Pucklechurch,' she told him. It did make sense for one person to know her route though it was most unlikely the mare would throw her. 'I'll be gone for a few hours and will lunch out somehow. It's too nice to stay indoors,' she explained and Walter was satisfied.

She rode out of the yard, trotted through the village, nodding to acquaintances, then eased the reins and let the mare have her head to canter. It was a glorious day and she sat straight, savouring her beloved countryside. She rarely went into Bristol if she could help it. She decided she had become a genuine rustic.

Sarah did not hurry. She was having one of those gentle, soothing rides which settles the nerves and restores harmony to the spirit. At the top of the high land, she walked her mare then, looking ahead, she frowned with puzzlement. How odd, troops around, but why? She rode up, then halted as one lifted a hand imperiously.

'Good morning, ma'am. Who are you? Where are you from and where are you going?' he asked stiffly.

Sarah knew better than to take offence. Soldiers only did their duty, especially ordinary rank troopers.

'I am Mistress Penford from Yate village, on

193

a pure pleasure ride as it is such a gorgeous day,' she explained gently, then, fumbling in her tunic, she produced the pass James had given her years ago. The soldier examined it carefully, looked up at her, memorised her face, dress and mare, then handed the pass back. This lady was who she said, he was satisfied.

'Have you seen anyone on your ride, ma'am?'

Sarah shook her head. 'Not a soul since I left my village. Why? Is anything wrong?'

'No, mistress. We have simply been posted here to pick up any Royalist strays from the Battle of Worcester. We are taking all the military prisoners possible to get information. If we capture Prince Charles then that will be a very fine thing.'

Will it, Sarah asked herself? And will you execute this one too without a proper trial?

'He has vanished?' she asked innocently. She was never one to miss a chance to grab information. What was good enough for John Thurloe was also fine for Sarah Penford.

'He made his escape, damn him, after Worcester. Once he realised he had lost, he went but we'll get him,' the soldier growled. 'If you do intend riding straight ahead, ma'am, I think I should warn you, you'll shortly come across a convoy of wounded men. They will have top priority on all the tracks.'

'Of course,' Sarah agreed instantly.

'But remember though, ma'am, there will also be Royalists on the run and they may still be trigger-happy. You can use that pistol I hope?'

Sarah threw him a hard look. 'I can and I'm very accurate as well, as it happens.'

She nodded her head politely and rode on but the sparkle had gone from the day. She tossed up whether to return home in a large circle, then, annoyed, decided not to. Why should she? It was her land too.

She rode for another mile before pulling off the track to study the slow moving convoy. There were mounted men, walking wounded, and others who lay in carts. These jolted heavily on ruts and the men groaned or screamed their agonies. She bit her lip, feeling depressed at the spectacle. This was the other side of war. Not the glory of battle which men ranted on about. The escorting officer galloped over and halted with a flurrying jingle of chains. He studied her sombre face.

'Wounded men from the Battle of Worcester, ma'am,' he explained, turning in his saddle.

'Do they all go to Bristol?' Sarah asked him. The sounds were appalling and made her blood chill.

'They'll go to a hospice first, then to their homes, if they can,' he told her bluntly. 'Some will leave their bones in Bristol though,' and he nodded at a passing cart. 'Two of 'em in there are gut shot, pardon my language, ma'am.'

'You can't . . . ?' Sarah began and, of course, knew no one could. A pistol ball in the stomach or abdomen was fatal. 'Couldn't you at least give them something for their pain?'

The officer pulled a face. 'Nothing left to give,' he told her bluntly. 'They'll have to wait until we reach the city.'

'But those men at the rear are not wounded,' she said, pointing.

He flashed his teeth at her. 'Prisoners,' he grunted with satisfaction, 'all for interrogation so we can find that damned Prince Charles and finish the Royalists, once and for all.'

If they will talk, Sarah told herself. Great loyalty could make for stubborn tongues even with torture. She gave a deep sigh, depressed again. The prisoners stumbled past in tattered clothing, heads low, spirits even lower. Had these men once been proud, gaily dressed cavaliers? It seemed totally impossible. Now they appeared to be nothing but the dregs of society. Her heart went out to them and to all prisoners. Oh, she told herself. War is so stupid. Why can't men see this? Even animals only fought for the practicalities of food, a mate or home territory.

She turned off and rode at a slow canter, thinking deeply about what she had seen. James would have a different point of view. He would gloat at the prisoners. He would be the

196

first to chase after Prince Charles and Thurloe? She gave a tiny shudder. There was something about the man's name that chilled her. Why couldn't James break away from him and immerse himself in their business with Robert? She suspected why. He enjoyed working for Thurloe. In pitting his wits against the enemy, James thrived. Would to God something could happen which would make him change his viewpoint.

She crested a slope. She had been riding parallel to the track which fringed deep, unfriendly woods. How far they extended she had no idea; she was not too familiar with this region. The land crested downwards with a small stream at the bottom. This would be a good place to eat, then she knew her appetite had gone. The wounded men had done that.

Her eyes spotted movement and she stilled and concentrated then relaxed as she realised it was but two figures. A man and a woman sat by the stream's bank. Both of them were bathing their feet in the fast running water. She walked her mount down, intending to offer a brief greeting then water the mare and ride on elsewhere.

She saw the man had removed his hose and, with feet in the cold water, seemed to be experiencing an exhilarating sensation. He had long, spindly legs with puffed ankles. As she neared, it was easy to see a huge blister on one heel and the man looked at it ruefully.

197

Obviously he was unused to walking great distances. The woman appeared to be much younger and, with a piece torn from her underskirt, bathed the man's feet and ankles.

Neither of them heard the mare's silent passage on the springy turf. Then both turned and started, looking up at her quickly. Was that alarm in the man's eyes and why did the woman glare with such blatant hostility? Rude people, Sarah thought, deciding to ride more to the left to water her mare. Then she changed her mind. The man's face was haggard and he seemed tense and even frightened.

'Are you all right?' Sarah asked gently.

The woman glared, vibrating bellicosity but Sarah ignored her pointedly. The man regarded her thoughtfully, eyes narrow with unspoken questions.

She stared back at him. His face was ruddy and glowed from his exertions. He wore a leather jerkin and on his head was a battered felt hat. The woman was equally dishevelled. Her gown was torn on one side, wet and muddy at its hem. 'Thank you, but myself and my niece are resting,' the man replied at last, his voice mellifluous.

Sarah's ears pricked at the accent that was unusual to her. She guessed right away they were poor refugees from Worcester but her sharp ear also caught something else and she frowned slightly. She was not wholly familiar

198

with the Midlands' accents, but something told her that this man's speech was unnatural. It held the inflexion to a vowel denoting it was both laboured and false. Sharp instinct jabbed. This was no ordinary man. This was some senior officer, in disguise, struggling from defeat at Worcester.

'Where are you from?' she asked kindly.

The man never hesitated. 'From Worcester,' he replied evenly, as if this had been told before. 'Our home was demolished by guns and we were lucky to escape with out lives. We travel south now to join distant family.'

Sarah nodded to herself Her suspicions were correct; this story was told just a little too pat. Then the woman stepped forward boldly. Her antagonism vanished. 'We are hungry. Do you have any food to spare?'

The man frowned but stayed silent though, Sarah noticed, his eyes gleamed with hope. She dismounted swiftly and turned to her saddlebags. Was it her imagination but had fear flashed into the man's cyes? The woman though was suddenly more open. She licked her lips as Sarah opened her saddlebags, removing her lunch, handing it over to the woman quietly.

'Oat cakes, some bread, cheese and wine,' she explained. 'You are welcome to all. I'm not hungry now,' she told them without going into why her appetite had vanished.

The woman hugged the food as if it were

199

gold, then passed it to the man without hesitation. Sarah watched with amazement. It was the man who divided the food meticulously while the woman watched, her eyes wide with hope.

The man passed the woman her portion but, although obviously very hungry, she waited. He flashed her some kind of look and, only then did they both eat at the same time. She noted meticulous manners, slow eating until every crumb was gone. The man passed the flask to the woman who refused until he had drunk.

An odd something prodded at Sarah as the strange couple beamed their thanks at her. From the way they had eaten, Sarah realised both had been famished. It was providential for them that she had ridden this way.

The man stood and Sarah was stunned at his height. His body was lean, with no trace of fat. Once more he drank, then insisted the woman finish the wine. Their manners had been so dainty and refined, the suspicion enlarged but she said nothing. The man returned the empty flask to her, his eyes bright and twinkling, with sharp intelligence.

'Mistress, a thousand thanks. We were both very hungry indeed,' then he paused to stare at her thoughtfully before he continued. 'You may not know what you have done but I will tell you, this good deed of yours today will never be forgotten.'

Sarah knew. Those careful good manners, even though starving; his refined speech now with all trace of an accent wiped away. His height, general poise and assurance. Very carefully Sarah turned to look around but they were alone. She turned back to the man, smiled gently and slowly gave a graceful curtsey. Her eyes never left those of the man. His twinkled in return and he gave a gentle nod with his head, while a slow, warm smile crept over his face. Then he moved forward and took her hands in his own. He stank of dirt and sweat, his ragged dress was disgusting but nothing could hide a natural, courtly manner. He stood looking down at her, strong, unafraid and very dignified.

'I would like to know the name of a kind lady who stopped, fed two very hungry people and who asked not one question afterwards,' he said gently.

Sarah blushed. 'I am Mistress Penford from the village of Yate. My husband James has a partnership in a spice business,' she replied, then hesitated. What she had said was true, but it was only half a story.

The man knew something had been withheld. With a twitch of his lips he spoke again. 'Where did your husband stand in the wars, Mistress?'

Sarah did not hesitate now. 'He was a Captain for Parliament,' she told him with quiet firmness, 'and indeed, he works now at an activity from which I am precluded. I ask no questions so I can tell you nothing as I am ignorant,' she replied thoughtfully. 'And even if I did know, I doubt I'd tell you because I love him very much and a man must do what his conscience dictates. A wife can also do this,' she finished with a wide grin.

'What would your husband say if he knew about today's encounter?' the Prince wanted to know next.

'He would be thrown into a proper state!' Sarah laughed. 'But he'll learn nothing from me. I am a grown woman, a mother, and a landowner in my own right. When I married it was never to become a man's chattel. I have a mind and will of my own and I do exactly as I choose as long as this does not go against the laws of the country or damage my husband and family.'

'Well answered, Mistress Penford,' the Prince replied and chuckled. 'It's people like you who give me heart and hope again, especially after Worcester.' He turned, beckoned to the woman and flashed her some silent order. She obeyed instantly and fumbled in a small pouch that was held by a cord around her neck. Sarah had never guessed she had anything there because it was hidden under a dirty, coarse top. It struck Sarah it was exactly in this place she too had carried so many messages all those years ago. Only those vital ones had rested in her body's other more secret hiding passage. There was no doubt but female breasts could have more uses than one.

Something passed from the woman's hand to his. He closed his fingers as if, from feel, he could identify the object, then he opened his hand and gave it to her. It was a small gold medallion with the royal crest at the top. There was a tiny, thin loop so that the object could be worn, hidden or clipped to a shirt.

'You are generous, sir,' Sarah said, smiling with pride, taking his gift. She guessed this Prince did not have much left to pass over to anyone if he meant to escape, survive and fight again another day.

'No, I'm not,' he contradicted firmly. 'You could have ridden by and not stopped. You could have galloped away for soldiers. You did neither. You . . . helped!'

'Oh!' Sarah gasped. 'I nearly forgot, sir, do not go up this slope. There is a patrol over the crest about two miles away. They are looking for you. I suggest you move in that direction,' she pointed. 'There are some thick woods with a track which appears to run their length. I don't know where it goes I'm afraid but I doubt soldiers would wait there.'

Prince Charles bit his lip and his expression became stern. Then he looked down at his swollen ankles. 'I'm not used to long walks,' he said, trying to make a feeble joke.

Sarah bit her lip. 'I dare not let you have my horse,' she said slowly, anxious not to appear

203

mean. 'She is my special mare and just a little too well known. Also, she is getting old and I doubt whether she could carry two.'

'I see,' he murmured. 'Troops looking for me,' and he managed a lop-sided grin. 'Well, if they want me, first of all they have to catch me!'

'I would suggest you and your companion get into the woods as quickly as you can. There are soldiers everywhere,' she said and informed him about the wounded convoy. She continued to hold his gift in her hand, suddenly deeply troubled.

He sensed her agitation. 'You don't like it?' he asked, nodding at his medallion.

'Oh yes, it's lovely but . . .' Sarah halted and looked deep into his eyes. 'I think it's only right you should know I was a courier for Parliament when Prince Rupert held Bristol. My work all aided his and your father's defeat. Do you still want me to have this?'

Prince Charles smiled gravely. 'Not only are you kind and generous but also brave and honest. If God had seen to give my poor father more fighters like you, then he might be alive today. However, be that as it may, far too many Englishmen have died for my liking and the load upon my back is great. I will come and take up my crown. It's mine by lawful inheritance and have it I will but when . . .?' He shook his head. 'Who knows? It might take years.' He stopped and looked into the

204

distance then his gaze rested on Sarah again. 'If you had such strong Parliamentary sympathies that you worked against my father, why have you helped me?' he asked with frank curiosity.

Sarah could not help but give a snort of annoyance. 'I did not work as I did, taking risks with my life, to live now under what is turning into nothing but a dictatorial regime. It's always us ordinary people who are at the receiving end of things with no redress whatsoever. We cannot do this, that or the other because of what a handful of men say in London and it appears it is going to get worse. What kind of a life are we going to have, sir?' she snapped, nostrils flaring indignantly.

The Prince chuckled. 'What a warrior you would have made!' then he became very serious. 'Do you think there are many like you?'

Sarah realised this was an important question. She considered thoughtfully. 'Perhaps not right now. It's just all hot air grumbles but you know we English are inclined to take rather a long time to stir into action. I think though, if matters become worse, as I predict they will, eventually there will be a groundswell of opinion against Parliament. It won't happen this year, or even next. I can't guess when it will happen but happen it will in the future,' she replied and eyed him carefully. 'Whatever you plan to do.

sir, should have a long-term aim. At the moment, Parliament and Cromwell are simply too strong but Cromwell cannot live for ever.'

'He has a son, Richard!'

Sarah paused. 'I know nothing about him,' she said slowly, 'but unless he has his father's calibre and can control the Puritans, then that will be the time for you to act. It might mean a long wait though,' she ended quietly.

He considered her words. They rang with truth and only confirmed his own suspicions. He gave a great sigh. 'I have time,' he told her, 'and I have patience, but what I don't have is either the will or the wish to see more Englishmen die fighting each other. That I abhor.'

Sarah threw another look around. They were still alone but she knew this could not last.

'I think you should move, sir, and get into those woods,' she told him, pointing. 'Who knows when more soldiers might not appear and what I can guess, so might others.'

'Wise words,' the Prince said, and flashed another of his looks at the woman who had remained totally silent. She moved, gathering up his hose and he sat down to put them on. Sarah watched him, then mounted the mare and looked down at them both.

'I'll ride back up to that crest. If it's still safe I'll wave. If no wave then you must try and save yourselves, somehow,' she offered. It was all she could do under the circumstances. With another polite duck of her hand, she spun the mare around and rode briskly for the top of the crest, looked around with great thoroughness, then, standing in her stirrups, waved back down to him. For a few seconds she watched the couple start to trudge in the direction she had indicated then, feeling happy and sad at the same time, she turned to ride home. Prince Charles Stuart had given her much to think about.

CHAPTER TEN

James was puzzled. It had all started after his return home following the Royalists' latest defeat at Worcester. Sarah had, as always, been delighted to see him and their lovemaking that night had been passionate and long-lasting. He could never get enough of her after his absences but, afterwards, when they lay, his arm around her, he had sensed a subtle difference.

During his week's home leave, he watched his wife surreptitiously. She often had spells when she was distant, sometimes even to the point where she stood and stared blankly at the wall. He was an astute man and, having lived by his wits for many years, he was also a shrewd guesser. This time though he was baffled. He knew better than to ask an outright question. Sarah was exceedingly touchy about her privacy and independence and, he had to admit, she never once questioned him. Twice he felt pique. If Sarah had a problem why couldn't she share it with him? Two heads were always better than one. On the other hand, what could there be to arouse such distraction? He was baffled, confused and just a fraction alarmed.

After one brief trip into Bristol to see a political contact, about whom Sarah knew nothing, he found her, again, absorbed in heavy thoughts. That evening, they sat together on their settee, quietly companionable but James wondered how much of her attention was present. It was not that their domestic atmosphere was heavy, but rather foggy. He decided to tell her what he could of an incident which amused him and which also aroused his admiration.

'Here, seen this?' he asked, knowing perfectly well she could not have.

Sarah studied the poster, her eyes opening wide with surprise then she bent her head to read.

WANTED

One thousand pounds reward for the recapture of Charles Stuart who is a long, dark man above two yards high and who is

**thought to be wearing an old, felt hat, a
leather jerkin and green breeches.
Thought to be accompanied by a female.
Capable of imitating local accents.**

'Well!' Sarah gasped while her mind raced.
The description was so accurate. Who had
told? She made herself reread the poster,
aware James was studying her face. He was so
quick and sharp; it would never do for him to
realise she had met the Prince and even helped
him. She managed not to swallow as a wave of
nerves consumed her, because, during the past
few days, Sarah had finally reached a
momentous decision. When she remembered
her courier work, she recalled how she had
lived with excitement, thrill and risk. Now she
knew she was so bored that, without some
other interest, her marriage could become
stale, despite her love for James. There was
more to marriage than bed. Yet how did she
start to work for the other side? It had been
easy before. James had made the subtle
arrangements.

Her mind had swiftly gone to her husband.
She would be putting herself in the opposite
camp, yet, why shouldn't she? James was, in
many ways, as bigoted for Parliament as the
Puritans were for their religion. He had
anathema against royalty and monarchs that,
at times, was totally unreasonable. Her mind
had considered possible allies, all of whom had

209

been dismissed. Walter had always been James' man. Robert was a puzzle. His early experiences had left him a silent, deep individual. She loved him dearly and knew this was reciprocated but, with him, she had always felt there were some subjects best not discussed. The Pair, of course, were quite apolitical. She guessed there were village inhabitants whose loyalties were against Parliament but she knew none in depth. Also, her early work had taught her to be secretive for her personal safety. She stifled a sigh of exasperation. She must think about all this again and not in front of James.

'That's an awful lot of money,' she managed to get out at last.

James had been studying her, baffled. She had a secret from him! He was amused and also hurt again. Rack his brains as he might, he could think of nothing important enough to drive his darling wife into such frequent, brown studies.

'What's happening in the country now?' she asked, turning to give him her full attention; all problems swept away temporarily.

James decided to play this irritating game her way. He'd find out in due course, he told himself.

'Well,' he drawled, 'Prince Charles has made a fool of us!' That held Sarah's immediate attention. She sat up straighter, frowning. 'What do you mean?'

210

'He has run rings around Parliament,' he told her, then had to grin. There was nothing he admired and respected more than audacity. 'We've now found out most of the details though I expect there'll always be gaps left we'll never fill. After Worcester, the Prince escaped to spend the first night up an oak tree, of all places. The local squire, Colonel Lane helped him.'

'How do you know?' Sarah asked quickly. Would he answer?

James gave a discreet cough. 'We questioned him,' he told her, then shook his head. 'No, it was not torture, more I should say, a bit of bragging on his part! The Prince acquired a passport in the name of William Jackson and a girl, Jane Ludd, went with him as companion and guide.'

A girl, Sarah asked herself? That was superb disguise then. She had thought her middle-aged. 'What happened?'

'He headed for Bristol and we know he had help but the names are a mystery,' James replied coolly. He knew perfectly well, even with no fighting, the English would take sides, as always. 'We had Bristol's outskirts ringed, thick with troops but he still managed to slip through. He went down to Abbots Leigh and . . .'

Sarah interrupted. '*Of course* ordinary people helped him. Many did not hold with his father's farce of a trial to say nothing of his

211

execution,' she said, then wished she'd kept her mouth shut. Had she sounded too anti-Parliament?

James gave her a long, thoughtful look. He was not unduly perturbed at her hot words because he'd heard them in numerous other places. He too had disliked the situation and made his feelings felt, but to no avail.

'Charles Stuart worked his way down to Lyme then Southampton and finally Charmouth, hunting for a Continental ship. Now here comes the bit I do admire. He had time on his hands so went to church. He had the cool nerve to sit and listen to the parson rant on about him. The sermon said that help in his capture would obtain merit for them all with the Almighty.'

Sarah pealed with laughter. She could picture the scene after meeting the man. 'Go on,' she chuckled again.

'Then, if you don't mind, he took lodgings at the best inn where we had forty of our soldiers staying. That takes guts of the highest order.'

Sarah did not miss the admiration in his voice. Later she must test him again. 'And?'

'He called himself Barlow while at the inn and left it, roaming to Stonehenge and Shoreham. He's probably seen more of the country than me,' James mused before he continued. 'He did eventually find a ship. He had also acquired a small coterie of like-

212

minded followers. They told the ship's captain they were merchants in debt.'

'Did he believe them?'

James nodded. 'Captain Tattershall, with whom we have also had a few words, did believe him. Why shouldn't he? He demanded sixty pounds payment in advance plus another two hundred guineas as insurance. They paid him, so Charles Stuart sailed merrily off to France, and there he can stay and kick his heels as far as I'm concerned.'

Sarah did not miss this. 'Why hate him still? I think he has shown himself a brave and resourceful man.'

'That's as maybe,' James told her firmly, 'but he is still a prince and wants to be a king.'

'Oh, James. You are getting hidebound!' Sarah told him gently.

He thought about this then gave a little nod. 'Probably so, because I've seen just too many good men killed. It's not something a man can ever forget, especially when they have been fellow countrymen. There is nothing in this world worse than civil wars,' he told her in a hard voice.

Sarah knew better than to debate or argue. This was something quite beyond her ken and she could imagine how such scenes and losses could turn a man's viewpoint into something quite inflexible. On the other hand, there was the other point of view. She decided to test him out.

213

'I don't like the way our life has changed,' she began smoothly. 'We are not allowed to celebrate Easter, Whitsuntide or any other festivals. The last Wednesday in each month has to be a Fast day. What rubbish! And what kind of country do we now have when soldiers and even constables are allowed to force their way into private homes, snooping? Do you realise it is now an offence for two sweethearts to take a walk together on Sunday? Then there is no cleaning, no fires to be lit on Sundays, no this, that and the other. What about the cows to be milked on Sundays? Look at how many soldiers Parliament is employing to do all this spying. Look how people's amusements are banned! No stage, bowls or football; no one to use the maypole; no cards or dice why, I could go on and on. Is this what you fought for? Be honest, James?'

No, he told himself, it certainly was not but it was normal for a pendulum to swing too far in the opposite direction before it stabilised.

'No, I didn't,' he told her frankly, then looked deep into her eyes, 'but we must all give it time, Sarah. Even Rome was not built in one day. You mark my words, it will all come right in the end.'

It won't, Sarah added to herself as her heart sank low. James was as adamant as ever. He would never change, so now her views opposed his? Certainly she must keep them very secret, as he kept matters from her, and always had done. She was glad she knew where he stood as her resolve crystallised. If there was anything she could do to break this Puritan stranglehold, then do it she would. Any reckoning could be dealt with later, but she knew she could not live with herself if she sat back and did nothing. Her heart ached for James and his blindness but she said exactly nothing. However, remembering the past, she continued to probe but more delicately now. Information was never wasted, no matter what kind.

'What is Cromwell really like?' she asked softly.

James paused to sort his thoughts out. 'I like him,' he said thoughtfully. 'He is a brilliant army man and he has to juggle the army against the Puritan faction. Cromwell himself is very sincere with his beliefs and what he wants for the Commonwealth, as he prefers to call England. Don't forget also that he has to follow the advice of a Council of State. He is, personally, a very tolerant man. He's allowed all the Jews to return and he's said that Roman Catholics and Anglicans can still follow their religion, in all their forms, as long as this is done privately. He's not interfered with other eccentric Sects either.'

Sarah shot her question at him as he paused for breath. 'But is he a good civilian leader?'

James was unsure but had no intention of admitting this. There was so much he could

215

not tell Sarah. Not for the first time, he wondered whether he had been wise to continue working for John Thurloe. It was not as if he really liked the master spy. They merely rubbed along because of their identical beliefs. Yet it was not easy to make the break. Thurloe's arm was exceedingly long.

'If I approached you to be a courier now, Sarah, would you?'

She did not hesitate. 'No!'

'Do you resent my connections?' he asked quietly.

Sarah pulled a face. 'Of course I do,' she said firmly, 'but you must do just as you think fit even if we might disagree,' as she now knew they did. 'When can you leave that man though?'

'When my work is finished,' he said and swiftly debated how much to say. 'If Charles Stuart intends to live on the Continent for a while, he has to be watched. He has little money, we know. He will eventually be forced to sell jewellery and he might even be reduced to penury. On the other hand, there are still far too many sympathisers in England who could send him funds.'

That's enough, James warned himself. Even those limited words would arouse Thurloe's wrath because Thurloe rarely talked to anyone. Certainly his right hand never knew where the left would move.

'As you seem to have become antagonistic to

216

Parliament, I'll tell you no more,' he told her, but not unkindly.

Sarah bridled. 'You don't trust me?' she said archly.

He threw her a wry grin. 'I never did,' he replied honestly. 'I trust no one.'

'Not even Martin, when he lived?'

'Certainly not and you can take it from me, it was mutual. It's the only way to survive because espionage is a dirty business.'

This did shock Sarah but also showed her how to act. Circumspection was not enough. Total secrecy was vital. She averted her gaze and leaned back in his arms. Doubt assailed her. Did she really want to get involved in something so morbidly secret? Then it occurred to her she had no contacts, so how could she? Perhaps she was letting her imagination run away with her. Dear God, was she going mad through inertia and boredom?

The next morning, James made one of his mysterious departures, simply kissing her, smiling wanly with a shrug of his shoulders, then was gone. Sarah wandered idly through her home, getting in the way of The Pair, peering in at the children with their private tutor, and, finally, deciding to ride.

She had a new horse that Jack had brought on. A sixteen-hands gelding because the mare was getting old as was James' stallion. She rode out of the yard and headed towards open countryside. The prospect of a gallop lifted her spirits. She nodded to the villagers whom she knew and was surprised to see a stranger loitering not far from her home. Remembering Fletcher, she felt a twinge of alarm but dismissed it. She was armed, as always.

Sarah threw a snap look at the man. He was dressed in the dark, sober clothes the Puritans preferred their citizens to wear. His hair was cropped short and his whole person was neat with black coat and breeches topped with a crisp, white shirt. She thought how dreary he looked and then eyed her own sober dark green riding skirt and jacket. Oh for some gay ribbons and fancy lace. Damn the Puritans, she thought yet again.

She threw him a nod before pushing into a brisk canter, moving easily but not with a light heart. She was still so confused and uncertain. She heard a thunder of hooves and the stranger drew alongside.

'Good morning,' he said politely.

Sarah muttered a curse. She wished to ride alone. Now what did he want?

A number of the village houses had lodgers. This must be one of them. She hoped he would go away and very quickly.

'I know you are Mistress Penford,' the man said and threw her a sharp look.

'What if I am?' she asked ungraciously.

He was not at all disconcerted. 'My name is Simon Forrest.' He introduced himself and, with his reins in his left hand, he extended his

218

right with palm open. Sarah looked over and caught her breath with amazement. The small medallion was not of gold, like hers, but otherwise quite identical. 'I was instructed to show you this.'

Sarah pulled on the reins and halted her horse. She gave the man a long, thoughtful stare, eyes wary with suspicion. 'Where did you get that?' she challenged.

'From the same source as you received yours except the metal of mine is not of the same quality,' he told her smoothly.

Sarah was taken aback. Her recent muddied thinking had never anticipated anything like this. 'What do you want?' she barked at him, one hand hovering near her pistol meaningfully.

'That is my correct name though I admit to using others at times,' he told her quietly. He did not miss where her hand lay and he became wary. He had already deemed it prudent to make a few enquiries of his own and he now knew this was no lady to trifle with. 'You helped Prince Charles when he needed it badly. He gave you his token; like mine. Now I am to contact you to see if your sympathies still lie in the same direction. The Prince is a most thorough man. He also has an excellent memory for names,' he hinted.

She picked her words with extreme care. 'I understood the Prince was ensconced on the Continent?'

'That he is,' Forrest agreed pleasantly. 'He still wants to know though who is for or against him. Have you changed your mind, lady?'

Sarah slowly shook her head. 'No, I've not,' she admitted, 'but Parliament is extremely strong and I can never imperil my family.'

'We'd not want you to do more than establish a connection with a contact and help us through the family spice business.'

Sarah was astonished. 'What do you mean?'

'For the future!'

'Don't talk in riddles!'

'Let me explain then,' he continued calmly. 'It is true Parliament is strong and Cromwell also, even though it's also common knowledge his health is not the best. That situation though cannot be expected to continue forever and one day there will be a change. We want a place where messages can come into England and to be passed on to the right people. Your firm deals with ships from the West Indies, the Spice Islands and even India, to say nothing of the Continent. You have a half share. Your adopted son works in Bristol. We would like to infiltrate one of our men into this firm. A man in a position to extract a message and pass it on.'

Sarah was stunned with the simplicity of it all. 'What about this contact?'

'It would be helpful for you to establish a relationship with a trusted courier of ours for, say, emergencies? But your husband is

Cromwell's man, isn't he?'

Sarah flared up immediately. 'He was a soldier. He's just a salesman now, travelling around for the firm,' she invented rapidly.

Forrest read her instant agitation. 'No harm will ever come to a man doing that,' he told her. 'Are you game?'

Sarah made her decision and tumbled off the centre of the post from where she had been sitting indecisively. She had to help make a better England for her children and just hope that one day James would see sense.

'I will,' she replied firmly.

He beamed at her. 'That's splendid! And no harm to your family ever!' he promised. 'Now one day, in the near future, you will be given a verbal address. We want you to go there and you'll be shown an identical medallion as proof of loyalty. This will be your only contact. As to the other, you will also be given the name of someone whom we would like employed in the spice firm.'

Sarah touched lips that had suddenly gone dry. Now it was upon her, action instead of mere thoughts, her blood stirred with excitement and apprehension. She gave a little swallow then, eyes glowing, threw him a grin. Quite suddenly, what had been a miserable day to start with now throbbed with anticipation. Thank God James was away so he could not read her new mood.

James took a deep drink from the tankard, stretched his booted feet before the fire and eyed his companion. He had been startled when the discreet knock at his door had been followed by the immediate entrance of an apparent stranger. The disguise was superb and, for a second, he had been caught flat-footed.

The other finished reading James' neatly written report, compiled with meticulous accuracy. 'Good,' Thurloe grunted, 'concise and to the point. I wish I had more men like you. Are you satisfied though?'

James considered before he replied. Although he had worked for Thurloe for so long, he realised he did not know the man. Who did, he asked himself ironically? There was not even a vestige of friendship, for which James was thankful. 'Yes and no,' he replied. 'Charles Manning and John Lane are nicely placed in Charles Stuart's court, if that is what it can be called. Neither of them knows of the other's existence. Each thinks they work alone, though it might pay to put Lane more in the picture.'

'Why?' Thurloe barked. Penford was an enigma to him. There were times when he could not reach him; his mind was too devious yet he had a brilliance quite unequalled at this work.

'I think he happens to be the better man,' James told him quickly. 'He's more in control of himself. He doesn't panic easily and he would be a hard one to break.'

'You don't think this of Manning then?'

James shrugged. 'He's a good average agent but only that. Better than most, but it's often crossed my mind to wonder how he'd hold out under interrogation.'

Thurloe considered that. 'They're being paid a thousand a year so they'd better come up with the goods,' he grumbled, but more to himself. Natural French speakers were still thin on the ground and Manning was excellent in that tongue. Better even than Lane or Penford, come to that.

'What about Willis?' James asked quietly.

Thurloe gave him a wolfish leer. 'That was one of my better moves,' he admitted with pleasure. 'As you will know, Sir Richard Willis was a devoted Royalist when Governor of Newark and the best thing King Charles did was to fall out with him after we took Bristol.'

'Because he just happened to be Prince Rupert's close pal?'

Thurloe confirmed this with a nod. 'King Charles never forgave Rupert for losing Bristol so his friends became tainted with the same brush.'

James had managed to work this one out for himself but it was always nice to get an answer confirmed. This was the first time Thurloe had unbent enough to confide in him. Dare he hope the man might be mellowing?

'Willis was approached, I'm not saying by whom and, after a bit of talking, we managed to get him to agree to stay a Royalist but act for us too.'

James gave a snort. 'I don't trust turned men,' he grated. 'They can be treble as well as double agents.'

'True,' Thurloe conceded, 'but money talks a pretty strong language to someone like Willis who just about bled himself dry for the King. Naturally, I don't trust him one iota but use him I will.'

Neither will I trust him, James thought grimly. He knew Thurloe would never betray an agent but neither, on the other hand, could he ever trust even his own shadow. He was simply too deeply involved with spying. James often thought all his natural instincts had long been smothered with the urgent need for total secrecy at all times. He guessed that in Thurloe's famous black book would also be lodged names and details of all double and treble agents as well as Royalists who turned for pure, financial gain, not political beliefs.

Thurloe eyed Penford, alias Hawkins. He was one of his best, if not the most excellent agent he had. He admitted that, on the rare occasions he talked, it could only be to someone like James Penford.

'I've been hearing other bits and pieces of

news too,' he began, and James stiffened with expectation. 'Some of the younger sons of the aristocracy might try to make trouble for us later on. I've heard rumbles about a society they might form. It's to be called the Sealed Knot society.'

'With a view to an uprising?' James asked with interest.

Thurloe grunted. 'If it conies about, the fools won't get far. I know every thought and action,' he laughed but no smile reached his cold eyes.

'Any idea who would be the figurehead?' James wanted to know.

Thurloe had to ponder at that. 'I would guess either Penruddock, Grove or perhaps both of them acting together.'

James turned these names over in his mind. Thurloe seemed unconcerned which indicated any potential aristocratic rebellion would never get off the ground. He almost felt sorry for the aspirations of these young men. Why couldn't they accept such a cause was wasted time, energy and lives?

'I understand Edward Hyde chose exile with Prince Charles so he's safely out of the way but what about Monk, sir?'

'Ah! Yes! Monk!' Thurloe said slowly, this time with an edge to his voice. 'Now that man really does puzzle me. Although I agree he sides with us now, I often wonder whether he is a soldier first or a Royalist. After we captured him, I was amazed that he became a Parliamentarian, so trust him, never! What's his game?'

James knew something of this officer. 'I don't think he has it in him to go in for dual roles.'

'That's as maybe. Monk is one whom I watch very closely,' Thurloe said. 'There is another man whose name you should have. Simon Forrest.'

James was surprised. He had never met the man but he knew of him. He had also heard of his Royalist views which, though discreet, were known to those who mattered.

'What about him, sir?'

'He's been seen in your area,' Thurloe replied bluntly.

James was startled at that. 'What, when?'

Thurloe continued. 'And knowing him, he's not there just to take in the scenery either. I have my suspicions that, in a very quiet, tactful way, he is sounding out opinion; trying to find those who would support a King Charles II. Although we know most of the people who helped the Prince escape from Worcester, we do not have every name, more's the pity. Where ordinary people helped, it was easy for them to vanish into obscurity again. It's these people, the majority of them commoners, who bother me. I don't like such unknowns. I want names and details in my black book. Get 'em!'

James ran this startling thought around his

226

mind. 'I wonder if he's setting something up for a Bristol insurrection?'

Thurloe threw him a short nod with a cold glower. 'Of course he is and I want to know everything. It's your backyard. Find out for me.'

'On the other hand, he might just be back tracking the Prince's escape route to tidy up any loose ends,' James suggested. 'Charles Stuart is nobody's fool. He'll have memorised names then, later, notated them. We do know he took a list with him to France but where this is hidden, your guess is as good as mine. He might even have memorised the list, then destroyed it.'

Thurloe's mind worked elsewhere. 'I have a hunch that Forrest has been detailed to set up a line of communication with the Continent. He'll be picking operatives with connections, ordinary people, the most difficult to discover, who'll lie low until needed. Sleepers.'

'Very hard to trace,' James murmured. 'Where was he last seen and dressed how?'

'In Bristol, and he looked like any Puritan. He left the city by a north gate and my operative then lost him, the fool. We've not seen hide nor hair of him since but he's out there somewhere and not just exercising his horse.'

'Difficult!'

'You'll not be short of funds,' Thurloe added. 'I'll step up your expense account

227

because we both know money talks, long, loud and clear. Pay your informers above the normal rate to loosen tongues. I don't like to be away from the capital for too long. Cromwell's health is not what it might be and that son of his . . .' Thurloe's lips twisted scornfully.

'Tumbledown Dick?' James asked. He too had a very low opinion of Richard Cromwell whose idea of life was riding, hunting and hawking. Politics, business and work did not enter his head. 'He'll never make a leader without some drastic alteration.'

Thurloe's mind had reverted back to the original problem. 'I'll brief Willis. Someone might just let something slip if he has become our double agent but . . .'

James shook his head. 'I'll never rely on any information from him,' he said flatly. 'I don't trust those who change their colours so quickly.'

Thurloe gave a rare, deep sigh of frustration. Neither did he. If only there were more men available like Penford. His mind switched to something else. 'Cromwell's life might be in jeopardy too. He's not liked too much and I've heard rumbles of assassination threats from more than one quarter.'

'Who?'

'Many,' Thurloe told him. 'Secretaries, Anabaptists, Independents and Quakers to say nothing of Royalists. No one now knows where

Cromwell goes nor when. I've arranged a permanent bodyguard for him with armed sergeants in his coach at all times. He'll never use the same route twice either nor stay more than one night at lodgings.'

James was stunned. 'It's as bad as that?' He felt something cold touch him. He had worked, fought and risked his life to make the Commonwealth, the Republic of England, but now there was an evil cancer loose. He remembered Sarah's change of heart, her hot accusations. How many now thought like her? Was it him who was out of step? Then his resolve hardened. There would never be a king in the country again; there could not be when so much fine blood had been spilled. He gave a deep sigh and felt Thurloe's eyes on him.

'It's a bit of a bloody mess, isn't it, Penford? But we soldier on. Get the information I want and I don't care how you go about it. Just get it.'

CHAPTER ELEVEN

Robert felt frustrated. He felt a great internal urge for expansion because he could see vast potential. It was true their spices came into Bristol from many countries, yet he felt they could do better. The trouble was, Sarah and James, the majority shareholders, were both in a rut. More to the point, the two of them seemed involved in their own private worlds. It was true they listened to his views and considered them, but were far too cautious in his opinion.

He had grown into a strong man. He was not tall like James, whom he regarded as a fine big brother but he had enormous shoulders. When he reached his full growth, in his thirties, he would be bull strong. His dear Sarah, his surrogate mother, even though she was only six years his senior, would also discuss ideas with him yet, recently, she did nothing. She too appeared to be constantly lost in a small private world of her own.

'Can't you do or say something?' he asked.

Walter debated. Since the Fletcher affair, he and Robert had become close in a way that surprised both of them. They were friends, trusted each other, exchanged ideas and were drinking companions when Walter rode into Bristol. Walter fully approved of Robert. He was close-lipped, very much his own man, had picked himself a fine girl and was going places.

'And you want to go to sea, eventually?' he asked.

Robert nodded enthusiastically. 'My girl will wait, she understands. Also, I'm sure I can do more for the firm, especially going to India. We should take advantage of the East India Company's joint stock system now they trade as a corporation. The profits they distribute to shareholders will grow and grow, especially when Bombay comes under their influence. It's no good relying just on the West Indies and it takes a long time to sail to the Far East, the Spice Islands. There are spices in India that we should have. There's cardamom, turmeric, garam masala; there's cumin from the Mediterranean, coriander. Oh! There's fenugreek, chillies, which are the seed pod of the capsicum; so many spices for different foods but we are stuck on peppers and common spices. Different, hot foods can be made. And we are being hidebound. We are not adventurous enough,' he cried, beating a fist on his other palm.

Walter knew Robert was talking over his head but he could understand his annoyance. 'The ports are certainly open now for all shipping,' he agreed thoughtfully, 'and a lot could be done but the business belongs to the partners. If you feel so strongly, why don't you invest your own savings in shares with the East India Company?'

'I'll probably end up doing just that. Sarah and James simply don't respond when I talk to them. It's as if they're both miles away with private thoughts.'

That was also accurate, Walter thought. His officer, as he still considered him, was at home only now and again, and Walter knew exactly what such absences meant. He was suddenly glad he was not asked to ride with James.

What did the future hold for England now? Walter had, over the long weeks, thought much about the past because it was from there the future was made.

There had been no repeat of his outburst, the solitary act that had driven two stubborn people together, but he often wondered uneasily how matters stood between them. With the master away so much, working obviously where and for whom, the Mistress had changed. She was even withdrawn with him, not quite so open and chatty, as if she nursed some problem. He was glad his home life was simple, yet he could not help but worry a little for these people whom he had grown to love like close family. Now here was Robert consumed and agitated.

'Invest your money as you think fit,' he advised. 'I'm not going to speak to anyone for you. It'd not be wise; more like interfering. Why don't you wait and see which way the wind blows in the near future. We live in times of great change.'

Robert eyed him. 'You mean politically. I don't like politics much,' he admitted slowly.

'You should do,' Walter chided. 'It's your life that's affected, like mine.'

Robert agreed he was correct but, ever since that sordid affair of Master Martin's death, he had felt squeamish reluctance to involve himself. There were still odd days when he wondered what had happened to his mother, especially after Fletcher's death under Sarah's mare. He supposed she was long dead too. As always, when his thoughts reached this gloomy point, a flashing vision of Jane Benson would, luckily, float into his mind. Today was the monthly day when Sarah normally rode into Bristol to see him. They might lunch together or simply stroll around or discuss spices.

Sarah was, at that moment, only two miles away, trotting along steadily. She supposed Bristol would be its usual, unpleasantly crowded city but, at least, the Parliamentarians had cleaned it up a bit, which was one credit point for them.

There were days now when Sarah vibrated with internal agitation. She was well aware that when home, James would, now and again cast her odd, long looks and she always struggled to be her old self. It was guilt though—the actual fact she had volunteered to place herself against him that made this so. It seemed to her his absences were far more prolonged than they used to be. Certainly she never knew when he would arrive home nor for how long. There were some days when she nearly despaired. It seemed that all her life her country had been engaged in political struggles, with never a true ending in sight.

As she neared the city gates, other riders and carts converged until her horse was slowed down to a very slow walk. A number of riders became grouped around her, leaving the left

233

side free for a procession of carts of various shapes and sizes.

One particular horse walked, shoulder to shoulder but, lost in thought, she never looked at the male rider.

'I thought you were never going to leave the village,' he said abruptly, in a low voice only she could possibly hear.

Sarah stiffened and shot a look at him. She had never seen him before in her life. His dress, that of some kind of journeyman, was strange to her and she presumed he was some artisan, looking for craft work in the city. She was puzzled though because she fancied his tone was a little familiar.

'You don't know me?' he asked.

Sarah bridled. Such impertinence. 'Should I?' she asked coldly.

'It's me, Mistress Penford, Forrest!'

Sarah's eyes opened wide with astonishment. She was flabbergasted. She certainly would not have known him. 'Well!' she gasped, too shocked to say more.

He grinned smugly. 'I thought the disguise was pretty good myself but not that brilliant.'

Sarah had to grin. He looked so pompously sure of himself, like a little boy who had scored a victory at some game. How naive males could be at times. They had neither subtlety nor artifice. She flashed a rapid look around but the stream of citizens ignored them; all intent on entering the city. Perhaps being

234

in such a noisy, good-humoured, chattering crowd was an ideal place for secrecy.

'What do you want?' she asked, but kept her voice low for the sake of prudence. She had learned much from James.

'I can't stop long,' Forrest told her, 'even in disguise. I'm going to pass you a slip of paper with a name and address. This is he whom we'd like you to slip into the spice firm. The man is an excellent clerk so I'm sure it would be quite natural for you to place him there. He will work hard and loyally for you. There is, on the back, another address who will be your Bristol contact. A person only ever knows one other, when we can arrange this, for security,' he explained.

Sarah did not enlighten him that she already understood such precautions. Was he trying to teach her to suck eggs? She felt a twitch of irritation that she hastily smothered. Here was the opportunity she wished for.

'The person at the second address will identify themselves with the medallion. They are completely trustworthy . . . to us.'

Forrest paused, then eyed her shrewdly. 'Prince Charles indicated you are not inexperienced at such work?'

Sarah's eyebrows elevated. Charles Stuart did indeed have a good memory. She said nothing though and waited for Forrest to continue.

'It might be helpful if you and the contact

can work something out whereby you meet on a regular monthly basis. In the event of emergency information, we trust you'd find an excuse to ride into Bristol with this. You'll always have the excuse of going to the business,' he added smoothly.

Sarah stared at him. Was it her imagination or did Forrest have something a little oily about him? Why did she feel a tiny prickle of something? Was her instinct and imagination working too hard? Yet, she remembered, James never ignored that which was natural. He called it gut-feeling. It had saved his life on more than one occasion. Perhaps, she rebuked herself, it was because she had been out of touch with such work for so many years. It might also be the fact that Forrest tried just a little too hard and was bombastically smug with it—attitudes which had always annoyed her.

'When you have memorised details, burn the paper,' Forrest told her just a shade too bumptiously.

'Don't try to give me lessons!' Sarah snapped back at him.

He realised he had antagonised her, and he knew all about her as well. He went to pull aside. Let the contact do the work. 'I leave now. I don't wish to enter the city,' then, abruptly, he swerved and was gone.

Sarah was taken aback at this abruptness. He moved into another sidling stream, before vanishing. Casting another swift look around, she opened the paper, read both sides, committed all to memory and, carefully, thoroughly, ripped the small paper into a myriad shreds. They fluttered down, immediately lost under hooves and boots.

Now excitement filled her and Sarah took a deep breath. So it had started. She felt just one, strong remorseful pang for James and pushed it away. She was her own woman too. She rode into their firm's yard, which backed on to a wharf. It was piled high with baled goods, recently landed and she saw Robert checking the import against a cargo manifest. Her heart warmed at the sight.

He turned and saw her, his handsome face breaking into a beaming grin of welcome. He thrust the list into a youth's hands, snapped some order at him and bounded over to her, all long arms and legs but with a torso, slowly filling out. She felt dwarfed by his width. Despite being a head shorter than James, he still gave the appearance of strength and power.

'Sarah!' he cried and enveloped her, almost making her ribs crack in a bear hug of delight. There was a wonderful rapport between them that had started on the day of Martin's murder. This had then been further nurtured after Robert's shooting and Fletcher's death. Sometimes Sarah wondered if her own son, Peter, would ever arouse in her the affection she had for this adopted son.

'Put me down, you great bear!' she laughed as he lifted then swung her around.

They chatted amiably for a while but Sarah sensed he was a little on edge. She was a good guesser.

'The East India Company?' she asked quietly.

'Yes!' he replied firmly. 'I was carrying onto Walter about it and how you and James are being stick-in-the-muds!' he teased but with an edge in his voice. 'Anyhow, I'm going to invest my savings, and yes, Jane agrees with me.' He paused to eye her mischievously. 'And I think her father might not be averse either.'

That made Sarah take notice. Although she considered Benson a typical, stuffy, slow-moving lawyer, she knew he was no fool. She had also learned he was cautious with money. Then another thought struck her. 'Walter here?' she repeated after him.

She knew the two were friends but how odd for him to ride in today. Was it coincidence? She gave herself a little shake. It had to be. Walter was as dedicated to Parliament as James; then a new thought flitted into her mind. Was it at all possible that Forrest was under scrutiny? If so, where did this leave her? Had they been seen together? She felt Robert's eyes on her and knew she must think about all this later. It would not do for her to go into a brown study before him. There were times when Robert could be every bit as discerning as James.

'Do you have enough workers here?' she asked, turning to look at the recently landed goods.

Robert shook his head. 'There's a mountain of paper work,' he admitted, 'which I hate doing anyhow. I want to be out there!' he said, nodding towards where the river went down to the sea. 'I want to sail to faraway places and see plants with my own eyes.'

Sarah knew the day was coming when he would up and go. He was of age. They had no right to stop him; then another interesting thought entered her mind. If Robert *was* away, sailing the seas on someone's vessel, any man she planted for Prince Charles would, if clever enough, have an open hand, without rousing suspicion.

'You and your old sea,' she teased, holding her breath. 'I might be able to help though. I've heard of a man who wants work and who is educated.'

Robert was all ears. He had a feeling there would be no objections when he sailed away to explore some of the world and a good man as manager, suitably supervised by Sarah, would give the perfect excuse.

Sarah continued, reading his mind only too well. 'His name is John Browne, with an "e" and he's lodging at the Golden Cock Inn while looking around.'

239

Robert made a snap decision. He had a hunch this was a blessing sent to order. 'I'll send a boy around right away, interview him and, if he's any good, he can start right away, on trial.'

'Then,' Sarah said slowly, 'you'll be on the first available ship. As what? Agent? Factor?'

He smiled tenderly. 'Either would do to start with.'

'Oh very well. You and your old sea. Serves you right if you get sea sick,' she teased, feeling fresh guilt. This was all going too smoothly to be true, because she knew Charles Stuart would never send her a dud man. Too much was at stake for him to slip up in any way. 'I hope Jane understands this wild urge.'

He flashed sparkling white teeth at her and she thought how she loved him. There were days when she forgot he was adopted. He was so much part and parcel of past life. 'She does!'

On this point, Sarah was dubious. She knew, only too well, how irksome and tedious home absences of a husband could be and sea voyages took months, sometimes even a year or more. Still, she reminded herself, that's their problem.

'I can't stay,' she told him gently. 'I have another call to make. If you go through my saddle bags you'll find some comfits The Pair have sent.'

He hastily opened his package and

immediately started chewing a ginger man. Then he carefully packed the saddle bags with the spices and peppers The Pair had become used to using. Sarah mounted, smiled down at him, then turned and headed forward. She had a rough idea of the other address and knew this was the most important part of the day. It was not often she came to the small village of Clifton and she took time to study the houses. They were a mixture of two- and three-storied ones, partly built from brick and almost on the old Elizabethan style. It was not a flashily rich area yet it was a long way from being poor.

She found the house, studied it, then slowly dismounted and tied her horse's reins to a post. It was a small property, but discreet; one which might have top quality boarders. Holding her long brown skirt up at one edge, she climbed two stone steps and banged a brass doorknocker.

The door was opened with a sharpness that told her she had been observed. The woman who faced her seemed incredibly old with a wrinkled face but she was clean, wholesome and dressed in the correct Puritan-coloured clothes. Her apron sparkled white while her skirt was jet black. Two dark eyes regarded her and narrowed while Sarah felt a minute something touch the pit of her stomach.

Checking they were unobserved, she opened her hand and flashed the medallion. The woman also looked around and did the same.

'Come in,' she said shortly and hastily shut the door.

Sarah followed, rather puzzled. There was something just a tiny bit familiar, which she could not immediately place. She normally had an excellent memory for faces too. The old woman took her into a small room for sitting. It was clean but sparsely furnished, almost utilitarian in concept. Sarah stood and scrutinised the old woman. The neck was as wrinkled as the face and pouches of sagging skin showed she had once carried more weight. Her body was thin with bowed shoulders. Sarah sensed there was a tenseness about the woman, almost fear coupled with resignation.

The woman indicated a chair and slowly Sarah sat, perching on the edge. She had the distinct feeling she was expected and unwelcome.

'You don't know me, do you?' the old woman asked abruptly.

'Should I?' Sarah replied, playing for time. There was something not quite right here. 'Who are you then?'

The old woman swallowed heavily and took a deep breath. Sarah listened intently but the house appeared to be empty apart from the two of them.

'Bessie!'

Sarah was staggered, shocked into silence and immobility. A hundred names could have been thrown at her but this would never have

242

sprung to mind.

'I don't believe it,' Sarah whispered, showing downright shock and disbelief. There was not the slightest resemblance to the old Bessie, then her mind flashed back. She remembered James' words on that day after Robert had nearly died. He too had described a hag of a woman. Then there was another ghastly memory of Martin slumped forward, the knife's haft protruding from his back. 'No!' she cried in protest. Was this someone's idea of a deadly macabre joke? She tensed, ready to spring up and depart.

'It's true, what's left of me,' Bessie said very slowly. 'Even Robert does not know me.'

Sarah gasped, shocked for a second time. 'What do you mean? You're not supposed to see him or speak to him. My husband did warn you,' she cried hotly. Then she realised Robert did not indeed know his mother. He would have said before now. 'You are a wicked woman!'

'And a fool, but I've paid as I told your husband five years ago,' Bessie said huskily. 'He came to see me. There was murder in his heart too. I could feel it floating from him. Then I heard you married and adopted my boy . . .' She paused heavily 'That was good,' she praised. 'You've done well for him. I sometimes stand on the road and watch him from a distance.' She halted again. 'How do you think I felt, when I knew it was you

243

coming?'

Sarah's mind worked rapidly. Forrest had not come into the city with her. His departure though had been a ploy. He had entered by another gate and warned Bessie while she had been with Robert. She worked it out. There had been ample time. Her jaws clamped together. Forrest had used her. He could have warned her but, she argued with herself, if she had known, would she have come anywhere near? Be honest, she chided, you'd have gone in the opposite direction.

'You know my story so I'll not repeat it,' Bessie continued in a heavy voice. 'I worked hard in that inn. I slogged my guts out and saved. A penny here, another there, the odd tip and gradually I built up a precious little nest egg. I found a better place and could earn more. Then I could have been happy, content to stay at that job, but it was not to be.'

'I don't understand?'

'Blackmail!'

Sarah was deeply shocked for the second time. 'You'd better explain,' she said grimly.

Bessie took time to put her thoughts into order. 'I thought the past was all long dead,' she began slowly, then shook her head, 'but it never does go away really, does it? No matter how hard a person works and tries to redeem themselves, there's always something ugly to rear its head when least expected. A man approached me one day when I'd gone to

244

market. He knew all about me. How, I don't know,' she said wearily. 'He mentioned Martin Penford, you, Fletcher, Robert even, plus various incidents which must have happened to you and about which, of course I knew nothing. He said it was simply laying the groundwork. He said, like your husband, although I did not kill my old master I was an accessory and could still be tried and executed. He said as Master Martin was an old, highly-thought-of Parliamentary agent, those in power now would be delighted to learn about me.'

An ugly suspicion surfaced in Sarah's mind but she stayed silent. 'Go on.'

'He said he suspected I had always had Royalist sympathies, which was true. I never held with Cromwell and the Puritans and, possibly, must have made a wrong comment to some person at an inopportune moment. I was terrified. It seemed the nightmare would never leave me. It seemed I was to go on paying for the rest of my life. He wasn't cruel, just very determined. He said he'd provide a house and all I had to do was receive and send messages, pass them on to one person only and receive them from another. He said I would not be paid, because of what I'd done in the past and I had to earn trust again, but if I obeyed, caused no trouble, the house would one day be mine.'

'This house?' Sarah asked quickly.

Bessie nodded. 'It's a good one. There is no other way I could save enough to buy a place like this. I thought, if he kept his word, it would give me somewhere in my old age now I'm alone,' she said but without whining. 'Sometimes I take in a short-term lodger, sent by him with a code word, but not often. I think I'm here for future use.'

Sarah turned all this over. It had the ring of authenticity. She doubted Bessie would have the guts to lie again, especially to her.

'Out of the blue, this morning, I was warned you were coming. I nearly fainted with shock and horror and then I felt sick. I thought I'd vomit but I was also astounded. To think you were now on the Royalist side—and I did wonder if it was some kind of trap . . . ?'

Sarah shook her head. 'It's certainly not that.' She had worked it all out. How dared Simon Forrest! It was obvious that, in the back of his mind, he intended to blackmail her in the future too, either with the Parliamentarians or her own husband. Most women, in such a position, would pay handsomely for silence. Her marriage could be threatened; the lives of her children too; even the innocent Pair. Her cheeks flamed scarlet and she itched to meet Simon Forrest again.

'Describe the man, Bessie, and give his name,' she said, forcing herself to be calm. There must be no error.

Bessie complied. There was not. Sarah felt

246

some of her natural hate for the old woman evaporate as she stared at the pitiful figure whose eyes were wide with fright and where tears hovered. There was no point in taking vengeance upon her, as James had so rightly said years ago.

'What would you do if you had a critically important message to get to Prince Charles?' she asked quietly.

Bessie was mystified. 'I use a pigeon. There are some on the top floor. I don't know where the birds go but the few messages I've sent seem to arrive. Now and again, I receive a confirmation, just to check the system works.'

'Good!' Sarah said coolly. 'Ink, paper and quill, please, Bessie. Two can play at being devious and I might just be better at this game than Mister Simon Forrest . . . your blackmailer.'

Bessie hastened to comply and watched as Sarah thought, then wrote a brief message, She checked it, rolled it into a tight cylinder and placed it inside the pigeon's leg container. How providential she had learned all about this from James, she thought.

'The birds, Bessie?'

Bessie led her up to the attic from which came soft cooing. There was a large, wickerwork cage with six birds, all settled and content on a long perch. Bessie selected a bird and Sarah strapped the tiny cylinder on one leg. Bessie then took the bird outside, through

247

the loft's door, tossed it aloft and they both watched. Sarah only hoped there were no hawks around, especially trained ones.

The bird circled three times then broke away and soon vanished into the sky. Sarah turned to Bessie. 'If that odious man Forrest calls again, asking questions or anything, you can say I've been but nothing more. However,' Sarah said, a wicked gleam in her eyes, 'I don't think it will take him long to want to see me.'

Downstairs, Sarah let Bessie give her refreshment. Some of the shock and sting of the past was going. James had never liked working with Martin. Now she was in a similar position because of politics. Personalities were of no consequence; all had to be sacrificed for the greater cause.

'Where has that message gone, Sarah?' Bessie asked timidly.

'Directly to Prince Charles whom I just happen to know personally.'

Bessie was speechless for a few seconds. If it had been anyone else she would have disbelieved such a statement. Not Sarah. She knew her too well of old. Quite suddenly, Bessie felt a rare warm feeling flood into her. 'Sarah,' she began uncertainly, 'I know it's early days but, perhaps some time, we could just visit and talk . . . women's talk?'

Sarah understood and knew she could not snub. The past was history. They were now comrades in arms but, she told herself grimly,

God help her if James ever found out.

'I'll call regularly, once a month and bring country food. Also I could do with a new outfit. Is there a dressmaker handy?'

'As it happens, right next door, my good neighbour, Mildred Cook.'

'She knows nothing, I hope?' Sarah asked quickly.

Bessie shook her head firmly. 'As far as she's concerned, I just take in suitable lodgers to help make ends meet.'

'I'd better be on my way, Bessie,' Sarah then said. 'In a month's time.'

She rode back to her village in a thoughtful frame of mind. It had turned into a weird day, with a vengeance, yet not wholly unsatisfactory. Her wish had been answered. She was wanted, for herself and her skills. The only great heartache was James. Was it possible, dare she hope, that one day he too would change his mind? Her heart went out to the lonely prince, exiled from his land, whose only hope rested with the likes of her? It made an awesome responsibility but, Sarah knew from the past, she worked well when the load on her shoulders was great. Her main difficulty, the enormous problem, was going to be concealing everything from James' sharp eyes and clever brain; plus, she reminded herself heavily, the fact that her marriage might even be at stake. Where would she stand if put to that awesome test? It was something upon which she preferred not to think. Let that day arrive and she'd deal with the problem then only.

CHAPTER TWELVE

Sarah awaited the reaction and took certain precautions. She dug out her little pistol, cleaned it and rearmed it, hiding the holster, when she rode under her long riding shirt. She made a point of riding out each day, always on the alert, knowing perfectly well how Forrest must feel. He would be boiling.

Luckily, James was still absent and, she hoped, neither Jack nor Walter took undue notice of her renewed riding activities; it was the shrewd Walter who caused her the most concern. He was the one whom she must fool because there was very little which missed his eyes. Always at the back of her mind, was the awareness that Walter was James' man. She was glad James was away; it would have been impossible to ride alone if he were home. It was going to be difficult finding a regular excuse to ride into Bristol, monthly, without him wishing to accompany her. She taxed her mind in deciding the new clothes she must have made to make the necessary excuse. The trouble was, with the Puritan's ridiculous dogma, there was a limit on the different clothing considered suitable. Damn them, she told herself yet again.

She rode a new mare, which Jack had schooled and to which she was giving the final touches. As always, she rode far from the village, reckoning that Forrest would not approach her near to habitation and she herself, wanted isolation. He came after nearly a month, approaching from an acute angle. He rode straight to her so Sarah halted to face him. On the man's face was a set, furious look. He did not beat around the bush either.

'Well,' he snapped. 'What is it? I've been told to liaise with you?'

Sarah had wondered how her message would be dealt with. Obviously, the prince anticipated she was more than capable of dealing with the situation herself. It would have been imprudent to send a man for disciplinary purpose.

'You've been contacted by Prince Charles?' Sarah asked quietly, eyebrows elevated.

Forrest was taken aback. He had, and he did not like the tone of that which had come back to him. There was something wrong and he was uncertain. Like all bullies though he resorted to verbal force.

'That's nothing to do with you. You were engaged on the understanding you'd be a simple courier. What were you doing sending a personal message to our leader?' Forrest snarled. Obviously, it had all gone to the woman's head and now he must crush her into obedience. What had worked once before could not fail a second time. He opened his mouth to roar at her then noticed her narrow eyes, set lips and stern jaw. He hesitated fractionally, acutely aware this woman was of a different metal to the old crone.

Sarah decided to get in first. 'Don't think you can blackmail me,' she rasped harshly.

Forrest gasped, the wind snatched from his sails with a vengeance. 'I know your game and it won't work with me,' Sarah shot back at him. She could see he reeled from this unexpected attack. 'You may have successfully blackmailed Bessie but not me! I saw through your game right away. You fool! Do you think Prince Charles will tolerate such tactics? He's had a full report from me, and what about the money you are supposed to pay Bessie?' she snapped, taking an educated guess. 'It's lining your pockets, isn't it? Well, the Prince has been informed of that too. As if he'd have helpers without remuneration! You must think we are stupid!'

Forrest stiffened with shock. He had not imagined she would see through his trick. He counter-attacked rapidly.

'It's time the authorities were informed about that stupid old woman and . . .'

'You'll sign your own death warrant then,' Sarah promised quietly. 'I asked the Prince not to deal with you but send you to me. You

252

miserable scum. How dare you pretend to be on the Royalists' side when all you're doing is feathering a little nest for yourself. People like you make me sick. Well let me tell you this and you'd be wise to pay attention. You utter one word, by any means, about Bessie or me, come to that, and I'll promise you, you'll be staggered at my influence with Prince Charles. There'll be no room left in this country for you and neither on the Continent either. You've shot your bolt through greed. You will die.'

Forrest felt fear. He did indeed know how long were the tentacles of the Royalists even now, when they were politically weak. They had their methods to enforce silence. He knew he had gone too far but who would have thought she'd find out. How? How strong was her influence with the exiled Stuart court?

How was it possible for someone unimportant like her to have such influence? Then something occurred to him and he cursed. Why hadn't he considered this before? Her medallion token was of pure gold, his only of a base metal. This meant she was indeed privileged; he had slipped up badly. He had only himself to blame for queering what could have been a highly lucrative pitch.

Forrest was unused to resistance. His charm had always been enough in the past to enable him to wriggle from predicaments. Now his temper burst. He was finished with the Royalist cause and he knew better than to try to wheedle into Parliament's graces. Anyhow, he loathed their political aspirations. 'You bitch!' he snarled, leaned from the saddle and struck out at her face. Revenge of some kind he would have.

Sarah reacted with a speed that shocked him. Her hand darted under her loose shirt and appeared with a small pistol. For a second he stared at it, mesmerised, horrified to realise he was within range. His next move was automatic and stupid. He dived for his own saddle pistol.

Sarah lifted her weapon, coolly sighted and fired. There was a loud bang and her mount half reared, startled, not yet trained to such noises. Forrest let out a yell of pain and shock. Her pistol ball had struck in his upper arm, the flare of pain violent. He lurched in his saddle, swearing savagely and knew he was beaten. His right arm was useless and, he suspected, the ball might have broken the bone. If it had not, he was left useless.

'If you bother me, mine or Bessie again, I'll see you dead,' Sarah told him in a calm, cold voice. 'I'll get in first before Prince Charles,' she added for good measure. 'Now get out of my sight and my life.'

Forrest hesitated only momentarily. She had no other pistol but he was in no fit state to use his own. It took an effort of will to stay on his horse. He turned a face, savage with anger on her. 'You'll pay!' he growled.

'Don't bluster,' Sarah retorted and waggled the empty pistol. If only they could be made to fire more than once, she thought. She too had her normal saddle pistol but did not wish to use this. She wanted the moral victory from one weapon.

Forrest cursed violently, which left Sarah unmoved. Muttering more foul words, he turned and walked his horse away, mind churning; bitter with defeat. An excellent source of revenue had been stripped from him but, more to the point, he had stuck himself out on a precarious limb from which he could not, at the moment, see a safe retreat.

Sarah watched him vanish, then slowly walked back home. She knew she had acted correctly. Now she must take her pistol back to her private room, clean it and hope it would never have to be fired again in anger. At the same time, she decided it would be prudent to carry it always. Should she have killed Forrest instead? Could she have done this? She knew not, under the given circumstances but she knew another message must be sent to the exiled Prince, and that would have to be by a pigeon from Bessie's. Thank God she had worked out suitable garments to have made, to provide her with the appropriate excuse for Bristol trips.

As she entered the yard James appeared with Walter at his side. She threw him a delighted smile, dismounted, then flung herself in his arms. It was always so wonderful to have him back and never more so than right now. How she longed to confide in him and, suddenly, she was torn in two.

'What's all this then?' he teased. 'I'm handsome, debonair and dashing but this is almost too much!'

Sarah collected herself. She must always remember his astuteness. There had been the prickle of tears at the back of her eyes but, with an effort, she stifled them and switched her thoughts to a safer topic. 'How long are you home?'

He pulled a face. 'Just tonight,' he told her in a low voice. Walter already knew because, for ever at the back of James' mind, was the knowledge that the country was not perhaps as peaceful as the majority thought. Now he learned Sarah rode into Bristol alone and this bothered him.

'You should go with her,' he had told Walter after some thought.

Walter was uncertain. 'I doubt the mistress will take kindly to having an escort again, sir, and I can't make her, can I?'

James had realised his difficulty. There was also the eternal problem of Sarah's desire and insistence upon independence. 'Follow her?'

That made Walter pull a face. 'Easier said than done, sir. What if she sees me? What do I say?'

James took his point. Walter eyed him

thoughtfully. 'Can't you stay at home, sir?'

'I wish I could,' he began. There were days now when sometimes all this riding was more than irksome. It was exhausting. There was also the matter of watching his back. Thurloe seemed to do nothing but throw problems at him, which appeared to increase, not diminish. Also, at the back of his mind, was the subtle awareness that Sarah was not quite her old self.

That night, when they had made love, each enjoying the other to a full extent, he gently started to talk as they lay together.

'What's your great secret?' he began in a soft voice.

He felt her stiffen as she lay in the crook of his arm. 'What on earth do you mean, James?'

'Well,' he tried again carefully. 'You do have one, don't you? You're not the girl you were this time last year.'

Sarah pulled away and sat up, turning to look down at him. His face wore a placid, almost serene look that did not fool her. Was it possible he knew something and had started to pump? Unease filled her but she kept a bland expression on her face and did not make the mistake of breaking eye contact.

'So do you,' she countered in a soft voice, waiting anxiously.

James thought about that. Her non-reply confirmed his suspicions. Now what could she know that he did not? His mind swiftly raced

257

over a number of subjects. Was she pregnant again? She had vowed she only ever wanted two children and he had done his best to comply.

'That's my work,' he replied slowly and waited.

Sarah took the bull by the horns. 'What possible secret can I have living here?' she countered.

'Had a nice trip to Bristol last time?' he asked softly.

Sarah got out of bed, tossed her hair, which had grown long, into another position and pulled up a chair to face him. 'Robert was well,' she told him, 'but itching to go to sea. England is too small for him. Anyhow I think he'll be getting a clerk who might be good enough to become manager. His name's John Browne, with an "e". If Robert is right, he'll then be off.'

'So Jane is prepared to wait?' he asked. Still she had not given him a direct reply, which, for forthright Sarah, was almost ominous. He nodded, as if answering his own question, aware of her eyes on him. Was it his imagination or did something trouble her? 'So you won't be going into Bristol at all then once he's off to sea?'

'Oh but I will,' Sarah told him firmly. 'I can't rusticate here all the time and where else can I go?'

That's a strange answer, James told himself

and wondered why he felt such a sick feeling. Something nasty hovered at the back of his mind.

'I've found a dressmaker,' Sarah added hastily. His eyes had narrowed like they always did when confronting something unpleasant. Dear God, she thought wildly. If he once suspects, but then, how can he? He'd never forgive her for changing sides so blatantly yet how could she do otherwise? The country was in a mess, thanks to men just like James and his odious Thurloe. It flashed through her mind to wonder whether Prince Charles had someone like the spymaster? Who coordinated the information he received? 'Even the Puritans can't object if I get a better wardrobe,' she explained hastily.

'Who is it?' he asked softly.

Sarah started to bridle. He was interrogating her. 'Why?'

Now they looked directly at each other, eyes locked, neither willing to break contact first. 'My question is reasonable. I am your husband,' he told her, a little bite entering his voice.

'I'm not a six-year-old, James,' she threw back at him, 'and neither am I one of your suspects!' she added, starting to get hot under the collar with indignation and guilt. Oh, damn him, what had started this off? Walter? But he knows nothing, he can't do, she told herself wildly. Forrest? Impossible! If he had any sense, and he certainly was not stupid, he would have left the area in a hurry.

'So you won't tell me?' he persisted, half sitting up himself.

'No!' she replied with rising anger. 'For goodness sake! Since when have you been interested in dressmakers? I don't quiz you about what Thurloe says to you!'

It wouldn't do you any good if you did, he told himself. She was getting worked up over something and the ugly thought reared its nasty little head for the second time.

Even then, he knew he could not air anything like that. 'Sarah,' he whispered, 'can't you confide in me?'

'I don't know what on earth you mean!'

'I think you do!'

She glowered now but he saw her bottom lip gave a little tremble. Whatever her secret was, it clashed with her conscience. Oh, how well he knew this stubborn, independent wife of his.

'Last time I was home, you were abstracted most of the time, so whatever bothers you isn't new,' he said with a heavy sigh. Again the thought reared its head and enlarged a little.

Sarah gave a shake to her head, stood, walked to the window and stared out into the night. He was too clever for her but what lie could she tell that he would believe? It hit her this might be something which could go on for a long time and that was dangerous to any marriage. She had not thought of this when she had agreed to Forrest's request. Now he was out of the way, she could still back down. She doubted it would be held against her and she now had the method to get a message through to Prince Charles. Her other half argued as to why she should. Didn't she have the strength of her convictions? Did she back down at the first little obstacle? But it's not little, berated her conscience; it's my marriage!

'When are you going to stop working for . . . him?' she asked sharply, turning back to him abruptly.

He was taken aback, not expecting a flanking attack. For a few seconds he had no answer. He needed time to sort out words. 'When I can,' he compromised.

They studied each other, both sharply aware they were now lying in their teeth. A barrier had risen, high, not quite unclimbable but getting more impossible all the time.

'You lead your life, James. I'll lead mine, thank you very much!' Sarah said finally. She knew it was a pathetic statement but her mind had ceased to function. His eyes had appeared to probe into the hidden depths of her soul. She walked back and climbed into their large double bed. He made no move to fondle her, instead he held himself rigid.

When he made no move, feeling incredibly hurt and rejected, Sarah turned on her side, half curled into a ball and willed sleep to come. Instead, she found herself staring into

261

the room's gloom. Her heart thumped uneasily and she bit her bottom lip as tears hovered. He had turned against her, she knew it, she could feel it, sense it. It was horrible, hurtful and hateful. She yearned to turn back to him, rest her head on his broad chest but, if she did, she'd break down and blurt it all out. If only he was not so dogmatic politically.

James lay rigid, then turned on his right side away from her. He was sure his heart was going to break. She had done nothing but prevaricate in a skilful way. That meant only one thing. His heart was heavy with misery at the thought of her being with another man? Was it his fault? He examined his conscience. He did spend too much time away from home, yet it was his work. His mind reflected on the fact that most agents paid an awful price for what they did. Somehow though, he had never expected this to happen to him? He would have sworn he had her total love and loyalty and he writhed with bitterness and rabid jealousy. He had to find out who the man was then . . . He baulked. He could call the man out and kill him or be killed. But if Sarah now loved this stranger, she would hate him even more. How though, could he do nothing? He toyed with the thought of setting Walter on to guard her secretly, but what if Walter demurred. Working for him in the old days secretly was one thing, spying on a wife was an entirely different matter. Dear God, he thought to himself, I'm paying a price heavier than I can bear. Without Sarah, I don't really want to live. The Pair could raise the children with Walter as guardian. He knew he could not go on without his Sarah. From that first meeting, all those long years ago, there had never been any other female. For a few seconds, he felt an enormous lump lodge in the middle of his throat. Surely to God he was not going to cry?

A resolve began to rise. There were two things he could do. Resign from Thurloe and come back to fight for his marriage because it was certainly worth fighting for. He'd done his share for England. Let Thurloe get someone else. He had savings, he was not short of money and there was always the spice business, particularly as Robert stood poised to sail the high seas.

They lay there, two stubborn, troubled people; quite unable to communicate as each was consumed with dark thoughts.

When Sarah woke in the morning, he had gone. She lay there for a few minutes, heart aching, but she made herself get up. Today she should ride in to see Bessie. Deep down she felt an awful, internal sickness but, she thought grimly, I started, I'll carry on to the bitter end, come what may.

When she took her horse and rode out, Walter eyed her retreating back. The master had left before the cock crowed, without two words to say to him. Now the mistress looked as if the world was coming to an end. Surely to God, those two were not at loggerheads again? He felt his heart slump. One thing was for sure though, this time they must sort it out together. He did not wish to be involved. In a thoroughly put-out frame of mind, Walter strode back down to his own cottage which was always cheery and peaceful. He knew he had much to be thankful for.

*   *   *

Bessie opened the door and smiled nervously as Sarah stepped in. She was still uncertain as to how far she could go in offering friendship to Sarah Penford yet, so often her days were incredibly lonely. To while away the time, she would often walk into the city, go down to the dock and stare for hours, on the off chance Robert would appear. She longed to rush over, tell him who she was, but she would never do it. Apart from giving her word to Master Penford, she was astute enough to realise that Robert might find it impossible to understand or accept what she'd done so long ago. Robert had always had a very soft spot for Martin Penford.

Today she sensed a certain difference with Sarah, almost a stiff rigidity, and she wondered uneasily if she was the cause. But Sarah accepted a drink of wine and Bessie decided to bring her up to date.

'I've had a bit of news, Sarah,' she said in a low voice. 'A pigeon came in directed to me with the rider to tell you. Parliament has had a spy in Prince Charles' court in France.'

Sarah brightened. James. Was this his doing?

'His name was Charles Manning but he was found out. I don't know how though. He had been sending very detailed messages to Parliament.'

'Really?'

Bessie continued; she had Sarah's complete attention now. 'The Prince has been a fair man. He ordered a proper trial and then Manning broke down and confessed everything. He pleaded he did it for poverty but do you know, we also found out Thurloe had been paying him a whole thousand a year.' Did Sarah know who Thurloe was?

Sarah's wits snapped into action. 'First, who is Thurloe, and a thousand a year? That's a fortune!' she gasped, genuinely astounded.

'Thurloe is the top man for Cromwell,' Bessie explained, pleased to be able to bring Sarah up to date. 'But always be careful because of him. He's a very clever man and a great danger to the Prince because of his agents.'

Don't I know it, Sarah thought to herself. This was a crazy, double-edged game she had started to play. Had she been mad to consent in the first place? She made herself concentrate as Bessie looked at her, a question in her eyes.

Bessie was puzzled. Sarah had not heard. Wool-gathering was no good. 'I said I'd not seen that awful Forrest man again.'

Now Sarah was fully alert. 'You won't, because I shot him.'

Bessie was stunned, momentarily lost for words. 'What happened?' she asked anxiously.

Sarah explained briefly 'So there'll be no more blackmailing.'

Bessie nodded to herself. 'Now I understand. I've been given a new contact and I just thought they'd moved Forrest elsewhere.' She paused as suddenly she knew she had to step on to some very thin ice. 'Your husband is Parliament's man. He works for John Thurloe?' she stated quietly.

Sarah understood in a flash. It was incredible how so-called secret information travelled. 'What I do is unknown to him,' she explained gently but firmly 'just as what he does is not related to me.'

Bessie frowned. 'That must make life hard when you are wed?' she probed.

Sarah bit her lip. 'Sometimes too hard, but he won't change and neither will I.'

To that, Bessie realised, it would be better to make no comment. She changed the subject. 'I've arranged to take you into Mildred Cook, the dressmaker.'

Sarah was glad to hear this. The sooner she had a legitimate excuse the better, just in case her suspicious husband took it into his head to have her followed. She could put nothing past him.

Bessie hesitated again, and Sarah had the impression she was formulating words to be spoken with finesse. 'What a state this country is in,' she began gently. 'First the Parliamentarians have their underground movement then, when they are in power, we have to start ours. So it goes on and on. Silly, isn't it? Perhaps also rather tricky.'

Sarah frowned. That was double-talk if ever she'd heard any. 'Are you trying to say that if my husband should change his politics, it might be held against him?'

Bessie gave a little shrug. 'I'm a lot older than you, Sarah and war breeds terrible hatreds and resentments.'

Thurloe, Sarah thought, she's given me a warning about him? Yet there was no chance of James changing his mind, was there?

'Parliament has had its troubles too,' Bessie continued quietly. 'There's been a big row between the army and Parliament. It took Cromwell all his time to smooth things down.'

Sarah had not known this. James must be aware though and, once more, the gulf between them stretched wider. Divide and rule was her next thought. Was it possible Prince Charles could utilise any such quarrel,

267

then she realised the impossibility. She remembered his spoken words; his horror for all who had died already. That man would only cone back through negotiation; he would refuse to carry more English blood on his shoulders.

Bessie eyed her and smiled wanly. 'Sometimes I too wonder if it is all worthwhile for the likes of us to get involved,' she said understandingly.

Sarah felt her heart warm suddenly. She pulled a moué, gave a little shrug to her shoulders and managed a thin smile. 'But without us commoners, what could they do on their own? Nothing I think!'

'It's going to be more difficult for you, though, Sarah, if your husband is still rigid politically,' Bessie told her carefully.

Later she rode to the business before going home. A strange man, middle-aged, with early grey hairs, introduced himself quietly.

'I'm John Browne, mistress. Thank you for doing the necessary. Master Robert is out right now but he said, if you called in, you were to have these spices,' he said, lifting up a small packet.

Sarah studied the man. Because his introduction had come through Forrest, she was wary, yet as she looked into his brown eyes and studied a placid, kindly face, she relaxed. It was true; an exterior could hide many faults yet she felt no antagonism from him. He seemed almost too kindly to be involved in anything yet he too was a Royalist. She leaned from the saddle, to speak privately.

'Nowadays my husband is away a lot, but, if he should come back to run his share of the firm, you would have to be very careful,' she warned. 'My husband misses nothing. He is totally against monarchs.'

Browne understood. He nodded meaningfully 'I would see precautions were taken,' he promised. 'I am the only one who knows what comes in where and when.'

Sarah believed him. This was no flippant youngster or arrogant Forrest. It relieved another worry from the back of her mind although, she told herself, she could not yet see the day when James would be a true civilian. However, it was always prudent to cover all possible options.

'Work well here,' she said kindly, 'and anything else does not concern me, does it?'

'At the moment no!'

Sarah blinked. Now what did he mean by that? She went to question but thought better of it while he watched her unblinkingly with straight eyes. Sarah took a deep breath. It was obvious someone had started planning somewhere, but to do what? Surely no man was fool enough to contemplate an uprising yet? She shook her head and left, deeply immersed in her thoughts, oblivious to the watcher.

Walter was puzzled. He had expected to see Robert and been disappointed that he was out; then his attention had been caught by Sarah's arrival. He was also disconcerted to understand the direction from which she had come? Then what had she found necessary to say so secretly to Robert's new man? He felt troubled, uneasy, but knew he would neither do nor say anything to the master. If there was trouble in the offing between husband and wife, there was no way they were going to involve him this time.

He followed her at a considerable distance then, making a snap decision, veered off to the right and moved into a gallop. Sarah was riding slowly, obviously immersed in deep thoughts. With luck, he could get home before her, which might be much better than following at her rear.

His ploy did not work out because Sarah increased her pace, suddenly anxious to get home, so that the two horses converged together one mile from the stable yard. Sarah was surprised to see Walter then reflected that, as Robert's friend, he had visited Bristol to see him but left earlier.

'I didn't see Robert,' she told him.

'Neither did I,' and Walter managed a forced smile. 'I think he had gone to see his betrothed. That's strange, mistress!' and he pointed.

Sarah followed his gaze then halted. Her

property was a blaze of light this evening. Although it was dusk, it was not strictly necessary to make a beacon of the property.

'Something's wrong!' Walter snapped and galloped forward.

Sarah followed hastily. Certainly, there seemed undue activity. As they skidded to a halt, hooves sending sparks from the cobbles, Jack ran over, white-faced, highly alarmed with The Pair fluttering at his heels.

'The horses!' Jack gasped. 'They've been stolen.'

Sarah sat stunned. Their horses had been increased to make a breeding herd of top-quality riding animals. It had been Walter's excellent idea, approved of by both James and Sarah.

Walter vaulted to the ground, looked around, then flashed a look at Sarah.

'My children!'

The Pair answered in unison. 'Inside and quite safe, Sarah. A gang of men came across the country, opened the gate and took the horses.'

Sarah was bewildered. 'But how?'

Jack explained. 'They drove three of the mares out first, including your old favourite, Sarah and, of course, master's stallion followed. Once they were all out, the men just drove them off with pistol shots. I was here alone. I could do nothing at all,' Jack told them, distressed beyond words.

271

'It's all right, Jack. One man against many . . .' Sarah shook her head. 'Walter?'

'It'll be really dark soon. We can do nothing until the morning,' Walter remarked, yet he was puzzled. Horse-stealing was rare. A horse was so valuable that offences for stealing them were severe. Something did not ring true. He frowned, troubled, without knowing why.

'We can go out at first light,' Sarah said swiftly. 'Split up to cover all directions.'

Walter threw her a look. He opened his mouth to point out there were only two men available. It would take time to get more from the village. Sarah forestalled him.

'I can track with the best man,' she stated firmly, 'and I'm not sitting here twiddling my thumbs while my dear old mare is out there and, Walter, don't argue. I'll go alone if necessary.'

Walter could see she meant it. He looked at Jack for moral support and received none at all. Jack was too distressed with what had happened when he was in charge. The fact that he had been alone cut no ice with him at this moment.

'I'll get some more men first thing,' he extemporised wildly.

'Too late,' Sarah told him. 'Those horses will be moved on at first light and they'd hear many riders following. The thing to do is for us to leave the moment there's enough light to track. We split up, the three of us, take two

272

pistols; one for signalling, the other for protection. Whoever fires first, calling for help, brings the others.'

Walter did not like this at all. He could see innumerable flaws. They must have more men. 'I'll still arrange for other men,' he told Sarah firmly. 'And they can come after us,' he added quickly to forestall more argument.

Sarah turned that over and gave a slow nod. Why hadn't she thought of that? 'Good,' she said shortly, 'but we three leave as dawn breaks.'

CHAPTER THIRTEEN

Thurloe was in one of his difficult moods, James told himself, as he sat before his superior's desk in London. So that's going to make two of us, he added to himself grimly.

John Thurloe was annoyed. Disagreeable news had reached him only the other day that merely confirmed something Penford had said to which, at the time, he had not, perhaps, paid sufficient attention. Such lapses infuriated him.

'Manning is dead,' he grunted.

James switched thoughts, startled at this, perplexity showing on his face. 'What happened?'

'The fool was found out somehow. Charles

Stuart gave him a trial, found him guilty and had him executed. You were right to doubt his moral fibre because, at the end, Manning grizzled for mercy.'

James said nothing, turning this over in his mind. He was not unduly surprised. The trouble was, although Manning's French had been so impeccable, his moral fibre had been less. Thank God he'd placed two separate men in the exile's court and that neither man knew of each other. This explained Thurloe's mood and I'm going to make it worse, James added to himself.

Before he could get a word in, Thurloe started again. 'Why haven't you done anything at your end? Also did you know someone shot Forrest?'

'No, I did not!' and again James was startled. 'Where?'

'Again in your area. There's someone there playing a dirty, double game. I want to know what's going on,' he growled.

James snatched the opportunity. 'Well, you'll not find out through me. I resign!'

Thurloe's eyes opened wide with astonishment. He sat back in his chair, steepled his fingers together and put an unreadable expression on his face.

'What's biting you, Penford? After more money or something?' he provoked.

James knew him when in such a sarcastic mood. He also knew he must tread warily. Yet

274

why shouldn't he provoke in return? He had nothing to lose now and he'd never liked this man in the first place.

'Grow up,' he rasped back.

Thurloe sat forward abruptly, anger glowing in his eyes. He could not last remember when he had been so addressed. 'I'll overlook that but you'd better do some pretty fast explaining,' he threatened.

James did not reply immediately. How far could he and should he go in opening his heart? What did Thurloe know of love? Had he ever loved anyone? He knew nothing about the man's personal life and did not, he reflected, want to.

Thurloe was equally disconcerted. Penford's statement was the bolt from the blue and, at this time, was the last thing he wanted. He eyed his man, debating with himself the best tactics to use. Force? He mentally shook his head. With some men it worked but not with these ultra-tough cases. Penford had seen and done it all. He was not just a trained soldier, he was an experienced and blooded one. He was more than capable of getting up, slamming a fist at Thurloe and, with his awesome power, breaking his neck. Artlessness? That was a possibility, yet Penford knew all the mental tricks going. After all, he had used them for Thurloe. So what was left, he reasoned with himself, but basic truth and reasonableness.

'Why?' he asked and this time his tone was

gentle, man-to-man, confiding, requesting, almost soothing.

He did not fool James for one second, yet he was not untouched by this about-face. His heart hurt him so much, he was so deeply troubled and worried, he ached to confide in someone and who was there apart from Walter? He lifted miserable eyes to the spymaster.

'My wife,' he managed to get out with a groan, 'she's changed. Been like that for a while now and I think it's my fault . . . and yours.'

'What the hell does that mean?' Thurloe asked, downright astonished.

'Another man, because I'm hardly ever at home,' James grunted, then shook his head, his emotion almost overpowering him.

Thurloe was shocked. Penford was near the point of breaking down. He would not have believed this possible.

'If you want to talk, you'll find I can be a very good listener, man,' he said in a kind voice few had ever heard.

'Christ!' James blasphemed. 'I feel like bawling my bloody eyes out like a kid!'

Thurloe stood, opened the door and growled at his clerk. 'No interruptions of any kind!'

Then he came back and dragged his chair around from the back of the desk where he usually kept it to impose a barrier between himself and subordinates. First he went to his private cupboard and removed some brandy, pouring them both a generous measure. James took a heavy swallow, feeling the spirit chase down to the pit of his stomach.

'Now, start at the beginning. I've usually found that's the best place,' he encouraged.

James took a deep breath and related his feelings, emotions and suspicions. He took his time, not missing a detail nor exaggerating and Thurloe never interrupted until James paused to take another gulp of the brandy.

'Sex life all right?' Thurloe asked bluntly.

James lifted watery eyes and nodded. 'That's perfect. It's afterwards. We used to talk, confide in each other, and have no secrets . . . apart from my work for you. Now . . .' He shook his head. 'Some man somewhere has caught her eye. She meets him in Bristol and . . .' He could not finish and took another drink.

Thurloe turned this over. He recognised the ring of authenticity. Certainly Penford was now of no further use to him. Any person with emotional problems was a menace to themselves and all around. It was a shame though. This man was just about irreplaceable. He wondered if the problem could somehow be resolved and he could get Penford back again, then he shook his head. The man would hardly wish to leave his wife alone again. Women, he muttered to himself. They have their uses. At times their work is brilliant yet there was always the ugly head of sex and emotion to contend with. He sniffed and scratched his head thoughtfully.

'Are you still with us though?' he asked softly.

James sat up straighter. The brandy had settled his nerves. 'I'm no traitor and damn you for even thinking that!'

Thurloe lifted a placating hand. 'I had to ask. So would you if you sat in this chair.'

James gave him a strong look. 'I've heard rumours that some want Cromwell crowned as king. I don't hold with any of that.'

'Why on earth not?' Thurloe asked, frankly puzzled. 'If we must have a king, why not one of choice instead of inheritance? It makes more sense.'

'But what happens when Cromwell dies? Where does Tumbledown Dick come in?'

'You never did like him,' Thurloe mused.

'I'm not alone either. He's a wastrel. God, I'd almost rather have a king back than Richard Cromwell, sir,' he said hotly.

Thurloe saw the man was more himself again. He was going to get argumentative. 'In your head is vital information,' he pointed out evenly. 'Many would kill for it.'

James understood. He looked long and hard into Thurloe's eyes. 'I know all about your black book as we both know. I think, from now on, I'm going to be apolitical. Somehow, the

278

game sticks in my nostrils,' and he flared them as if there was a bad smell nearby. 'What I will do is this though, sir. In the highly unlikely event I change my political colours, I swear, before God, that the information I have will not be used by anyone else.'

Thurloe gazed back into his eyes, his own narrow, hard and probing. 'I believe you too,' he admitted slowly. 'I wouldn't to a thousand others but you, yes! I'm sorry you're going,' and he grimaced, 'but an unwilling man is no use to me. One day, if you can sort out your home life and if you feel domesticity palls, you know where to contact me.'

James felt himself sigh with relief. It had all gone far better than he had dared to hope. He had been prepared to argue, debate or use physical force, but leave, he had determined he would. Sarah was more precious to him than England, when it came down to the crunch.

'I'll give you a piece of advice, sir, for what it's worth. You'll never have a decent England with the Puritans. Get rid of them or, if you can't do that, clip their wings but do it hard.'

Thurloe grunted. 'That's easier said that done!' he grumbled though he knew again he had heard the truth. There was much that he too now disliked yet he could see no way yet to deal with this conundrum.

'It's been a long time,' he said slowly, going back down the years. James's thoughts mirrored his and he nodded ruefully. Somehow, although his heart still ached savagely, a great weight had lifted. He stood and looked quizzically at Thurloe. 'You are a great man,' he said slowly, meaning every word. 'Will England ever know, understand and appreciate?'

Thurloe was taken aback yet again. Penford had never shown sentiment before but he was not displeased. He too stood and they faced each other, a yard apart. James offered his hand first. Thurloe grasped it.

'I'm going home,' James said simply.

'Get off then, you brandy-soaked bugger!' Thurloe rasped but a twinkle showed in his eyes. 'And Penford!'

James turned at the door, eyebrows lifted warily.

'Watch your back!' Thurloe barked.

James grinned, feeling unexpected comradely warmth. 'And you too!'

*   *   *

Sarah threw a look at Walter, her lips tight. It had been a sleepless night. The loss of their horses was a bad blow and James would go berserk to find his precious stallion gone. Even though old, his stud potential was still extremely good. She was devastated to lose her mare who had been part and parcel of her life for so many years.

280

'Arms, mistress?' Walter asked bluntly. He did not like this at all. It was true an urgent message had produced information that help would arrive shortly but the mistress was hell bent on going now, this very second when dawn had barely broken.

'I've my small pistol under my tunic, one around my waist and this,' Sarah told him. She bent, lifted her skirt, displayed a black riding boot from the top of which protruded a thin-bladed, but very lethal knife. 'Stop fussing like a mother hen. We are wasting time.'

Walter flashed a look at Jack and gave it up. 'All right, split in three directions. The Pair will keep watch here and send the other men after us when they turn up.' He had debated whether to send a pigeon for the master but events were moving far too quickly.

Hastily Jack reconnoitred the immediate area. The hoof tracks were bunched for half a mile, then split into distinct groups. Sarah studied them. The stallion's very large hooves were easy to distinguish. 'I'll go after him,' she said firmly, brooking no argument. 'The other groups you men can follow.'

Walter's grim face displayed his feelings but he knew better than to say anything. Sarah wore her implacable mask. She considered it better to follow the big black because the animal knew her well; he accepted her scent as she had established a friendship with him. She was also worried. A stallion, separated from all

281

of his mares, could turn into a dangerous animal who might have to be shot.

The air was chilly, almost raw and she shrugged herself deeper into a short coat and walked her mount forward. Around her head she had tied a black scarf and her clothing was also of that hue. She hoped these shades would be difficult to pick out at a distance.

The mist hung in patches and the grass was sodden but made tracking very easy. Overhead, the early sky was patchy with clouds but she thought the sun might get up later and disperse the mist.

Her horse's hooves squelched as she walked him slowly forward, bent at the waist, intent on studying the ground. She thought there were five animals ahead with the stallion and she guessed the robbers must have used whips. If the stallion had been hurt, his temper would be highly aggressive. An enraged stallion could be far worse than a bull who only had horns to attack. A stallion had hooves plus wicked teeth and was formidable at the best of times.

The land ahead was relatively flat, interspersed with clumps of trees, still in their autumn leaves of browns and reds. After riding for what she estimated must be about a mile, Sarah halted to listen and study her mount's ears. They flickered backward and forward; the horse held his head high but she was uncertain. Did this mean there was someone around or was the gelding frightened because he could scent a stallion? If the black came thundering towards them, it was quite likely he would attack a contemptuous gelding. The fact she was astride meant nothing.

She should be on a mare, she berated herself. Should she ride back and change mounts? She dithered uncertainly, then shook her head. It would take too long, then her lips twitched. Both Walter and Jack had also missed this valuable point.

Her horse suddenly passaged nervously sideways for a few steps and Sarah tightened her reins. At the same time, she bent forward and unfastened her saddle holster as something walked over her grave. Then, cutting through the morning air, came the harsh, brassy screech of an infuriated stallion. She caught her breath, shocked that she was so near. By straining she thought she heard men's voices, low, muted, but angry. The stallion was playing up. Serve them right for taking him.

She made a snap decision and quietly slipped from the saddle but took the large pistol. She eyed her horse. As soon as she released the reins, he would be off at a gallop, away from the stallion's proximity. If she tied him, he would only rear back and snap the reins. She debated what to do for the best, then the matter was taken from her hands.

With a small explosion of unexpected sound, a horse and rider burst through the mist, cantered up and halted one horse length from her. Sarah's mount reared, grabbed his freedom, spun on his hocks and bolted with terror.

'I thought the stallion would flush you out alone, you arrogant bitch!' Forrest snarled.

Sarah jumped with shock and froze as he slid clumsily from the saddle. His right arm was bent at an awkward angle, half supported, but there was no mistaking the menace of the pistol held firmly in his left. She kept carefully still. On Forrest's face was a mask of hatred and triumph.

'You think you know it all,' he growled at her, 'but I'm way ahead of you now!' he leered.

Sarah's heart stopped thudding while her mind raced. Oh what a fool she had been. Forrest's revenge! Of course, taking their horses when she and Walter were absent was the perfect excuse to divide and rule. Why hadn't she thought this theft through? She had gone off half-cocked and now look at the mess she was in. There was something very ugly in Forrest's eyes and she was under no illusions.

He stepped forward and jabbed the pistol in her belly. 'Move very slowly and put that pistol on the ground. That's right, drop it!' Forrest ordered. When she had complied, he jabbed again. 'And the one under that tunic,' he snarled. 'You won't fool me a second time.'

Sarah had no option but to obey. Her mind raced frantically. If she called for help, she would be dead before her voice had died away.

Finally she stared Forrest in the eyes.

'Now it's my turn,' he snapped triumphantly. 'You are going to pay,' he threatened. 'You certainly finished me with the Royalists, you cow. I had a good thing going but it's no more, thanks to you. And I'm persona non grata as well. A man can't live on fresh air alone and now I have to go elsewhere. It's going to be the West Indies for me . . . and you! Yes! Don't look startled. I've worked it all out. The men here will be more than content with the horses, but it's you and you only I want. I'm taking you with me. Oh, don't let wild ideas flash through your head about help coming. I'll have you drugged and you'll be shipped aboard as freight. Then, you'll be mine and, when I'm bored with you, I'll pass you on to whoever wants you. You'll make a fine whore, I reckon.'

Sarah felt this was all quite preposterous except for the maniacal gleam in Forrest's eyes. She kept very still. There was one slight chance only, but how to put it into action?

'Turn around and walk ahead,' Forrest grunted, jabbing again. 'This'll be in the small of your back so don't get fancy ideas of running into the mist.'

Sarah kept a straight look on her face. Was this the chance? If so, when to try? She must act so, lowering her head as if in submissive defeat, she obeyed silently.

'Walk forward . . . slowly!' Forrest warned.

Sarah obeyed and trudged, eyes down, peeping from their corners. She could sense he was half a step behind. The pistol kept touching her back. How far away were the other men in his gang? Where was the stallion? When should she act? She stepped forward again and let herself trip, arms going forward to save herself. It looked a genuine stumble and Forrest halted. 'Up!' he barked.

Taking her time, she started to scramble to her feet but her right hand slid under her skirt. Moving swiftly and innocently she grasped her dagger and, as she stood, innocently pulled her skirt down, half turning at the same time.

Forrest waited patiently, so Sarah gave another half-stumble, which lurched her at him. Her left arm frantically knocked the pistol arm aside as she turned while her right brought the dagger up. Without the slightest hesitation she rammed it straight into his stomach, then shot aside instinctively. His pistol barked, more from a reflex action of shock than intent, because already he stood wide-eyed. Forrest looked down at the dagger protruding from his stomach and the belching blood.

Sarah kicked out, one of her feet hooking around his. She jerked and Forrest fell heavily, landing face down, driving the knife home even further as Sarah fled. She ran like a maniac then, after some paces she stopped. She opened her mouth and screamed frantically for help. Surely the men must hear her?

The stallion certainly did; so too did the men around him. Men and horses halted as the shrill, blood-curdling scream split the air and the horse recovered faster. He reared high, snatching the restraining rope from the men's hands, spun on his hocks and bolted for freedom.

Sarah panted from shock and exertion. She looked around. The mist was becoming even more patchy and she was not wholly certain which way to go for home. Then a strange sound approached. A rumbling, thundering sound and she froze. There was violent snorting and she guessed. Which direction? The stallion burst through the mist, almost on top of her. The animal braked to a halt, reared high, enormous hooves towering over her. The black ears were flat against the horse's skull and the eyes rolled with rage. Then her scent rose up sharp and clear. The stallion dropped down on all fours, bounced a few steps then, still on edge, nosed her, the rope dancing from around his neck. She was safely familiar. She was the person who had always used soft words and offered titbits.

Sarah kept very still and gently stroked the black nose, breathing her scent deeper into the stallion's nostrils. She eyed the rope, looked at the stallion's back and made a decision. She had never ridden him and bareback? The

287

thought was frightening but she could not continue to stand. The other men could appear at any moment. She grasped the rope's loose end, patted the huge, crested neck and eyed the stallion's back. It seemed mountain high and would he stand? Already he had started to dither his front feet, still agitated.

Sarah grasped hold of the withers. 'Stand!' she said firmly, bounced on her toes and laboriously, ungainly, slithered over his back. Hastily she straddled him, then the stallion's patience evaporated. With a snort he shot forward and Sarah frantically grabbed his mane again. His back felt slippery, but the power and grace of his paces! No wonder James raved about his favourite horse.

The stallion burst into a gallop, head swinging low, heading unerringly to his home area. Sarah was a passive passenger. She could do nothing but sit and pray; yet she revelled in the thrill of the horse. He was incredible. His steps were explosive and she gulped, frightened out of her wits yet enjoying the wonderful sensation. He went faster and faster, eating up the distance, tearing across the last field and Sarah's heart rose in her mouth. A shut gate faced them. The Pair had thought to be helpful; then her eyes opened with a new shock.

James stood there, holding his horse's reins while The Pair gabbled away. From out of the thinning mist, a wild, black apparition hurtled towards him. On the stallion's bare back, crazily, wildly, shrieking was Sarah. His heart rose into his mouth. He dropped the reins and sprang forward to open the gate but knew he would be far too late.

The stallion took off. Great hocks pressed and the black body soared up and out, clearing the gate easily. Sarah rode the jump, beautifully balanced, then the stallion landed. His hooves struck sparks from the yard's cobbles and he lurched. The inevitable happened. Sarah shot from his back, flew through the air and, by the grace of God, landed face first in the muck heap.

"Sarah!' he bellowed. He'd never been so terrified in all his life.

She sprawled inelegantly, her nose flaring at the stench of soiled straw, then he grabbed her, pulled her upright and clasped her in his arms. 'Are you all right?' he cried, still shocked out of wits, while The Pair stood nearby, white-faced and horrified.

'Yes,' she gasped, 'but I stink!'

'Serve you right for rolling in the muck heap,' he told her, waiting for his heartbeat to slow down. Dear God, what the hell had been going on and why? The Pair's garbled explanations had left him too confused for thought and the strange men from the village, hurrying after hoof prints, only added to his confusion.

'Help me up!' Sarah told him then standing,

starting to shake from delayed shock she looked up at him. 'Oh James!' she cried. 'It's been awful!'

'So I gather,' he said dryly, taking a deep breath and turning to The Pair. 'I think a hot bath is in order,' he hinted broadly. Mary and Nellie exchanged looks then turned and trotted into the house to put pans of water on to boil. James escorted her back inside, one arm around her shoulders, which had now started to shake.

Walter appeared, threw a questioning look around, assessed the situation, then let the stallion loose again. He was the best one to get his mares but with Walter following. The other men hastily turned their horses to his wave and followed. Sarah saw and was satisfied. It would not take Walter long now and Jack would soon join him. There might be a fight with the other men but, she suspected, it would turn into a half-hearted affair once Forrest's death became known. Now, for the first time in hours, she could relax.

'Bath first, then talk!' James said bluntly, then sniffing himself from where he had held her, 'And me too I think!' he added dryly.

It took them an hour to get themselves clean and into fresh clothes, then they retired to their private sitting room with some ale. Sarah drank deeply. From outside there were many sounds that she identified as horses returning. She was quite satisfied. By noon, the property would be back in order again, the whole episode resigned to history but, she reminded herself, with Forrest's death to be explained to the sheriff . . . and James.

She eyed him thoughtfully, over the froth of her drink, He stared at her, lips twitching a little but whether with amusement or barely concealed irritation, she was uncertain.

'Well,' he said finally, 'how about telling me?'

Sarah chewed her lip and did, omitting any reference to past dealings with Forrest. That was the tricky bit. She knew she could never lie satisfactorily to him, yet how could she tell the truth without going too far? It hit her how terribly tricky her situation was because James continued to regard her without blinking. What was going on in that clever head of his? She swallowed with apprehension.

'So, a man's dead,' James remarked slowly, crinkling his nostrils. He knew perfectly well he'd been given some watered-down version of a story. Oh why didn't Sarah realise she could not fool him? Once more, the old heartache surfaced.

Sarah made a decision. She would go so far but not one step more. 'I know who the man was,' she started, picking her words with incredible care. 'I'd had trouble with him before. It was his idea of revenge. Stealing the horses was but a blind to draw me out.'

'What sort of trouble?' James asked quietly.

291

'And who was the man?'

'His name was Simon Forrest.'

James sat up straighter with a jerk, astonished, mind reeling. 'Him?' he gasped.

Sarah was quick. 'You know him?'

Now it was his turn to ponder carefully. He knew he would never break his oath to Thurloe, his honour was too sacred for that and he realised he had given himself away. He muttered a low curse.

'You do know him?' Sarah prodded quietly.

'I know he was a Royalist man and that recently someone shot him,' James told her. A suspicion showed its head. Was it possible? But why? Surely to God Forrest wasn't her lover? He was not all that much older. He was personable with charisma but not Sarah's type of man, he would have considered. On the other hand, his absences, through no fault of his own, had left the field clear for a bold man to attract Sarah's attention. If his deduction was correct, she had shot him, but why? Had Forrest attempted to go too far too fast? He felt fresh pain in his heart. How far *had* those two gone? Where did all this leave him now that Forrest was dead? He wanted to take her into his arms and reinforce the deep love he had for her. The past was the past. Everyone made mistakes and, knowing his beloved, forthright Sarah, she would soon be consumed with guilt at an extra-marital affair.

She continued to regard him thoughtfully

while his mind, for once, hesitated as to how to proceed. Finally he made his decision.

'I've left Thurloe,' he told her in a gentle voice, 'which means I'll be at home now.'

Sarah was flabbergasted and delighted, then shocked. Her mind revolved. Why? How had he managed this? Was it safe? From what he'd related before, John Thurloe was not a man to trifle with, so how had he managed to break free? Where did this leave her with her new work? James would obviously take up the reins of the business so how could John Browne operate safely? Did this, by any chance, mean James' political views had changed through some unknown event? A thousand questions stormed at her.

'That's nice to know,' she said delicately.

James felt fresh hurt. In a clairvoyant flash he realised his announcement did not entirely please her. Did this mean that Forrest was not her lover? There was another, somewhere in Bristol? Perhaps Forrest had come between them? He writhed.

'What is it, James?' she whispered. She had not missed the confused look in his eyes and, something else. If she hadn't known better, she would have sworn disappointment had shown.

'Who is he? Can you tell me? I'll not do anything to him,' James promised wildly. 'I just want the chance to win you back again because, Sarah, I love you so very much,' he grated and felt that awful lump lodge in his

293

throat once more.

Sarah was baffled. She frowned. His words were nothing but a riddle. 'Who is who?'

He took a deep breath. He must be calm. He must not rant or rave. He must ignore the painful heartbeat but he must know so he could fight and win back his wonderful wife. 'Your lover?' he managed to get out at last, shoulders slumping hurtfully.

Sarah's jaw dropped. 'My what?' she croaked. Had she misheard him?

He took a deep breath. 'I know you'll not want to tell me. Just give me a chance, my darling. Let me court you all over again. I love you so much it hurts here like a physical wound,' and he touched his heart while, he could not help it, his eyes misted.

Sarah was speechless. Her eyes took in his abject misery and she shook her head while her mind revolved. What on earth had put this idea into James' head? It was incredible. If she had not known him so well, she would have thought it an unpleasant joke. 'My lover?' she repeated, shaking her head. 'But I don't have one except you!'

He looked up, holding her eyes, hardly daring to believe his ears. She held his gaze firmly, sitting bolt upright, the half-empty tankard tipping slightly. He wanted to believe her, oh so desperately, yet how could he?

'No?' he said, his voice echoing disbelief.

'Of course I don't!' Sarah snapped at him

with some asperity. 'What on earth put such a crazy idea into your head? Is it because of . . . ?' Then it hit her. 'That's why you've resigned!' she shot at him. 'What does Thurloe know?'

James lowered his head, put his tankard down and moved both hands expressively. 'He knows because I made an ass of myself before him,' he told her in a low voice. 'I just about broke down but he acted damned well. I've changed my opinion about him too.'

'I don't believe what I'm hearing!' Sarah protested. 'What on earth put such an idea into your head in the first place?'

James took a deep breath and looked over at her very steadily. 'Because you've been distant with me for a long time now. Even after we'd made love, I knew your thoughts were far away and I was totally excluded. You've always been so open with me in the past, my darling. So what else could I think? Because I was away so much I deduced you'd found someone else. It broke my heart and that's when I saw Thurloe. All I want to do is win you back again. There's never been another woman for me and I don't think I could go on without you!' he confessed.

Sarah put her tankard down, walked over to him and knelt to take his hands in hers. 'Oh James, you big silly fool. There *is* no other man. There never has been and there never will be. You are all the man I have ever wanted

295

and I love you dearly but . . .' she hesitated, aware of the immediate quagmire.

'So what is it then? You've only been half a person,' he rebuked softly. 'Can't you tell me?'

Sarah puffed with her cheeks. This was getting very difficult indeed. She sank back on her heels, still holding his hand but from where she could look right into his eyes. 'It's not easy,' she told him thoughtfully, then frowned. He was quick, sharp and intelligent. 'You have never been able to tell me about your work,' she hinted and waited, almost holding her breath.

Now it was his turn to frown while he set his mind to work. Why did she look at him like that? Those words carried a hidden meaning. She knew something but was unable to confide in him but why should that be? He released her hands, stood and started to pad backwards and forwards across the room, his mind now highly alert. For the first time in many days, he knew he was thinking clearly.

He went back, right back and remembered Sarah's change of views, her hot words. He coupled these to his work and open antagonism to monarchs. He remembered Thurloe's news about Forrest. Who had shot him and why? Then this attempt to abduct her for revenge. What kind of revenge? How great was the offence? So if Forrest was a Royalist . . .? And his mind hunted around, gathering up loose threads and starting to weave an understandable pattern at last. Suddenly, the work was complete. He turned, looked down at where Sarah still squatted and gave a gasp. 'Well I never!'

Sarah looked at hint wryly and slowly stood to take his hands in hers. 'Now do you understand why I cannot, will not talk, even to you . . . unless your views have changed?' she asked hopefully.

He shook his head slowly but firmly. 'I doubt they will ever do that.' Then another thought entered his head. 'It's a dirty game, Sarah, and not one for a woman,' he told her in a low, worried tone.

'Not perhaps on the periphery,' she replied carefully.

So she was just a courier, he told himself. Well, that wasn't too bad though there would be moments of risk. However, now he had worked it all out, and discovered there was no rival, his head lightened and he felt years younger.

'From this moment I follow no creed,' he told her gently. 'I'll not get involved, I don't want to. Also, I'll not betray Thurloe. He trusts me,' he added quietly, 'so I don't want to know anything, at any time. On the other hand, though,' and his voice dropped low and grim, 'your safety is paramount to me. If anyone hurts one hair on your head I'll crucify them no matter who they are, their rank or wealth.'

Sarah knew he meant it. She was disappointed he had adopted a fresh neutral stance. How she could have benefited from his experience and wisdom but she too knew when not to press.

'Can you tell me if you have someone on that side, powerful enough to back you in an emergency?' he asked with insistence. It was vital her back be covered. There'd always been Thurloe's help he could call upon.

Sarah turned over her answer. She could see no harm in reassuring him. It would make their life easier. There was obviously much trust to be built up again.

'Yes,' she whispered, and mischief twinkled in her eyes. 'Prince Charles Stuart!'

'What!' he gasped. This was the last name he'd expected. 'But how could you . . . ?'

Sarah chuckled. The atmosphere had lightened. It was now like it had been in the old days. 'He's been a kind of friend since I helped him after Worcester.'

He was speechless. Words failed him completely. He shook his head to show his amazement, 'You helped him?' he managed to get out at last.

Sarah related her story to which he listened in stunned silence, then shook his head. 'No wonder we never caught him when ordinary people worked for him!' he marvelled. 'Well, one thing's for sure, you won't ever get a better backer than him but Sarah,' he said,

298

dropping his voice to a serious tone, 'trust no one but him.'

'I don't!' she said with a grin. 'I too learned from you.'

She paused and eyed him, head slightly to one side. 'You won't . . .' she began hopefully.

James shook his head firmly. 'No,' he told her quietly. 'You're on your own. I've had a gut full of it all. Just you be careful, never become complacent and be wary about your contact in Bristol. No, don't jump; it's obvious that's why you go. Remember, people can be turned with the flash of money. Always protect your back,' and he stopped to give her a look filled with love but implacably firm. 'I hope you and your ilk fail.'

'Oh James!' she wailed softly, her eyes becoming large and hurt.

'I mean it,' he repeated. 'I don't like monarchs and never will, so this subject is now closed for all time.'

Sarah took a deep breath. He had been honest. She knew where she stood and she respected as well as loved him. He had thought the very worst yet he had thrown up all that he held dear to win her back. What greater love could he have for her, than this? She went to him, nestled in his arms, laid her head on his chest and revelled in listening to the steady drumming of his heart Oh James, she whispered to herself, you're implacable now, but time will tell.

299

PART THREE

1658

CHAPTER FOURTEEN

James ate the last mouthful of a delicious meal, then, taking Sarah's hand in his arm, they strolled to their sitting chamber.

"The Pair are getting old,' he said in a low voice to her, as he closed the door.

Sarah nodded. 'But are you brave enough to suggest they retire?'

'Not likely,' James quipped, 'but we could get a couple of girls in from the village to help so there's little heavy work for them to do,' he suggested.

'Now why didn't I think of that?' Sarah complained with chagrin.

'Because your head is stuffed full with that other rubbish!' he teased as they sat comfortably together on their settle.

Sarah was forced to smile. Now they were in their thirties, they enjoyed a full, happy life together which, at one time, neither had dared to envisage. James was a respectable businessman and the spice business had grown. John Browne was the trusted manager because now Robert spent his working life at sea. His wife Jane and their children did not seem to mind in the least so Sarah guessed each homecoming was a wonderful, tender occasion. Certainly, not long after Robert sailed off again, Jane would announce another pregnancy. It seemed a crying shame she had been through so many miscarriages.

Walter and Jack had both been luckier with their broods. Was it because they lived in the healthier country? Yet Jane expressed no yearning to have a house near to them; neither did Robert. He could not bear to be parted from water and sometimes she pulled his leg, saying he should have paddles, not legs.

Sarah was happy. She had her work and now enjoyed her regular visits to see Bessie. It had taken time for a gentle friendship to grow and flourish but her monthly visits were something which both of them enjoyed. Mildred Cook had been used until Sarah's wardrobe was bursting but, once James knew her activities, secrecy from him meant an alibi was no longer required. She still used the dressmaker, whenever a new garment was needed; yet Sarah knew Mildred was not her kind. She was too small, too pert and too nosy.

There had been a slight problem with James working in the firm, when she wanted to speak to John Browne but, fortunately, these occasions were rare. She was aware James knew of her acquaintance with his manager and, knowing him, had probably put his two and two together very early on. He never said anything to her though and was tactful enough to vanish when she and Browne conversed; not that this happened often. As far as Sarah could see, the years rolled by with no improvement in the Royalists' position at all. Sometimes she almost despaired.

She looked around the room that she had brightened to make into a comfortable, warm place—their refuge from the world once the children had retired. Sarah had thrown homemade, coloured scatter rugs around, while James had added his own, more martial touch. One wall displayed old weapons, pikes and swords that he had arranged in a pattern. It was rather stark to Sarah's eyes but it pleased James, which was more than enough for her.

They regarded each other, eyes soft and loving: two happy people, utterly content with each other. Sarah wore an old pair of Robert's breeches, which she found so practical for riding. The village had been scandalised the first time she rode out in male dress but she did not care. If James didn't, the village could get lost. For Bristol riding, Mildred Cook had made her four long riding skirts that divided in the middle. Although not as comfortable as Robert's breeches, they were a vast improvement on an ordinary skirt.

James wore what Sarah considered to be nothing but a Puritan uniform. Starched white shirt, minus lace or ruffles, with black coat, breeches and boots. Sometimes she thought the men's dress was positively funereal. His complexion was a healthy tanned brown-red, like hers and he had acquired a little more

305

weight since he had ceased riding all around the land.

He was adamantly neutral, although he never interfered in what she did. Sometimes though, Sarah had the suspicion he or Walter kept a discreet eye on her activities. Certainly James rode into Bristol with her and, at times, accompanied her but always left her well before Clifton village. She wondered how much he had managed to guess. Quite a lot, she mused. If only he would help. Why did he insist upon keeping this ridiculous apolitical status?

'I'll get really fat if I don't watch out,' he joked and patted his stomach, then threw her a piercing look. 'He's dead.'

'So!' Sarah sighed. 'It's come at last.'

James nodded. 'In many ways, I'm very sorry because he was a great man and history will one day confirm this. England will not meet his like again in a hurry. Look what he did for warfare? He improved it beyond recognition. Look at the way horse breeding has changed, just because of Oliver Cromwell.'

Sarah was forced to agree. It was he who had decided that lightweight, fast horses with men only protected with leather, were far superior to men in metal protection. He had certainly revolutionised the horse and his stud was famous. On the other hand, she viewed him as the enemy. 'Maybe he was a brilliant soldier, but he was a rotten civilian head of the country. It was a good job he refused the Crown but I think he lost all control recently.'

She fell silent, thinking deeply. 'Who takes his place?'

James grimaced. 'Son Richard!'

Sarah groaned. 'He is worse; he is useless.'

James agreed but did not say so just then. He remembered what he had once said to Thurloe about Tumbledown Dick. He pulled a face to himself.

Sarah had been studying his expression. 'You don't like him either,' she accused. 'This is the first time we've talked politics in years. James, please be with us,' she asked in a soft voice. 'Look at the mess the country is in. There are soldiers whose pay is so much in arrears, they've had to take to crime to survive. Unless someone does something, and very quickly, there is going to be anarchy. It will be like the dreadful days when Stephen and Matilda fought for the country.'

'Not quite us bad as that,' he demurred. But he agreed with her. He knew perfectly well the country was in such a financial mess, that it was racing towards total bankruptcy. Many people were stating, openly too, that when Cromwell closed the Long Parliament of '53, it had been unconstitutional. Therefore Parliament had never been legally dissolved. Now, he had heard something of which he strongly disapproved. There was talk of a costly, highly elaborate funeral for Oliver

307

Cromwell, which England simply could not afford.

Sarah sensed his involved thoughts were slowly working their way to some awesome conclusion. She waited with baited breath. 'I still don't like monarchs,' he grumbled.

Sarah said nothing. This time silence would work more than any speech. 'They are ornaments,' he growled, 'or else they think they are creations of the Almighty who don't have to answer to ordinary mortals.'

Sarah looked down at her hands though her eyes twinkled. How like James to go through his grumbling routine first. She held her tongue but looked at him, twinkles in her eyes.

'Stop smirking!'

She gasped. 'Who, me?'

'There's no one else here. Oh, very well then,' he said in a tone so low she almost missed his words. When she realised what he'd said, she clasped her hands together with joy. He held up one of his. 'But first, I go to see Thurloe.'

Sarah went pale and flinched. 'Why? That awful man!' she protested hotly.

'No, he's not but you'd never understand because he's a man's man. Anyhow, I gave my oath long ago and I just want to make sure he knows I'm going to keep it. I'll divulge nothing to your lot which I was party to through him.'

'But that's years and years ago,' she said quickly. 'You'll be out of date and out of

308

touch.'

'That's as maybe but I'm still going to see him,' he replied coolly. Sarah did not like this but had more sense than to argue. James could be very adamant when he chose and, suddenly, she saw his point of view. 'Very well, go your own pig-headed way,' she replied sweetly.

He decided to change the subject. 'Now, you have a contact in Bristol. Just the one, I take it?'

Sarah pursed her lips. 'Actually I have three now.'

He shook his security-conscious head. 'That's two too many!'

'Not under the circumstances,' Sarah told him and paused: 'Actually one has not been there since I started.'

He gave a sigh. 'I think you people have been playing at resistance,' he told her quietly. 'Look at that crazy fiasco in '55? It was doomed from the start and I won't be a party to a side that goes in for such unrealistic planning. Those young aristocrats paid for their so called uprising. I think those who organised it, Penruddock and Grove, wanted their heads examining in the first place. The time simply was not right. Look at what happened!'

Sarah bit her lip. He was right again. The ill-fated Sealed Knot Society peopled by young, hot-blooded aristocrats had risen in their pitiful rebellion. She knew that John

Browne had been instrumental in getting arms to them via the firm's ships. What would James say when he learned that? It was an uncomfortable question.

'The bulk of those young men were executed and the remainder sent to Barbados as slaves,' James said. 'What a pathetic waste of life. The whole affair was slapdash from the start and the leaders should have been shot for incompetence. Were you in on that?'

'Not really, just with messages,' she explained.

'I didn't know until it was all over. I'd certainly have advised against it. Thurloe, of course, would have known from the beginning.'

'How on earth . . . ?'

'Because he knows everything and don't you ever forget that. The Royalists don't seem to grasp how efficient that man's organisation really is, the fools. I happen to know that for a long time he's had access to open all post.'

Sarah had not guessed that and her face became grave. 'You've not sent anything that way, have you, Sarah?' he asked quickly.

She shook her head. 'I don't operate in that fashion.'

'How do you? I have to know if I'm to help?' he pointed out.

Sarah took a deep breath. 'You are then with us, James?'

'I've said so, haven't I?' and his tone was

mildly exasperated. 'Do you think Thurloe has planted me to spy on you, is that it?'

'From what you've told me about him, I'd put nothing past him.'

'Well, he's not,' James stated, 'and that's the honest-to-God truth. Now talk, Sarah; I need details if I'm to advise or help.'

Sarah still hesitated. She had become so security-conscious herself, it was second nature to be discreet. 'We have Edward Hyde in exile with Prince Charles to help with the planning but the Prince will only operate through negotiation. No more fighting,' he says.

'Showing more sense than his late father then,' James grunted.

Sarah seized the chance. 'That's just it. He is not his father. He is his own man and when he becomes king, as he will, he understands he can reign but that, from now on, Parliament must rule. His father's execution plus his personal experiences after Worcester, to say nothing of his penury in exile, have all contributed to make him the man he is. He's nobody's fool either,' Sarah said sagely.

James considered and gave a tiny shake to his head. 'That's all very well but negotiation is better done with an army at a man's back, for insurance purposes, if you take my meaning. The whole linchpin of any operation is going to be Monk. His army is exceedingly powerful. His men are loyal to him and him alone. He has his famous Coldstreamers, the Haselrigs and Fenwicks and . . .'

'Hold on a moment, I'm not with you,' Sarah interrupted. 'Who are they?'

'They are a splendid body of men who were originally recruited to be Cromwell's personal bodyguard. They are called the Coldstreamers from the name of a stream where they were stationed in Scotland. Now if Monk ever marched south with these men, to back up negotiations, then, and only then, will your people get anywhere.'

'I don't suppose you know Monk?' she asked innocently.

He grinned. 'I did and I also knew the two Fairfaxes, father and son,' he told her, going way back down the years now. 'Though only a humble captain, my type of work meant I mixed with many people, especially those in high places. Thanks to Thurloe.'

'What do you mean, thanks to him. If he hadn't wanted information to suit his own ends, you'd never have met them,' she said acidly.

'True but, my word, you do dislike John, don't you?'

'Yes!' she snapped.

He was puzzled. This was the one critical flaw with females. They always brought emotions into anything. Two men could fight each other to the death but still shake hands afterwards even if it was with their dying

312

breath. Two women would be on their way to heaven—or hell—still intent on clawing each other's eyes out. He shook his head with amusement.

'And what do you mean calling him John?' Sarah said scornfully. 'That's not what I call him,' she muttered with genuine anger.

James lifted a hand. 'Let's change that subject, shall we?' he asked mildly. 'Let's get down to the nitty-gritty I think. Has it entered your head that when Charles Stuart comes back, there might be trouble among his supporters?'

Sarah frowned, completely baffled at this. She shook her head, so he hastened to explain what was perfectly obvious to him. Was it because she was female again?

'He'll come back a very poor king to start with,' he commenced smoothly, 'which means he will have no money whatsoever to reward loyal adherents; even with the best will in the world. When Cromwell won the war, many Royalists lost their land and properties, correct? They were given to the parliamentary faithful and have, for years, been owned by the original recipients or their sons if the former have died. It is over twenty years, don't forget, since most of it started. How can these sons now be dispossessed just because a king's come back? It's not *their* fault, is it? Sometimes also land and properties have been sold on. They have changed hands two or even three times. It is not one bit of good loyal Royalists thinking they are going to get everything back just because Charles gets his throne again. They will get precisely nothing but the glory for what that is worth.'

Sarah gasped. 'I hadn't thought that through,' she admitted slowly and bit her lip. 'So does that mean Royalists would start internal fights? Surely not?'

James considered carefully. 'It depends upon how loyal some of Charles' followers are when put to the acid test or whether they have supported him to line their own nests, with rich pickings. It all makes a very tricky situation for Charles Stuart even before he gets his crown back. It needs a person with vast knowledge of home and foreign affairs to smooth the returning monarch's path and there is one only.'

Sarah sat bolt upright, disbelief in her eyes. 'You are not daring to suggest . . . ?'

'Of course, John Thurloe.'

Sarah snorted. 'That's utterly ridiculous, quite preposterous and downright stupid!' she flared at him. 'He'll be caught and executed and serve him right.'

James let out a bellow of laughter. 'Want to take a bet on it?' he cried, holding his side with amusement.

Sarah looked at him stiffly . . . 'I think you'd better explain,' she said frostily.

James became serious. 'I'll tell you why not.

314

Because in his black book are the names of traitors to the Royalist cause as well. Royalists are not all angels, far from it. There have been many with their eyes glued to the main chance— their own chance. Look at Forrest, to start with. Thurloe knew all about him.'

Sarah was shocked. 'He did, but when?'

'From the word go,' James told her bleakly. She simply must understand what she was up against. 'In the book will be the names of all the two-faced Royalists and who is the first person who will be offered a list of their names, for his own life?'

'I don't believe it! The duplicity of the man!'

'The common sense, more like,' James told her. 'That's espionage. Know both sides to survive. Prince Charles also knows all about Thurloe *and* he'll know about the book. When he does manage to get his crown back, I predict he'll imprison John Thurloe and then the haggling will start. At the end of the day Thurloe will not only walk free but probably work for the new king as well.'

Sarah was totally outraged at the very idea. She bridled, her cheeks went red and she was almost too angry for words. 'They say women are two-faced, but you men!'

James smiled at her. 'That's the name of the game. Now you understand why I call it the dirtiest one invented by man, don't you? Anyhow, enough of my predicting the future; if I'm to work with you, after seeing Thurloe,

315

then I'll want a few facts. Your Bristol contact, man or woman?'

Sarah took a deep breath. 'Female,' she said. This bit might get nasty so she'd give no names until she had to. She'd never forgotten how vitriolic James had been after Martin's death. What would his reaction be to learn her contact was Bessie? It did cross James' mind to wonder why she gave no name but he put this down to her security and nodded approvingly. 'And you say you have two others?'

Sarah nodded and again felt uneasy. He anticipated her. 'John Browne's one, isn't he?'

Again Sarah was surprised. She pulled a face. 'Were we so obvious?' she asked with worry.

He shook his head. 'No, it's just that you always made a gentle beeline to him when visiting the firm for me and it didn't take me long to puzzle out his standing, especially as I remember you placed him,' he grinned. 'Now the other man, who's not been with you from the start.'

'Walter!'

He was stunned. 'Hamlyn?' he exclaimed. 'Good God, I'd never have guessed him. I'd have sworn he was Parliament's man to the death.'

Sarah shook her head. 'Probably as a single man, but a married man gets a different view point,' she explained, then continued, 'especially when he has children and looks ahead to their future. It was Walter who counselled against the earlier plot. He said it could never get off the ground. No one listened to him of course. He was too new, still too suspect.'

James nodded thoughtfully. 'And the arms came in to Bristol on the ships with goods for the firm?' He thought a moment. 'So what does Walter actually do?'

Sarah moved her shoulders. 'Nothing at the moment, like me. There *is* nothing we can do, which is the frustrating part. I visit my contact monthly and hope to receive news or instructions, but never do. I sometimes think it is all a horrible waste of time and I get depressed with it all. Walter often escorts me,' she explained. 'By doing this, he knows where I am and who the contact is though he's never actually met the person.'

'I think I'd better meet this lady,' James said shortly.

Now Sarah knew she was against it. 'How do you propose to work?' she said, turning the conversation, frantically stalling for time.

James, as always, saw through this. Why did she hesitate? He decided to play the game her way though, for a moment. 'I think someone should go over and visit the prince. Find out what type of negotiations he has in mind and with whom. There should also be a discussion about Monk which will, later, mean a visit to him. I presume you can arrange an egress to the prince for me?'

Sarah nodded quickly. One pigeon message would do that trick. She knew there was nothing for it. James had to be told. 'I can do this through my Bristol contact.'

'In that case, the sooner I meet your mystery lady, the better.'

Sarah took the bull by its dangerous horns. 'You already know her. It's . . . Bessie.'

James went stiff and cold. He pulled himself up very high in his chair and his jaw set as ice entered his eyes. For a few moments he did not speak but Sarah read hatred across his face and she broke into a sweat. What if he turned the opposite way now? 'James?' she whispered.

'My God, you Royalists must have been desperate to scrape the bottom of that barrel,' he sneered, his tone very ugly.

'Oh, James, please! It wasn't like that at all. Bessie had no choice in the matter because she was blackmailed into it by Forrest, many years ago.'

James relaxed a fraction but his expression was still hostile. 'You'd better do some pretty quick and fancy explaining!'

Sarah did. She went back over the years and spared nothing. He listened in total silence but his face was a mask. Know him as she did, Sarah realised she could not now read him. She was aware though that he sat tight on his chair, explosive and under rigid control. For the first time, it flashed through her mind that

318

her husband could be a very dangerous man to cross.

'You see, she had no choice initially then later she enjoyed the work. It's given her the security of her own home, which is hers by title deed. I helped to arrange all that long ago after the Forrest business. Mr Benson did the conveyancing for her but he knows nothing as he was always so strong for Cromwell.'

James stayed silent and she studied him with awe and apprehension. 'James,' she cried, 'don't just sit there. Say something, for goodness sakes do!'

He let his breath out in a long sigh and slowly relaxed. 'I'd never have guessed her,' he said slowly, 'and, of course, I don't like it,' he admitted firmly, 'but if you are satisfied, then I will be too.'

'Thank goodness for that,' Sarah sighed with relief. 'I was so worried about telling you. I too was hostile to start with but, over the years, we have become friends. After all, it's years since Martin's death, isn't it? Do you remember when I had all those clothes made? That was through her neighbour who is a genuine dressmaker.'

He threw her a look. 'Does this woman know anything?' he asked shrewdly.

Sarah shook her head. 'Bessie's never told a soul, especially her. I only discuss sewing matters with Mildred Cook. She's a widow with no children. I must admit, I don't

319

particularly like her but that is probably just me. She's one of these small, pert, chatty females and I've never liked that type.'

He did understand. He examined her. Noted how she had brightened up and was less tense. Poor, dear Sarah, she must have agonised for years yet nothing had stopped her working. It was this spirit that had attracted him in the first place, on that day long ago when, as Massey's scout, he had abducted her, to her rage.

'You realise that this means I'll probably be away from home for long periods again, don't you?' he asked in a gentle voice.

Sarah nodded slowly. 'Just as long as something is sorted out and sooner rather than later. Do you know, I can hardly remember a time when England was at peace with itself. The children have never known this and that's all so horribly wrong. Now Cromwell is dead, surely it is the time to act positively? Go and see whomever you like if it will help. I certainly feel as if I'm just marking time down here,' she told him heavily.

'I'm not a wonder man,' he hastened to remind her, 'and don't forget, I was Thurloe's man first. You can bet all this will be known over in France. I'll only get into that court with your introduction. The prince will have learned a thing or two about security himself by now,' he added thoughtfully to himself as much as her. 'I might even have to do some kind of apprenticeship to prove my worth and trust, but I'll do it.'

*   *   *

'Well, Penford, and what brings a yokel like you up to the big smoke again?' Thurloe mocked.

James grinned. 'You're getting old and crabby,' he retorted.

They glared at each other. Not with the hostility of two dogs over a juicy bone but, more from force of habit than anything else. Neither of them could have managed a jovial greeting without suspecting an ulterior motive. 'You are wearing too,' James added for good measure.

Thurloe was not to be outdone by anyone. 'And you're as fat as a pig.'

James was uncomfortably aware that this was truth. He tried to suck in his stomach. Thurloe chortled, 'Still shows!' he leered. 'I suppose you want to guzzle my best brandy again?' he grumbled but stood and went for his little private store.

He was not ungenerous but he watched his old agent as he took an appreciative swallow. 'Well, what do you want? If you think I'm having you back to work for me, you've another think coming. You're not fit enough to start with.'

James said with what he knew was irritating

321

blandness. 'I am starting work again . . . for the Royalist cause.'

Thurloe nearly choked on his drink, spilling two precious drops. 'Did you say . . . ?'

'You heard me the first time,' James told him. 'There's never been anything wrong with your hearing in the past and I doubt there is now even though you show your age.'

'You always were a cheeky bugger, Penford. Never did show me the respect to which I am entitled. Now what's all this nonsense? You, working for the Royalists? Since when have you been a turncoat? Come off it, man. Don't ruin my day before it's started properly.'

'My coat was turned when you put that idiot Richard in his father's place and stopped paying the troopers,' James said coldly.

Thurloe stopped drinking. He held the small tankard halfway to his lips, for one of the very few times in his life, thoroughly shocked and bemused. 'But why? He's not all that bad, with guidance.'

'Balls!' James retorted. 'He's the most useless man this country has ever bred for starters. At least Prince Charles is straight and if he came back under specific conditions, he'd pull the country together again. Richard won't, and let me tell you, the people are fed up with the Puritans. They should have been given the heave-ho years ago. I did warn you.'

'I'll defend and back Richard to the best of my ability at all times,' Thurloe told him coldly.

'In that case, welcome King Charles II!'

Now they glowered at each other, two strong men with opposing views but who had the greatest respect for each other.

'Richard will go down and you might just follow him,' James warned. 'I know you've not abused your power financially but there are other affairs from which you don't come out smelling of roses. Selling those young aristocrats into slavery on Barbados.'

'I'll survive,' Thurloe replied wolfishly, 'and as to Barbados, that was all legitimate. Those idiots were conspirators and I can prove it.'

I bet you can, James told himself and I know damned well you will survive, as I told Sarah, but the going, in between, will get rough.

'You sent them into prison and exile without a proper trial though,' he said aloud, in a more gentle tone.

Thurloe replied with a snort which showed his opinion.

'I'll fight tooth and nail to stop a king coming here again and I'll do the same to Monk if he comes down on that side,' he said coldly.

James could see he meant it and he gave a tiny shake to his head with a deep sigh, 'You always were pig-headed,' and he paused, flashing a look at Thurloe. 'I expect I'll be around to pick up the pieces because, Thurloe, there are times when a man is glad of a friend, who is unrelated. What if, when the king comes back, and coming back he is, you're in prison? What about your family? Thought of them at all?'

'My private life's none of your damned business,' Thurloe snapped, then, reading genuine concern in the other's eyes, he let himself mellow a little. 'My first wife died and our two sons went in their infancy. I've four sons and two daughters by my second wife Anne. She's Sir John Lytcott's daughter. If anything should happen to me . . . but it won't . . . they'd take care of 'em,' he said firmly, then threw a questioning look at James. 'What about your domestic life? All right now, I presume? How come you only have two children though?'

'And you can mind your bloody business now,' James shot back at him but not maliciously. 'We've deviated,' he added. 'I'm not with you but, rest assured, I'll divulge nothing which might relate back to the old days. I gave my word, I'll keep it.'

Thurloe nodded. 'I know you will.' He grinned cagily. 'You don't know anything now, anyhow,' he crowed, but suddenly his face became serious as if something had just crossed his mind. 'However, it might be prudent for me to know to where I can send a message, just in case I wanted, shall we say, a chat?'

James frowned. Now what was he up to? Thurloe did and said nothing without a reason. 'Send it to my man Hamlyn. Use the old code. I think I can still remember it.'

Thurloe nodded. He opened his mouth as if to say something, then changed his mind. James was puzzled and watched him with narrow eyes. 'All right,' he drawled. 'Now what is it?'

Thurloe fixed a bland expression on his face and muttered a silent curse. The trouble was, the two of them had worked together and known each other for so long that Penford was the one man from whom it was difficult to keep secrets. Initially, they had mutually loathed each other. Only political equilibrium had enabled them to work in harness but, over the many, long years, respect had grown and now the tentacles of a delicate friendship had surfaced.

'Clear off, Penford. You've said what you came to say and you needn't think you're staying here hours guzzling my best brandy.'

James stood slowly Thurloe was hiding something. Something which might concern him but, rack his brains as he might, he was baffled. Did the wily old devil still have plants in the exiled prince's court? That had to be it, which meant any move he made would be known forthwith. Well, he told himself, two can play at that game. And I can be every bit as cagey as you.

'We'll meet again,' James promised, 'but I don't know when.'

Thurloe simply sniffed but, as James reached the door, he called out. 'Keep your powder dry!'

James gave a chuckle. 'And you watch your back, you devious, old bugger!'

CHAPTER FIFTEEN

James was in a mood, Sarah knew and she hoped he was not going to be too difficult. He rode in silence, almost a petulant look on his face, and she had to smother a grin. He looked just like his son when forbidden to do something.

'I don't like this,' he grumbled.

Sarah eyed him archly. 'Well,' she said sharply, 'in that case go home and find a better temper.'

James threw her a stiff look, saw the gleam in her eyes, opened his mouth to retort but thought better of it. Sarah was as tense as a spring and he knew he was the cause. 'All right,' he muttered, just loud enough for her to hear, 'what's the drill?'

Sarah took a deep breath. A quarrel now would be the final straw. She mellowed her tone. 'I don't go to Bessie right off. I usually call in at Mildred Cook's first, leaving the horses outside, then I go into Bessie's house around the back.'

James thought about that. He supposed it was one way to eliminate any possible watchers but it was rather juvenile. He had enough tact to pass no comment though. Sarah was in a harsh mood. She would row for the sake of it and he did not feel like a fight with her, so soon after returning from the capital and Thurloe's abrasive tongue.

They halted their horses, amid curious stares from the locals, and James tied the reins together, hitching the ends around a post. The house door had opened while he did this and, when he joined Sarah, the little lady was eyeing him with frank curiosity.

Sarah performed a hasty and perfunctory introduction. 'We'll go and see Bessie now,' she said, and went to walk down the passage to the back door as was customary.

The tiny woman, with sharp black eyes, half blocked her passage. 'She's not in I don't think.'

Sarah halted and frowned uncertainly. This was unusual to say the least, and anything abnormal required investigation.

'That's the funny thing,' Mildred Cook continued. 'She went out very early on and has not come back yet, I'm sure.'

'How odd!' Sarah commented and wondered why, yet again, something about this sparrow of a woman irritated her. 'Perhaps she went to market?'

'No, Sarah. It can't be that. She hasn't taken in lodgers for ages so she doesn't need the provisions she used to have. You know how lame she is with the joint ills. She can't walk far without her stick.'

Sarah knew most of this and wondered why she felt uneasy. 'I'll still go in and see whether she's left a message for me somewhere,' she said pleasantly but with firmness.

'I'll come with you then,' Mildred Cook said quickly.

James had stayed quiet, listening to the conversation, not understanding the circumstances. What he did realise though was that Sarah had gone on to the alert. She also did not like the other woman. Why? He decided to intervene.

'There's no need for that,' he said pleasantly but firmly. 'I'll escort my wife.'

The little woman turned to him, held his eyes only for a moment, then broke contact quickly. Her instinct warned her to back down before this strong, powerful man. There was a distinct air of authority about him that made her uneasy. 'Oh, very well,' she grumbled. 'Have it your own way. I'll get the back door key,' and with barely concealed bad grace, she opened a drawer and placed it in his hands.

James flashed a look at Sarah, and she stayed silent as they scrambled over a low back fence and approached the back door of

328

Bessie's home. As James put the key in the lock and turned it, Sarah moved closer. 'Something's not right,' she hissed. 'Bessie never goes out at this hour of the day, though I agree she has become lame.'

They stepped in, James removed the key, reinserted in the lock on the inside and turned it firmly before removing it and placing it in his pocket. At the same time, he took out his pistol, ran a swift check over it and took the lead. Sarah felt the hair at the back of her neck tingle. James had become ultra alert yet she too was disconcerted. Bessie out and not come back? It was strange.

James entered the downstairs sitting room and flashed a look to Sarah. 'Is everything normal?'

She nodded and stood listening. 'The house sounds empty,' she murmured, now deeply puzzled.

James examined the downstairs thoroughly, then went up the stairs, Sarah at his heels. He started to open doors and peer inside each small room. There was only one door left, on the side of a short flight of stairs that went to the attic. He opened that door, peered in, and then stepped into the room, Sarah at his heels.

She flashed a look around, gasped and stilled. Bessie was in bed and sound asleep, at this hour of the day. She opened her mouth to speak but, with a gesture, James silenced her. He padded to the inert figure and looked down for a number of seconds before bending lower. Sarah frowned with bewilderment as he sniffed at Bessie's face. Suddenly, her hand flew to her mouth. She knew.

'She's dead, isn't she?' she gasped in a hoarse voice.

James straightened, threw her a nod, then looked around very carefully. Finally, he holstered his pistol and eyed Sarah thoughtfully. His eyes noted every minute detail. Sarah stepped forward and laid a hand on Bessie's cheek. It was very cold and she withdrew it quickly, as if ice burned.

James came back, picked up Bessie's hand, felt its stiffness, calculated the room's temperature and made his deduction carefully.

Sarah felt tears rise. She now realised how much she had come to love Bessie. She had been a good friend and they had enjoyed many quiet hours of conversation together, which had had no connections with politics. 'Oh James,' she moaned. 'What shall we do? I'd better go and tell Mildred Cook.'

James' fingers moved and clutched her arm, pressing until they nearly hurt. 'Are the pigeons kept on the roof through the attic, up those other stairs?' he asked.

Sarah nodded. The birds. She'd have to do something about them. They could not be left to starve. But they were birds trained to go too and from certain places only. Could they be retrained for their home? She had no idea.

330

'When the pigeons are released with a message, can they be overseen?' James asked suddenly.

Sarah furrowed her brows. This had never entered her head. 'I suppose it might be possible,' she murmured, not thinking straight. She was desperately upset. She had never dreamed Bessie's heart had been so bad. She had lost a cherished friend and the tears welled.

James started to pad backwards and forwards across the room, moving as softly as a cat. Sarah frowned, then caught her breath. When James behaved in such a fashion, it meant he was immersed in deep, complicated thoughts. She felt the hair on the nape of her neck tingle and a shiver slid down her spine.

'James, what is it?' she whispered as fear rose high.

He turned to face her, his face grim. 'Now just you pay attention to me. You are to do exactly as I tell you. No questions now. I want us out of here at the double. We'll then ride and you'll stay quiet while I think this through. Then I'll tell you.'

'But . . . ?'

'No buts!' he snapped coldly. 'You are to walk out of this house but lame,' he told her firmly. 'We never went upstairs. That's vital. You are lame because you tripped over the edge of that rug. Don't forget, as you are supposed to be lame, you'll have to make a big deal of mounting your horse and grimace with pain when in the saddle. No talking though!' and his voice rang with urgency.

Sarah was completely bewildered as he took his pistol out again and threw her a questioning look. She took a deep breath and nodded without having the slightest idea what it was all about. All she could think of was that dear Bessie had died from what must have been the most awful heart attack. What on earth had come over James? He acted as if he expected the devil to come up the stairs at any moment. She gave a shake to her head, swallowed with a gulp and obeyed him to the letter.

Mildred Cook met them as they came over the fence, James supporting Sarah who leaned heavily on him.

'Goodness me! What's happened?'

James got in first. He could see Sarah was too numbed with shock to be coherent. 'My wife tripped on that rug. She's hurt her ankle so I'm taking her home, right now.'

'Oh you poor thing!' Mildred Cook said sympathetically. 'Come in and rest and I'll get an apothecary.'

'There's no need,' James replied in such a blunt tone that further words died away abruptly.

James helped Sarah outside and, acting to the best of her ability, Sarah swung awkwardly into her saddle, pulling a face as if in great pain. James clucked around her, as would any concerned husband, then, throwing a brief nod at Mildred Cook, he mounted and led the way from Clifton, back through Bristol.

Once they were out of sight, Sarah straightened her riding posture and turned to him. 'James! For God's sake, what's going on?'

'Later!' he grunted. 'I want to think. Just follow me and shut up!' he said harshly.

With that Sarah had to be content though, as they rode from the city, tears cascaded freely. Bessie dead! Her numbed mind kept repeating the words over and over again. James rode hard and fast, heading towards their village, then he sheared off at an acute angle, which made Sarah frown.

Finally she understood. They were going to the ruins; the place where they used to meet for utter privacy, all those years ago. Finally, James reined back to a more sensible pace to allow the horses to cool. At the Court, they dismounted; he secured the horses, and looked around.

The deer still lorded it over the park but the Court's ruins had been taken over by the wild. Weeds proliferated, hiding the worst of the rubble, softening the wreckage. He found a half-standing wall, pulled up some weeds, tossed them aside and patted it.

Sarah sat slowly. 'What is this all about?' she asked him wearily.

He eyed her thoughtfully. 'Bessie was

murdered,' he told her bluntly.

Sarah stared at him speechless, her eyes growing wider and larger, his words taking time to register. Then her shoulders slumped miserably. She cried freely and heavily, and he let this run its course. Finally, there were no tears left, and she subsided into miserable sniffs. He passed her his kerchief and she used it freely then, still with a gulp or two, lifted reddened eyes to him.

'Explain!'

James saw she was in control again and started. 'Bessie had been poisoned. Did you see that small glass by her bed? No, I thought you missed it. You also missed that stain on her lips. Someone had given her something to drink with poison added. They wanted her out of the way I was on edge in case whoever did it came back to collect her body. Mildred Cook is in it, up to her neck, of course. It's my betting she is a parliamentary agent and has been so for years. Just a sleeper but an effective one with a back-up team of men for when she needed help.'

Sarah was stunned. Her mouth opened to question, then she snapped it shut again. James was far too experienced to make some ghastly mistake, surely?

He continued remorselessly. 'You say we went in on the normal day, so that woman knew you were coming. She did not expect me though and, more to the point, we were much earlier than usual. We did not call in at the firm first, which you told me, had always been your normal practice. I bet if we'd gone at the usual time, her body would not have been there. She'd simply have vanished.'

'I can hardly take this all in,' Sarah gasped.

'What I'm saying is that Cook must have been planted years and years ago. Like I was,' he explained more kindly now. 'She knew all about Bessie. Every time a bird went off it would be intercepted by someone, somewhere with a hawk.'

Sarah frowned. 'But how could that be?' she argued. 'The messages did get through, that I do know,' she insisted.

'Simple,' he told her. 'At some time, some pigeons, trained to go over to Prince Charles' agents, were intercepted. They were not killed but kept for just such a situation. The hawk killed and brought down Bessie's pigeon, the message was extracted and read, then replaced on the leg of a captured bird.'

Sarah gasped. It was all so logical and she flinched. 'So there's never been anything private at any time. That horrible man has known all! But why now?' she protested.

That had taken him a little time to work out. 'Because Cromwell is dead. Richard is destined to be Protector and no one wants the Royalists to start rocking the boat during the transition period.'

'I hate Thurloe!' Sarah snarled. 'He's killed

my friend. I'll . . . I'll . . .'

'Do nothing at all,' James told her calmly. 'I intend to go and see him again,' he said grimly. Thurloe never sullied his own hands. He was far too clever for that but he did have others who, for the right price, would do his dirty work for him.

'Bessie didn't deserve to die like that. Was it painless, do you think?'

'Yes,' he lied quickly. The body had been lain out too neatly, too straight.

'Oh!' Sarah gasped, as something else entered her head. She flashed a look at him. 'What a good job Robert never knew!'

He nodded agreement. 'Thanks to Walter's advice. As it is, there's that house to dispose of, if, as you say, it was hers. It really belongs to him and we'll see it goes to him. We'll have to cook up some elaborate story with Benson.'

He saw this had distracted her. He boiled inside but she never guessed. That bastard Thurloe, he told himself. All the time he was chatting me up and giving me his brandy, he had just this in mind. I'll crucify him, he thought. Dragging my wife into this, perhaps imperilling her safety. He itched to get on a horse and ride to London but, from long practice, he kept his expression bland and unreadable even to his wife.

'What can we do?' she asked finally.

'Nothing,' he told her practically. Then he gnawed his lip. 'Correction,' he added. 'If you

336

are up to it, I'd like you to go back to that house tomorrow with Walter, of course.'

Sarah was horrified. 'Oh, I couldn't!'

'It would help if you could. First of all, there are those pigeons to rescue and, don't forget, they go to where they can do good and they'd be safer sent off from our end. No hawks.'

She nodded, biting her lip. 'I'd forgotten the birds,' she said miserably.

'I'd also like to make quite sure that Bessie's body has been removed. Could you go up into that room again? Walter would have to stay outside though because if he escorted you inside, suspicion would be aroused that we'd seen through everything. You'd have to think of an excuse,' he pointed out,' because of that Cook woman.'

Sarah's heart plummeted. Even the thought of the idea was nauseating but she nodded wanly.

'Good girl,' he praised, then eyed her gently. 'This is the dirty side,' he reminded her.

Sarah took a deep breath. The tears had dried up, she was in control again and over the shock. 'Bessie's body?' she had to ask though.

He hesitated. He guessed it had already gone into the river somewhere, heavily weighted and would be well sunk. 'That will be seen to,' he extemporised smoothly. There were some things it was better for her not to know.

Sarah had started to think again. 'If Cook

had refused to let us in, that would have aroused our suspicions,' she commented carefully. 'I never did like her but I did not know why. I wonder with whom she works? She might even report direct to that hateful Thurloe of yours.'

He let that pass. He too was puzzled. Why should Thurloe bother himself with the fate, or otherwise, of one insignificant sleeping agent? Now that he had calmed down, he realised Thurloe's game was always aimed at the top people. Unless there was something afoot about which he knew nothing. He reflected on their recent meeting. Twice, he had fancied, Thurloe could have told him something but each time had refrained. This had to be it, of course. Damn the man, he told himself. I'll have something to say to him this time, he added grimly.

'I'll have to go away, Sarah. Perhaps even for a few weeks,' he started gently. 'When you ride out, always have Walter with you.'

She eyed him wanly. 'Oh no! We've not come to that again, have we?'

He gave her a slow nod. Perhaps she had been right for years. Perhaps the country would be more stable with a change at the top? It still stuck in his throat that this must come about through a monarch again but, he added to himself trying to be fair, Republicanism, even when called The Commonwealth, had not worked. Now it was time to give a monarchial system a try again and just hope that kings had learned what Parliaments were for.

'Will you be gone for very long?'

He shrugged eloquently. 'I'll have people to see. Years ago I had connections. Good ones too. There are people out there,' he waved one hand vaguely, 'who owe me for past favours. Now the time has come for me to collect but after I've seen your prince.'

Sarah understood. 'In that case, when we get home, you'd better have my token for identification. It will take you straight to where you want to go, better than anything else. Mine's of gold. Others were made from base metal so mine opens more doors, right to the top,' she explained wearily.

He took her hands. 'We've had some strange meetings here,' he said gently, 'yet I like the place. I consider it ours.'

Sarah looked at him wanly. Tears had suddenly started to prickle again. He knew it and was trying to take her mind off the worst of what had happened. Oh! How she loved him, and she slipped into his arms.

He took a deep breath. She was getting maudlin again. He knew he must distract her before he rode away. 'I'd like to make love to you here, one day.'

That did it. She pulled back and sat up straight. 'What, with all these nettles around? Thank you very much but I'd rather not. It's me that's underneath, don't forget!'

He put his tongue in his cheek. 'There is more than one way,' he suggested delicately.

'James!'

*   *   *

James had no appointment; no way of getting a swift message through so he did the only other thing. He rode up to Thurloe's private home and simply hammered on the door. The servant was askance at his demanding tone but, after a quick consultation, took him into a large, well furnished sitting room. Thurloe joined him after only a short delay and entered, slamming the heavy door, thunder on his face.

'What the hell do you think you're doing coming here?' he barked angrily. 'There's a time and place for everything. My private life is kept quite separate from my public duties. I've a good mind to have you kicked out and your arse booted from here to Whitehall!' he bellowed in a rage. He was shocked to learn Penford even knew his private residence.

James strode over to him, halted one yard away and balled his fists with rage. During the ride, his mood had oscillated between hot and cold temper. Now Thurloe's words were the final straw. He shot out his right fist. It slammed against Thurloe's jaw and flung him against the wall. James went after him, fury on his face and, before Thurloe had a chance to collect his wits, let alone call for help, James seized his throat. With one great hand he slammed hard, fingers pressing.

For one of the few times in his life, Thurloe panicked. He hit out, ineffectively, his blows landing but without enough power. Thurloe felt his senses going, there was a warning red mist before his eyes. In wild savagery, he brought up his right knee in an emasculating kick. James dodged, released his grip and slammed it deep into Thurloe's ample belly. The man gasped, bent over and started to suck for air, frantically then slowly, he toppled and half fell over a chair.

'You fucking bastard!' James roared at him. 'No one threatens or endangers my wife. I've half a mind to kill you, here and now.' Thurloe's brain still worked. Although he had always known Penford was dangerous, it had never entered his head that the man would turn on him. He struggled to get air into his lungs, kicked out again, threw out both of his fists, then they were brawling; James too angry to be professionally neat, Thurloe too much in fear of his life to connect properly; neither of them young men in their twenties. Within a minute, they both had to stop, draw apart, sobbing for breath, sweat streaming down their faces. They were like two enraged bulls who had only paused, by mutual consent, before battling to the death for the cows.

341

'What do you mean?' Thurloe bellowed back. 'I don't even know your wife!' he raged, hitting out left and right in quick succession.

'You knew when I was last here. You'd already planned it, you swine,' James ranted back, his words followed with his own blows.

For half a minute, they stood and exchanged punches, added with a few kicks for good measure, neither of them concerned with rules or ethics.

'I don't know what the bloody hell you're on about. You've gone mad!' Thurloe shouted.

'Don't lie! You'd already arranged it!'

'I'm not lying. You're insane!'

Again they had to halt, both panting heavily, James' eyes narrow hot dots of savagery. Thurloe's wild with fright and fury. Both had their fists up but, Thurloe knew, Penford was the fitter, stronger man. Should he call for help now? He opened his mouth and promptly received a blow right in the centre. He felt a tooth loosen. Swivelling his tongue, he spat it out. It clinked on a piece of the floor not carpeted. The little tinkling sound halted both of them. They stared at the tooth, still bloody from its drastic extraction.

'That's my good tooth,' Thurloe shouted, half bending. 'I don't have many left like that.'

'Tough!' James bellowed unsympathetically. 'I'll shift a few more, then I'll break your bloody neck for good measure!'

'What the hell is this all about?' Thurloe

raged at him, lifting his arms defensively again. His strength had nearly gone. He was no match for Penford at any time, let alone in this temper. Then words registered.

'Why am I a fucking bastard? At least, tell me?' he roared.

James paused and eyed him hotly. He thought Thurloe had more balls than to protest innocence. His lips curled sneeringly as he eyed the man's jaw again. 'I've done nothing to your wife. I swear it!' Thurloe shot at him.

James pulled his intended blow short. He stood, feet braced, his right fist only inches from Thurloe's mouth. He glowered into the man's eyes and it hit him. The innocence registered there was genuine. For a second or two, sudden, sharp doubt assailed him. 'But she's dead. Poisoned!' he threw back.

'For Christ sake, *who* is dead?' Thurloe bawled, sensing the other might be ready to pull back but only if he had the right answers.

Now violent doubt hit James. He lowered his fist, his face brick red, covered with sweat from effort and fury. Thurloe's was the same but more from shock and the thrashing he'd been receiving. 'Bessie!' James shouted and waited.

Thurloe struggled to push his wits into gear again. Jesus, Penford had a punch like a horse's kick. He gingerly tested the rest of his precious teeth then, moving slowly to show he

343

had finished fighting, he half collapsed in a chair.

James watched him, hawk-like, then warily copied. They sat, three feet apart, each tense, both quite ready to spring up and fight again though both would prefer not to. It had dawned upon them collectively, they were unfit and out of condition for brawling.

'Bessie?' Thurloe repeated, frowning heavily. 'Bessie of no last name?'

'Her!' James grated.

Thurloe looked over at him and James saw complete confusion, too genuine to be acting. His own doubt suddenly swelled. 'You mean, you didn't order her killed?' he asked doubtfully.

'Of course I bloody well didn't!' Thurloe shouted back. He was recovering his wind but was still rather afraid for the first time in his life. One wrong word and Penford would be at his throat again. On a second time, John Thurloe knew he would die. He had no strength left to combat animal rage and, even if he called for his servant, Smythe would be ineffectual against Penford. By the time outside help arrived, he would be well and truly dead.

James suddenly knew he told the truth. His shoulders slumped a little. Then who had done it and why? Where did this leave Sarah? Should he have left the house? Could Walter cope?

344

His breath was expelled in a rush of air and he shook his head slowly. 'As it happens, I believe you, Thurloe,' James said slowly then, studied the other's battle wounds. 'I've given you a hammering for nothing,' he added but his look was sardonic and totally unashamed. 'Won't hurt you,' he finished, with an edge.

'I'd like to put you . . . !' Thurloe began, then held his tongue. If he made too big a deal of all this, Penford would mock him for the rest of his life. 'You madman! You of all people should know better than to go off half-cocked. Now you'd better explain what the hell this is all about because, I tell you, I know nothing!'

James took a deep breath, worked out where to best begin, then told the story from the moment they met Mildred Cook. Thurloe heard him out, frowning more deeply with each word. When James had finished, Thurloe shook his head.

'That was *not* my doing and that, Penford, is God's own truth!' James was bewildered. 'But I'd figured it out that you knew everything . . .'

'Of course I did,' Thurloe snapped. His tongue kept going to the tooth's empty socket. It felt as large as a chasm. 'Your wife was playing at it, that's why I never interfered. I reckon if she was busy involved with Bessie of no last name, then she'd not make trouble elsewhere for me. Mildred has been my sleeping agent for years and she alerted me to

Bessie of no last name. Anyhow, what's the connection there? Don't you think I'd better know?'

James took his point. 'Bessie was the mistress of the man who murdered my brother Martin back in '45.'

Thurloe went stiff with interest. 'I never knew that,' he replied, voice piqued. 'Well, that is interesting. Go into detail.'

James did, and told the whole story from before his brother's death, right up to the discovery of this body. 'It did cross my mind later, to wonder if it was your wife who'd shot Forrest before she knifed him. Hm! Your lady wife does not believe in playing pat ball, does she?'

'No,' James grunted, 'and she hates you too.'

Thurloe was not at all disconcerted. 'So do many and they can go and jump into a fiery furnace,' he retorted. 'Well,' he continued, 'I'll start an investigation but, I repeat, that woman's death did not come through me. I go for the bigger fish and you should know that!' he snapped. God, his face hurt. He'd need attention with plenty of arnica before he went to bed and what his wife would say, he didn't like to think. This would have to take place at his home.

James did not like this one bit. 'I prefer to know my enemies,' he began slowly, biting his lip, thinking hard, then suddenly he looked sharply at Thurloe.

'I reckon you have some renegades on your side, out for their own ends, as Forrest was out for his, under Charles Stuart's name.'

That had already entered Thurloe's head. 'You might just be right and, rest assured, I'll be looking into this first thing,' he said grimly.

James eyed him. Both of them, with energy expended, were more calm and reasonable. 'I reckon you could do with a drink of your brandy,' he suggested smoothly.

Thurloe was taken aback. 'Why you . . . !' he roared back at him. 'You come in here, hammer me, then sit there and hint for my brandy!'

'Oh get it out, man, and stop bleating,' James grunted. 'You'll be all the better for a thrashing,' he grinned. 'Anyhow brandy will remove any infection in that socket!'

Muttering and grumbling, Thurloe went to a glass cabinet which fitted into a corner of the room. He returned with a tall decanter and two glasses. 'You're always drinking my brandy,' he muttered. 'Never see the colour of yours though!'

'I'll bring you a bottle when Charles Stuart has you in prison after he's returned,' James mocked and knew he would.

Thurloe was quick off his mark. 'And when he's released me, because of my little black book, how about you and me going on a bender?' he questioned, and now there were twinkles in his eyes, one of which had swollen beautifully.

James lifted his glass, raised it high, grinned, despite a badly cut lip, and swelling face. 'Done!'

'Don't forget!' Thurloe growled but knew Penford wouldn't. 'I'll arrange for us both to bed down in an inn somewhere. That way the women can't wail!' he chuckled, his good humour restored quickly. 'Hell, man, have you always hit like that?' he wanted to know, touching various sore, swelling portions on his face.

James chuckled. 'Only when I get real mad,' he conceded. 'You didn't do too bad yourself but you're fat, flabby and old,' he mocked.

Thurloe unaccustomedly rose to his dangled bait. 'I'm not old,' he snapped, 'I'm just wearing nicely.'

James let it drop now, his thoughts reverting to the original reason for coming.

'Find out whose behind everything, John,' he said calmly 'I'm going to be away a bit,' he added smoothly. 'I don't want to be looking over my shoulder for my wife's safety.'

'All right, James,' Thurloe agreed. He too wanted to find the guilty parties and, when he did, this time he would dispense his own justice. But where was James going? He knew better than to ask. Anyhow, it wasn't necessary. He'd find out in due course. James knew that perfectly well and ignored it.

Thurloe did not know about Sarah's gold medallion. Any conversation he had with Prince Charles would be extremely private and the same with Hyde and Monk. Now they were on Christian name terms and had tested each other in battle, they were almost benign. They sprawled, legs extended, quite comfortable in each other's presence as they drank Thurloe's brandy.

'I think,' James said, slurring his words a little. 'I'd better find somewhere to sleep this lot off then I'll go home to Sarah and tell her everything. It might be politic, with her regarding you as the devil incarnate.'

Thurloe grunted agreeably. He certainly did not want Mistress Penford riding up to the capital like a mad bull, most likely with a dagger in each hand, to carve out his guts. 'Good idea,' he rumbled and belched. ' 'Nother, James?'

'Don't mind if I do?' he slurred happily. What a very nice day it had turned out to be.

*   *   *

Sarah had put off going into Bristol for another day. From what James had deduced, Bessie's body would have long gone. Also she did not fancy the trip but, she agreed, it would look very strange, and arouse suspicions, if she failed to make another enquiry after her friend's disappearance.

349

'That's odd, mistress,' Walter said, frowning and pointing, 'here's the master back. That was a quick trip.'

Too quick, Sarah added silently, so what's wrong now? She eyed James' posture. He slouched in the saddle. Where had his military stance gone? He had been hurt and that was not his horse. 'James?' she cried with worry, and ran up as the strange horse halted uncertainly.

Walter helped him dismount and James looked at them. 'God, I've still got a rotten head,' he moaned.

Sarah looked at Walter not understanding. He did, and a grin slid over his face but he kept tactfully silent.

James looked at the pair of them. He saw that Walter understood. There was amusement in his eyes but Sarah was frightened. 'I left my horse at an inn and borrowed this nag,' he said, nodding. 'Mine sprang a shoe. I've ridden for hours,' he grumbled, 'and I've a mouth like a bird cage.'

'James, what is it? Are you sickening?' Sarah asked, her voice cracking with alarm. She saw Walter frown a warning at her, and failed to understand. As James walked heavily towards their back door, he caught her arm. 'Go easy, mistress,' he advised.

Still Sarah failed to grasp his meaning. Walter took a deep breath and shook his head. How incredible it was that the mistress could still be naive. 'He's been on a drinking bout. He has a bad head and his temper won't be the best until he's had a night's sleep,' he advised. 'Not many could ride from London half-cut because I bet that's where he's been.'

Sarah's head whipped from Walter's face to James' retreating back. 'James . . . drunk? I don't believe it! He rarely drinks to excess!'

'Take my advice, mistress. Cool it for today,' Walter warned her firmly.

Sarah was amazed but gave a brief nod. What could have happened to get James drunk, especially at this time, she could not imagine. She fidgeted and fussed but saw Walter's words were true. James slept heavily all that day and, that evening, when she went to bed, he was waking up. Bright-eyed and bushy tailed. All very well for him, she thought tartly.

'Have you been into Bristol yet?' he wanted to know.

'In the morning,' Sarah replied coldly. 'Who were you drinking with?'

He grinned merrily. 'Just with John,' he explained. 'We cleared up well over a pint of brandy between us. Good stuff it was too.'

Sarah was speechless, collapsing on her side of the bed. 'You don't mean . . . Thurloe?'

He nodded happily. 'Yes, me and my pal, John.'

Sarah exploded. 'Well, how could you? That dreadful man who I'd like to . . .'

He grabbed her. 'You listen to me,' he said and went back to the moment he hammered on the man's doorknocker. Sarah listened with stunned amazement, How could two men try to half kill each other then end up drinking, the best of friends? It was beyond her but was that because she was female, she asked herself? She considered his words. 'I'm glad he wasn't responsible for Bessie's end,' she said slowly, 'but I can't say I'm overjoyed to know there's a renegade somewhere; another Forrest,' she told him soberly.

'That's why I came back. To warn you personally and I'll have a word with Walter before I leave at dawn. Now you go to sleep, I have some figuring out to do on paper, then I'll memorise and destroy it and I'll see you . . . well, I don't know exactly when but, I'll be back,' he promised and kissed her as she lay down, mind revolving but almost too tired to take it all in. Tomorrow, she thought, was another day.

*   *   *

'Well mistress, I was wondering when you'd come and see if Bessie had returned,' Mildred Cook stated calmly as Sarah faced her, Walter two paces behind, expression stiff.

'I've been busy,' Sarah prevaricated. How could this little woman stand here quite so blandly, telling lie after lie? 'I'll just pop in.

Will you let me have the key?' Sarah asked, with a sweetness she certainly did not feel.

'Go in?' Cook asked, with a frown.

'Yes,' Sarah said coolly, holding out one hand.

'Why?'

Sarah took her time in answering, letting the full power of her personality clash with the other's eyes. 'Is there any reason why I should not?' she parried.

The other was flustered, taken aback and slowly, the drawer was opened and the key passed over. Sarah flashed a look at Walter who then carefully positioned himself outside, both ears highly alert, eyes everywhere for intruders.

They had discussed arrangements on the ride into the city and Sarah had her little pistol, carefully concealed. She opened the back door, entered, but did not lock it. With a straight face, she left the key in the lock, then withdrawing her pistol, she examined downstairs. It was exactly as before. Mildred Cook had not made the mistake of dusting. Softly, Sarah mounted the stairs, feeling sick at heart. Carefully she examined each upstairs room, then halted before the one door left. Gingerly, with heart thumping, she opened it and made herself step inside. It was, as James had forecast, empty of anything except furniture. The bed had been carefully made, the linen clean, but the same layer of dust lay thick and heavy.

Sarah's heart slowed its beat and her shoulders slumped. When had they taken Bessie's body; where was it? James had been too swift with his answer. Surely to God they were decent enough to give it a Christian burial or, she bit her lip, had Bessie ended up in the river? Dear, sweet Bessie, what a mess she had made of her life through one single error when a young girl. The repercussions from this had followed her down through the years. She had more than paid.

Cold anger started to grow in Sarah's heart. Revenge reared its very deadly head. The vengeance of a female is poles apart from that of a man, it is far more dangerous with its implacability. Sarah stood, thinking deep, ugly thoughts, turning it all over in her mind. Damn all men, they had no idea how to act properly where females were concerned. James would not approve. John Thurloe would loathe her, and she did not care one damn about either of them, right now.

The board gave a minute creek and a wicked smile twitched her lips. Silently, she withdrew her dainty pistol and tiptoed forward. On earlier visits, she had noted the loose stair floorboard. She had carefully climbed the stairs, walking on their sides so her progress had been silent.

She counted under her breath then, with a sudden unexpected jump, opened the door and came face to face with Mildred Cook. The little woman had the fright of her life after one look at the other's face and steady pistol. 'As I thought,' Sarah said slowly and coldly.

Mildred Cook panicked. 'I just came to help . . .'

'Help murder me too?' Sarah shot at her.

The little woman blanched white. 'What do you mean?' she stuttered wildly.

'You'll see,' Sarah snarled and waggled her pistol. 'Back downstairs, gently and slowly. I'm quite a good shot with this actually so don't get silly ideas. We have to have a little talk first.' And it won't be about the birds and the bees, she said to herself, wondering why, at this time, such an idiotic thought flew into her head. Was the stress making her hysterical?

'Sit!' Sarah ordered, indicating a chair in the sitting room. She took one opposite, taking pains to remain within pistol range. Not that she expected any resistance. James' deductions had been only half correct. There was far more to this than met the eye and Sarah had a shrewd idea what it was.

'Why did you murder Bessie?'

Mildred Cook struggled to regain control now the initial shock was over. She was badly afraid. This was a side of Mistress Penford she had never known existed, despite wild stories which had floated to her, which she had dismissed as being fanciful. Now she was not so sure. Rumour had it this lady had killed

355

once. From the look on her cold face and the hatred in her hard eyes, she was more than capable of repeating any past act.

'I don't know what on earth you mean,' she snapped, fighting to gain the upper hand and save her life. 'Bessie disappeared on a walk. She never came back.'

Sarah took time in replying. 'Bessie was here on my visit a few days ago. She was lying upstairs on her bed, quite dead, from poison.'

Cook stilled and her heart began to thud with fresh fear. So they *had* gone upstairs before the two men she had hired had been able to take the corpse away. She clenched her teeth, mind racing frantically. 'I think you're touched, Mistress.'

'I think you are an evil murderess,' Sarah stated.

'Why should I kill Bessie? We'd been neighbours and friends for years.'

'You knew she was a Royalist courier just as you are in Thurloe's pay,' Sarah replied evenly, not missing how Cook's eyes opened even wider with alarm. 'But you were never satisfied with the pay you received. You wanted more. You wanted Bessie's house when you knew it was hers in title deed. You thought you'd get rid of her, by poison and then apply for the house under the Parliamentary rules of normal sequestration,' she accused.

There was utter silence from Mildred Cook.

356

How could this woman know? Who had told her? No one knew but herself. Even the men she'd hired to remove Bessie's body had known nothing. For a good sum, the right price, they had no objection to removing a corpse and slipping it in the river. Anyhow, there had been no time for them to talk and how could they, without implicating themselves?

'You are quite evil,' Sarah continued remorselessly. 'And you are going to die yourself because Bessie was my dear friend. I will not let her go unavenged.'

'Rubbish!' Mildred Cook snapped. 'You can't prove a thing.' She snorted with indignation, though her fear had started to grow and enlarge: 'My word is as good as yours in a court.'

'I think not,' Sarah replied coolly. 'The men who took Bessie's body will talk freely and easily for a reward of five hundred sovereigns.'

Mildred was thunderstruck. It was an unheard of sum. 'You're bluffing!'

'Try me,' Sarah said sweetly. She had nowhere near that sum but this vicious woman was not to know. 'I repeat, this house is not yours. It's one owned by Parliament and you live here free, while you work for them. You've had hot, greedy eyes on Bessie's ever since she told you it belonged to her,' Sarah threw at her.

Mildred Cook shook. Now her fear rose

357

high enough to make her quiver. How did this mistress know all this? It never entered her head that Sarah was a good, logical guesser.

'You've worked it out that Parliament's time with a Protector is slowly coming to an end, if not this year then perhaps next. You decided to strike and get in first to secure your future. Once this country has a king, there will be no room for you and your kind, no remuneration and certainly no house. You decided to take Bessie's, gambling solely on sequestration because she was a Royalist. It nearly worked too. It was your bad luck that myself and my husband came in extra early that day, before you had chance for your ruffians to remove her body. You're finished. You too are going to die and there are two ways you can go about it. Whichever you take is up to you. I'm quite indifferent, just as long as you stop breathing,' Sarah told her with ice in her voice and her pistol still very steady.

Mildred Cook had the sense to know when she was beaten. She lifted her head, with the last vestiges of pride. 'I don't understand.'

CHAPTER SIXTEEN

Walter felt relief when Sarah appeared. He beamed at her, then stilled. She wore a bleak, almost cruel expression yet, from her eyes,

358

something glowed which sent a chill down is back. He looked uneasily at the two horses then back to Sarah again.

'Right, Walter,' Sarah said briskly. 'The pigeons are on the top floor of that house there. The front door I've left open so you can get in. I'd be obliged if you will get the birds first.'

Slowly, Walter removed the two wicker baskets attached to the rear of his saddle. He felt sudden, very deep unease but couldn't finger where the danger lay.

'Mistress . . .' he began, but Sarah forestalled him. 'The pigeons, Walter, please!'

Muttering under his breath, he looked around again. 'It's all right, Walter. I'm not going anywhere. I'm not going to be abducted or harmed in any way. I promise I will stand here, before everyone's eyes and pat the horses' noses.'

Walter, reluctantly but unable to think of a satisfactory protest, finally obeyed. Before he entered the house, he looked backwards again. The mistress stood stroking the noses of the two horses while the citizens of Clifton passed, going about their lawful affairs.

He thundered up the stairs, burst into the attic, grabbed the startled birds and hastily packed them. Then he rushed downstairs again, as fast as he could, the baskets jolting, the birds cooing their protest. Outside, it was exactly as it had been five minutes ago. So why

359

did the chill down his spine grow? What was going on?

'Let's go, mistress?' he said, as he finished tying the baskets each side of his saddle.

Sarah turned to him. There was nothing on her face but a cold, implacable, cruel mask. 'We will wait for five minutes.'

Walter opened his mouth to argue hotly. 'Why?'

'Because I say so, Walter.'

'But Mistress . . .' he tried again.

'Walter. Shut up!' Sarah shot at him. 'We are going nowhere . . . yet!'

Walter dithered. He stood on one foot, moved to the other, shot rapid glances around, fingered his pistol and kept flashing concerned looks at his mistress.

'Right!' Sarah said at last. 'You will come with me, back into that house. No, not the one the pigeons came from.'

Walter wanted to bawl and shout, stamp and rage but did nothing except draw his pistol. Quite confidently, Sarah opened the door as if with right, then stepped into a room on the right, before Walter could get in first.

'Good God!' Walter exclaimed as he looked at the woman on the floor. He knelt, felt for a pulse, then looked up at Sarah with considerable alarm. 'She's dead!'

Sarah's eyes were narrow, cold and calculating. 'She'd better be!'

Slowly Walter stood and regarded her

360

carefully. 'I think you'd better tell me what's going on, Mistress. This body will have to be reported to the authorities.'

'We'll report it to Lawyer Benson first though,' Sarah told him bleakly. 'I gave her the choice. Of being arrested, tried and publicly executed for killing my old friend Bessie for greed or, going out the easy way; no fuss, no frills, no baying crowd, no public execution. As I thought, she still had enough of the poison left. She took it herself.'

'Good God!' Walter gasped. 'But . . . I don't fully understand.'

'Of course, you don't, Walter dear. You can't help being just a man,' Sarah cooed very sweetly, feeling enormously pleased with herself and delighted that Bessie had been avenged. 'You see, it's like this,' and she explained very carefully going right back to James' attack on Thurloe. 'I knew very well this wasn't a man's work but James had become blinkered. Once he was away I was able to see the wood for the trees. Bessie was my friend. It was up to me to avenge her. I have done just that. It's quite simple, really.'

'Is it?' Walter asked. It's not to me, he told himself wildly. The master would throw a fit and Thurloe? His mind revolved with awe. She had defied Thurloe! She had killed his intelligencer. Dear God, didn't this woman ever learn? Now what a mess she'd made and who was to clear it up? It would have to be

361

him. The master would not be back for . . . he had no idea.

'We'll place all the facts before Mr Benson and Bessie's old house will go to Robert with a suitable excuse. And then I want that odious, bigheaded know-all in London to know *exactly* what has happened to his agent. I want it publicised, long, loud and very clear.'

'What on earth for?' Walter gasped. This was total insanity.

'Just so long as he knows that he does not get his own way, every time, with every woman!' Sarah snapped. 'So see to it, Walter and do not argue any more,' she barked.

Walter was frozen to the ground. 'I can't do that, mistress.'

Sarah fixed him with a very cold eye. 'You will,' she assured him.

And he knew he would. Should he try and get a pigeon to the master, Walter asked himself wildly but, if he was already in France, it would take ages for the message to reach him. Also, and more to point, it would distract the master at a time of critical negotiations. He took a very deep breath, shaking his head with considerable agitation and felt more unhappy than he had in years.

*   *   *

'Oh!' Sarah said. 'It's a message from Mr Benson. He would like me to call in this

362

morning,' Sarah explained, showing the note to Walter. He was distinctly stiff with her now, did not trust her one inch and was on tenterhooks for when James returned. The Pair and Jack were perfectly well aware that something had happened but had no details at all. What they did know was that Sarah was smug yet, now and again, her eyes were red, showing she had been crying.

Bessie was never far from her thoughts and, without her revenge, Sarah knew she might have broken down completely because everything had gone horribly flat. There was no need to ride into Bristol any more. There was no James to talk to in the evenings. The children were engaged with their school work. The Pair knew nothing of the involved life she had been leading. Jack was also ignorant. Only Walter knew, and he was being difficult, bloody-minded and nearly downright impossible. She could hardly go to the privy without him appearing to guard her. Damn all men, she told herself. Damn them, damn them, damn them!

So a visit to Bristol, even to see that stuffy lawyer was, at least, the prospect of an outing to break up this awful mundane routine. Walter would be coming with her, she knew and now did not mind.

When she entered Benson's office he stood to greet her and Sarah was instantly aware that there was something amiss. The man moved as if on edge and when he sat on his chair, it was as if it were liberally covered with sharp thorns. For a fleeting instant, she wondered what on earth could be wrong now. Her conscience was perfectly clear about Mildred Cook's suicide. It was by her own hand when she was not on the premises, and was therefore, to her logic, nothing whatsoever to do with her.

Benson though, being a man and an incredibly stuffy lawyer, might, she realised, have other ideas. This made her bridle indignantly and she too found herself sitting tense, jaw held just a little too high, eyes narrow and ready to flash sparks.

The lawyer stifled a groan. It did not need much education to see the mood Mistress Penford was in. He heartily wished he could deal with her husband. At least, man-to-man, they could have a reasonable discussion. Right now, this strong-minded lady looked ready to eat him if he said the wrong words. And that, he reminded himself, knowing her opinions only too well, was what he was about to do. Rack his brains as he might, there was no other option. Then, to make matters worse, was the other matter. He suddenly wondered why on earth he ran a legal practice. Surely there were more benign ways to make a living?

He cleared his throat, still trying to sort out his words. 'About the house of the deceased,' he began carefully. 'I have checked the title, it

364

was in the name of Bessie Dixon and you say the deceased had a son, Robert, whom you and your husband adopted.'

Sarah felt her irritation start to grow. Of course they had adopted Robert. He'd seen to it. Why must lawyers make a mountain out of a molehill? She stared fixedly at him and gave a cursory nod. What was the matter with the man this time?

'Well,' he began and took a deep breath.

'Oh for goodness' sake, Mr Benson, do get on with it.'

He did. 'Parliament has sequestrated the house.'

Sarah was stunned. 'What?' she gasped. 'How dare they?'

'Easily, I'm afraid,' he told her firmly. She must be made to understand the legalities and formalities of the situation.

'That's wrong!' Sarah said, raising her voice with anger. 'The lady was murdered as you well know.'

'That's as maybe. She was still a Royalist agent, albeit mostly a passive one. Parliament has the complete right to take anything from those who work against her.'

This was something which had never entered Sarah's head. She stared at him with disbelief, hardly able to believe her ears. Then her temper rose in a sheet of flame.

'Oh!' she gasped. 'This is all that dreadful man's doing. I can see his greedy hands, they

365

are everywhere. It is outrageous. It's disgraceful. How I hate, loathe and detest him,' she cried, standing up in her temper, red-cheeked, eyes aflame with every hair on her head quivering wrath. She was far too angry to hear the far door open.

She did see Benson turn colour. He went white and lifted one hand placatingly, throwing a hopeless look to her rear. Sarah turned quickly and glowered at the intruder, how dare one of Benson's clerks presume to come in when she was here on private business.

The man looked over at her. Sarah's eyes raked him. He was older than her by a few years and wore the stark black and white Puritan dress, though the cut and quality of the material were superb. There was a trace of fat around his middle and his jowls were starting to get a little fleshy. She looked into dark hot eyes, the colour of which she had not seen often, and now they were narrow and cold.

'I don't know who you are but how dare you come in here right now!' Sarah cried then turned back to Benson. 'I'm astonished you can't control your clerks,' she snapped. Then she whipped around again. 'Get out, out, out, I say!'

'That man has done more harm to this country than anyone for years,' she snapped, turning back to Benson. She had not heard the door shut; she simply presumed she had sent

366

the other packing with his tail between his legs.

'John Thurloe has been the bane of my life for over a decade and now he snatches dear Bessie's house,' she raged on. 'Well,' she snapped, pausing to take breath, 'it will be over my dead body. I'll fight him tooth and nail, all the way down the line.'

Benson had turned white as he continued to stand helpless before her tirade. He flashed a pathetic look behind Sarah. Her eyes opened wide and again she turned. Her breasts heaved with indignation. 'I told you to go!'

The man stood stock still, and now his eyes held amusement. 'My,' he murmured, 'you do indeed have a temper, Mistress Penford. I had heard, but didn't reckon it was as bad as this!'

Sarah stamped two feet nearer to him. 'Get out, for the last time,' she hissed, almost shaking with her anger.

The man swiftly lifted a hand, palm outwards in peace. 'Mistress, you might just be interested to hear me out about that house,' he replied soothingly, then he glanced over at Benson and gave him a nudge.

Sarah was mystified. Why had she received a warning prod in her mind? She half turned and saw Benson meekly head towards the other door, open it and depart. But this was his office, his practice. What power did this man have to drive him out? At least, this now explained Benson's nerves and agitation.

Sarah concentrated on the stranger. 'Who

367

are you?' she snapped bluntly.

The man removed an imaginary hat with his right hand then performed a courtly bow that would not have disgraced any cavalier. 'John Thurloe, at your service, ma'am.'

Sarah stared at him transfixed. *This* was Thurloe? Surely not! Thurloe lived and worked in London. Thurloe was a wicked evil man. This gentleman could, when a certain expression alighted on his face, be called benign, charming and a complete gentleman.

'I don't know exactly what your game is . . .' Sarah began, voice going cold again '. . . but I'm not interested in playing it!'

He laughed then. A rich, deep bellow which echoed around the room. 'Now I'm here, she doesn't believe I'm me!' Thurloe chortled, holding his sides.

Sarah hesitated uncertainly. Surely this was a weird joke of Benson's? 'Thurloe?' she questioned, hesitantly.

He nodded, highly amused at this unusual situation. Most people backed away when his name was mentioned. The sight of him could make people cross a room to avoid him. This lady did nothing. He could almost swear he could see wheels turning in her mind. He studied her expression with deep interest. First there was uncertainty, next came hesitation, finally realisation started to dawn then, at last, he saw the real lady. Her eyes went narrow, hot and hard. Her cheeks flamed red. Her jaw jutted and she seemed to draw herself to a greater height.

'Why you obnoxious, thoroughly disgusting, hateful man,' Sarah rasped at him. 'For years you have been a thorn in my flesh. I've had your name flung down my throat until I have become sick and tired of hearing it. And what do you mean getting my husband drunk on your brandy? How dare you send him home in that state? He could have fallen off his horse anywhere along the line, and broken his neck but that wouldn't have worried you, would it? Mister high and mighty, selfish, dogmatic, hateful John Thurloe. I hope the King hangs you in the end. I'll come and dance before your twitching body too,' she added for good measure. Her hands itched to attack him. She thought about her little pistol but how could she draw it on him when he appeared unarmed. Even the devil expected one chance. She glowered at him, fumed, boiled and raged, teetering on her toes, on the verge of slapping his face.

'Sarah! Sarah!' he tried to begin.

'Don't you dare to Sarah me,' she raged at him again. 'You don't even have manners! I'm Mistress Penford to you.'

He laughed at her, highly delighted with this spirit that did not disappoint him. My God, he told himself, James married a tartar with this one, but what an ally at a man's back, he marvelled.

369

'And I've heard a lot about you too,' he told her, 'which means you are Sarah to me and there's nothing you can do about that either, is there?' he taunted with glee. He was now enjoying himself. Initially he had been put out, downright angry at realising what he had to do and where it was now necessary for him to go.

He indicated a chair. 'Why don't we rest our legs?' he asked smoothly. 'Surely you're not afraid to sit and be here with me . . . alone?' he challenged, with a leer.

Sarah bristled again, teeth clenched as she struggled not to lose her temper any more but remain logically calm. This was a dangerous man, she reminded herself. Many had died because of him. His power was awesome. Even James was impressed with it and, she thought back, James was convinced this man would survive the transition back to a monarchy. It was rare for James to be wrong, so what made this man tick? Slowly, she sat then, reading his mind, reclined right back in the chair but prudently kept one hand on her waist. From its position, she could easily snatch her little pistol and blast this man to hell and back if he tried anything.

She did not fool Thurloe for one second. She did lift his respect even higher. 'You were an excellent courier for us years ago,' he said with sincerity. 'You ran great risks and, if caught, we could not have helped you. You'd have died like Hannah Rhodes. Now though, working for the other side, which did grieve me when I learned of it, you have only played at the game, which is just as well. You see, it has become even nastier over the years. I'm not saying that you would be too faint-hearted,' he said quickly, seeing her bristle again, 'but it's not something I'd advise anyone to do unless they have a natural hardness, even cruelty, just here,' and he touched his heart.

'Like you?' Sarah asked acidly.

He was not at all put out. 'Like me,' he confirmed coolly. 'The hardness which knowingly sends good men to die. The cruelty which has no pity on friends.'

Something stirred in Sarah's mind. An uneasy feeling touched her heart. She stared deep into his eyes. Was he telling her something?

'If one hair of my James' head is harmed through you, I promise you this, I'll hound you to a very early grave and, being female, you'll find out what cruelty is,' she promised. 'I'd emasculate you, just for starters.'

She paused. He must be made to understand. 'No protection, no bodyguards would save you. I'd wait, months, years, the rest of my life then, when you were on a downer . . . and no one is exempt from depression . . . then I'd strike. This is no threat, John Thurloe. It's a sworn promise.' She waited a few seconds. 'I hope you have the wit to realise this.'

371

He did. He smiled and this time it reached his eyes. 'I have always known the female of the species is the more dangerous but now I'll vow something to you, in my turn. No harm will comes to James through me or anyone connected with me, if I can help it. You see,' he halted uncertainly now, as if baring his soul would disclose a state secret, 'I like James. I'm proud to think he is my friend. I have so few real ones,' he told her, in a wistful voice. 'I've led a hard, dangerous, devious life and there is, as yet, no end in sight for me. Perhaps there never will be. I don't know,' he mused, this time ignoring her probing eyes, talking to the opposite wall. 'Some might think my immediate future is uncertain. I know better. I shall push for Richard Cromwell to the very end before I capitulate. Then I'll be sent to prison while many, perhaps even a mob, will bay for my neck, the fools,' he grinned at her. 'Everyone knows about my little black book. What they do not know is exactly what is in it?'

'Which is?' Sarah shot at him, trying to catch him out while he appeared sentimental but he was far too astute and clever for that.

He laughed. 'Enough to hang many good Parliamentarians and even more good so-called Royalists. I bet, right now, James is making sure Prince Charles understands this,' he grinned. 'Oh, your prince will have to go through all the motions of treating me as public enemy number one but, when he releases me, as rest assured he will, James and I will go on a long-promised bender.'

'I know,' Sarah said but this time in a more mellow tone. Why, she marvelled, when he wants to, this man has incredible charisma. If he keeps on like this, I'll be falling under his spell. She took a deep breath. No, I won't, she vowed. She glared at him. Immediately he recognised the signs of battle. With a few swift words, he was aware he could flatten this. Should he? How about letting her rant on a bit more before the put-down? Then he decided against it. Such humiliation might turn into even more devastating hatred and this lady was not one to cross with impunity.

'That house,' he said quietly.

Sarah scowled pugnaciously, belligerence coming from her in an almost touchable aura.

'I'm giving it to your husband and to you, for past services rendered.'

Sarah was stunned. Her eyes opened wide with disbelief. Now what trick was he leading up to? She frowned and showed her wariness. He approved. He nodded sagely.

'In my position, I can now do more than some people realise. By giving that house to you and your husband, for services rendered— even taking into account your present new views—it means you'll be able to sell it and Robert can thus have what is rightly his.'

'Oh!' Sarah gasped, a smile appearing. 'That's wonderful!' she exclaimed, then she felt herself flush uncomfortably. She threw him a sheepish look. 'I think it's now my turn to apologise,' she said in her forthright manner. 'When Mr Benson told me about the sequestration, I was ready, able and very willing to disembowel you personally.'

He laughed at her chagrin. 'So I gathered.'

'I'm sorry,' she said and meant it. 'I went off half cocked.'

He smiled back at her. 'Not a wise thing to do,' he said and waited. He could see she was going to come out with something else.

'I hated you for years,' Sarah said slowly, with feeling. 'I can't say I exactly like you . . . yet. However, I have a suspicion this might come if we were ever able to get to know each other better and, of course, without dirty politics,' she ended, a bit sadly.

He was touched, sitting right back in his chair now, thoroughly relaxed and enjoying himself. He studied her carefully. She was not exactly what he could call a beautiful woman, yet there was something about her, which held a man's eyes and now he understood. It was her spirit, her honesty, and her fire. No wonder James had thrown in the towel with him, years ago. Now he understood why the man had nearly broken down into tears.

He leaned forward then, looking deep into her eyes. 'I have an apology to make too,' he began with genuine sincerity. 'Your Bessie did not deserve to die in any way, let alone by poison and, I regret, although I have conducted an investigation, I cannot yet help you.'

Sarah nodded to herself. For once someone was ahead of him. 'I sorted that out,' she replied and told the story.When she had finished she regarded hint carefully. 'It was all thoroughly nasty,' she conceded. 'But Mildred Cook took her own life rather than face public consequences.'

He was amazed. He turned over her story, thinking hard, nodding thoughtfully to himself now and again.

'It was a fitting justice,' he agreed, 'so that should be the end of the matter, but it might not be,' he told her carefully.

Sarah went stiff and cold. 'Explain?' she asked, her voice going a little hoarse with dismay.

'Mildred Cook had a son,' he replied. 'I can't tell you any more than that because I don't really know.'

'I'd no idea she'd ever married!'

He eyed her. 'She wasn't. He was a by-blow but, from a couple of little snippets I heard last year when rumour reached me, the son might not be a very nice person. I don't know what he looks like. I don't know his name. I do know he exists or, at least, he did last year. At the time, I must admit I took little notice of what I thought was nothing but trifling gossip. The man who passed this on, one of my agents, is now dead so there is hardly any chance I can enlarge upon this.'

Sarah licked her lips. James must know about this as soon as he returned. Sons could have the very nasty habit of turning into personal avengers no matter how loose was their relationship with a mother.

'I'll tell James as soon as he . . .' she paused, nearly letting the cat out of the bag.

He decided to tease her. 'Oh, he's back from the Continent,' he drawled cheekily.

'How could you . . . oh! agents somewhere?' she fished hopefully.

He chuckled. 'Agents everywhere,' he confirmed. 'Even down at the Isle of Purbeck to pick out those men who travel to France through the Channel Islands.'

'You know everything!' she could not help but marvel.

'I try to, to survive,' and now there was blatant mischief in his voice.

Sarah shook her head. 'I don't know how you remember them all,' she said, with respectful amazement.

'God gifted me with an extraordinary memory,' he told her. 'I bet your man is on his way down here right now,' he finished for her. Then slowly, almost reluctantly, he stood and Sarah copied. She felt so much different to when she had ridden into Bristol. She guessed they must have talked for nearly an hour and now she viewed this man with fresh eyes.

Thurloe took her hands in his. 'I have to go,' he told her in a soft voice, 'I have work to do,' he sighed. 'Richard Cromwell to chivvy, not that I think it will do any good but I'll try, to the bitter end. I have to,' he said simply.

Sarah nodded to her thoughts and he waited with interest. 'James is right. You'll survive,' she told him with a grin. 'It's obvious you're going to spend some time in prison but, yes, when you come out, when the new king frees you, go on a bender with James.'

'Sarah, a thousand thanks. My true friends can be counted on half of the fingers of one hand,' he told her and waggled his right hand expressively. 'One day I hope to count you as one of those too.'

Sarah dimpled at him. Why, she thought, when he wants to, he can ooze charm! 'Time will tell,' she replied enigmatically, tongue in cheek, eyes twinkling.

'May I?' he asked gently and bending, kissed one cheek. 'Hm!' he murmured. 'Nice, nice!'

'Oh, go on with you,' Sarah shot back, embarrassed, flushing like a young girl but rather pleased at the same time.

'My salutations to James and make sure he has not forgotten his first promise either,' he growled, resuming his gruff, cold exterior but throwing her a wink. 'Benson!' he roared. 'Where the hell are you, man, sulking again?'

Walter was confused. Surely the world had gone stark, raving mad? He had ridden into Bristol with a fairly affable mistress but the return was astounding. She had ridden back, cantering very happily, humming a little tune to herself, blithely indifferent to everything except some private thoughts.

As he took her horse's reins in the stable yard, he eyed her. 'You did sound happy, mistress?' he fished politely.

Sarah threw back her head, laughed and beamed at him. 'Oh yes, it's nice to be kissed by a charming gentleman when my husband is absent. Wake him up a bit when I tell him too,' she said mischievously and awaited Walter's reactions. He could be very stolid at times, even incredibly old-fashioned morally.

'Kissed you!' he echoed, his face going stiff.

'Oh yes,' Sarah told him, delighting in the torment in his eyes.

Walter did not hesitate. He knew perfectly well it was none of his business but the master should know what went on behind his back. That was only right and proper.

'Who was he?' Walter growled coldly.

'My friend, John Thurloe!'

'Eh?' Walter gasped, quite speechless, then his brow darkened. Fancy her lying with such an outlandish, utterly impossible name. 'Mistress!' he grated, starting to get angry.

This was not at all fun, though she seemed to think so.

'Yes, dear John,' Sarah trilled happily, eyeing Walter, her head on one side. 'And if you don't believe me, ride into Bristol and ask Benson who visited me in Benson's chambers!' Turning on her heel, she left Walter flat-footed, decidedly unhappy, horribly confused and riddled with suspicions. Very well, he told himself grimly, I'll do just that at the first opportunity.

*   *   *

James was away another two weeks but now Sarah did not mind. She could feel, in her bones, that something dreadful was slowly coming to its inevitable conclusion. Walter had, she knew, ridden into Bristol leaving her in Jack's care. Upon his return he was abashed, awestruck and tongue-tied. Serve you right for your suspicious, dirty mind, Sarah told herself with glee. How naïve men could be at times with their sewer minds. Nothing but overgrown boys, she added to herself for good measure.

She was on the verge of retiring in their bedchamber, when she heard the sound of a weary horse walk into the yard below. Peering through the window, she watched him dismount and her heart started to glow. By the time he had plodded heavily to their room she was waiting, clad in a loose white nightgown.

'James!' she cried and flew into his arms. His hug was as powerful as ever but she could see lines of fatigue.

'I'm sick of the saddle,' he told her as he stripped his outer clothes. 'God, it's cold out. We are going to have a bad winter I think,' and eyed her. 'I'd give much for a hot bath.'

'You'll have one too,' Sarah told him and, flinging on a robe, scuttled along the passage and down the stairs. The kitchen fire never went out and hastily she put pans of water on to boil. Jack opened the door and peered in. 'Help me get these up to our room, Jack,' she asked and, ever-obliging but in his usual silent manner, he took the quickly boiled water. James already had the hipbath waiting and, as the water was poured in, he eyed it with pleasure.

While he soaked, then scrubbed, Sarah watched him, feeling good, warm and happy again.

'What have you been doing?' he asked, making conversation really. There was little she could have done now. She must think her life empty and dull. He'd have to get something organised for her.

Sarah was filled with glee. She decided to tease. 'Oh, seeing my new lover.'

He stilled, lifted his head and stared at her, uncertain. The room was gloomy as the candles were at his end. He could not read her

380

face nor see her eyes. 'What's that supposed to mean?' he asked with rising irritation. He wanted to sleep for at least a whole twenty-four hours.

'What it says,' Sarah chirruped back with fun.

He grunted. Not at all amused. 'And who is lover boy?'

'Dear John,' she replied saucily.

He stopped and now concentrated on her. 'I can't see you properly,' he complained. 'I'm not in the mood for jokes.'

'I'm not joking about the lovely, sweet kiss I had in Bristol,' she trilled back.

He stood up, water cascading in all directions and stepped out onto the towel she had placed down. She handed him another and he started drying himself, hair tousled, body still muscular and fairly fit but showing a slight line of fat around the middle.

'All right,' he told her, 'I don't know what this joke is about but I'll play the game your way. Which John?' he asked keeping his voice amicable though he suddenly felt like smacking her bottom. Didn't she realise an exhausted man was not the wisest target for fun and games especially at this hour?

'Why, your John, of course!'

'Sarah! Pack it up!' and now there was a distinct edge to his voice.

She did, and stepped forward, handing him his nightshirt. 'John Thurloe,' she added

381

sweetly.

He froze and nearly dropped his nightshirt. He opened his mouth, looked at her with disbelief, then took a deep breath. 'I planned on going straight to sleep but I think I'd better sit in that chair and you tell me what it is that is bubbling out of your ears,' he said with total resignation.

Squatting at his feet before their bedchamber fire, she did. He listened in amazed silence, for once, at a complete loss for words. Finally when she finished, he spoke, still shocked. 'If anyone else had told me this tale, I'd have called them a raving liar.' He studied her carefully now, admiring her looks which, to him, were so lovely. 'My God, yes,' he murmured, 'that's you all over and to get John eating out of your hand like that,' he marvelled. 'But I'm glad you made friends with him. He's going to go through a rough patch before he emerges cleaner than snow.'

'Can you tell me anything?' she wanted to know, squeezing on to the chair, half sitting on it and his knees.

'I had a long talk with Hyde; another with Prince Charles and then I went to Scotland to see Monk.'

'All that riding! No wonder you're exhausted!'

'It's coming, that's definite, but it will still take a little time to arrange. If we are not a monarchy next year, then we shall be in 1660.

Monk will not move until he considers the time absolutely ripe, which makes horse sense. He'll probably wait for negotiations to be completed with Sir John Grenville. Apart from bemusing John Thurloe, you didn't do too bad a job on Charles Stuart either. He remembered every detail of that meeting down to a description of exactly what he ate and drank. That man has some memory. I think it might rival John Thurloe's too.'

Sarah was quietly appalled. 'So long,' she complained. 'I bet a woman could organise it sooner.'

James grinned at that. 'There's much to be discussed,' he pointed out. 'Bruised egos to be massaged. Finances to be considered. One thing, there's jealousy now with Parliament's army. They think Pierrpoint and St John are pushing too hard for Parliament. There's a strong murmur of evil counsellors and of John's personal power over Richard Cromwell; all the kind of talk to play into the Royalist hands. Just let the rot ferment and bubble next year and I predict, it will boil over in '60.'

Sarah frowned. 'Haven't I heard there's to be a new election for Parliament? What if the Cromwellians seize power?'

James chuckled. 'If that should happen, it will be providential because you can bet the Royalists will be barred from taking their rightful seats. That will be the one act, above

383

all others, to make that pot overflow. Monk has already told me he will never allow rightful men to be stopped from taking their legitimate seats at Parliament.' He mused a moment before continuing. 'There's also something else. Richard Cromwell is hated. He knows this and he's the type of weak fop who gets upset when he's not liked. How Oliver fathered the likes of him is a mystery.'

Then there was the other matter, which he did not like. Mildred Cook had an illegitimate, mysterious son? 'Never relax your guard,' he told her suddenly.

'I've no intention of doing that,' Sarah reassured him. 'After Fletcher, Forrest and Mildred Cook, I'm prepared to peep behind each dandelion before passing it with my back.'

She related to him, John Thurloe's wisecrack about a first promise. He understood. 'I've bought a small cask of very best brandy with me. I'll take it to him in prison and when he's free . . .'

'You two go and get drunk!' she completed, amused but being female, not quite understanding. How could men enjoy making themselves so ill for the next day?

He studied her and gave a short nod. 'Now I'm clean I'm going to bed, but first I want you. Now!'

'I saw that ten minutes ago,' she retorted. 'If it gets any bigger, it will trip you up!'

PART FOUR

1660

CHAPTER SEVENTEEN

'Well,' James drawled to her, still giving little shakes to his head. The brandy had been more powerful than he'd anticipated and John appeared to have a better head.

'So, it's long live King Charles II,' Sarah said thoughtfully. 'I can hardly believe it. We are at peace, surely?'

They were not quite, but he had no wish to upset the happy look on her face. John Thurloe had passed him the information discreetly in his quite comfortable prison room.

'Be careful yet, James,' he'd advised. 'There's another group of hotheads around who refuse to accept the monarch. Just like the Sealed Knot Society, these Fanatiques could cause a bit of bother before they are controlled.'

James groaned but was not surprised. There would always be agitators, no matter who was in power.

'I suppose they'll flare up like a dying candle,' he mused aloud, 'before spluttering away to nothing.'

'Something like that,' Thurloe told him. He was amused at this situation. There were firebrands crying for his head, saying he was fermenting something himself to put Richard back in power. Some people, he told himself, are too dumb to live.

'Where's your little black book?' James asked with a grin. 'Where you and no one else can find it,' John Thurloe shot back quickly.

James bellowed his laugh. 'Now let me see, you were arrested on the 15th May and put in charge of a sergeant-at-arms. Today's what, the 5th June. When do you anticipate being freed?'

Thurloe did a swift little sum. 'I bet I'm out of here no later than, say, 29th,' he chuckled. 'The trouble is, as far as both sides are concerned, I know just a little too much about everyone. When you think about it, I should be assassinated!'

James blanched. 'Don't say things like that,' he cried in agitation. 'Many a true word spoken in jest,' he pointed out.

'Except . . .' he was told by the other, laying stress on the one word. '*Where* is my dear little incriminating black book?' He chuckled. '*That* is my insurance.'

James grinned. He had no idea where the notorious book was and did not wish to know either. 'You're enjoying this, aren't you?'

John Thurloe looked at the stone wall. He was glad it was the decent weather. Even so, there was a nasty smell of must and damp around. To be imprisoned in the wet, cold months must be hell. His conscience did not trouble him though. Anything he'd done had

388

been for his beloved England. 'Not really,' he replied slowly, 'because it means I've failed. Everything for which I worked, laboured and planned with care and forethought, has gone down the drain. I still don't hold with monarchs. I still think we could have made ourselves a decent republic but the time wasn't right. The people were against it. The army was ready to revolt at the end and the country's coffers are pretty near empty. The whole thing has become one mess. Then there's the fact of all those who died; families who became divided when political beliefs clashed; fathers versus sons; brothers against each other. So many dead—for nothing,' he replied sadly.

James eyed him. If he didn't know better, he'd have thought the brandy was making the other maudlin. He reflected back down the long years too. Some of the memories were horrific. There were days, times and places, which he preferred not to remember. He had a vision of Martin. How horrified his brother would be if he were alive now. Martin could never have adapted to the present new situation. 'Charles Stuart has learned,' he commented slowly. 'He won't make his father's mistakes. He's too bright for that and not arrogant enough.'

'He'd better not,' his friend growled. 'We've chopped off one king's head which makes a very nice legal precedent.'

'There will still be some blood-letting. The regicides,' he pointed out. 'I've heard some of them are going to flee to make a new life and a new country in the Americas. Those who choose to stay might end up losing their heads.'

'And you?'

James gave a sigh of satisfaction. 'No more politics for me. From now on, I'm nothing more than a very simple spice merchant. I've had enough excitement to last me the rest of my life while, you,' he grinned, 'will shortly be hand in glove with the crown, I suppose?'

He'd ridden back home in a euphoric cloud, wondrously happy, realising this was mostly from the savage spirit. By God, that brandy had been good and, he grinned over at his wife, there was the promise of another session to come.

Sarah regarded him indulgently. 'I think what you need, is a long bracing ride in the morning. That will clear your head. I'm having reservations as to the good of John's friendship if there's too much of this,' but her tone was mild, she was pleased to see him happy. There had been so many periods of worry and stress, so many long, uncertain separations, too many dangerous episodes; it did not really seem possible that peace had come with the new King.

The next morning they were up early, though Sarah was amused to see that James

390

lacked his normal bounce. There was a mist that gave token of a good day to come once the sun had dispersed the clinging film.

'It's a bit early to go out,' James grumbled. He knew he was not himself but there was Sarah, bouncing around all vim and go.

'Do you good,' was her unsympathetic reply as she mounted her horse, one of their better ones but not, in her opinion, as good as her old mare.

Still mumbling, James straddled the big chestnut he had taken as his personal mount—a keen, almost flashy animal, but one with an excellent turn of speed when needed.

He wore old breeches and a patched shirt and Sarah was dressed almost as disreputably. She had packed saddlebags with a picnic meal because she had a good idea what they might end up doing in some private place. 'Come on, let's ride up near to the next village, then cut across to the ruins before we go farther out,' she called to him, leading the way.

James shook his head, trying to remove the last of the cobwebs. He'd never known alcohol remain with him so long but, he grinned, it had been worth it. He knew he could not spoil the ride. It was so long since he'd seen Sarah so relaxed and carefree.

As they trotted along, a fox passed them, eyeing them warily before continuing to his earth, a bird between his jaws. The birds were all about, twittering and yet, of humans there was no sign. As Sarah led the way, he marvelled that they could be so near to two villages, yet see and hear nothing. It was peaceful, clean and fresh, making him realise London was a pesthole. People were welcome to the capital.

They rode slowly for fifteen minutes, Sarah in the lead, and he wondered where they were going, then started to smile as they crested a slope and she halted. Both, peering through the mist which clung in little patches, smiled at each other and dismounted casually. Sarah waved a hand expressively and he nodded. It was on this very spot, all those years ago, she'd been riding when he met her, as scout for Massey's dragoons, on the expedition to relieve the men trapped at The Court.

They stood together, idly remembering, while both horses lowered their heads to snatch at the grass as if unfed. He tied the reins together and looped the ends over a low branch so they could stroll a few paces.

James eyed the grass. It was sodden with the night's dew and she read his mind.

'No thank you,' she told him quickly.

He grinned, they were so much in tune with each other now. He took a deep breath, savouring the wet air, enjoying the tang of freshly turned soil somewhere near to hand, the odours from plants and grasses.

Sarah looked casually at the tied horses then studied them more intently. It was always possible to learn much from any animal's reaction to given circumstances.

'James,' she said quietly but he ignored her. He thought he had spotted a four-leaf clover and was bent, turning tiny leaves aside with great interest.

'James!' Sarah said again, this time with more insistence in her voice.

'What?' he grunted. No, there were only three leaves; not taking any notice of her, then a sudden sharp tone in her voice registered. He lifted his head sharply, straightening up.

'What is it?' he grunted.

Sarah did not reply, simply pointed at their two horses. Their mounts stood with ears pricked sharply, taking a great interest in something hidden by the mist on their right flank.

He sucked in a deep breath and focused his attention, flogging his wits back into action. One horse, his own, lifted a hoof and snapped it down a little impatiently.

'There's another horse somewhere around,' Sarah murmured in a very low voice. 'Who could that be at this time just here?'

James strained his ears and muttered to himself. Suddenly he was as alert as in the old days, his instinct jabbing hard. It did not seem possible for anyone to be near, yet the horses' alert behaviour indicated otherwise. The mist was still patchy but he fancied it was lifting in odd places.

'I'm sure I just heard the chink of metal,' Sarah whispered to him, suddenly feeling something cold slide down her spine.

'Walk very quietly back to the horses and mount,' he hissed at her, leading the way.

They swiftly unfastened and mounted their horses, settling themselves into their saddles. Automatically, both checked their girths for tightness and looked at each other. Sarah was baffled but could feel quiet alarm.

James was furious with himself. He had been warned. The land was not wholly at peace yet. He had lowered his guard much too soon with hotheads on the rampage. That this might be useless would cut no ice if they were after revenge for parliament's defeat, and who better for a target than someone like him? The part he had recently played was now common knowledge and, even without that, James was very well aware that, over years, he had made many enemies.

'I don't like this,' Sarah murmured, biting her lip. 'Do we ride home?'

He shook his head. 'We don't know who's out there yet or how many,' he told her quietly, straining to hear. What a crass fool he'd been. It would have been simple to follow him back from London when he was under the influence, yet, he questioned, why hadn't he been attacked then? To the Fanatiques, he was a prime target. It then flashed into his mind that this reasoning could be erroneous. What if any target should be Sarah? What was it John Thurloe had mentioned to her? Something about Mildred Cook having an illegitimate son? What if this young man had joined the Fanatiques? He knew perfectly well there were many men who could take revenge, for anything, just for the hell of it all. Killing released some satisfying urge in their blood.

'Do you have a pistol?' he asked quietly.

Sarah bit her lip and shook her head. 'Why no, now we're at peace I thought . . .' and her words trailed off miserably. 'What about you?'

He nodded and indicated his saddle holsters, but two pistols, although lethal when used correctly, were not very effectual against many. Pistols took so long to load and prepare and he did not have his sword or any other suitable weapon for use on a horse.

'But who can it be?' Sarah asked with worry now.

'I never told you, I forgot, blame the brandy, but it might be the Fanatiques. A wild, rebel Parliament sect, rather like the old Sealed Knot Society,' he told her quickly, thinking rapidly. From the direction their horses' ears pointed, a way back to their home was out of the question if they rode in a straight line. He had no intention of telling her that it might be she who was the target. Even if this deduction were correct, it would be futile adding more worry because, he could see, Sarah was apprehensive. With a flash of understanding, he realised she had come to the end of a very long line.

'Now listen carefully,' he told her in a low voice. 'When I give the word, we'll move away at a hand canter. Don't gallop until we have to. I want to find out how many there are. If only two, then we'll face them with my pistols. However, if more than that number, we have to outthink and outride them.'

Sarah licked her lips, which had gone very dry. She felt sick at heart, her morale slumping to rock bottom. She had been so deliriously happy when they awoke, her whole world settled firmly in place and now this. Dear God, wouldn't danger ever end?

'Which direction though?' she asked him doubtfully.

He thought a moment, working out angles, riding terrain, possible cover from trees and other factors.

'We have some advantages on our side,' he told her calmly, even though his mood had changed to rage. He was terrified for her safety. It had flashed through his mind to order her to ride away while he faced them. This had been dismissed instantly though. She would never obey. 'First of all, we've guessed their presence, thanks to our horses. Secondly, we are very well mounted and thirdly we are top-class riders. What I intend is for us to burst into the open, weigh up the situation and, if more than two, we turn and ride like hell for the court's ruins.'

Sarah frowned her bewilderment. 'Why there?' she asked. It could be dangerous under hoof for the horses with all the rubble, most of which was now hidden by weeds.

'The moat,' he said quickly, then saw her blank expression. 'We'll jump it where we both know it's narrow and . . .'

She grasped his plan now and took a deep breath. Then she understood. 'And we turn to one side, ride alongside the old moat where it widens and . . .'

'Yes,' he grinned wolfishly. 'They'll put their horses to where it is unjumpable. That way we reduce the odds in our favour.'

Sarah gulped. It sounded fine in theory. She just wished she had her mare. The jumping ability of this mount was of an unknown quantity. Then her nostrils flared angrily. Shock and fear were overtaken with temper. How dare these hooligans from some crazy sect spoil her lovely day? Her spine stiffened, her lips set and, watching this mood change, James was gratified to see her jaw stiffen belligerently. It crossed her mind to wonder how these riders had followed James and why, when, in a swift, clairvoyant flash she saw it all. 'It's me they want, isn't it?' she hissed back at him. 'Something to do with that stupid woman's death because of Bessie's murder?'

There was no time to explain more. James realised he did not really need to. As usual, it had not taken Sarah long to work out the permutations and reasons. He lifted an eyebrow questioningly. She threw him a nod in return and they clumped heels to flanks. Their horses shot forward in a harsh, still jolting canter, breaking from the mist unexpectedly, into the clear.

'There they are!' someone bellowed and a pistol barked.

'One!' James muttered to himself and flashed a sharp look around, counting the opposition quickly. His heart sank as he saw there were four of them. Muttering foul oaths to himself, he looked over at Sarah. 'The ruins!' he bellowed. 'Ride!'

Sarah felt her heart thundering wildly. She could still not properly believe what was happening; it was preposterous, sickening, insane. She heard bellows behind, oaths being roared then, quite plainly, 'That's the bitch!'

It took all her effort to control her horse who was startled by the noise to the rear. They cleared the last bit of ground to enter the outskirts of the park. James thundered alongside her, his larger horse much faster.

James eyed her with fright. She was white-faced, eyes running at their corners from tears; from shock or their speed? He didn't like to think. 'Keep going,' he encouraged, 'but let me take the jump first!'

The ruins approached at what was, to Sarah, a horrendous speed. How could they possibly

398

jump? They were as mad as their pursuers.

'Follow me!' James shouted, turning his horse, collecting him together, driving and releasing the reins at the last moment. His horse soared up and out, going very high, stretching, measuring the distance. Sarah became a passenger. Her horse copied, oblivious to her orders through reins or legs. She held her breath, terrified out of her wits. It was an impossible jump. The animal could not make it. For a fleeting second, she looked down on broken rocks, stones, weeds, brambles then the ground came up, hard, and fast. Her horse pecked slightly, Sarah lurched, grabbed a handful of mane for balance then her animal turned, anxious to copy the leader.

James threw a snap glance backwards and spurred forward, racing alongside where the moat widened. It was, he thought grimly, a feeble chance. Surely they would see his ploy?

'Now turn!' James cried, waving his left hand. Sarah copied, anxious to comply, anything to get away from this nightmarish mess. James carried on cantering then, working hard with his hands, he controlled his horse, spun it around, and stared, grim faced.

Sarah, panting heavily from fright fear and exertion, turned after him. She was just in time to see what happened. Two of their pursuers led, with the others at their heels. Their two horses jumped together, driven on by the riders. It was at a point which no horse could hope to clear. Midway, the animals knew this. One's hooves touched the far side, his hind legs scrabbled wildly then slowly, inelegantly, horse and rider toppled backwards. The second horse was no jumper at all. He simply vanished into the moat's depths, landing with a screaming cry.

The other two riders struggled to halt but their chase had meant a flat-out gallop. Both of their horses, witnesses to what had gone on, sensibly refused. One stopped dead, so violently, his hooves ripped up the grass, leaving long brown earth stains. That rider went head forwards into the moat, landing on the rubble and weeds. The fourth was slightly more lucky. He too shot off headfirst but quicker, and with more instinct, he tucked himself into a tight ball. He landed heavily, cried out in agony as a bone broke, was whiplashed by the nettles and finally stopped, jerking savagely, against a pile of rubble.

'Off!' James cried, and was out of his saddle, running, both pistols in his hands. Sarah was slower and had the presence of mind to snatch the two sets of reins and hastily knot them together. Then she ran after James, slowing at the moat's edge, peering down apprehensively.

James carefully slithered down and bent over first one body then another. At the third man he stopped and gave a long hard look, shook his head then went on to the fourth. He

400

was young and now terrified. He was in great pain from a broken leg, the bones of which, from the tibia, protruded through his breeches.

Sarah cautiously scrambled down to join James. He flashed a look at her. 'The bag is two dead, one going and this one,' he said a little callously.

This was a side of James she had rarely seen. He was now the hard, cold, trained military man who neither asked nor gave quarter. She swallowed nervously, wanting to hold his arm but deciding not to while he held pistols.

James stopped a yard from the younger man. 'You are members of The Fanatiques?' he barked.

The young man had never known such pain existed. He looked up at the cold devil facing him, tears streaming down his face. He was suddenly very young, very unsure and his whole world had collapsed.

'Answer me, damn you or I'll kneecap the other leg,' James roared at him, lifting a pistol and taking aim.

'Yes, yes! Don't shoot my other leg!'

James gave a long hard sniff. 'You're Cook's bastard son, aren't you?' he challenged. 'And don't lie!'

The young man began to cry like a child, sobbing wildly, nearly out of control. 'Giles Cook!' he confirmed, shoulders shaking, yelping between his sobs as each movement brought fresh agony to the shattered tibia bone.

'Why?' Sarah cried. She flung a look at James, her eyes asking a silent question. 'John did tell me,' she said slowly, 'but it seemed too far-fetched to be believed.'

He spoke in a low voice, for her ears only. 'Revenge is never that. He might have known his mother's plans, even if he wasn't party to Bessie's death. He'd have inherited a nice place and Cook did die because of your pressure.'

Sarah's fright vanished as her spirit rose. She glowered down at the young man. 'Serve you right!' she snapped at him.

'And all members of The Fanatiques will not meet with the new King's pleasure,' James drawled slowly. He nodded his head backwards. 'Two of your companions are dead. Their necks are broken as are those of their horses. The third one is on his way out. His ribs are stove in and I guess he has a punctured lung so, if this was all your bright idea, you are responsible for three deaths,' he stated very coldly. 'How does that fit on your head?'

It didn't. Giles Cook had never imagined such an ending for his careful plan. He wanted to weep, howl and rage but dare not move because of his leg.

James handed Sarah one pistol. 'He's not

going any place but watch him nevertheless,' he drawled. I'll go and see to the third man,' he drawled.

Sarah understood in a flash. She took the heavy pistol and held it firmly in both hands. If she could carry a secreted small pistol in the old days, so could a man but Giles Cook did not. All he could think about was the sweet agony of his leg. 'Help me!' he wailed, tears streaming down his face.

James strolled back. 'Your other mate is now dead too. I congratulate you on a tally of three. And now we come to you, don't we?' he said in a cold, very hard voice. He hefted his pistol thoughtfully as he took that back from Sarah. 'Go and get the horses,' he said softly. 'We'll have to ride around until we can find a place where we can lead the horses over the rubble.'

Sarah shot him a puzzled look but obeyed. When she had climbed back out again James went forward. He looked Giles Cook straight in his brown eyes. 'You're evil,' he said slowly, 'you're not fit to live,' he recited, 'but I'll do for you what you'd not have done for my wife and myself.'

James waggled the pistol. He put it at half cock, then looked around. Eighteen inches above Giles Cook's body was a small, natural ledge. James carefully rested the pistol there, the butt towards the injured man, then he stood and, with a nod, indicated it. 'There's an

403

escape, if you've the balls to take it. If you don't, you'll be in hell for a long time with that leg and, when it's recovered, you'll then spend the rest of your life in prison. How does that thought fit? Locked up, no sun, no fresh air. No females for sex. Incarcerated for the rest of your life and you're young, you have a good thirty years left . . . while you breathe. Or do you want to show you are your mother's son after all? The choice is yours,' he stated bleakly, then without a backwards glance, scrambled back up out of the moat.

'No, don't go, Penford!' Cook wailed, but, gasping, sobbing, he knew he was alone with his own choice to make.

James joined Sarah, took the reins and led his horse forward. He strode on without a word, hard faced, ears cocked, head high with jaw rock hard. Sarah said nothing. This was not a James to talk to. She bit her lip, followed and felt her heart hammering against her ribs. Suddenly, there was a loud explosion and James halted in his stride. He stood stock still while his horse, head held high, tried to pull back on the reins. 'Hold him,' he grunted to her and turning, strode back purposefully. He was gone for two minutes before coming back to take his horse.

'That's another one out of the way,' he grated.

'But . . .'

'I left him my pistol and invited him to

follow his mother's example. I offered the alternative of agony with that leg, plus incarceration for life.'

Sarah started to tremble as reaction set in. 'But where does it stop?' she wailed as tears flooded suddenly. 'It's crazy. A feud, a vendetta goes on and on, even down the generations. We'll never be free; we'll forever be looking over our shoulders. I can't stand any more of it, I can't! I can't!'

He stopped and, ignoring the horse, snatched her into his arms. 'Shh!' he crooned, understanding her misery. 'I bet it's over right now. This second. This instant.'

'But how can it be?' she sobbed.

He gave a tiny shake to his head. 'Let me tell you,' he began. 'All right, there is this crazy sect in rebellion, just copying the Sealed Knot Society all those years ago, but do we hear of them now? We haven't in years. They died a natural death and, when they were active, it was not the ordinary people they were after.'

'But we are ordinary,' she interrupted, crying bitterly, giving great sobs.

'True,' he agreed, 'but these circumstances were totally different. Think! This was simply another repeat.'

She lifted red eyes to him, confused and not understanding. He hastened to make himself more clear.

'Giles Cook was but copying his mother. Although she acted alone, as far as we'll ever

405

know, she must, at some time have told her son; perhaps verbally or even with a letter which he received afterwards. He's probably been stewing and fretting for a long time because he did not know exactly who you were. Then, of course, my activities recently have become common knowledge and, hey presto! he learns about you at last. Nothing simpler than to gather a gang of like-minded ruffians and try this crack-brained scheme. Exactly what he hoped to gain, I simply don't know. People who are off mental balance behave illogically to folks like us. We simply don't think the same.'

'But there will be others. I know it!'

He shook his head. 'No, I don't think so. Any more of these crazy Fanatiques will head for bigger game. And anyhow, don't forget, we have the most valuable priceless ally on our side. I'll get a pigeon off tomorrow. A message will be taken to John and, when he is released, which will be before the month's end he says— and I believe him—we'll have the backing of the most powerful organisation this world knows. Even the King won't have better protection.'

'John Thurloe?' she asked, still sniffing, wanting to believe him desperately. 'You're not just saying this to quieten me down?'

He shook his head, looking deep into her eyes. 'No, I swear what I've said is the truth,' and he meant every word. He too wanted peace of mind now. 'Believe me?' he whispered hopefully.

Her crying had stopped. She looked backwards. 'I suppose that means we'll have to go home and . . .'

'I'll see to things,' he told her gently.

'I want to believe you,' she whispered. 'I feel I've had enough of everything.'

'Come on,' he told her, taking her arm. 'I think the horses can scramble down here and up the other side. Home we go and you look forward to a happier future.'

The sun burst out suddenly. Immediately the ruins took on a different, softer aspect. Sarah stared at him hopefully. He kissed her, then taking a deep breath, she led her horse down, after his. At the top, after the scramble up, they remounted. Riding together, hand in hand, they rode home.

Chivers Large Print Direct

If you have enjoyed this Large Print book and would like to build up your own collection of Large Print books and have them delivered direct to your door, please contact **Chivers Large Print Direct**.

Chivers Large Print Direct offers you a full service:

✧ **Created to support your local library**

✧ **Delivery direct to your door**

✧ **Easy-to-read type and attractively bound**

✧ **The very best authors**

✧ **Special low prices**

For further details either call Customer Services on 01225 443400 or write to us at

Chivers Large Print Direct
FREEPOST (BA 1686/1)
Bath
BA1 3QZ